To Eva,
Hope you enjoy
this "journey"
         Diana Rivers

JOURNEY TO ZELINDAR

Book 986 of the Hadra Archives
JOURNEY TO ZELINDAR
The Personal Account of Sair of Semasi

Written by Diana Rivers

LACE PUBLICATIONS

Library of Congress Cataloging-in-Publication Data

Rivers, Diana, 1931–
Journey to Zelindar.

I. Title.
PS3568.I8316J6   1987   813'.54   87-11226
ISBN 0-917597-10-9

©Copyright 1987 by Diana Rivers. All rights reserved. Reproducing or transmitting any part of this book in any form or by any means, mechanical or electronic, including photocopying, without permission in writing from the publisher is forbidden. Printed in the United States of America.

First Edition. First printing. Cover design by Lace Publications. Cover illustration by Ellen Sandi Strack.

Lace Publications/POB 10037/Denver CO 80210-0037

All characters in this book are fictional and any resemblance to persons living or deceased is purely coincidental.

ISBN 0-917597-10-9

ACKNOWLEDGMENTS

This book is for all those women, myself included, who like to read fantasy and adventure but are so often disappointed at finding themselves written out of the center of the action. It is also for the many encouraging friends and acquaintances at women's festivals, writers' conferences and elsewhere who have heard me read a few chapters and wanted to know when I was finally going to get it all between covers so they could read it themselves.

I want to take this opportunity to thank all my writers' group, especially Judith Foster, for careful listening and thoughtful criticism. I also want to thank and acknowledge Alice (Beetz) Popcorn for typing and midwifing the first half of this manuscript while laughing uproariously, though not unkindly, at my very creative spelling, and Su Henry for typing and midwifing the second half with such deep personal involvement and commitment that on occasion she even went to Semasi herself to do research so she could give me the benefit of her valuable and detailed criticism.

I am deeply grateful to Merril Mushroom. Without her persistence and insistence that I send this manuscript to Lace it would still be lying unfinished at the bottom of a drawer. Most particularly I want to express my gratitude to Chris Christoffel whose loving kindness and patient encouragement helped me overcome my technology-phobia long enough to make friends with her computer so I could get my hand in at doing the final corrections myself.

TABLE OF CONTENTS

Letter to Jorkal i
Section I 1
Section II 103
Section III 191
Final Letter 299

The following is to be delivered to Jorkal of Zelindar, Keeper of the Hadra Archives.

My Dearest Jorkal,

   I trust to the Goddess this letter finds you happy and in good health. Here is the account of my time among the Hadra, written as you requested for the archives of Zelindar. I hope you think it suitable, for only at your urging would I have undertaken such a task. In fact, when you first, asked I had not thought to do this. As you know, I am no writer and have set down only those few pages needed to please my tutor. The enforced idleness of winter with so many long hours before the fire made the doing of this easier. Snowbound days here grow wearisome, and the library is small. Also, your words pulled at me and gave me no peace.

   To the best of my ability, I have tried to record honestly all that befell me, setting down even those private parts that in Eezore would have been considered shameful to reveal. I know the Hadra have no such delicacy and would feel that these things have their rightful place in my tale. Indeed, it is these parts of my experience, as much as any others, that have caused me to be where and as I am today.

   I have written the following journal in the style of such books in Eezore, leaving the flow of narrative intact, but adding some needed information in afternotes at the end of each chapter. Most of these afternotes are definitions and the rest commentaries. The inclusion of this material would have overweighted the text. Some of it, more over, may have been unknown to me at the time the story occurs. Much of this information is already familiar to the Hadra. I am including it here so that this account may be of use to any, now or in the future, including new Neshtair.

   I must tell you, Dear Friend, that the writing of this was far more difficult than even I anticipated. Truly, I think the adventures set down here were not nearly so hard in the doing as in the recording. Having done both, I would rather struggle to move logs and stones to shape a building, than struggle again with words in the shaping of a story. Many times I thought to stop part way, but Quadra kept at me to finish and Tarl also, for she has been learning to read as I write this. I hope with the safe delivery of this manuscript into your hands, that my debt to the Hadra shall have been honorably laid to rest. As it must be.

Much love to you always,
Sairizzia of Eezore
Sair of Semasi

i

SECTION I—EEZORE TO SEMASI

PART 1—EEZORE

I was going to the ocean to die, as I had seen it in my dreams so many times on that dread night. Now, looking back in search of the true beginning of this tale, that is the picture that comes to me over and over—sharper and clearer than all the rest. I see myself, a small ragged figure trudging along the side of the road with many weary miles stretched out before me.

I had never been to the ocean and knew little of it except what Old Marl had told me. She used to talk much of her childhood by the sea, but that was before the Shokarn* slavers captured her people. It has been long years since Marl was a girl, being near a hundred when she died and that ten years back; yet I knew the ocean was ancient and enduring. I was sure it would still be waiting there for me. Marl used to call it the "eternal waters". When I listened to her stories, I would try to imagine a body of water so large I could see no land on the other side, no matter how high I climbed, or how far I looked.

Now it called to me, always west, following the sun by day and the Great Star Triangle* at night. I would end my life there, my body floating on that vast expanse of water, peaceful at last. In a way I was already dead, for among the Shokarn of Eezore*, a woman so used is no more among the living. They will not look at her, nor speak to her, nor give her aid in any way. So I thought I had no choice but death, and still with my old stubbornness, wanted some choice of place—that it be mine not theirs.

It seems I am getting ahead of my story here. How was it that I, who was so young and advantaged, could see nothing before me but the choice of one death or another? I think it was that same stubbornness, crossed with the luck of being born a woman. Women in Eezore are trained to be submissive and obedient. I was neither and had no wish to be. I was wild and willful and must have been born so, as some are born with blue eyes. It was fortunate for me that my father was no tyrant, but a kind, indulgent man, who loved me and was much inclined to give me my own way. Also, he was a dreamer and it was hard for him to stand against so strong a will. So in my father's house I saw a certain freedom, whereas outside it I saw none.

Of my mother I had little knowledge. She died at the start of my second year trying to give birth to a baby that did not survive her. My father would never speak of her. A look of grieving crossed his face at any mention of her name. I overheard the servants saying that he had loved her far more than was proper for a man to love his wife, and that this was why he had not done his duty and remarried. They seemed to think it was from grief his business affairs had gone astray and our house had not prospered.

Once I heard Old Marl saying, "What a pity to lose her so young to birth-fever. She had more power in her little finger than most who claim to be witches and healers will know in their whole lives." When she noticed me sitting in a corner she fell quickly silent and turned aside all my questions. The other servants, when I sought to ask them, drew away afraid. No one would speak to me of my mother's powers.

After her death I was given into the care of Old Marl, who had been my mother's nurse. To me she became a friend and companion and something more. She was the guardian of my wild spirit. She made no try at teaching me to be a proper lady. Instead, she told me many of the old stories and taught me many things, not all of which would have pleased my father. As we had not much other company, we went about together, the oldest and the youngest of that house. Sometimes at dusk we would go out on the balcony to watch the sunset. Then Old Marl would say longingly, "The sun goes home to the sea." I knew at such times that she was remembering her own childhood. Once I asked her why she had not run away and gone home. She pulled up her skirts and showed me the deep purple scars on her legs. "I tried to," she said, "and this is what they did to me."

"In my father's house?" I asked, horrified.

"No," she said quickly, "your father is a kind man. Others are not." She shook her head and turned away, clearly finished with my questions. I never spoke of it again, but I understood then why she sometimes went with a limp.

When Marl died, then truly, I was motherless, for my father had not married again. The other servants found me too strange for closeness and I thought them too tame. I was much alone after that. I deeply missed Old Marl, but did not long for other company.

Most girls in Eezore are given little learning, so I found them dull companions. As my own mind was hungry for knowledge, I begged and pleaded with my father until he got a tutor for me. After that, I read and studied much, taking books from my father's library and being gone with them for hours. Our house was large, with many long-abandoned places that I made my own. That was my school, and though it was not much, I knew I would have no other.

I grew up active and restless. Dresses and skirts, and all that went with them, I found so tiresome and confining that, at last, I gathered my courage and asked my father to let me wear boys' trousers. He was shocked at first and would not hear of it, but, as was my way, I persisted. He finally gave way on the agreement that I must never go dressed so before visitors or in the street. That was an easy promise. When my tutor was not there, I would put on my pants, take my books and go about to my secret places; tangled corners of the courtyard garden, the small room at the top of the west tower, even high lookout places on the roof that were dangerous from neglect. From there I could see out over the whole city. On clear days I could even see the high tips of the Rhonathren* mountain range that was the far eastern edge of my world.

I had those books and the old house dog for company, or the garden birds—peacocks and pigeons—and so was quite content with my life and my freedoms in that house. I knew well enough what it was like for other girls in Eezore.

* * *

I did not always stay at home in those years, but learned some of Eezore and even a little of the land beyond her gates, for my father would take me riding in his carriage. Eezore was a beautiful city with it's fine parks and gardens, or so it seemed to me when I was young. It was awesome, too, with great stone buildings, wide avenues and parading men at arms. I also saw ugliness there and suffering as well, beggars and slaves and dark narrow streets twisting away from the wide ones, but I thought little of all that at the time. Once, coming home from the country we passed the Bargguell*, that great refuse heap that lies outside the city gates. My father said to me, horrified, "Do not look, Sairizzia. Turn away."

But he was too late. I had already seen what looked like a woman's naked body, bloody and mangled, with a great shaft like a lance handle, protruding from between her legs. I turned my face against his chest and whispered, "Oh, Father, what was that?"

He sounded old and weary when he answered, "The Zarn* is fighting a rebellion on the Balmori River*. That is one of the river women that the troops have brought back and done so to." He shuddered then and said with great bitterness, "They should be made to bury their own work."

This all seemed to me strange and terrible beyond comprehension, but I, who was always so curious, had not the courage to ask more. For a while after that I had no eagerness to go out and preferred the peace of the courtyard garden to all the wide fields beyond the gate.

* * *

At fourteen my father began to talk of marriage. Each time I made great protest saying that I was not yet a woman and still had much studying to do, and also that I did not want to lose him so soon, or whatever else I could think of that would gain me time. This went on so for the next few years. I think my father was not too anxious himself, for he did not press the matter much, but I am sure that friends and visitors must have thought him a lax and careless man.

When I had to appear before visitors in the presenting room, they were always amazed that a girl my age was still at home unmarried. They would say so quite plainly, discussing possible matches in front of me as if I were a fancy horse to be paired off and had as little knowledge of words. I would sit there, awkward of tongue and hot with anger, stiff and itchy in my dresses, until I could slip away to my room. Safely there, I would call my maid to help free me from that imprisonment of clothes.

In this manner I was still living as a child in my father's house, reading books and wearing boy's trousers, when most girls my age were married and making their first or second babies upon the world. This could not go on forever as I well knew, but I, who had never obeyed anyone in my life, could not imagine obeying a husband.

When I was seventeen, my father became more urgent and my protests more desperate. At last on my eighteenth birthday he said, "Daughter, I have found you a good husband. You will be married before this month is out. It is no use to protest this time, for it is done." Then he added, as if to soften the blow, "You will go to a finer house than this shabby one and be far better provided for." That was no comfort to me. What did I care if our tapestries were faded and the rugs worn and the meals simple as in a tradesman's home? I wanted nothing more than those familiar walls.

I was angry and afraid and so shouted at him, "I will not go! You cannot make me some man's wife!"

At that he grabbed my arms and shook me, a thing he had never done before. "Sairizzia!" he shouted back. "You are a woman now and not a child. You will go where you are told. You will marry this man. It has been fairly agreed to. He wants you and you are paid for."

My arms hurt under his hands. He had never treated me so. I was trembling. "Father, you must give back the money," I pleaded.

He released me then and said more quietly and with great sadness, "I cannot, Daughter. It has already been paid out to save this house from the money holders."

I stopped struggling after that and looked down at the floor. My eyes filled with tears. I had been sold to save my home, and so, one way or the other, would have to leave the place of my childhood.

* * *

During the next month, I had to be fitted for my wedding gown many times and many weary hours. Our house was filled with the chatter of the women who did that work. From them I learned much, though I asked nothing, moving will-less this way and that at their command. I had lost much of my spirit at that time and felt like a walking doll.

I heard it said that Lairz Mordal, the man I was to marry, was captain of the guards and from a very powerful family in Eezore, cousins to the Zarn. I also heard that he was young and handsome. Apparently he had seen me on the street and in my father's carriage, and so sent his aunt to make the match, paying quite a high price for my beauty, in spite of my age. Those sewing-women were much impressed with the sum. They thought me very lucky to have made such a fine marriage. I, on the other hand, who had never had reason one way or the other to think on my looks, now wished myself ugly as a toad if it would have won me my freedom from all that. My father I did not speak to at that time, nor did I ask him anything at all.

The day of the wedding my father came to tell me the carriage was ready and waiting for us. He seemed sad but tried to smile. "You are very beautiful, Sairizzia. I have never seen you so."

He turned me to face the mirror. My long blond hair, which I usually wore pulled back, had been piled and swirled high on my head, studded with jewels and flowers. My face was powdered to an unnatural whiteness and my lips painted a hard, bright red. I did not like the look of that woman in the glass and shook my head.

He kissed me on the forehead, saying, "Many maids are afraid before their wedding but learn to be happy. In the end you will see that this was best." I turned away and would not look at him again.

I went to that wedding sullen and resistant, pained by those clothes. While others said how beautiful I was and how fortunate, and drank and feasted and had their enjoyments, I saw my little freedoms bargained all away. But when I crossed that threshold to my husband's house, some part of my spirit returned. I promised myself that, though I had reluctantly given my hand, I would never give my body or my soul.

* * *

My new home was indeed large and grand, more even than I had expected. It had huge stone columns at the entrance, imposing enough for a palace. Its inner walls were of dark, carved wood and its rugs were all of thick-weave from Balmori. Yet none of it gave me pleasure. There I was watched and supervised and attended to in a way that left me little freedom, and so I longed for my old private places, however shabby they may have been. I should have been grateful, I suppose, that my husband's mother did not scold or beat me much and my husband's father did not force me to his bed. Both I had heard were common for new wives. But gratitude has never been my virtue. Instead, I was angry at being expected to love this stiff cold stranger who was now my husband. And, indeed, I did not love him. I even refused him in the bed, thinking if I persisted so, he would be forced to send me home. I knew well enough why men needed women, for in my father's house I had often sat in my secret corner of the kitchen listening to the servants talk. He would not keep me long if I was no pleasure, of that I was sure.

Lairz did not struggle much with me. After each try he would say, "I will not force a wife who is unwilling." I, who was in many ways such a child still and knew little of the world, in spite of my studying, thought I was winning and had only to stay strong. I did not see then that it was pride, not gentleness or weakness, that made Lairz act so. He had bought a wife in the proper way and wanted her to come willing, even eager to his bed, not drugged and forced like some soldier's catch. For that he was willing to wait. All this I understood later. At that time, I had little knowledge of this man I had been sold to in marriage and, in truth, I did not try for any. I heard his words but did not see his claws.

Things went on so for a while. At the end of the second week Lairz said, "You have one more chance, Sairizzia. Most wives are not treated with such patience." His voice was thick with threat, yet I kept my calm. When I refused him the next night, he turned away easily, and I went to sleep in peace, thinking it was over. Later he shook me awake with rough hands. I sat up dizzy in sleep, not knowing if it was night or morning.

"Get up and dress fast, "Lairz said harshly. He lit one candle. When I reached to ring for the maid, he grabbed my wrist with such force I gasped in pain. "Dress yourself this time," he told me. He did not help, but stood watching with a hard, closed face while I fumbled sleepily, scarcely able to see by that one flickering light. My hands shook as I pulled on my clothes.

"Hurry," he said to me. "you are too slow."

"Where are we going?" I spoke in a whisper. Fear choked my words. Never had I seen him in such a mood.

"We are going for a walk."

"Before breakfast?" I asked, amazed.

"You will get your breakfast soon enough," he answered with a strange laugh.

I moved as quickly as I could, thinking it best to humor him now, since I had held out against him in bed. Even then I held some hope that he was sending me home, but kept that hidden to not provoke him more.

When I was ready, he signalled me to silence. We left by narrow back stairs I had not seen before and met no one from the house. The street also was deserted. Lairz took my arm in a terrible grip, and we walked quickly in what seemed the direction of the north gate, though by streets and alleys I did not know.

As I was in pain, I said, "Please let go, Lairz. You are hurting my arm."

Instead he gripped me harder, saying, "That will not worry you soon, Sairizzia." He spoke no more words, but a cruel, wolfish grin was on his face.

Being unused to the city at night, I felt uneasy on those streets. I might have clung to a companion, but when I glanced at Lairz he seemed far more frightening than the dark, and so I went stiff and silent as if in an evil dream. When we came to the barracks at the foot of the north gate, I had a terrible foreshadowing, though I still understood nothing except that Lairz was both pleased and angry, and that it concerned me in some mysterious way.

"What are we doing here?" I asked, pulling back.
"I am going to present you to some of the men in my command," Lairz said with a peculiar eagerness. He was smiling, but there was no warmth in it. Stepping forward he said something to the guard. The man nodded and went before us to open one of the doors and light some torches. We entered a long narrow room that stank of sweat. Eight men were sleeping there. They moaned and cursed at the light, but when they saw Lairz, they looked startled and tried to rise.
"Relax, men. You may stay as you are. I am here as a friend and not your captain and have even brought you a present." Then he thrust me into the room and pushed me forward, saying, "She used to be mine. I do not want her any more. You can have her for whatever you want."
"It is me that does not want you!" I shouted, suddenly furious at his lie in spite of my fears. Those were my last words of childhood.
Lairz gave me a hard shake, saying, "That will not matter much to you now." Then he turned to the man on the first bed. "Well, Koll, you look to be a big man. How is your appetite?"
The man he called Koll blushed and grinned, seeming pleased. The others laughed loudly. Then Koll looked at me so strangely that I tried to shrink back against the door, but Lairz pushed me toward the bed.
Koll stood up saying slowly, "Whatever we want, Captain?" There was a look of greed on his face.
Lairz nodded and said with that same cold smile, "Yes, Koll, whatever you want."
Suddenly I understood. I remembered tales I had heard of the soldiers being kept from town women so they would be more fierce in battle to rape and plunder. I saw again the body of the river woman so wounded in her private self and flung on the Bargguell. Terrified, I turned and ran for the door, shouting, "No, Lairz!"
He grabbed me again and said quite softly, looking straight at me, "Yes, Sairizzia. Some men do not mind using force." Then he pushed me from him so hard I stumbled and fell against Koll. Instantly, Koll clamped his thick arms around me and held me tight while I kicked and struggled. The others came laughing and shouting as if to some sport and grabbed my legs.
"Good luck," Lairz called out. "She fights well. When you have

finished you can throw what is left on the Bargguell. I will leave word for the gate to let you pass."

I do not know if Lairz stayed to watch, but those were the last words I heard him speak. Koll threw me down on that hard floor. I screamed and struck out at him, but hands rushed to gag me and hold my wrists. Those others held me down while Koll stripped off his clothes and mine. I felt many hands pull my legs apart, forcing them open against all my strength. Then Koll threw himself on me and rammed his way inside. I screamed against the gag. I was still a virgin and the pain was terrible.

When at last he climbed off me, there was another to take his place, and then another. They held me down for each other, turn and turn about, shouting jokes and encouragement. I heard Koll bellow, "Save me another turn!" Then there was a last terrible tremor in my body, as if spirit and flesh were wrenched apart, and I fell back with the limpness of death.

After that, one man kicked me and said loudly, "You have left me a dead thing. I have no wish to fuck a corpse." I believe he kicked me several times more. Though I knew this was happening to my body, I did not truly feel it, nor did I care.

From what seemed like a far place, I heard a new voice saying, "She was not a corpse when she came here."

Someone else answered, "Hey, Mica, you did not help us much this night. Do you not like the ladies?" Then many others shouted at him, too, teasing and taunting.

"I like them much better alive," he said coolly.

"You could, at least, have helped to hold her."

"There seemed more than enough hands for this work. I was waiting my turn, and now there is nothing left."

They all guffawed at that and another shouted, "I think that was a virgin the captain threw us. There is a mess of blood on everything."

Someone else answered, "Gods, it has been a long time since I had a virgin."

And another replied, "Sweet hell's fire, man, that was no virgin by the time you had her!"

That, too, was followed with a roar of laughter, and in that way they went on jesting over my body, until the voice that was named

Mica, broke in, "Since I lost my share in this sport tonight, at least, let me carry the body to the Bargguell."

At that there was more laughter and a voice quite close said loudly, "Well, boy, enjoy yourself. There may still be some bit of pleasure left there."

I heard steps approaching, and opened my eyes, fearing some new horror. What manner of monster was this that wished to so use a seeming corpse? My glance met the soul-sick eyes and stricken face of a young man, looking at me with terrible pity. He seemed about my age, not at all the same rough sort as the others. My eyes flew wide with surprise at his appearance, then with a groan I fell back into a stupor. I felt myself being picked up, and rolled onto his shoulder. The rest cheered and whistled, flinging open the door for our passage.

The air was cold. It was still dark. I heard Mica speak to the guard, and the door in the gate creaked open. I was barely conscious, but I knew that this man was not cruel, and carried me as gently as he could. When, at last, he laid me down in that dreadful place, it was on something soft and warm that he wrapped around me. Then he knelt by me a moment, kissed my forehead and said almost in a whisper, "May the Gods have mercy on you, child, as men have none." After that he pressed something into my hand and was gone.

All this I observed from a distance, as if my mind and body were separate beings. For a while I lay among that stinking refuse in a sort of floating trance and from there slipped into a dream-filled sleep. In those dreams I saw my body floating as a tiny speck on the vast ocean waters. Many times that night I had the same dream and each time felt with it a great sense of peace.

11

AFTERNOTES

Shokarn — The light-skinned ruling class of the four Zarn ruled cities between Yarmald and Tashkell. They are mostly uppercaste, merchant caste and guards, thought some are farmers, and some from impoverished families even become working-caste. The Shokarn are said to have originated somewhere in Tashkell on the other side of the Rhonarthren mountain range and to have swept down in conquest, overrunning the native Kourmairi and driving them almost to the sea before the Redline was laid down to protect Yarmald. Such is their reputation among other peoples for being ruthless conquerors, that in some places, the word Shokarn is held to be a curse.

Great Star Triangle — A triangle of three bright stars that is a sure guide westward on clear nights. The uppermost star is thought to be the Great Star itself.

Eezore — The largest of the four Zarn ruled cities, the others being Maktesh, Pellor and Nhor. It is said that Zarn rule in Eezore is more absolute than in othe other cities and has been established for a longer span of time.

Rhonathren Mountains — The long forbidding mountain range that is the eastern boundary of the Zarn held lands.

Bargguell — A hugh garbage heap outside the walls of Eezore where refuse of any sort may be dumped, sometimes even bodies. In Eezore the word Bargguell is often used as an insult such as, "You are fit only for the Bargguell," or "That is Bargguell-meat you sold me," or "The Bargguell must have been your mother." Such insults are not taken lightly.

Zarns — Hereditary Shokarn rulers of the cities of Eezore, Maktesh,

Pellor and Nhor holding sovereignty (often disputed among them) over the lands between, from the boundary of Yarmald on the west to the Rhonathren Mountains in the east. The Zarns are considered more than kings, having absolute life and death power over their people and claiming mythic or sacred origins, with a line of descent from Rhaais, the God of Battle. They are related to one another by carefully arranged marriage sales, and are both adversaries and allies in their conflicts with other peoples.

Balmori River—A wide river west of Eezore. It flows through and irrigates the fertile Balmori valley or plain. The people of that region, mostly Kourmairi, have long been in rebellion against the rule of Eezore.

PART 2

ROAD TO THE SEA

I woke in the first gray light, cold and in pain. Looking about me, first with amazement, then terror, I suddenly groaned aloud for I remembered where I was and all that had happened. Indeed, at that moment I wished myself dead, but my body, it seemed, had been too strong to do me such a kindness. Instead, I sat up slowly, holding my head. It was then that saw myself to be wrapped in a man's greatcoat. There was a bag of bread by my hand, and my clothes were piled beside me. I had been left at the far edge of the Bargguell, away from the city gate.

A sickening stench thickned the air. All around me were piles of refuse of every sort, even the rotting carcasses of beasts. Glancing over my shoulder, I saw the remains of what might have once been human. I turned back quickly and would not look that way again, for I knew that sometimes executed slaves and criminals were thrown here. That had always seemed to me a dreadful way to end. Now, I myself had come to this, and at my husband's hands.
There seemed no hope for my anywhere. What was I to do? I could not return to the city. There was no shelter for me there. I would be stoned and beaten and no doubt thrown again on the Bargguell, for a raped woman in Eezore is no more than garbage and already a dead thing. Yet, I must go somewhere, and quickly, too. Even now, as the sky was turning blue, I could see those great dark birds circling and hear their cries. The birds-of-death would soon be swooping down to feast. They would not hesitate to pluck the flesh still living from my bones, if they found me lying there.
I pulled on my clothes, or what scraps of them were left me. Then I struggled up and stood for some moments, sick and dizzy, swaying on my feet, with no thought of where to go. Suddenly my dreams came back to me, and I saw clearly what I must do. I would make my own death. I would follow the road west to the sea. That, at least, would be a clean end and one of my own choosing.
Looking back for a last time at the walls of Eezore, I said aloud to that city I had thought beautiful, "This—this stinking refuse heap is your other side." Then I picked my way down through the rubble.
When I set out, I kept the road in sight but myself hidden off to the side. Soon I came to a small stream. There I washed as best I could, trying to rid myself of my own blood and the stench of the Bargguell. As my skirt had been hindering me, catching on brush and brambles, I tore it near in half, and taking some strips from the hem, I bound it to my legs in the manner of trousers. That was a great improvement and gave me far more freedom to walk. The greatcoat I rolled and bound with another strip to carry more easily over my shoulder, as I knew I must keep it with me. That coat was my only shelter for it was early spring still and the nights could grow quite cold, even if the days were warm. All this was a terrible effort. It took much time and most of my strength. The sun was already warm on my back when I was able to set off again.

Of the next few days I remember little. It was not strength but will that moved me forward, the dream of the ocean drawing me on, keeping me alive to seek my death. I dreamt of it many times and thus woke able to stumble on, one foot before the other, knowing that somewhere, hours or days in front of me, was peace. Meanwhile, I was in constant pain, especially between my legs. My shoes, which were ladies' shoes made for crossing carpets and stepping in and out of carriages, hurt my feet dreadfully. They soon wore through and had to be abandoned. I tried walking with my feet bared, and when that grew too painful I tore the pockets from the greatcoat with much difficulty and bound them on. The only food I had was the bread Mica left me that quickly grew hard and stale, and some few nuts I found.

I moved as a ghost or a walking corpse through the land, always hiding from other humans, going sometimes by the road and sometimes off to the side as seemed safest. Where the road passed through farmland, there were few people about, but I had to skirt several villages, fearful each time that I would not regain my way. Once a pack of dogs ran at me barking. They would have been on me had I not picked up a stout stick to ward them off.

There was some moon at the time so I went on at night when I was able. When I could walk no more I curled up in the greatcoat and slept behind the hedges. For one whole day I rode hidden in the straw of a farmer's wagon thinking this a great piece of luck. It had gone for some ways and I was just dozing off, when there was a loud command to stop. The wagon was quickly surrounded. I thought the men to be soldiers from the tone of their questions. There were shouts and cries and much commotion in the distance and the smell of burning was thick on the air. The farmer's voice when he answered was a frightened murmur. Hardly breathing in my place of concealment, I lay in a cold sweat, fearful that they would soon be stabbing about in the straw with their swords. After much shouting back and forth between the men, they let the farmer pass, for soon I could hear the clump of the horse's hooves on the bridge and the flow of the water beneath us.

After that I slept from exhaustion, lulled by the sway of the wagon in spite of my fears. It was not till late in the day, that I slipped off, when the farmer turned down the lane to his own house and barn. With painful envy I watched him go, sitting behind his plodding horse, being carried home. The lamps were lit already in that house.

Having rested for that day I went on at night, following the Great Star Triangle, and so passed safe and unknowing through most of the dread Drylands in the coolest time. I was only vaguely aware of the sparseness of the vegetation and the strange shapes of it by moonlight. When it grew too hot the next day, I rolled myself into a gully under the shelter of some shrubs and slept.

* * *

Some days away from Eezore, four or perhaps five, the road forked, the right fork bearing northwest. Having moved west, mindless and thoughtless all those days, I now stood frozen before a decision. The new road was smaller and less travelled and so seemed safer — also, it pulled at me. I felt much drawn by it, but as my only guidance up until then had been to go west to the sea, I was afraid to change direction. So I stood, wavering on my feet, not knowing how to move, until I heard the sound of horses coming fast behind me. I had scarcely time to make myself secret, flattened behind some bushes, when a small troupe of the Zarn's guards rode by, very smart in their dress uniforms of black and gold, going west by the straight way. My decision was made for me. I got up, dusty and shaken, and took the smaller road.

The land which for a ways had been hilly and wooded now became flat or rolling, but I could see mountains far beyond, blue with distance. This new road was not so well paved, having many cracks and holes. In places it broke up altogether, and for a stretch would be dirt only. Here I walked openly on the road, feeling less endangered.

Before noon I came to an amazing sight, a red band that ran across the road straight in both directions, over the land as far as the eye could see. It was wider than a person's height and seemed like a threat or warning, a barrier of sorts. I stood staring at it, open-mouthed.

Then out of the dimness of the past it came back to me. I could hear Old Marl saying, "There is a red line now that protects the Yarmald. The slavers go no more to the sea." That was many years ago and had meant little to me at the time, for it was told as part of some fairy tale with giants and sea monsters and other wondrous and unreal things. Now I found myself standing before that line and it blocked my way. Plainly I could not go around it. The line had been laid down into the far distance—all trees and brush and grass having been cleared from its path.

Again I was faced with a choice, this time whether to sink down and die at that spot or go back to Eezore for my death or cross that line at my peril. Suddenly, I heard myself laughing aloud. What did it matter anyway. I was seeking my death. This was as good a place as any. With the fearlessness of despair, I took those four quick steps and was then standing on the other side, breathing heavily, but unharmed.

Nothing had happened. I was not struck down by the guards of the line, nor hit by lightning, nor attacked by wild beasts. The line itself was only a thing of paint. I even pressed my fingers to its surface. For the moment I was safe and quite alone there, except for a few lizards that scurried to hide under the rocks. The sun shone fairly, a sweet gentle breeze was in the air and I even felt a sense of ease and lightness, as if I had crossed to some place where Eezore had less power.

* * *

I had gone but a short way past that line—no more than a mile or so—when again I heard horses in back of me and this time the sound of women's voices. There was scant room to hide, for at that place a steep rise came down almost to the road, so I had to make do with a ditch grown high in brambles.

It was a small group of riders that passed by me, ragged and brightly clothed, with several extra horses, some hugely loaded, and even a few dogs. They were laughing and singing and shouting to each other as they rode, not at all like that tight silent guard from Eezore. A little ways past my hiding place, one of those horses that was so burdened, stopped in the road, and the whole clamorous troupe stopped with it.

I fully expected the whip to be laid on that reluctant beast so they could all move on and leave me to continue my death walk to the sea. Instead, with more shouts and laughter, they leapt from their horses, which I now saw them to be riding without advantage of

17

saddle or bridle. I had scarcely time to be surprised at that, when one of their number turned back to take the packs from the stalled beast, and I saw that person to be a woman. I almost gasped aloud in my amazement. Never before had I seen such a woman—though I now think if any in Eezore had come on me dressed in my trousers they might have been equally amazed.

I could see her clearly for she had stopped quite close to my place of concealment. She was dark skinned, bare to the waist, wearing nothing but ragged leather riding pants that scarcely covered her. All she had on her chest was a silver triangle on a chain and several strings of bright beads, yellow and blue and orange. Braided in with her long dark hair were feathers and shells and more strings of those same bright beads. Adding to the wildness of her appearance, she had little bits of white fluff caught on her hair and pants. The horse and packs were dotted with this as well.

She swung the packs off as lightly as if they were filled with feathers and tossed them into the grass. I had never seen a woman move so—like a dancer and a warrior in one. For just a moment, she looked in my direction. Though I knew myself well hidden, it felt as if her mind touched on mine and I was seized with waves of fear. Then she turned back to the others without comment, and I could breathe again.

The freed horse, meanwhile, snorted, trotted off a few steps and rolled in the dirt, making great clouds of dust over the scene. Another of the riders ran at it, laughing and shaking a blanket. The animal jumped to its feet and trotted farther off. The rest of the riders, six or seven in all, were busy freeing the pack horses. The horses they had been riding and those with no burdens had already moved off to graze.

Watching from hiding, I now saw that all of those riders were women—or so they seemed to be—though that was hardly credible. If so, they were indeed the strangest women I had ever seen. Most of them appeared to be young, close to my own years. They were darker than any Shokarn, almost as dark as slaves, but seemed to wear no brand* of caste or class. Their clothes were untidy and random, no better than a slave's clothes and with no hint of modesty, yet full of bright colors: bits of weaving and embroidery, ribbons, belts and sashes. Like that first woman, most wore beads, feathers and shells. Caught in all their ragged finery were those same bits of white fluff.

Moving with the freedom and assurance of men, those women were soon done with their work. Now, instead of going on, they spread out blankets, unpacked their food and set about enjoying a lunch by the side of the road. From my place in the ditch, I spied on them in a fever of curiosity, but also, in great fear of being discovered, for I could not safely move from there. They seemed to me as frightening as men, perhaps more so. Several times they appeared to look in my direction, and once one of their dogs ran toward me. The woman in leather pants called it back. It came to sit before her and she talked to it as seriously as if it were a person. Then another woman came to settle next to her. This one had large dark eyes and short black curly hair bound back by a red sash. They made their lunch together, sitting close, sharing bits of food, touching hands and sometimes kissing as if they were lovers. If I had not seen their bare breasts, I would not, from their behavior, have believed they both were women.

All this was so extraordinary that I had constantly to question my sanity, but stronger, at that moment than my amazement or my fear, was my terrible hunger from the smell of their food.

It seemed a wanton cruelty to eat before me with such relish. All those days from Eezore, food had mattered little and I had survived thus far on that stale bread and those few nuts I gathered. After all, I was the walking dead looking for my final rest. What did it matter if I ate? But my body had its own ways and reasons and was at that moment causing me great pain from hunger.

The woman with the red band began talking earnestly to her friend and looked several times toward my hiding place. Then she gathered up some flat breads and fruit in a cloth and came toward me. I was seized again with those waves of fear. She hesitated. Her friend said something to her, then she set down the cloth on a flat rock and turned away.

Mad with impatience for them all to leave, I had to dig my fingers into the ground and bite my lip to blood to stop myself from moving out of hiding. The women began calling in their horses and repacking them. They moved with a fast efficient ease, yet to me it seemed an eternity before they all mounted and rode off, their dogs and other horses running loosely alongside. Even after their dust had settled and their voices faded, I lay in that ditch, my arm pressed in pain against my belly, fearing a trap.

When I crawled out at last, ripped and torn by thorns, I was so weak that my hands shook as I opened the cloth — three flat breads and three peaches. I crammed them in my mouth one after the other, barely remembering to spit out the pits. Then I licked the cloth and finally sucked on it. After that I stared at the emptiness in my hands, thinking ungratefully that out of all their bounty they could have left me more. Almost immediately my stomach cramped from too much food too fast, and I sat clutching it until the pains passed.

When I went on at last, I felt both better and worse from that strange encounter. Before I had been numb, a moving corpse, but now, having eaten, that part of every creature that wants to live had been reborn in me. With it had come an awareness of the hunger and the thirst, the ache in my body, my torn feet, the absolute weariness with which I moved, the terrible pain between my legs, and worse than any of it, the overwhelming shame of what had befallen me, all of which I had been dead to for days.

I felt a peculiar anger toward those women. How did they know I was there? What right did they have to treat me as one of the living? And their arrogance — the insolence of the way they dressed and moved and rode, seemed like an insult. Yet I was being drawn along that way, not only by the sea, but by that strange troupe of women as well. I could almost feel their touch on my mind pulling me after them. If it had not been for the Zarn's men, it might have been safer to turn back and go by the other road. No, I was too weary and the pull too strong.

Next morning I found another little packet of food set neatly on a flat rock. I ate hungrily, but not so fast this time, and again felt that mixture of anger and gratitude. Why was it not more? Why had they left me anything at all? All I wanted was to die in peace.

By evening the air was changing. It was cooler and smelled of salt. When I found the next packet, I was expecting it. I sat down on a rock and ate more slowly, even enjoying the taste. This gave me some strength, so with the aid of a sharp stone, I ripped out a sleeve from the greatcoat and rebound my tortured feet. After that I sat there some little while feeling the evening fold around me, and that night I dreamt again of the sea.

Shortly after sunrise of the next day, I was up and walking, going openly now on the road. The land around me began to turn strange, with huge mounds of sand on either side. In places, sand drifted to cover the road itself. Soon I could hear the distant thunder of the great waters. There was no mistaking it. The air was moist. It had a wildness in it and also a taste of salt. Overhead a flock of large, gray-white birds startled me with their loud cries. I watched them dip down past the hill to disappear in the direction of the ocean's roar.

Weary as I was, I felt a certain thrill and also dread. The road had been growing steeper for some time now and more difficult to climb. It went up a last hard rise where suddenly it forked. The main part curved to the right and a smaller branch plunged down steeply to the left. There it lay before me, a wide scoop of golden sand, and beyond it, endless blue framed between red cliffs that rose steep on either side — my death, vast and beautiful before me.

If there had been any strength remaining in my body, I would have run down that last slope to greet it. Even with my dead eyes, I knew this to be the most wondrous sight of my life. But I was hardly able to stumble forward. On torn feet I crossed the hot sand to stand at last in the sea itself.

Wild and thunderous it rolled in at me in long lines out of that far reach — cold, so cold, that after the first terrible salt-sting in my cuts, it bit into my bones and numbed them. This is what I had walked for all those days. There was no other side. I was at the end of my journey, the end of the road — home to the sea at last.

I unbound my skirt so it would easier take me under and began to wade out into the water. It rushed at me, drew away, and rushed at me again, a wild thing foaming at the edges, so fierce that if I had had any fear left, surely I would have been afraid. But fear, like my life, was over for me. On the other side of that rushing water lay peace.

I kept walking until the sand was pulled out from under my feet. Then a great wave crashed over me and I was being sucked away face down in the water. Instead of peace I felt panic. The force of the water drove me this way and that. Another wave and then another crashed over my back and covered my head. My body began to fight for its life, struggling against my will and the sea. My hands grabbed at air trying to pull me up, and my lungs were bursting. This was not the death I had dreamed of.

* * *

AFTERNOTES

Castebrand — All those who live in Eezore or in lands under the sovereignty of the Zarn of Eezore wear a castebrand as mark of their rank. The brand is applied in the first year after birth. Colored dyes as well as heat being used, it is difficult and painful to remove. Removal without official permission is illegal and can incur severe penalities — even death.

Highborn and upper merchant castes are branded on the back of the neck. Free farmers, artisans, artists and tradesmen are branded on the wrist. Bond-farmers, working-caste and slaves are branded on both wrist and forehead, thought the forehead brand is not applied until the age of thirteen in the event that the family is able and willing to buy back the child's bond. After thirteen, the person is considered adult and redemption is near to impossible.

There is little movement from one caste to another except for the occasional fall from higher castes to lower ones due to family misfortune or the incurring of the Zarn's displeasure.

PART 3

THE HADRA

Just as a painful darkness was closing over me, I felt many hands upon my body and heard voices all around. Soon I was being dragged back onto the beach, where I was suddenly dumped down and some violence begun upon me. When I opened my eyes, I saw the woman from the road, the one in the leather pants, sitting astride my chest. She was pumping water from me with great force. Choking and coughing, I turned my head with effort and spit out a mouthful of sea.

When I turned back, that woman looked straight into my eyes and said some words I did not understand, but in my head I heard her saying *, /You are a fool./ The other one, the one with the dark eyes, had been crying over something. She knelt and gently touched my face.

The woman seated on my chest said, "Tarl," pointing to herself. Then she said, "Halli," and pointed at the other one.

I nodded and looked up. I saw then that I was surrounded by a whole circle of women, the riders I had seen on the road that day, or others just as strange and fierce. They seemed quite menacing, peering down at me and blocking out the sky.

Wanting to be free of them, I said in Shokarn, not knowing if I would be understood, "Tarl, let me up." Instantly she stood up, brushing the sand from her pants. Halli helped me to my feet.

When those two stepped away a little to speak with each other, I saw my chance for freedom. I started to run past the others back down the beach toward the sea — the sea that had for so long been my hope. But my body was too broken to do more than stumble a few steps and my wet skirt dragged at me, wrapping around my ankles and holding me back. Tarl was on me in an instant. She pulled me down so that I fell with my face in the sand. I shook my head wildly, spitting out sand, and striking at her as best I could with whatever strength remained. All my struggles, of course, were useless. The other women came to her and, holding me easily with their strong hands, and so once again I was overpowered. Now I was much afraid of what they would do, for though they were clearly not men, they did not seem like women either, but more like some dangerous unknown creatures. I could not imagine what fate I would meet at their hands. The cold merciless sea seemed safer and kinder to me then.

They conferred with each other over my body and there even seemed some argument among them. Then a big one, who seemed older than the others and named herself Zarmell, took some things from her sack. She mixed a little red powder* and some liquid in a cup and held it out for me to drink. I shook my head and would have knocked it away had my hands been free. At that, Tarl motioned for Zarmell to hold my head. That one was very strong. I had no force left to set against her. When she gripped me with her big arms, Tarl pried open my mouth and poured in the whole dose. I wanted to spit it out, but she quickly clamped her hand over my lips and when I tried to bite, she held my nose. I had no choice but to swallow.

Almost instantly I felt limp. The drug seemed to dull my fears as well as my will to fight. I watched with a strange sense of distance as Tarl stripped off my skirt, ripped pieces from it and lightly bound my wrists and ankles. The rest of them released me. Halli wiped the sand from my face. With almost no effort, Tarl picked me up, slinging me over her shoulder like the sacks of corn I had seen carried into my father's kitchen. In this manner she started up the beach, shouting and whistling loudly. Suddenly a horse trotted up beside her, as if summoned, and I was rolled onto its back. Water was still running from my nose and mouth, my own salt tears of frustration mingling with the waters of the sea.

I had come so close to freedom and now I was a helpless captive among these strangers. Would I be taken back to Eezore, or was I to be some sport for them here? Though there seemed a little kindness among them, clearly the one that had carried me was of a tough, hard sort, and had scant mercy. With shame I thought of myself, lying head down, having the whole length of my legs bared to other eyes, a thing that in Eezore would have been a deep disgrace. The moment I thought that, some words were said and my nakedness covered by a cloth, tucked in around me by many hands.

We went by a steep road which curved away from the sea and up to the cliff top, though from the way I was lying there was little I could see. When we gained a place where the ground was flat, I was taken off the horse in the same rough manner by Tarl and carried into a round stone building, followed by the others. Tarl rolled me onto a big bed. Several of the women came forward quickly to remove what remained of my wet clothing. As I had never willingly undressed before strangers, I began to struggle again. Tarl shouted something, then, together with Zarmell, she bound me hand and foot to the bed posts. The rest of them set to cutting away that wet and rotten fabric. At this I should have felt terror, but all I was left with was a dull despair.

Meanwhile, the one called Halli, sat down beside me on the bed. She took my face in her hands and looked deep into my eyes. I tried to turn my head away, but she had a firm grip, and after a while I heard her saying in my head, /Trust us. We will help you. We will not send you back./

She said it many times though without seeming to move her mouth. There were tears in her eyes. I began to feel sleepy and my exposure to strangers did not seem so dreadful anymore.

When they had stripped me to the skin, one of them rubbed me dry with something soft, then quickly slipped the quilts over my nakedness. After that, each woman came and pressed her fingers against my forehead. The last one made a circle in the air with her hand that appeared some form of blessing. They all left me then, save one very old woman. She told me her name was Yima and sat herself down in a corner to doze.

Lying there, a strange lassitude came over me, as if thought of escape or death could wait for the morrow. Since I was bound to the bed I had little to do but contemplate the ceiling, which was indeed extraordinary. It was strangely covered with either a tapestry or a painting, a large wheel or circle of brilliant colors — yellow in the middle merging into oranges and reds with violets and blues at the edges, all woven into intricate, concentric patterns. As I stared at that circle everything seemed to flow toward the center with a rippling motion and then as surely all flowed out again. In and out, like breathing, or like the waves of the ocean I could hear below me. At some moment, I knew it was their red drink that gave such free motion to those colors, and in the next moment, I knew I did not care. I gave myself over to it and floated out onto the sea with those waves of color.

* * *

I reawakened awash with pain, drawn back to consciousness by the sound of voices speaking words I could not understand. When I opened my eyes, it was to a scene so odd I felt as if I had awakened in a dream, and for that moment had no memory of how I came to be there. It was full light already in that place. I was lying bound on a big bed in the middle of a round stone room under a strange bright ceiling. All I was wearing was a long shirt of some thin, white fabric. Standing all around me were savage-looking women, some half naked and some in long robes. I would have shut my eyes again, feigning sleep, to give me time for thought, but they seemed instantly aware of my awakening.

One of them came forward quickly. She said, /Good morning./ though without speaking aloud, and laid her hand on my forehead. At that moment I remembered her name was Halli. I remembered, too, all that had passed before and how I had come to be a captive there.

Glancing about me warily, I saw among them some others whose names I knew: Yima, the old one, who had sat with me after my capture; Zarmell, whose rough, strong grip had subdued me; and Tarl, the one who had carried me on her shoulder and who was still dressed in those wretched leather pants. Looking at them I felt some apprehension. However, it was clear that whatever plans they had for me, I was as yet unharmed.

I could see they were discussing my fate. Not wanting to lie there while they talked over my body, I struggled to sit up, but fell back instantly as my hands were tied. With that, I felt a rage of helplessness at being so bound.

"Release me," I shouted, furious at them. I had suffered enough at the hands of men, I would not be treated that way by mere women. As if my thoughts had sprung into the air as words, Tarl threw back her head and laughed. She poked the woman standing next to her, who also laughed, and soon they were laughing all around me. I could hear the words "mere women", echoing about the room, or rather not the words, but the idea itself if such a thing were possible.

I ground my teeth and would have struck one of their laughing faces had my hands been free. They seemed to be making sport of my helplessness. I feared they would leave me bound for their amusement, but Halli shook her fist to silence them. Then she untied my wrists and ankles, rubbing them gently with some salve. My limbs were stiff and swollen and pained me much when I began to move. Halli spoke some angry words to the others. When she turned back to me, she stroked my hair gently and said without words, /You must not try to kill yourself again./

I looked hard into her face, wanting to understand how she could speak inside my head. She smiled to reassure me, and I saw that in spite of her rough appearance she was quite beautiful. That day, she had put on a sash of blue and gold to bind back her hair, and was wearing a short tunic of the same colors. Her long legs were altogether bare. No woman in Eezore would have gone so dressed in public, yet on her it seemed quite fitting.

/You must eat something,/ she told me. The rest of them drew back, watching, as if it had been agreed that she should take charge for now. I shook my head, but she propped me up on some pillows, poured a bowl of soup, and came to sit by me. She looked so sadly and tenderly into my eyes, that I could not resist and so slowly began to eat. That soup was a good vegetable broth, warm and nourishing. My body responded with instant gratitude in spite of my stubborn head.

While I ate, Tarl paced about the room, appearing perturbed and glancing several times in my direction. At last she stopped and looking straight at me, asked in my head, /Who are you and why are you here?/

With that I flung down my spoon and shouted at her in anger, "I came to the ocean to die! It was you that stopped me!"

The moment I spoke those words, the scene in the guard barracks rushed back into my head, as clear and terrible as if it were newly done. At that instant many things happened. Halli screamed and dropped the bowl. Tarl shouted, "No!" and threw herself down on the bed, pulling us both into her embrace. She pressed us tight against her as if to be our shield from harm. The rest of the women were moaning or crying out or bent over in sudden pain. I had to see that horror in the barracks rebounding back at me from many other minds.

I shut my eyes then and turned my face against Tarl's side, waiting to be denounced and stoned, now that all knew my shame. To my surprise there was no angry outcry. Instead, each woman seemed to be struggling with her own private agony. When calm was restored at last, they came forward one by one to gently touch some part of me—my hand, my foot, my hair—and say a few words I could not understand, but felt were kind. I knew then that I was safe, at least for the moment.

Halli was crying. Tarl's body shook. Meaning, no doubt, to be comforting, she held me tighter still. I felt cramped and twisted with my face pressed against her side. Also, she smelled heavily of sweat and horses and I longed for a little distance. No sooner had I thought this than Tarl released me. She sniffed under her arms, laughed and stood up. I blushed deeply, seeing that my rude thoughts had been heard as clear as spoken words. In Eezore, to comment on a person's smell was thought a dreadful insult, but Tarl was laughing. Halli was laughing, too, the first time I had seen her do so. She pointed at Tarl and shouted something to the old woman, Yima, who also began to laugh. Soon they were all laughing, again, all the women in that room, laughing with the abandon of children while I stared at them, uncomprehending.

At last Tarl came over to me, prancing and snorting and tossing her head. /So, I am as smelly as a horse?/ she asked me with amusement. She was not at all angry and even seemed to be enjoying herself. With many humorous gestures she went to the window and stripped off her pants, under which she wore nothing. Leaning far out, she tossed them into the courtyard. With that there was a roar of approval in the room. Afterward she poured water in a basin and set about washing, lathering under her arms and between her legs with no more shame than if she were alone. I tried to look away from her nakedness. There was a mocking insolence in all her motions that drew my eyes and, indeed, seemed meant for me.

I thought they had all forgotten me, so quickly did their moods change. They seemed like birds who fly this way and that without direction, but in a while Zarmell came and stood by me. She said something in Shokarn I could scarcely understand. I do not know if the words would translate as doctor or healer or woman-of-herbs, or perhaps all three. I nodded to show I had caught her meaning. She patted my knees, and spoke again in faulty Shokarn, "In order to heal you, I must see the place where you are hurt." This time I understood the meaning more than the words.

"No!" I shouted at her, shaking my head violently. I was afraid, remembering the strength of her arms. My body became rigid and my legs clamped tight together. It seemed like the offer of another rape. I felt that this should be my private pain and not tampered with by any other.

Zarmell shrugged and turned away, saying something to Yima. That one left and came back shortly with a cup of tea which she offered me. This I drank gladly, for the salt water had left me with a desperate thirst. The tea had a sharp, pleasant taste, sweet and sour at the same time. When I felt my muscles softening, I had a flash of anger, for I knew I had been tricked once more by their brews. I glared at Zarmell. She shrugged again and stood waiting, a small smile around her eyes. When none moved to force me, my own inner voice said, you have already been raped and left for dead. What does it matter now if some woman looks between your legs? It was my turn to shrug. Indeed, it seemed these women would have their will of me one way or the other.

I lay back trying to ease my fears. As Zarmell raised the covers, the others turned away to give me privacy. Yima sat by my head, taking my two hands in her old wrinkled ones. She chatted rapidly to distract me, not a word of which had meaning for me. After a time I understood that in some way she was sending me mind-pictures, scenes from her past and from that land; mountains and streams and flower-filled fields, and then a city so beautiful it made me gasp in wonder. There were buildings of white stone and huge trees under a bright sky. It was built on hills between a bay and a river.

/You must go to that city,/ she told me in my head.

I answered her, /If I live, I will./

"Zelindar*," she said aloud. The name rang in my head like bells. I wandered those streets only vaguely aware that Zarmell had parted my legs and was applying ointments and compresses to my private self. She finished, pushed my legs together and patted me gently. "Now keep them closed," she said as she covered me. There was a soothing coolness where that raw hot pain had been. I was about to thank her when she reached for my feet, and I drew them back with a gasp. She stood waiting again, watching me with patient amusement until I held those torn feet out to her for healing.

When Zarmell was done, Tarl came over to me. She was dressed in a long embroidered robe of some soft white cloth that lay quite beautifully against her dark skin. She bowed this way and that as she let me understand with a mocking smile that she had covered her nakedness to not embarrass me. At that I blushed angrily, feeling even more like the fool among them.

Just then, another woman came in wrapped in a dark cloak. I had not seen her here before and took her to be about forty. The others looked toward her expectantly. Tarl spoke with quick words and many gestures, no doubt explaining the manner of my coming among them. Indeed, I caught some pictures of the scene on the beach, which seemed from Tarl's head, not mine.

The woman nodded several times, then came and stood looking down at me with the appearance of a fierce old eagle. I found it hard to meet her gaze, so instead let my eyes wander to the pendant that lay between her breasts, a large silver double-triangle set with blue stones. A similar device was worn by several of the women*.

When she had seen whatever it was she had need to see, she said in Shokarn, "My name is Quadra. I am councillor here. How are you called?"

"Sairizzia," I answered her. It was the first time I had spoken my name aloud in that place.

"Sairizzia," she repeated, frowning and shaking her head. "Sairizzia? The Hadra will never be able to use such a name. It is too fancy. We will call you Sair."

I was about to protest this casual loss of my name, but something in her look silenced me. She continued as if that matter were quite settled. "Well, Sair, I hear you would throw yourself into the sea. You must give us a chance to help you heal. If at the end of a month with us you still want to kill yourself, then you may do so and none shall stop you, for that is each person's right. But next time, you

30

should take rocks and a rope and do it better. For now you must promise us to wait that month." She fixed me with a hard stare.

I felt some compassion under her stern manner and so took her hardness as a challenge, not as cruelty. In the same tone I answered, "I give you my promise, Quadra, and if in a month I need to throw myself in the sea, I shall come to you for the rope."

At that moment a fierce, angry will to live was born in me. I stared back at her until she laughed and looked away.

Quadra made a motion with her hand for the others to leave and for me to lie down again. When they all had gone, she came and sat by me on the bed.

"Rest now, Sair," she said.

After that, she spoke no more to me in Shokarn or in any language, but took my hands firmly in hers and sat there in silence, sending me strength. I trusted her hands, and after that was no longer afraid of those women.

* * *

When I opened my eyes again it was evening, but I could not be sure if it was that same day or if some days had past, nor did I much care. The Great Star Triangle was high in the heavens, framed at the top of the window arch, and the sounds of the ocean were all about me. Some one had brushed and braided my hair and made me clean. Yima was moving about softly, lighting a candle. She gave me another cup of tea and I slept again.

* * *

AFTERNOTES

The Hadra have no single word for their silent speech, but call it mind-talk, mind-speech, head-touch, mind-pictures or inner-speech. It is part of their powers, what they call their Kersh, further described in Section I, Part 4.

Yima-root — Dried and ground it makes a potent brew of many uses. I had been given a very strong dose to render me docile and lessen my fear. For more discussion see Yima's description in Seciton I, Part 5.

Zelindar — The main Hadra city in South Yarmald between Tarmail Bay and the Escuro River. For more discussion see Section III, Parts 8 and 9.

Double-triangle — Most of the Hadra wear double-triangles or circles and triangles, with precious stones inlaid or mounted at the center. The symbols have some significance in relation to Hadra origins and are often given as birth gifts.

PART 4

TIME OF HEALING

When I woke next, there was a soft gray light in the room. Rain was pounding on the stone roof and sheets of rain washing at a slant across the windows. It seemed to me it had been raining so for days.

This time I remembered where I was and how I came there, though not how long I had slept. Someone had dressed me in a loose robe of bright green and bound my hair back with a sash. To my surprise, I found myself alone for the moment and so free to observe my surroundings without distraction.

I could see that the building itself was not round as I had first supposed, but eight-sided and made of soft red stone much like the stuff of the sea cliffs. In shape it resembled the domes of Zelindar that Yima had shown me, save that it was smaller, being but one room.

Looking about me, all that I saw was done with a pleasing mixture of simplicity and grace. High, arched, many-paned windows were built into every other length of wall, with window seats in front of them and shelves of books between. Bright mats and cushions for sitting were scattered about and a large desk and chair of carved and polished wood occupied one wall. In the center of the room there were only a few small tables, holding bowls of flowers, and some bright rugs laid on the dark wood floor. It was very sparse and peaceful, an excellent place to read or study. No doubt, that was how it had been used before being occupied by an invalid.

When I looked up at the painted wheel above me on the ceiling, I saw it still still rippled slightly, though not near so freely as when I

33

had been drunk with their red brew. Watching the pulsing of those brilliant colors, I could feel some echo pulsing in my own body, some flow of strong returning life.

Slowly, and with care, I sat up to stretch and flex my muscles. Then I ran my hands over my whole body to see if I had mended yet. In spite of all my efforts to the contrary, I was very glad to find myself alive. My private self seemed to have healed well after that terrible abuse, and my feet were not tender to the touch. Suddenly I had a great longing to stand on them and see if I could walk again.

Just as I was struggling to rise, a young woman came in swinging off her wet cloak. Under it, she was dressed in a bright-striped tunic that was quite short, and soft high boots. Her youthful open face seemed strangely familiar. I knew instantly that her name was Kedris; that she was Quadra's daughter and about fifteen years of age—though how I knew any of this was not then clear to me.

"Good morning to you, Sairizzia. I am so glad to see you better."

I looked at her in amazement, for I had understood every word though she was not speaking Shokarn.

I was even more astonished when I opened my mouth and answered easily in that strange language, "Good morning to you, Kedris. Is it time for my lesson? How . . . ?" I asked staring at her.

Kedris laughed gaily and nodded, saying, "Yes, Sair, you have learned much while you were healing and have been a good pupil. That is Kourmairi* you are speaking. It is the language of the Yarmald* Peninsula. We Hadra* speak it some differently from the Koormir*, but still we understand each other." She spoke slowly and clearly to me, as if to a small child.

I shook my head in bewilderment. Too much had happened in my life too fast. Straining my memory, I seemed to catch flickers and glimpses of days spent in that room—faces peering anxiously, some gestures of Kedris', words said and repeated—but it was like trying to catch a view of the hills through the trees of the forest.

"More will come back to you as the time passes," Kedris said kindly. I knew she meant to reassure me, but I was afloat, like one swept away on a river with no landmarks.

"How long have I been sleeping?" I asked, almost afraid of her answer.

"A week and a half, almost two, much of it spent in a healing trance rather than sleep. Quadra has much skill in trancing and thought it would mend you faster. This is the first I have seen you truly awake."

"And how long has it been raining?" I was amazed at how easily I used and understood that Kourmairi tongue, though, at the time, it seemed soft and slurred to my ears.

"Almost the whole while you were healing. The spring rains have finally come."

Hearing this, I thought to be grateful to the Gods that those days unsheltered on the road had been clear and bright. At least the rains had not caught me on my way to the sea.

As I was again trying to rise, Kedris came forward saying, "Let me help you."

I took her arm and, leaning on her, shuffled about the room as if I were an old lady instead of a young woman but three years her senior. Though I was full of curiosity about this place I had come to, I had not breath nor strength to walk and talk at the same time. As we went by the windows, I tried to peer out at the scene, but little could be deciphered through the quivering dimness of the rain.

I thought to ask her the name of the settlement, and she answered "Semasi*" while the question was still forming in my head. She smiled, pleased and mischievous with my surprise at her quick response.

"Semasi," I whispered several times, loving the sound of that word.

Passing one of the stone window sills I noticed some strange ornaments there. They appeared to be carved curios of unknown ware, fine porcelain perhaps, made in bright, iridescent colors. I touched one and found it amazingly smooth and delicate. "Those are shells," Kedris told me. "Soft sea-creatures live in them. When they die their houses are left and we collect them from the beach."

"Shells?" I asked, cupping one in my hand. This seemed a strange tale. If Kedris had not had such an air of innocence, I would have thought she made sport of me.

As we went on, I noticed many more "shells" on other shelves and on the mantle, too, all adding the soft glow of their beauty to the room. I remembered then that my father had two such in his study, but I had always thought them the work of skilled human hands.

35

When we had gone the full way around the room I was weary. Kedris guided me back to the bed. While I sat there trying to catch my breath, she looked down at me with a worried frown. "You have been with us almost two weeks, Sair. You are not still planning to. . . ." She seemed stricken and could not finish. I caught her meaning easily enough.

"Never," I said quickly putting my hand on her arm. "That is over with." Hearing myself speak those words I knew them to be true. It had never been my choice to die. It was Eezore that had judged me a dead thing. My choice had been not to surrender my body on the Bargguell. Kedris smiled with relief, and I laughed with a sudden hard humor. "Yes, it would be a shame to waste a student you had worked on so hard."

"Oh," she said, blushing. There were tears in her eyes. I could see I had hurt her with my rough joking.

"I am sorry," I told her gently. "I only meant to tease a little." Then I lay back with a sigh, saying, "I must rest now for my body is still weak. Will you stay here by me, Kedris, and tell me about everything?"

"Oh, yes!" she said, seeming quite happy again. When she had tucked the quilt about my legs and come to sit by my side, I could see the eager child still there inside that earnest young woman.

Now, at last, I could ask the thing I had most wondered on and did not have words for. I turned to look at her, saying, "Kedris, I have only seen women here. Where are all the . . .?" Then I stopped, for there was no word for men waiting in my head. But she saw it in my mind and laughed.

"There are no men here. We are all Hadra."

"But where have they gone?" I insisted.

"There are no men here. We are all Hadra," she repeated.

Now I was filled with questions and asked amazed, "But how can you have children if there are no men?"

She smiled and said patiently as if repeating a lesson, "It is part of our old pact with the Koormir. We come together with their men at the spring and fall festivals, the Essu*. From that we have children."

I felt a lurch in my stomach at the talk of such a festival and asked quickly, "So you are without men the rest of the time?"

"We are all Hadra," she said a third time, as if that word had great significance.

I wondered then if they were nuns, though they hardly seemed so. In Eezore, only nuns in some closed religious orders were wholly free of men. I started to ask, "But then are you all . . .?" and found I also had no word for "celibate."

Again she caught my meaning. She shook her head and said smiling at me, "Oh, no, we are lovers of women."

I was shocked and could not look at her. There was no mistaking her meaning, for it had come to me in pictures from her head as well as words. Now I understood the close sitting between Tarl and Halli when I first saw them on the road.

"All of you?" I asked in a little voice when I could speak again. "Even Quadra?" Quadra seemed to me so austere and remote. I could not imagine. . . .

"Quadra and Jephra are companions*," Kedris said quickly.

"What does that mean?"

"It means that they are lovers, partners, comrades and friends, and will be so for some time, having gone through the bonding ceremony*." This she recited solemnly. I gave her a quick sideways glance to see if there was some evil to be seen under that youthful openness. At that moment Halli came in, her wet tunic clinging to her body. I was overjoyed to see her as if we had made some bond during my time of trance.

"Halli, help me," I implored, using my new speech with her. "I need to talk to you and must ask Kedris to leave." Though Kedris was but three years younger, I felt suddenly as if she were a child. I was embarrassed to be talking so in her presence.

"Is there something wrong?" Halli asked, looking from me to Kedris. I blushed.

Kedris shook her head and said, "Neshtair*." She took her cape and went out. Her face looked serious enough, but I could feel her inner laughter.

Halli sat down beside me, careless of her wet clothes. "I am very glad, Sair, to see you awake and feeling better."

I took her hand. "Sit here and talk with me, Halli, for I am in a great confusion. Kedris has just told me you are all . . . That all of you are . . ." I could not bring myself to say that word aloud.

"Muirlla*," Halli said with no hesitation. I stiffened at the sound

37

and looked down at the floor. In Eezore, it is a dreadful insult and means "woman's woman", though men who are very angry will fling it at each other in scorn. Then it is sure to mean a duel and some bloodshed. For a woman who is truly muirlla, it means death if caught.

"Muirlla, muirlla," Halli said again. "Come, Sair, it is not such a bad word. It even has a very pretty sound." Indeed, she said that word as if it had some music in it and was not the terrible curse I knew it to be.

As I still sat there not answering or looking up, she jumped to her feet and spun about swinging her arms and shouting, "Muirlla, muirlla!!" I tried to hold the pillow over my ears to close out the sound of her voice, but she pulled it away from me and danced off with it, singing with mock sweetness, "Muirlla, Muirlla, won't you dance with me."

I sat rigid on the bed, watching in spite of myself, while she danced about so gaily, singing that filthy word and, yet, looking so beautiful and innocent. Yes, innocent, in spite of. . . .

"Yes, innocent," she answered, snatching the word from my head. She stopped her wild dance and came to stare down at me. "And why not innocent? What should I be guilty of? Am I to stand accused before Eezore? Sair, they have raped you and dumped you on their refuse heap for the birds-of-death. How can you believe the meaning of their words? Why do you still give those words power over your heart and spirit?" Her gaiety was quite gone and her hands shook with anger. She swung about making a sound like a growl deep in her throat. Then she came to sit by me again. I still could not look her in the eye.

She shook me gently and said, "One day, Sair, you will go back and see Eezore as it truly is. You do not need to carry their garbage with you all your life. Leave it for them on their Bargguell."

I could hardly hear her words. "What is expected of me here?" I whispered, shrinking from her touch. She released me and moved away.

"Nothing," she said coolly, "but to heal in body and spirit and do your share of the work if you stay among us." I could see she was becoming weary of this. "You can live with the Hadra all your life and be celibate if that is your desire. We are lovers, Sair, not rapists. Or, if you need men, you can go to live among the Kourmairi."

"Do not be so quick to send her away, Halli. Some of us might find her quite attractive." Zarmell had come in during this scene and was standing in the doorway with her cloak dripping on the floor. She winked at Halli and then said to me, "It is good you have learned Kourmairi, Sairizzia, for I would be glad not to speak another word of Shokarn in my life."

I glared at her and answered, "As it was, I could barely understand you." I spoke quite rudely for I was angry at her constant teasing and wished to be hurtful.

At that, Zarmell raised her eyebrows and said sharply, "Well, even in Eezore working-caste and highborn Shokarn never understood each other very well. We almost speak a different tongue." With those words she brushed back her rough hair, and I saw on her forehead the dull purple burn of the castebrand, blooming like an old bruise. I knew then that I had been far ruder than I had meant to be and had been as rudely answered. I looked away fearing the anger in her eyes, but when I glanced back, she was grinning again and seemed not to be offended.

"Well, now, we must look to the patient," she said, pulling up the quilt and thumping on the soles of my feet. She nodded and seemed satisfied. "Healed well and sound with the blessing of the good Goddess and the help of Yima* leaves. I won't thump your other wound, but I must have a look at it."

Very reluctantly I lay back and parted my legs while Zarmell examined my private self, which she declared also well-healed and " . . . as pretty as any I have ever looked upon." With that she winked again at Halli and replaced the quilt. I found myself hot with shame.

"Is it true then?" I whispered, glancing from one to the other of them.

Zarmell laughed, "Ah, yes, the great discovery of the Neshtair, that we are all muirlla. Well, they get over it sooner or later. With this one I think it will be sooner."

Halli nodded. "I have been trying to tell Sair that the word 'muirlla' is not so terrible." Then turning to me she said in a teaching manner, "Actually, that word is not altogether accurate for us, as we are Hadra, and muirlla has in it the Shokarn meaning of

39

'woman's woman,' an owned thing. Though we are lovers of women, we are, first of all, free beings and owned only by ourselves."

Zarmell gave a loud snort of laughter and contempt, then shook her head, saying, "That is a fine fancy Hadra explanation, but in my life I have always been muirlla. I was born muirlla and so I will die. That is good enough for me. These Hadra think they are the best of everything." With that she swung on her cape and went out, leaving the heavy wooden door open to the rain. Halli shouted and rushed after her with no other word to me.

I lay back with a sigh. Clearly this was an old quarrel Zarmell had with the Hadra and no concern of mine, but I resolved to ask her later how and in what manner she had come away from Eezore.

* * *

As I was yet weak and the rain was constant, I could not be up much those next few days and was forbidden to go out at all. Having too much time to lie in bed and ponder, my wild imagination had its way with me. I was obsessed with the thought that all those women were muirlla, every one of them. Though I had little notion of what it meant for women to be lovers to women, still as each Hadra came in, I pictured her grappling naked with another. This was bad enough when only I myself was witness to these scenes, but the Hadra quickly became aware of my folly, for I could not shield my thoughts nor make them cease. Those women would come in and look at me with amusement, then smile and giggle and finally explode with laughter. They began coming more and more frequently to visit and soon were calling in their friends to share with them the contents of my mind. They would stand about me, laughing and teasing while I pressed the pillow over my head, attempting to hide my shame, and still I could not stop those vivid and distorted fantasies. For that time, I was often in a state of helpless embarrassment and hated them all for their teasing as well as their pleasures. My body had been stripped naked before their eyes, and now, even my thoughts were not private or my own. Then as I began to mend, moving about more freely and even going out some, this madness ran its course. The Hadra were forced to find some new amusement.

Now I was mad with questions, but as Kedris stayed away some days I could not ask her anything. Most of those others I did not trust enough. When Halli came next I greeted her eagerly and drew her down beside me on the window seat. I had been sitting there watching the ocean and enjoying some warmth from a pale new sun.

"Halli, there is much I do not yet understand in this place. Will you help me?"

She pulled away with mock surprise. "Am I to be allowed to sit so close?"

I put my hand on her arm, saying, "I think I am over my shock."

"Some Neshtair take much longer," she said smiling. Then she took my hands in hers and asked earnestly, "What can I help you with, Sair?" As she spoke, I thought how glad I was to be sitting next to her again.

"That is the first thing, Halli. What does it mean to be a Neshtair?"

"A Neshtair is a woman who comes to live among the Hadra. You will be Neshtair as long as you are here with us."

"And I can never become a Hadra?"

She shook her head and said with some sadness, "No, for you will not have Hadra powers. Not even your daughter will fully have Kersh* though she may have some part of it. Only your granddaughter can become Hadra and pass on her Kersh to her daughters."

I felt a sudden sharp jealousy for this non-existent granddaughter. "What is this Kersh you speak of?"

"Our powers, that as Hadra we are born with and then trained to use." She held up her fingers counting these off. "We can ward off harm meant for us so that it rebounds upon the sender, though we ourselves can do no harm without being injured by it. We can summon some aid in raising heavy objects, such as rocks or logs. This is helping us now in the rebuilding of Semasi. We can in some form talk mind to mind with other animals and with each other. Between us that is best used for simple sentences, for emotions and, of course, for the sharing of mind pictures, as you well know, for indeed you yourself have some part of the powers. Also, when we have children, we give birth only to daughters."

I was nodding, but wanted to hear no more in that direction, for

41

I felt a sudden uneasiness when she spoke of birth. "What is this place you call Semasi?" I asked quickly.

"This is an old settlement that was long abandoned. We have been here since last spring trying to resettle it. Semasi means something like 'view from the cliff above the sea' in the old language, the one that was spoken here before Kourmairi." She looked so soft and dreamy at that moment, I could not imagine her having the hardiness required for such work.

"And what brought you here, Halli? You seem less tough than those others."

At that she grinned and said quickly, "Oh, I am tough enough when I need to be." Then, after some moments of silence, she answered more seriously, "I came because of Tarl, but now I myself have come to love Semasi and would not want to live elsewhere. This time the settling will succeed. There are only thirty of us at the moment, but by next year we hope there will be fifty or more. Then we will be ready for children."

The mention of children made me uneasy again. I was about to ask Halli a question on some different path when a woman entered I had not seen before. She had a stern visage and graying hair, drawn back in a tight braid. This woman did not come forward, but stood by the door, looking at me silently and thoroughly, as if appraising my worth. It seemed she had little use for what she saw. She left again with only a curt nod and no word spoken. I looked at Halli in amazement.

"Who was that?"

"That was Jephra, Quadra's companion."

"I do not think she liked me much."

Halli laughed. "No doubt, but you are not the first Neshtair she has looked at so. She is known for disliking Neshtair, at least new ones. It will pass." Later I was to see in my dreams those hard eyes and that unloving face.

I sighed then and said, "My mind is weary, Halli, and can hold no more." I wanted to be alone with my thoughts. She kissed me lightly on the cheek and left me to myself.

For a long time afterward I sat there watching the sun brighten and break through. It fell across my hands, warm and healing, and lit in sharp relief the carvings along the window edge beside me. Cut in those stones were triangles and circles, some linked together and all bound by curling, leafy vines. These I traced with my fingers, amazed I had not noticed them before. Looking about me I saw other things that had been in shadow. The sun touched on small birds and creatures, on the cups and coils of shells, on leaves and flowers carved here and there among the stones and almost hidden by them. I saw the words "As it must be" carved in the arch of one window, framed by a pair of upraised hands, and discovered a chain of linked fish carved high in the arch of another. I had already read the words, "Oh, mother of waters, let me always be your child", cut over the door, but now saw for the first time a subtle tracery of waves on either side. It seemed that wherever I looked there were signs of carving, the work of unknown women; some sharp cut and clear, and others worn to roundness or almost worn away by the touch of many hands on that soft stone.

"Oh, mother of waters, let me always be your child", I read again. Those words touched me and for that moment I felt a deep connection with those who had lived and built here in another time. Those words and the carvings and the warmth of the sun all gave me a sense of peace and ease, as if I were not such a stranger after all. I gazed around the room feeling that I might, indeed, find my own place in Semasi. Eezore seemed very far away at that moment.

Later that night, waiting for sleep, I lay thinking of Halli's words, that I had some part of the powers. I felt warmth and wonderment at that, as well as a touch of fear.

* * *

AFTERNOTES

Kourmairi or Koormir — The dark-skinned native people who inhabited all of Garmishair from Tashkell to the sea before Shokarn invasions overran their lands, enslaving many of them. The words are often used interchangeably by the Hadra, but Koormir means race or people, and is also more formal usage, whereas Kourmairi means individual or several individuals.

In Shokarn held lands and cities, the Koormir, now, are mostly slaves and working-caste, though many of them are also artists, artisans, crafts people, small merchants and small farmers. Their existence under the Shokarn is often precarious and threatened, though some have managed to do well.

In Yarmald, behind the protection of the Redline, the Koormir live as a peaceful, tribally organized people in small farm settlements and in the two cities of Mishghall and Koormi.

Yarmald — Peninsula bordered by the Nevero Sea on one side and the Redline on the other, sometimes called The Hag because of its profile. It is believed to be the ancient Asharhan homeland and was Koormir territory until overrun by Shokarn invasions. At present it is inhabited by both Hadra and Koormir, existing peacefully in separate cities and settlements behind the protection of the Redline. There is little contact between them, save for the Essu festivals and the mutual maintenance of the Redline based on old agreements. For more information read Book 596 of the Hadra Archives — *The Redline of Yarmald.*

Hadra — Originally called Khal Hadara Lossien from the Asharhan words meaning "Daughters of the Great Star," a name that has been altered by usage and mockery to Hadara Lossi and, finally, to Hadra. These women have special powers or "Kersh", described in some detail in this Part. They inhabit the Yarmald Peninsula, living in their own separate cities and settlements. For more information on the origins of the Hadra, read Book 57 of the Hadra Archives, *Daughters of the Great Star.*

Essu — spring and fall festivals descended from old Koormir rituals of planting and harvest. This is a time of celebration when great license is taken, and all things can be done. It is only at the Essu that Hadra mix freely with Kourmairi, and even allow themselves to drink and to get drunk (burials are the only other exception). The core of the Essu is the Gimling, the nightly orgy where any woman can go who wants a child, but not a husband. For more discussion of spring Essu in Semasi, read Section I, Part 7. For discussion of Fall Festival on the Escuro River, read Section III, Part 6.

Companions — Two Hadra who have gone through a bonding ceremony together to declare a life partnership. They will share responsibility for each others daughters and be bond-mothers to those children.

Bonding Ceremony — A public ritual for the purpose of joining together the lives of two Hadra, who have declared themselves companions. The ceremony may be large enough to include the whole settlement, or a small one for friends and family only, but the Hadra do not consider it real and binding unless the councilor of the settlement is present to speak for the Mother, and seal the vows. It is a time of rejoicing, not only for the guests, but for those being bonded as well, for they have come to this glad and willing, not bargained for and sold against their wills.

Neshtair — Women who come to live among the Hadra, some in actual danger of their lives and others, who are discontented with their lot elsewhere. By Hadra custom, they are taken in, protected and made part of Hadra life. They are also free to leave if they choose. Neshtair are treated as equals in all things and can sit on council meetings, but they do not have Hadra powers, neither do their daughters. Only their granddaughters have that possibility.

Muirlla — Meaning "woman's woman," derogatory Shokarn word for women who are sexually enamored of other women. In Eezore,

45

such affections are against the law, and often worth one's life if caught.

<u>Yima</u> — A plant of great importance to the Hadra well-being, described by Yima herself in Section 1, Part 5.

<u>Kersh</u> — Hadra powers said to originate with the passing of the Great Star, and much discussed in this account. The meaning of "Kersh" is best described by Halli in this Part.

<u>Semasi</u> — Northernmost Hadra settlement in Yarmald, being rebuilt at the time of this writing after being long abandoned.

PART 5

SPRING IN SEMASI — HALLI

As each day passed, I grew more restless at my lack of strength and the slowness of my recovery. When Zarmell next came to see me I said with impatience, "When will I be well again? Why does it take so long?"

She shook her head, looking at me as if I were a troublesome or foolish child, though there was some admiration in her voice. "It took great will for you to get yourself here, Sairizzia, truly amazing — your body having been so brutalized and with little food and scant clothing and no shoes — truly amazing. And then to survive a drowning and still have the strength to fight us. You had nothing left afterward. You had used it all, Sair, the well was emptied. Now you must give it time to fill up again."

I gave her a hard, sharp look to show I was not impressed with all that, but she smiled indulgently at me. "Do not despair, Little One. It will all come back to you."

Impulsively she bent over and kissed me on the mouth. Then she patted my cheek and stepped back to look at me.

"So young, so young," she said shaking her head and smiling as if she had some secret with herself. She patted my cheek again as she left. In the doorway she turned and said, "I will see if I can find some help for your boredom . . ."

Later that day I was visited by a big hearty-looking woman of near my age. Her appearance surprised me, for she had crinkly reddish hair and was lighter skinned than most of the Hadra.

She gave me a quick mock bow and said, "My name is Ozal. I am told you grow restless in your imprisonment." With that she drew out of her sack a small, pear shaped, three-stringed instrument of dark polished wood.

With another mock bow she said, "If you wish I shall play you some songs on my ferl*. If not, I shall play them elsewhere."

"Oh, please," I begged, stretching out my hand.

"Ah, an audience!" she said with a glow of pleasure. Then she settled in the window seat opposite me, and leaning against some bright pillows, played a flow of wild and melancholy songs that made me both sad and very joyful. Her hands, which looked large and clumsy when lying at her side, moved on those strings faster than my eye could follow. When she finished I thanked her eagerly.

She set down her instrument, turned to me and said in her direct and forthright way, "Well, so you are the one from Garmishair?*" With those words she made a wide sweep of her hand. I shook my head, not understanding her meaning. At that she smiled. "Garmishair is a Hadra word and means all that lies over there, or everything that is not Yarmald."

I laughed then and said, "Yes, I am the one from Garmishair."

She nodded and leaned forward, looking hard into my face as if searching for some sign. "My grandmother also came across the line. She was a peasant on the Balmori River and walked here as you did after much abuse."

"Is it from her you got your red hair and light skin?" I asked

47

impulsively and then blushed, afraid she might think me quite rude for such a question.

She answered easily, taking no offense. "Yes, and from my mother also, for my grandmother was already swollen with her when she fled. So I am half Koormir and half Shokarn and all Hadra."

This last she said with much pride, then added with a shake of her head, "My poor mother, she raised me in Zelindar, thinking I would learn to be a city girl and not grow up a peasant like my grandmother. But the country is in my blood. When I heard Semasi was to be resettled I came here as soon as I could find a horse that would carry me north."

She stood up, stretching out her arms to show me her size. "I am too big for cities and feel too cramped and crowded there. These sea cliffs are more to my scale." From the doorway she called back, "Good-bye, Sair, the Neshtair from Garmishair!" Her laughter filled the room as she left.

Ozal came back the next day and for several days after that. Sometimes she brought with her a Hadra named Mirl, who played the flute and might have been her lover—though among the Hadra it seemed hard to tell lovers from friends. They played well together and even persuaded me to sing a few songs with them, something I had never done.

Ozal taught me other things as well, how to sharpen a knife, how to braid my own hair, how to play a few notes on the ferl. She also showed me the crock of sparkstone that was kept by the hearth and had me practice the use of it. After a while I could light a candle with ease. She even promised to take me later to find my own supply in the rock ledges above the orchards. All that served to lessen my restlessness a little.

Also, Kedris had come back and was now teaching me to read from the books in the library. She complained, saying, "You are too easily distracted, Sair. You were a far better pupil when you were sleeping." It was but gentle teasing. She was a fine teacher. I was an eager and industrious student, very pleased to resume my studies and satisfy my curiosity in those new books. We said nothing of what had passed before, though sometimes I saw her watching me with a small secret smile.

As I was sitting one morning at the big desk in the Zildorn, engrossed in a book of plants, Yima appeared with two cups of tea. Since I was well enough then to eat in the big hall, this was for friendship and for company. She drew a chair next to me and we talked of many things—the ways of Eezore, the customs of the Hadra, the history of Semasi. She told me how the first settling had failed due to some years of bitter winters. Having lived there as a young girl, Yima had many stories to tell of those times.

"To me, Semasi was always home. All those years away, I longed for her. So, old as I am, I was glad enough to come back." She shook her head and seemed to stare off into some far past. "Back then I had a great fondness for yima tea. It is from that I got my name." She laughed softly and I could feel the memories pulling at her.

When I sensed her back in the present I asked, "What is this yima that I hear spoken of so much?"

She turned to the picture in the book, a tall feathery plant with bunches of red berries. "It is one of our sacred plants and grows wild, a gift of the Mother. All of it is useful to us. The berries we eat fresh or dry them against the cold. They have a sharp sweet taste and are like sunshine for the body in the long gray days of winter. The leaves we use for a soothing tea—made dark and strong, it is our sleep potion and our pain killer. Those leaves are also good for healing compresses. But the red roots are best. Those we dry and grind into a powder. From that we make the brew that is for us a path to visions." I recognized this as the red drink forced on me after my capture.

Listening to Yima, she reminded me somehow of Old Marl, who had been my first teacher. Suddenly I thought of Marl with a sharp sense of loss I had not felt in years. I put my head down on Yima's lap and she stroked my hair. For that moment I was a child of eight, back in my father's house.

When I sat up again, she set her dark, wrinkled hand over my light one. "You are pale as a cave toad, Daughter, lighter even than when you first came to us. When it turns bright again, you must let the sun do some work on you, for that is the best healing of all, better than all our potions."

I laughed, for in Eezore that white skin was much guarded as a mark of caste and pride. Here it seemed of little use but to make me look the sickly one among those strong healthy women.

* * *

Each day brought different faces through the arched doorway of that stone room, some that I was familiar with and others that were new. I struggled to untangle their names, cursing myself for my forgetfulness. Ozal and Mirl and Yima and many others passed through in that first week or so of consciousness. Halli and Kedris I could count on. Quadra, I did not see again, nor Jephra either. Tarl came only a few times to see me and seemed nervous and uncomfortable. Yet each time she brought me something, some little present, a shell or a branch of flowering-lodi.* She would say a few words that were not well bound together and pace about until she left, as if that lovely spacious room were a barred cage. But I was always glad to see her and would hold her gift, staring at it long after she had left.

* * *

At last the rain ceased altogether, and the weather turned warm. Halli came in one morning with a stack of bright garments that she dropped on the bed. "You need some clothes, and I have far more than I can use. My mother and bond-mother worry for me here in this wilderness and send me too much of everything, my sisters, too."

"I cannot take your clothes, Halli," I said quickly as much from pride as goodness.

She laughed. "If you have nothing to wear, Sair, you will have to go about naked, and I know you are not prepared for that." Sweeping my objections aside, she thrust some clothing in my lap and said, "Try these on, and I will bring the glass."

Soon she had me dressed in a tunic of leaf green, a bright blue vest and soft loose pants of blue-gray stuff. She handed me the mirror and pulled my hair back to braid it. I found myself quite pleased with my new appearance. It seemed far more suitable for me than the dresses I had been expected to wear in Eezore. Later,

Ozal brought me some boots she said were too small for her, and Mirl made me a belt-pouch.

It was glorious to walk about again. The rains had fully brought the spring. The fruit trees were all in bloom and small new shoots of green were rising everywhere. The tree buds had opened in a soft green haze.

I still could not walk far, so often I sat in the public circle that was the central heart of Semasi. From there I could see the settlement spiralling out and rising slightly toward the hills. The old houses, the ones from the first settling, were built of the same red stone as my healing place. Most of them were domes. The new ones were of rough logs that Halli told me would later be replaced. The settlement itself was dotted with many small garden plots and large old trees. Around the edge of it, like protective arms, stretched the green-gold tarmar* fields, the common gardens, and the meadows where the horses grazed. Above on the hillsides, the orchards bloomed, and beyond them rose the wooded hills.

I would sit there for hours, watching everything from a bench in the sun, or if I grew too hot, then from the shade of the huge droopy-leafed Gobal tree* that grew at the core of the circle. Often I brought bread crumbs to feed the wild birds. There were always flocks of them there, pecking and chattering, fluffing in the soft red dust—the red and yellow ta-ta birds with their strange, rhythmic cry; the blue-green gorknail whose notes were sweet and piercing as a flute; and the round, short-legged loss, a clumsy, gray-brown ground bird much like the chickens I had seen in my father's yard. They mingled easily with each other and seemed not afraid of me, coming quite close to eat out of my hands and cocking their heads to look into my eyes, nor did they fly off when the Hadra passed*. I felt quite at home with those birds, for they reminded me of my father's garden and the pigeons and peacocks that had kept me company there.

Sitting in that circle it seemed I would meet every woman of the settlement, for sooner or later all passed through there and made some greeting. They were very busy, planting or building, shouting instructions to each other, and I was the lazy lizard among them in my time of healing. Sometimes even horses* came by seeming as free to roam those streets as the Hadra themselves. They would stop to have their ears scratched or snuffle in my hands for scraps of bread. For me it was amazing to observe a scene where there were no slaves or servants and all labored equally, though I could not discover who gave the orders. I was eager to join them and prove of some worth, and yet afraid. I had never tested my powers in such work.

Quadra came to me there one morning, wearing a striped and hooded robe that made her seem taller than I remembered and even more imposing. She had not spoken to me since that first day.

"It is the end of the month, Sair," she said gravely, and gave me a small, carefully wrapped box. When I opened it, I found inside three small stones and a piece of cord. The stones were of a size to weight down a bird and the cord not long enough to bind the stones. I laughed, thinking this to be a harsh joke, but she said to me quite seriously, "You must bury that box and say over it whatever words are right for you. That will be the end of your old life and your wish for death, if indeed you have chosen to live."

I looked closely at her to see if she were mocking me, but her face and her whole manner were almost solemn. I said with the same seriousness, "I have chosen to live."

"So I see," she answered, and this time there was a slight smile at the corners of her eyes. As she was turning to leave I put my hand on her arm.

"Quadra, why was I not stopped from going out into the ocean?" I had been pondering that question for some time.

She frowned at me and shook her head. "You are not easy to stop, Sair, from what you set upon. Also, those watching may have hoped that you yourself would hesitate and turn back before that power. But I am told you were very quick to do that thing. Maybe you needed to know for yourself that the sea is not kind or gentle to those who seek death in her arms. Otherwise, you might still long for that as one longs for a lost lover." She shook her head again, studying my face, then went on. "I myself was away at the time and so gave no council on that decision. If you wish to know more you must ask another."

I nodded, releasing her and thanked her for the box. Later I did as she said, waiting for a moonlit night to bury it in a small grove of pines above Semasi. The words I said are mine alone to know.

Now that I was almost well, I would have to move. The building I had healed in was not only a place for reading and study, it was also meant for ritual, meditation and ceremony, and was needed again for those uses. Kedris had told me it was built by the old settlers and was called a Zildorn*, the first building to be raised in any Hadra settlement. From her I understood that it was considered a great privilege to stay the night in a Zildorn. Clearly I had had more than my share of that privilege.

It had been decided by circle council that I was to live in a stone hut belonging to Seronis, staying until she returned or I could build shelter for myself. I had never met Seronis but had heard the Hadra speak with awe and admiration of her journey. She was exploring the region from Semasi north to the far tip of Yarmald, walking alone through the northland with only her dog for company. I could respect her bravery, but for myself, I wanted only to cling to my small safety. I had no wish to leave the Zildorn. I had never lived alone and was terrified by the thought of building shelter for myself though clearly it was time to leave. I thought of the Hadra saying "As it must be"* when faced with the inevitable, raising their hands to the Goddess to show they were in her power. I tried hard to feel some part of that acceptance.

* * *

The night before I was to move, Halli came to visit, sitting close by me on the bed. There was but one candle lit in the room. I had been watching the night sky in the arch of the window and repeating the words "As it must be," trying without much success to calm my soul or at least to sleep. Halli's entrance was a most welcome interruption. Indeed, she looked quite beautiful with her dark eyes and curly black hair. Her shirt was not fully buttoned and so lay open at the breast. By the light of that one candle, her skin flickered copper and bronze and gold. I watched her as she talked, the word "muirlla" haunting me as it had for days, yet my hands hurting to touch her skin. She, of course, could read my feelings.

"It is not so bad, Little One," she said smiling at me, and drew

53

her fingers lightly down the inside of my arm that lay bare on the covers.

I shivered, but did not move. She looked at me intently for a moment as if to see what I would do, then slowly leaned forward to kiss my lips. That kind of kiss, I had never experienced before. My mouth melted against hers and I could offer no resistance. Very gently she pulled the covers off my breasts. As I did not cry out or snatch them back, she ran the tips of her fingers quickly across my nipples. I was trembling, but could not stop her, nor did I want to. Hardly moving she slipped the quilt from my body. Her hands on me were like birds or butterflies, traveling lightly everywhere, even to places no other hands had ever touched. Very slowly, so slowly I could hardly see the motion, she lowered her head and brushed her hair across my breasts, touching each nipple lightly with her tongue. At that, a great shiver went through me, as if of heat and cold at once.

All in a motion Halli stood up and stripped off her robe. When she lay down next to me, pressing her naked warmth against mine, I shook like one in a fever, but did not try to stop her, nor could I move to touch her in return. I lay as one bound up in cords.

"Oh, you are so afraid, Little Sister,* so afraid," she said, wrapping me in her arms. I saw myself enveloped in a soft dark cloak of wings. When she kissed me on each eyelid, it was as if a silvery blue butterfly had settled there. For a while she held me trembling against her until slowly her warmth came into me — the spring sun over the fields of winter. Slowly, will-lessly I responded, my body thawing and opening after the long cold.

When my trembling ceased, she drew back and began kissing my face and neck, her touch light as the touch of feathers. Then she ran her fingers over me like the wings of tiny birds and with her lips touched me everywhere, even at the edges of my private self, so that I wanted to cry stop and more in the same breath.

All the sensations she woke in me were new. I had never desired a man, wanting mainly to avoid marriage. With my husband, I had kept all the doors of myself held shut and my mind alert. Now my mind was silent and my body moved unguided, having its own hungry knowledge. When Halli's fingers entered me and then her tongue, I lost all sense of being bound to earth. I was in the air — flying. I had no weight, only a great sense of speed and power and a knowledge of beauty so sharp, it was close to pain. I was the earth herself and I was looking down at the earth. The sun and wind were moving through me. The beauty grew almost past bearing and I felt the need to go higher, still further toward the sun. Suddenly all was torn by a shout or a scream, some terrible sound that was outside of me yet inside, too—the cry of a beast in agony.

When I came back to myself, I found I was sitting naked on the bed, soaked in sweat, yet cold all over as in death. Halli lay moaning on the floor. For a long time I stared at her with a vacancy of mind, then gently touched her shoulder. She shuddered and pulled away, withdrawing her flesh from mine. With that I remembered what had passed between us there. She had been loving me and at the moment of my greatest pleasure, the terror of the barracks had come back. I had blasted us both in my pain. With that bitter knowledge I ached to scream again, yet no sound came.

* * *

We slept that night clasped tight in each others' arms, but my spirit tossed restless for hours, pulled between those poles of joy and horror. I had not slept so with another person since I had been a small child, and Old Marl had held me safe against my nightmares.

When I woke the next morning, Halli was leaning over me, her face soft with concern. She looked in my eyes and said without speech /I am so sorry, Sair. Your body drew me in, and for that time I forgot what you had suffered at the hands of men/. At that moment, I remembered the pleasure far better than the pain and told her so, drawing her back down against me, her mouth on mine.

"Muirlla," she whispered smiling.

I nodded and smiled back as if she had whispered an endearment. After that we lay in bed a long time, being very tender and gentle with each other and talking softly in the manner of lovers.

Halli seemed most eager to tell me something and yet hesitant. Finally, like a shy young girl making an offering she asked, "Did my mind pictures please you, Sair? Did you receive them?" At first I was puzzled, but when I saw again in my mind those silvery blue butterflies, I nodded eagerly, knowing that the birds and butterflies, even the scenes of flying, had been her images—shared with me in loving. "That is part of Hadra love-making," she said softly against my ear. "We exchange mind-pictures with one another."

I was touched by her sweetness, but it pained me much that what had been mine to share with her that night had been my terror. I held her away a little to look into her face. "Halli, how is it you are able to speak so clearly in my mind?"

"There is a deep connectedness between us, Little Sister, that I felt from the start. Somehow I knew how to reach you when the others could not, though we all were trying."

"That day on the road—did you know I was hiding there?"

"As clearly as if you had spoken in my ear. I would have come to you then, but your great fear stopped me."

I laughed, remembering how strange the Hadra had looked to me then and how frightening—their wild clothes all tufted with bits of white fluff. Halli, seeing the picture in my mind, laughed with me.

"Whatever were you doing on that day?" I asked her.

"We had been on an expedition to gather lessmus fluff, a plant we use for stuffing pillows and mattresses and are also learning how to turn it into thread for weaving. It blooms in the fall and seeds only in the early spring, so it must be gathered then."

"But why had you gone across the line?" I could not imagine wanting to go back into such danger.

"Because the one place we have found it growing is by the edge of a salt lake in the Drylands. This time we brought back many seed heads to try planting near Semasi. Someday we may not have to go into the Zarn's land's to gather lessmus. As it was we almost crossed paths with the guard." I shuddered, seeing the guard again as they rode by my place of hiding, but Halli said in a quick hard voice, "It is they who should be glad we did not meet."

I thought then of Tarl throwing off those packs with such ease and remembered that it was her lover who shared my bed. "Will Tarl be jealous? Will she be angry at me?" I asked with apprehension for I was not eager to meet that anger.

Halli shook her head. "No, Tarl is not a jealous person. And, besides, what Tarl and I share you cannot come between."

At this I was relieved and also a little hurt. I asked no more questions, but slipped down, pressing my head against her breasts while Halli held me close.

* * *

We were sweet with each other after that and went about together like lovers—so much so that Zarmell felt called upon to say, "Well, Halli, you surely are a quick one. I had not thought to see her so easily cured." We even slept together sometimes, but whenever our desires drew us into lovemaking that same thing happened, blasting us apart, so that we both grew afraid of our passion.

At last Halli said to me, crying, "Sair, I am much drawn to you, but I cannot do this anymore. It is like being flung over and over against a knife blade."

Though I was in much pain from those words, I knew her to be right. So I agreed, and went away, seeming quite calm and holding tight to my pride. Afterward I walked out of Semasi as far as the edge of the woods. There I beat my fists to blood against a tree and cried with a fierce rage for what had been done to me in Eezore. That night I dreamt of Lairz, though I had not much thought of him since coming to Semasi. In my dream he was standing against a wall, stripped naked and trembling. I had a knife raised in my hand.

* * *

AFTERNOTES

Ferl—A small, three-stringed instrument with a high sweet sound useful for simple melodies. Because of its small size, it is often used for traveling.

57

Garmishair—The current meaning in Yarmald is all that is not Yarmald, all that is over there to the east on the other side of the Redline. The original meaning: everything from Tashkell to the sea, all of which was once Koormir territory.

Flowering-lodi—A small, wild fruit tree that grows in abundance on the hillsides of North Yarmald. It blooms with a profusion of delicate pink and white flowers bearing a sweet, pervasive scent. In its wild state the fruit is small, hard and bitter, fit only for deer and rabbits. Cultivated, it can be made to bare large, firm, semi- sweet fruit that keeps well through the winter months and forms a staple of North Yarmald diet for Hadra and Koormir both.

Tarmar—The common cereal and bread grain that is the basic staple food of Yarmald. To harvest, the ripe stalks are gathered when the seed heads are full and red-gold, then hung to dry over large, shallow, fineweave baskets. Within a few days of harvesting, the seed heads break open and release the grain.

Gobal Tree—A wide spreading, long lived tree, that often grows to great heights. This tree it is sacred to the Hadra. Their settlements are always planned around an ancient Gobal, which remains at the heart and center of the meeting circle. The Gobal tree is believed to be the companion of the Mother and as such to be especially favored by her.

As the Hadra neither hunt nor eat meat, creatures have not much fear of them and those around the settlement have learned to be quite tame.

Horses—Horses in Semasi are treated more like people from a friendly tribe than like animals. Once, before I understood this, I asked Tarl if the Hadra ever traded horses with the Koormir. She looked shocked, "No, never! We would as soon think of doing a trade in daughters or, for that matter, in mothers. You cannot trade what you do not own. They are our friends and companions, Sair, not our slaves."

Zildorn—Considered to be the central heart, both spiritual and secular, of any Hadra city or settlement. It is usually the first building to be built, located if possible on a high spot, visible from all sides. The Zildorn is intended to be a place of public pride and beauty, to be shared by all. As such, it is the focus for much decorative and artistic skills and endeavors. The building houses the library and the archives, as well as being a place for ritual ceremony, for special meetings and for study. For further discussion of the Zildorn of Semasi, see Section I, Part 4. For description of the Zildorn of Zelindar, see Section III, Part 8.

"As it must be"— A much used Hadra saying meaning, I have done all I can in the matter and now I turn it over to the Goddess.

Little Sister — Hadra term of endearment to a lover.

PART 6

SPRING IN SEMASI — TARL

Never in my life had I had my own home. Though this was but a crude stone hut and not mine for long, still I thought it very fine. I quickly lost my fear of living alone, and felt more freedom there than I had ever known in that grand and somber mansion that was my husband's family's home — and for me a prison.

It was clear that Seronis was no housekeeper. She had not much cared, using the place for shelter only and leaving me many cobwebs, but I worked hard to make improvements. I cleared the window-openings* of their debris, so I could see out in all directions and fastened up bright scraps of fabric for curtains. The stone floor, I scrubbed and oiled until it shone darkly under my feet. On the thick stone sills I set out clay bowls and bottles, filling them with grasses and bright flowers. The Hadra lent or gave me what they could from their own small stores. Soon that little hut began to glow around me.

I even acquired a cat for my new home, much against my will and my better judgment. Zarmell had asked if I wanted a cat* or dog* for company, as there were several in the settlement with no person. I shook my head, saying with conviction, "I am scarce able to care for myself. How could I care for a creature?" A few days later a large orange tabby came through the door, clearly claiming myself and the hut as her property. She was not easily dislodged. After a few days of struggle, I surrendered to being her person and named her Esla. She lay about among the pots of flowers, another bright ornament for my stone sills, and soon I grew accustomed to her company.

Of an evening I would sit on the broad stone stoop listening to the sea, while Esla purred in my lap. Sometimes Ozal and Mirl and others, too, would join me to make music there. With their urging I grew less timid of my voice and even had some joy in singing. Often Halli or Tarl, or both of them together, would come by to talk after the day's work. Tarl seemed less shy of me now that I was free and upright and not a bed-bound invalid.

If I were lonely I would go to the big dining-hall to eat with the others and do my share of the work there, though I was still wary of the Hadra in such numbers and felt somewhat a stranger among them. More often I ate at home, learning to cook for myself on my small hearth, a thing I had never done before. At first their food* was strange to me, but I soon became accustomed to it. As I grew skilled, I even asked one or another of the Hadra to join me at my meal. For that time, I was queen in my own small shelter and found much pleasure there. My peace was marred only by the fearful dreams that often came on me at night, sometimes of Lairz and sometimes of Koll and those others. Even these grew less frequent as the time passed.

* * *

As soon as I was steady on my feet, I went with Tarl and Halli back down to the ocean. The path to it was steep and rocky. Though the others went with ease, I had to force myself to set one foot before the other. Just as we reached the sand, strange wild cries sounded that forced me to look up. There, above us, was a long line of blue-gray seabirds. They flew past, dipping low over the ocean to skim the waves. Tarl and Halli called out and waved at them, seeming to greet old friends. "The kiri!" they shouted. "They are good luck. When they pass over you no harm will come to you that day." Seeing them, I thought of the seabirds that had passed over me that first day, the day I had come there seeking death.

How can I say what it meant to me to stand before the ocean again? Though I had been to it that one time for death and had watched it often enough from above, this was altogether different. In some way I was seeing it for the first time. It was as if I had yearned for the sea all my life and now, at last, was there—a pilgrim at the shrine. All that beauty and power together, the great rush and thunder of it crashing and turning, that blue that stretched out to eternity and pulled at my soul. I found myself crying, not from my old grief but from an overwhelming joy.

Tarl and Halli slipped away, leaving me alone with my tears, but when a decent time had passed they ran up on either side catching my hands. /Why stand there crying? Come in with us and learn to swim,/ I heard them say in my mind.

Now the waves seemed huge and threatening, far higher than my head. "No, no! I am afraid!" I cried, seeing those enormous waves bite into the shore. I held back, dragging my feet in the sand and fearful for my life as I had not been before.

But Tarl ran forward pulling at me, and Halli came on the other side. "Come out past the breakers. The water is still shallow enough there."

In spite of my great fear, I was hauled along resistant, spitting out water from the waves that crashed against us. Protest and struggle seemed useless against the Hadra when they had set their wills. Once past the breakers the water was, indeed, gentler and not too deep, moving in long, slow-rocking swells. There, I was able to catch my breath and calm myself a little.

/Lie back on our hands, trust us, we will use our Kersh and will not let you sink./ Since these were the same Hadra who had saved my life by pulling me unwilling from those waters, I could not think they meant me harm. I lay back against their hands, struggling to will away my fears. To my great surprise, I found myself afloat on the water.

After a while they slipped away their hands and then gradually withdrew altogether so that I was alone with the sea. I lay so for a long time, rocking on that vast blue belly under the bright blue sky and feeling a greater calm than I had ever known. Was this, perhaps, the true meaning of my dreams on the Bargguell and on the road? "Oh, mother of waters, let me always be your child." I remembered those words carved over the door of the Zildorn and chanted them softly to the sea as I lay stretched out on her body.

Walking back I found a shell spiral of pink and gold half-buried in the sand. I took it with me to remember that first swim, and from then on carried it always in my pouch. Later, Tarl and Halli showed me a few simple strokes. After that I swam every day, regaining my strength from that exercise and from the steep climb up the cliffside path. I also gathered many more shells, spending hours on the beach when I was free of other work. Some I even strung together and hung them from the roof of my hut so they made music, striking against each other when the sea wind blew.

* * *

Spring in Semasi meant much hard work and I had some difficulty with it. My body was strong enough, having made a good recovery, but I was not accustomed to physical labor. Never having learned the skill of it, I did not know how to pace myself. I would rush off to dig or hoe with all my strength and soon be weary. I felt even more the fool, seeing that old women like Yima seemed able to work for hours with little effort.

I was hoeing next to Jephra in the tarmar field one day, dusty, sweaty and exhausted. As I stood up to ease my cramped back, I looked about me and thought with disgust, /This is work for slaves./

Jephra answered me as promptly as if I had spoken aloud, "Then we must all be slaves." Her tone was biting, and so added to my other miseries was this intrusion into my thoughts and my shame for them. I stood staring at her, hot with resentment.

She went on hoeing methodically down her row, and said without stopping or looking up, "Sair, you might make a good Neshtair if you could ever forget your high-born Shokarn ways."

At that I shouted, "I did not choose my birth!"

Flinging down my hoe, I stalked out of the field. As soon as I was out of sight, I ran down the cliff path at risk to my legs and threw my dirty, weary body into the mother of waters. When, at last, she laid me back on the sand I was cleaner and clearer. Afterwards I walked for a while down the beach, gathering shells for my hut and watching the seabirds skim the waves.

Later in the evening cool, I finished my rows alone, not pacing myself against another. After that I tried to remember that I had only my own work to do. I did not have to do it faster or harder than the next one. I could stop when I needed to, swim when I wanted to. Things went easier for me then. My body, not pushed so hard, asserted its own wisdom and gained some skill. But from then on I tried to avoid Jephra. When I saw her watching me, I would cringe with embarrassment. It was as if my foolish words "This work is for slaves" were branded on my forehead.

* * *

Now that I was no longer trying to compete, I felt easier with the Hadra and more comfortable in their presence, all but one that is, that one being Tarl. I liked her. I even admired her, but somehow she made me angry, and I wanted to best her. If she lifted a rock, even with the aid of her Kersh, I had to try and lift a bigger one. If she ran, I had to try and run faster. Mostly she won, not caring, not even trying to, but I could not stop my foolishness. If we stood in line together I would bump her so persistently she would be forced to wrestle with me, or if she passed me I would block her way or grab at her. She must have felt some of that same antagonism, for we wrestled on the sand and the new plowed dirt, and sometimes in the way underfoot so that other Hadra would kick at us and grumble. However much I was beaten, I would still come back for more.

In spite of this small war between us, we often went about together, as we were much alike. We were both on the beach one day, and I had just stripped off my shirt to swim when Tarl called and whistled. Her horse, Timmer, came running up to her, tossing his head. This horse was a dark, handsome creature, named for the pine-covered Timmer Mountains that stretched south of Semasi, from Ishlair to the sea.

Timmer whinnied and snorted, prancing up against Tarl with such force I was afraid she would be trampled, but she slapped his neck and seemed to have no fear. After some words in his ear, she swung easily on his back and galloped off down the beach, her head bent close over his mane. Her black braid whipped in the wind behind her and her bright beads flashed. Clods of sand flew up from the horse's hooves like living things, and the kiri rose screaming and wheeling before them.

I watched her go with a surge of anger, so much did I want to ride that way myself. I thought she teased me with it, but when she galloped back she saw into my mind and shouted, "You can ride, too, Sair. You have only to ask the horse."

"Do what?" I shouted back, thinking this more mockery. She turned and trotted up to me.

"Ask the horse to take you for a ride," she said, looking down.

"But I do not know how to ride and there is no saddle or bridle."

"You have no need of those. It is better to ride by consent."

Tarl slipped off and came to stand by me. This seemed to me like more nonsense. In Eezore, people used saddles and bridles. There, horses went where they were made to.

Feeling the fool, but wanting much to try it, I said, "Timmer, will you take me on your back?" He snorted and pranced off sideways.

Tarl shrugged and said, "Well, plainly he will not, so you must ask another."

"There is no other," I answered angrily, for of course, there was only Timmer on the beach.

"There are horses in the fields. Picture one and call it in your mind. See if it will come."

Sure of failure, I shut my eyes and pictured the chestnut mare I had noticed that morning at the edge of the settlement. I asked in my head if she would come, and kept my eyes tightly shut until I heard the sound of hoofbeats on the slope behind me. When she ran up and nudged my arm, I felt a great swell of power such as I had never felt before. I petted and stroked her and whispered in her ear, gently touching the soft velvet of her nostrils. For some reason I felt close to tears.

"We call her Sharu," Tarl told me. "And she is not bonded with anyone."

When I tried to mount, Tarl offered me a hand, but I shook my head, wanting to swing on as I had seen her do. After several tries, Sharu grew uneasy and I was forced to take Tarl's help.

"You will learn soon enough," she said patting my knee, as I sat trembling and eager, a horse between my legs for the first time.

"What do I do now?" It seemed much higher from up there.

"Ask her to go slowly at first and hold tight with your legs."

We started down the beach at a walk, then went at a slight trot as I became accustomed to the motion and felt more secure. After we had gone at that pace for some turns I knew I wanted to run and would not fall off. I wrapped my legs around the horse, twisted my fingers in her mane and leaned forward. Sharu began moving faster. I could feel her muscles bulging under me and tightened my hold. Then the sea and the sand and the sky and myself and the horse were all one glorious motion flying together. Her hooves were like thunder coming up through the sand. We galloped in that way down the beach and back and down again. As we were going to pass Tarl a second time, I decided to turn right in front of her and gallop up the hill. Instead, I found myself lying on my back staring up into the gaping blue sky. Sharu was nudging me with her nose to see if I was hurt and Tarl was standing over me, laughing.

"It is best to guide not order," she said.

My body was not injured, only my pride. I jumped up and flew at Tarl, furious now, and she wrestled me hand for hand, not using her Kersh. I had the strength of my anger and was determined not to go down this time, but she still had some advantage over me. We grappled for a while until finally, I was tumbled on the sand. Pinning me with her weight, Tarl bent forward and kissed me roughly on the mouth. At that I twisted my head away and screamed, struggling against that grip, for suddenly it was Koll holding me down, not Tarl, and I was in the barracks again. Tarl gave a frightened cry and rolled over in the sand, doubled up as if in pain.

"Not me, not me!" she repeated again and again.

Then she was crying and would not look at me, but I heard her saying in my head, /Oh, Sair, I never want to seem to you like those men./

Finally it was I who had to comfort her. I turned her toward me

65

and stroked her hair and face. Then I pulled her into my arms. We lay so for a while with Timmer and Sharu watching over us. Looking at Tarl, so silent and turned in, I thought how different she seemed from the wild, arrogant Hadra who had galloped up and down the beach before me.

Just when I thought her sleeping she said softly, "If you can bear to do it, and it will not cause you more pain, tell me all that happened with those men so I may really understand, for I have only a jumbled notion of it." She had a quality of gentleness at that moment that I would not have suspected in her.

"Are you sure?" I looked at her hard, wondering if she truly knew what she had asked for.

"I am sure, Sair," she said answering my look.

Still it was no easy thing. I stumbled and struggled with the words and sometimes stopped altogether. Each time I heard Tarl's voice in my head drawing me on, /Say it all, Sair. Tell it through to the end./ So I went on until at last the words came of themselves, all in a rush, and with them a great easing for finally having spoken that terror aloud.

I told her the story as I have written it in this account, but it was more, for Tarl saw the pictures in my mind. When I finished, she looked at me with such grieving in her eyes that she must have had far more pain in the listening than I had in the telling.

Finally she said, "Oh, Little Sister, I had no idea what you had suffered. I have teased you and fought with you and made fun of you and I had no idea."

She drew me down against her and this time kissed me very gently on the mouth. When our bare breasts touched together, other things moved in me besides old griefs. A heat rushed up my body that gripped me between my legs and at the back of my neck.

When I dared to move again I drew back and brushed the sand from her breast, then slowly put my mouth down on it, taking that softness between my lips. I was not sure if she would let me, but I could feel her body quickly rising to meet mine. I knew then that this is what I had wanted. All those times I had fought and wrestled and tried to bring her down, all I had wanted was to touch her body. It was desire that had made me angry. When the sand began to scratch between us she slipped out from under me and pulled me to my feet.

"Take off your pants," she said impatiently.

We both stripped, then she took my hand and we ran together to the water to wash away the sand. After that she led me to a little cave at the base of the cliff. The floor of it was a thick mat of seaweed, dark green and crinkly. With a wide sweep of her hand she made a gesture as if showing me a spacious and well-furnished room.

"It is safe now, the tide is going out," she said.

I looked around doubtfully. "No one will come?"

"No one. We will put up a shield."

It seemed too wet and strange to me but with no hesitation Tarl spread herself out on that bed of seaweed, looking darkly beautiful. The sun was slanting in, filling the cave with a soft red-orange glow and making bursts of iridescence in the dark seaweed that surrounded her. Looking down at Tarl as she lay naked before me, sparkling with the wetness of the sea, I was filled with that same peace and fierceness I had felt standing before the ocean. But when she reached up to pull me down, I shivered and for that moment was afraid, afraid of her powers and the powers of that place and the strange force that was moving in me. Then she pulled again and I was down beside her, running my hands over her body while she lay very still, smiling up at me.

/This is what I wanted since I first saw you, though I did not know it then,/ I said in her head. Pictures of her flashed before me: Tarl as I had first seen her on the road, so ragged and arrogant, flinging down her pack; Tarl washing her brazen nakedness in front of me in the Zildorn and then dressed in that white robe; Tarl standing shyly in the doorway holding a branch of flowering-lodi.

She answered in my head, /I was blocking you, Little Sister. I was afraid of you. Your fierceness is too much like mine./ But she did not move to help me and there was still a little mockery in her eyes as she lay watching, as if to say, "This is what you wanted, Sair, laid out before you. Now what will you do with it?"

With that a shyness came on my hands and I was hesitant. I felt as if all the world was waiting for me to move. Even the waves seemed stilled. With Halli, it was she who moved and I who lay waiting. All had been secret and mysterious, done by candle light. Here it was all sunshine and the openness of day. I might have stayed frozen there forever had Tarl not shifted so that her legs parted slightly. Quickly I slipped my hand between them and that warmth revived me. She opened for me more, sighing and moving under my hands. Very gently I spread her other lips, opening her private self. Pink, lavender, purple, she was the color of sea shells inside. I slipped my fingers into that opening and felt her drawing me further. She was soft and moist like the sea creatures I knew from the tidal pools, the beautiful coral-colored Sharmir, the sea mouth that closes softly around your finger when you touch it.

I bent and put my mouth on her. She moaned and opened more. She tasted of salt like the sea. I moved my tongue, wanting to feel her pleasure, and when her body quickened against my mouth, I knew that same wild sense of power as when I had called the horse. At first I moved my mouth and hands trying to please, then my mind left and my mouth and hands moved with their own knowledge, faster and deeper, until with a sudden cry, Tarl wrapped her legs around me.

Afterward, as I lay next to her, she was still so long she seemed gone from her body. I grew afraid and kissed her eyelids until her eyes opened and she looked full at me. For a moment she seemed dazed, then suddenly, she smiled and said with some of her usual spirit, "Well, at least you have learned something useful since you came among us."

Then with a quick motion she rolled me over in the seaweed. She was not yielding now, but strong and willful. I was helpless under her hands and mouth, yet I was not afraid, perhaps because she had lain so open to me first. The seaweed no longer repelled me. I was in it, enmeshed in its fabric. The sound of the sea and the soft shifting light of the cave and the cry of the seabirds were all part of a journey that took me inward, through the dark, to a core of bursting color. This time when I cried aloud, it was with pleasure and not pain or fear. Then Tarl was holding me so tight against her we were one body, its heart beating very fast.

This time when the word "muirlla" came into my head I thought, "Yes, muirlla, yes. I will write it in red paint on the roofs of Eezore. They can brand it on my forehead!"

Later Tarl pulled me around so we made love to each other on that cool wet bed, two sea creatures in the setting sun. It was dark and cold when we finally moved from there and the water sounded very close.

"Little Sister, Little Sister," Tarl whispered softly to me as we struggled up the slope with no light, carrying our clothes. The horses had long since gone off to graze.

* * *

After that we rode and swam and wrestled and made love with the fierce wild pleasure of young animals. I felt that I had known Tarl all my life. Whenever the horror of the barracks came on me, she held me tight and sent me other pictures so that between us we could drive it back. After a time, it came to have less power.

* * *

So it came about that I, who had had no lovers ever and had wanted to throw my body into the sea, now had two, for Halli had not really deserted me. She was the humming bird in my life, and Tarl was the wild horse. I went about in a daze of joy, bumping into things, forgetting names, losing tools and being even less useful than before. I am sure the Hadra talked and grumbled about me, but I was the helpless fool before my great happiness, stumbling through my days in a blur of pleasure. I did not even notice that Tarl and Halli had little time for each other because of me. I had no sense then. I behaved outrageously and thought that that lovely spring would last forever.

* * *

AFTERNOTES

Glass — The only real window glass in Semasi, is in the Zildorn, and even that is in small panes, for it must be carried by horse pack from Zelindar or the Kourmairi coast city of Mishghall.

The Hadra seldom form as close a bond with cats or dogs as they do with horses. For the most part, the cats inhabit the grain sheds, living off rats and mice. The dogs of the settlement run about in their own pack, but know enough to do their hunting elsewhere.

As they have speech with all creatures, the Hadra cannot eat beast or fish or fowl, so their diet consists mainly of grains, vegetables, fruits and nuts. Two main staples are tarmar, which is an excellent grain of many uses and the fruit of the domesticated flowering-lodi, which keeps well through the winter.

PART 7

TIME OF CHANGE

When spring planting was over, the Hadra met in Council Circle*. There it was decided, that since none were planning to travel to the spring Essu on the Escuro River*, we of Semasi would make our own Essu at home.

Suddenly, the Hadra, who had worked so earnestly that spring, turned wild and playful. All set their energies toward the making of the festival. A bonfire was lit on the beach each night, that flared against the darkness and threw tall leaping shadows even to the sea cliff walls. Wrestling matches were held to the shouts and cheers of those watching, while horse races thundered up and down the sand. Even the dogs caught the madness as they barked and howled and ran about under foot. For eating, huge planks of driftwood were dragged together to make a feasting table and great pots of food sat bubbling on the fire. The drumming was constant, for when any at the drums grew weary, another took her place. As much yima root was drunk, those who sang and danced and made invocation to the Goddess did so with an untiring energy. If they grew too hot, they stripped off their clothes and ran screaming and shouting into the cold sea. Afterward they danced naked, their wet limbs flashing in the fire light.

Over this scene each night the moon rose, challenging the brilliance of the fire. Everything turned silver before her and the cliffs turned a silvery pink. Then loud shouts and cries would be heard for "Our sister moon . . ." to come dance with us and join our circle. For those Hadra already at the height of their visions, the moon had an even greater radiance.

None was exempt from the fever of the Essu, not even Quadra. At some moment I saw her silhouetted against the sea, her bare arms raised so that the sleeves to her robe slipped back, shouting words of praise to the Goddess. Later that same night she went about kissing at random and I, the Neshtair, was not missed. She kissed me full on the mouth, looking into my eyes like a lover. Then she put a flower in my hair which for those nights I wore loose around me.

When at last the Hadra grew weary, they sank down into a circle around the fire, body against body. Someone would begin by passing a kiss around the circle, then a caress, and soon all were entangled in pleasure with each other. It was often dawn before they closed their eyes and many slept where they were lying, until the sun drove them from the sand.

All this was mysterious and exciting and called to my wild spirit, but it was also frightening, as if doors had opened into another realm. Since I was wary of drinking yima root after my first turn with it, I watched this whole scene sober and would have been much afraid if either Tarl or Halli had not kept near me.

* * *

After a few nights of this madness, the fever abated and the fire became a time to smoke jol, tell stories and lie about together in the soft night air. The dogs were calmer, too and dozed against us. The horses did not run so wildly, but went to graze or stood nearby snuffling softly in the dark.

On the second such night when we all sprawled about, full with feasting, and the talk was at a murmur, I chanced to look at Quadra. She lay flat out, her mouth slightly open, her clothes awry and her legs bared. Seeing her so I felt some distress at her appearance, which seemed to me quite unsuitable for a councillor. Indeed, I thought it more fitting for an old drunkard, debauched on the streets of Eezore. With that thought there was a roar of laughter and Quadra sat up shaking her head. I was horrified that again my rude thoughts had burst into public view.

Quadra seemed shocked, yet it was not at me that she directed her sharp gaze, but at those laughing, saying angrily, "But why have you not taught her how to shield? Is it for mischief, you have not done so?" They looked abashed.

Halli said quickly, "I am sorry, Mother. We will do so tomorrow."

Quadra did not scold me for my thoughts, but went on quite sternly. "This is not fair or kind. You and Kedris must attend to it as soon as possible." Then she shook herself as if to shake off some heavy burden. "I do not wish to be Councillor any more this evening or to give advice on anything."

After that she turned to me and said, "Well, Sair, these Hadra are sometimes like bad children with their mischief, and we who are Neshtair often have much to endure."

"You are not Hadra?" I asked in amazement.

"No, no, I am Neshtair, though second generation. My mother escaped like you." She took my hand and said, smiling, "You are no doubt quite right, Sair, that I looked like an old drunkard laid out there on the sand. But it is my right, for this is my time of freedom. After all, I was not born a councillor. Often it is wearisome."

I blushed and could not look at her, so I asked quickly, "From where did your mother come?"

"Also from Eezore, but she was not uppercaste. She was a slave girl, abused and beaten and living with no hope in that cursed city." She shook her fist in the direction of Eezore.

"Tell us her story!" Zarmell shouted across the circle.

Quadra shook her head. "You have mostly heard it."

"Not I," someone called from the darkness.

"Nor I," said another.

"Tell it again," said several more.

Quadra leaned back against Jephra with a yawn. She took several puffs from the jol pipe Ozal held out to her. Kedris came to sit by her mother, looking at her with a clear and open affection.

"Please tell it again," she urged.

Quadra frowned. "Well, I will tell it then, but it is not a pretty story, at least not at the start.

"My mother, Chena, was sold by her family when she was very young and after that was sold many times, going from hand to hand. When she was twelve, another slave, a woman, tried to escape and was recaptured many miles from Eezore. She was brought back so the Shokarn could make an example of her, for that is how they do. All the slaves of that quarter were gathered together in the square to see her public torturing and execution. My mother was one of those forced to watch. I will not describe what they did to that woman. It was very terrible and her screams went on all day. At the end my mother was pushed forward with the others to look on the woman's face.

"That dreadful day changed Chena's life. But it did not make her submissive with terror as it was meant to. Instead, for the first time she thought of escape, knowing now there was a place to go. All that day she had heard talk of a red line that was dangerous to cross and of the strange Hadra who lived on the other side, women who were all muirlla, lovers of women. It was to Yarmald that the slave woman had been fleeing.

"From that day on, my mother had hope and a purpose. No matter how she did it or how long it took, she was going to make her escape across that line. But one lesson she learned from the execution: she would not die in that manner. If caught she would kill herself quickly. Death itself did not look so terrible, it was the dying of it that was hard. And even death seemed better than living a slave all her life. That woman, at least, had her peace at the end of it.

"As Chena was forced to look on the dead woman, she made a vow to that woman's spirit. /When I leave I will take you with me in my heart. When I cross that line, you can look through my eyes at freedom. I will never forget you. You are my mother now./ She picked up a little scrap of the woman's skirt. It was in that scrap she kept the rat poison she carried hidden for a year. It took her that long to escape. By then she was thirteen and had been raped by her master. She was carrying a child and knew she must leave soon or it would never be. I will not describe now how she managed, for that is a very long story, but will only say that her master had his share of that poison."

"And a good use for it, by the Goddess!" Zarmell shouted from the other side.

"What happened to Chena?" Ozal called out.

"She had not been well fed as a slave and had been able to take little food for her flight. When the Hadra found her, she was almost dead of starvation. It seemed but a little bundle of rags that Bettel found by the side of the road.

"It was the Hadra of Semasi who discovered her, for she escaped at the time of the first settling. They brought her back to life and nursed her through the birth of that first child, a wizened little creature, starved as he had been in her belly. As it was a boy, she went for a while to live with the Kourmairi on the Escuro River. As soon as she could find a home for him, she came back to live with the Hadra. There were no other children at that time so she became their pet. The daughter of all of them, she had as many mothers as she wanted." Quadra sighed again as if relieved to see Chena to safety. Then she took more puffs on the jol pipe and went on.

"She never grew very big. Privation and pregnancy together had stunted her. My brother, Dedo, also stayed small, a dwarf among those tall people of the river valley, though they did not mock or tease him for it. He was like a gift among them, loving and gentle and a knower of animals. It was almost as if he had the Hadra skill of speech with creatures. He never married, being a lover of men.

Now he is like a wise old man who sits on their councils and grows even smaller with the years.

"He and my mother were good friends. As she was so young when he was born and had not the raising of him, she felt more like his older sister than his mother. But by the time I came, there were so many years between us, he seemed more like an uncle to me and I saw little of him when I was growing up.

"After Dedo was born, my mother swore she would have no other children. Yet the longer she lived among the Hadra the more she wished to pass that life on to a daughter. Also she longed to give that dead slave woman a granddaughter, for she had not forgotten her. I was born when she was 26. By that time Semasi had been abandoned and Chena was living in Zelindar. She was full of fears when she went to the Spring Essu, but she prayed to the Goddess for a gentle man and a daughter. She got both. I was a big baby and gave her much trouble. But when I was born at last, and she saw me to be a girl child, she forgot her pains. She laughed and cried and named me Quadra for the woman who had died in the square that day. My younger sister was born two years later, and Chena named her Bettel for the Hadra who had first found her on the road."

When the jol pipe came round, Quadra took several long puffs on it before she spoke again. "My mother was one of the happiest people I ever knew. She was always amazed at the good fortune of her life in Yarmald and the miracle of her escape from Eezore. Her hard beginning gave her a strong joy for life. I remember her saying many times that nothing that happened after could ever be that bad again. She sang and played the stringed kerril* and told stories and was good at everything she made and did. Later, after the settling of Semasi failed, she sat on the Council of Zelindar as if she had been Hadra born. But she did not live to be old. Too much had been taken from her body too young. It is for her, for the brave little Chena, that I came back to remake this settlement." Quadra groaned and leaned back against Jephra, resting her head on the other's shoulder. Kedris put her head down in her mother's lap.

Quadra stroked her hair gently, saying, "And here is my daughter to follow after — Chena's granddaughter and a true Hadra."

After some silence Mirl asked, "Quadra, where is your sister now? Do you see her still?"

"In Zelindar. We are good friends and there is much love between us, but we are as unlike as can be. She needs the culture and the comfort of the city. I need to look out over vast spaces where I see nothing but what the Goddess made. When I go to visit her, I enjoy it for a day or so, but soon grow restless as a creature in a fancy cage. She does not come to see me much. The places I choose to live are too wild. We are the two halves of my mother, set loose to go our separate ways upon this earth."

Quadra had finished her story. She shut her eyes to show she wanted no more questions. In that lazy silence we were sitting up, stretching and scratching. Zarmell was re-lighting her jol pipe thinking to tell us some tale or other, and Ozal had just thrown another log on the fire, when Tarl sprang to her feet shouting, "Lar, riding fast this way!" And Ozal answered, "Yes, very fast. There must be some trouble from Eezore."

There was an alertness in the whole circle. Though I could hear nothing but the crackling of the fire, I knew the Hadra were all listening intently with their Kersh, their inner ear. Indeed, in a few minutes I, too, heard the sound of hoofbeats. Someone was riding fast down the road to the beach.

The Hadra were on their feet and crowded around Lar when she jumped off. I hung back by the fire watching, for her appearance gave me some fear. To my eyes, this woman they greeted so warmly looked like an arrogant young man of Eezore, an uppercaste Shokarn with a long, pale, bony face and white hands.

Her horse was breathing heavily and she herself had to stand silent a moment. When she caught her breath she said urgently, "The Shokarn army is gathering to march on the Redline*. They were to leave the day after I rode out." At this there were many groans, shouts, and exclamations until Quadra raised her hand for silence. Lar went on. "I could not bring you word any sooner. Ballis, who is one of their 'men', had much difficulty in leaving long enough to reach me. The army was being kept very busy, preparing to march. She will stay with them until they are on the way, and then when they are a day's distance, she will ride fast for home with word."

"She will be glad enough for reason to leave them," Jephra said bitterly. "Being one of the Zarn's 'men' is no great pleasure for a Hadra."

The others nodded and I shuddered at the thought. Then all their voices broke out again in excited questions until Tarl shouted for silence.

"How many men, Lar?"

"Not many. Less than two hundred, I think, but terrible new weapons, Sisters, things that burst and burn, a liquid fire that clings to the body. None on the other side of that line will oppose them."

There were more exclamations, and Jephra said over the clamor, "The Zarn's men had best look to themselves."

All this time, as they talked of Eezore and the Zarn's army, I watched Lar intently from my spot by the fire. She seemed very light for a Hadra, almost sickly white, but then as she was speaking, she stripped off the Shokarn clothing, took a bucket of water and began to scrub. Her own dark skin came in patches through the white. It was the first time I was aware that the Hadra had spies in Eezore.

"What does the Zarn want this time?"

"To re-open the old road to the sea. He hopes to reconquer Mishghall* and so have a port and power on the coast. Then he will be free to slave again in Yarmald. He has forgotten the lessons learned by his father and thinks that new weapons will blast him the way." She poured the bucket over her shoulders and looked up suddenly, straight into my eyes. I saw her flush with anger and I, myself, felt a rush of fear. "Who is that watching me? She is not Hadra."

"She is Neshtair and trustworthy."

"She looks Shokarn to me."

"I will speak for her," Tarl said quickly.

"She has seen me in my changes and she is Shokarn. None of you warned me."

Quadra put her hand on Lar's arm, saying, "She is a sister, Lar."

Halli quickly sat down beside me and Tarl went to stand directly in front of Lar. "She is lover and Little Sister to me, Lar. I have mind-touched with her. She is safe. As I am your sister so she is my sister. She also has much reason to hate Shokarn power." Tarl was looking intently at Lar, but Lar was glaring at me, her scrubbing suspended. Then Tarl must have sent her some mind picture, for suddenly she relaxed and strode around the circle, smiling at me.

"I am sorry for my rudeness, Sister. I have no love for Shokarn at this moment and was turning that on you. Welcome to Semasi." She gave me a huge, wet hug that left me flecked with soap suds and white body paint. Then she held me away a little to look into my face.

"And how are you called, Sister?"

"Sair. That is what I am called here. In Eezore I was Sairizzia."

"Sairizzia!" she exclaimed with great warmth. "Ah, so you are the woman who rose from death on the Bargguell and walked to the ocean. Already there are legends told of you in Eezore. Your name is a hope to women there." She stepped away and looked me up and down, nodding. "You will make a good Neshtair." Then she pulled me to her and hugged me again, wetting what parts of me she had left dry that first time.

"Come, Sister," I said to her. "I will help you shed your Shokarn skin."

So while the Hadra talked policy and strategy, I scrubbed away that whiteness, turning Lar this way and that in the fire light.

"We must call Hadra Council."

"There is no time to warn any but the river Hadra at Ishlair."

"We can choose line keepers and holders from Semasi and Ishlair. That will be enough."

"And we must warn the Kourmairi along the Escuro River."

"What help can the Kourmairi be in this?" Mirl asked sharply.

"That is part of our old bargain with them, though I, for one, could wish it were not so," Jephra answered.

Lar dried her face and said, "As soon as I have finished washing, I will ride on to Ishlair to warn the Hadra there and go also to the Koormir settlements."

"As soon as you are dry," Ozal said with rough kindness, "you will sit down here by the fire and eat some food. When we have a plan, I will ride to the settlements with it and warn Hadra and Kourmairi both. You will sleep here tonight."

When the washing was done, Lar thanked me with another hug. Mirl laid out a rug and drew Lar down to sit on it as Kedris poured her a cup of tea. Drying her back, I could feel her weariness under my hands.

Zarmell called out to her, "Lar, if you are not too stubborn and difficult, I will give you a rubbing with Lesh oil and herbs after you eat."

At this there were cheers and laughter and someone shouted, "Beware of Zarmell's rubbings. Sometimes they end in her cloak!" Lar looked up from her tea and grinned. "Well, Sisters, I am very weary and very glad to be home. Zarmell, this aching body would be grateful for some good healing at your hands, no matter how it ends."

Meanwhile, a lively discussion had broken out as to which road Ozal should take: the coast road with its dangerous pass through the Timmers and a hard, steep path after that, or the longer, easier way south through the foothills and up the valley road along the Escuro.

Jephra kept insisting, "The cliff road is too dangerous at night."

And Mirl would answer, "But the way by the valley takes too long. It is like riding backward."

This continued until at last Ozal shouted, "Enough, Sisters! I will go whichever way my horse and the Goddess see fit to guide me. Either way I have sense enough to get through safely."

While the matter was being settled, Lar kept looking about her anxiously, scanning the circle of firelight. "Where is Yima? Is she away? Is she not well?"

"I am here, Granddaughter." Yima came forward, bringing Lar a bowl of food.

"Why were you not here to greet me, Grandmother? I grew afraid when I did not see you."

"I was waiting for the business to be over. I had no wish to stand in the path of the Zarn's army."

Lar laughed and reached out for Yima's hand, drawing her down beside her on the rug. "Yima, sweet Grandmother, I am so happy to see you looking well and strong. The letters that pass between us come too seldom." She kissed the old woman on each cheek and then bent to kiss her hands, saying, "But I think of you much."

"And I think of you, too, living in that evil place. I think of you often and dream of you at night. Oh, Daughter's Daughter, I am so glad to look on you again safe in Semasi." With her fingers, she gently traced Lar's face and I could easily see the resemblance in their clear features and long, sharp bones. "This time will you stay a while among us, Little One?"

"As it must be, Grandmother, as the Goddess wills it."

"Oh, Lar, I have not much time left on this earth and long to spend some of it in your presence. Surely the Goddess would not begrudge me that."

"Come, Yima, let us not spend what time we have in quarreling." Lar said this roughly, but there was the sparkle of tears in her eyes.

Yima gave a deep sigh and put her head down against Lar's shoulder. Lar ate with one hand and with the other arm held her Grandmother close to her side. The discussion circled around them, with Lar sometimes entering in and sometimes seeming absent and far away. When at last she fell asleep with her bowl in her hand, Mirl laid her down next to Yima and covered them both with a cloak.

The Hadra talked of the Zarn's motives, the policies of Eezore, the rebellion raging along the Balmori River and the terrible measures being used to quell it, until Tarl finally burst out, "Sisters, how can we hold to any honor, living safe this side of the Redline and saying that what murder is done on the other is no blood of ours? Why must we wait at the line for that army? The Zarn is sending his men all the way to Yarmald. Can we not meet them elsewhere and drive them back to Eezore? Can we not clear some of the land between of that pestilence? The river people on that side of the line would be glad enough of our help."

"There are many among them who fear the Hadra more than the Zarn's army," Jephra said bitterly.

Quadra was frowning. "Tarl," she said shaking her head, "our Kersh is limited, a personal protection. It is not the weapon of an advancing army. Even to use it to stand at the line against that force of men will strain all our powers."

"But how many women like Sair suffer and die under that rule? Women like Chena, like Zarmell. Why must we wait here for those few who struggle through to us? Why can we not help open the gates? Are they our sisters only after they cross that line?"

"Tarl, I know as well as you and better the evils of Eezore. I have sometimes dreamt of tearing apart those walls stone from stone with my own hands. But that is fantasy. We have not yet the strength. Would you take on all of Garmishair, first the Zarn of Eezore, and then of Maktesh, and Pellor, and Nhor, and after that the armies of Tashkell*? There is no end to it. We are a new people, hardly a nation. The Zarns are very old in their power. It may be that our daughters' daughters will clear the land of that weight, but we are still too few."

"And I say we are cowards behind the safety of that line our grandmothers laid out for us."

Quadra was angry now and said quite sharply, "We must be mindful of our limits. Remember, Tarl, we are children of the Goddess. We are not the Goddess herself. Along with their powers all Hadra are trained to . . ."

"What do you know?" Tarl shouted suddenly. "You are not Hadra born!"

With those words there was a gasp from the circle and Tarl herself gave a sharp cry, saying quickly, "Oh, Mother, I am sorry. Forgive me my rash tongue which has outspoken me." She dropped down on the sand with her forehead on Quadra's feet and said again, "Oh, Mother, I am sorry."

Quadra shook her head. She quickly pulled Tarl to her feet, amusement and discomfort mixed on her face. "Come, Tarl, it is not so terrible. It is, indeed, a truth that you are Hadra and I am Neshtair, though you need not say it quite so rudely."

Zarmell jumped up and called out hard and mocking, "Sister, they think it the worst of insults."

And Jephra said sharply, "You should think, Daughter, before you speak with such a youthful, careless tongue."

Tarl bowed her head and said almost in a whisper, "Mother, I am ashamed to have forgotten you were councillor here."

At that Quadra laughed. "Well, enough, Tarl, but a councillor is not queen, you know."

Then other Hadra joined with their words from around the circle until Quadra said abruptly, "Enough of this. We have too much else to talk of," and made a motion for all to sit.

It was quickly decided that the settlements of Ishlair and Semasi should meet on the day after the morrow at the Escuro River. There they would come together at the council grounds to choose line keepers from among them. Those not chosen would remain as holders for the others after the battle.

That being settled, Ozal rode away to Ishlair with her heavy message and one by one the Hadra wandered off to their dwelling places or rolled up in their cloaks to sleep by the fire. I sat a long time staring into the glowing coals and thinking of what was to come. It seemed sure to me that Tarl would be chosen line keeper and maybe Halli, also. Clearly that loving carefree spring was over.

* * *

The next day all was a great haste of preparation. More meetings and consultations were held. Much food was prepared and packed. Clothes and bed rolls were made ready. Horses were chosen — or rather asked if they would go. And somehow, in the midst of it all, the beach was cleared as if there had never been a feast and festival. Even the coals from the fire were buried and all made clean again.

I had a great hunger to go with the Hadra and see for myself the Zarn's men blasted by their own weaponry. Some of my old anger boiled up in me again and I felt little fear. But I was told by Tarl and several other Hadra, that I was not to be allowed at the line or even in the camp.

When I argued this, Quadra stopped in her rush to tell me firmly, "You cannot go with us, Sair. The council has decided it. Your great anger would alter the energy and endanger us all. Speak no more of it, Daughter."

So I wandered about, restless and agitated, trying to lend my hand to the preparations for others to go where I could not. When I saw that I was of scant use in that state, I drew apart, going to the cliff above the sea for a little peace. There I sat staring down at the lines of waves. Suddenly I was flooded by memories of Eezore and found myself crying for the loss of my father. This was something I had not allowed myself to do before. I had left his house full of anger at being sold in marriage and had held that anger hard against him. Since that day I had not seen his face. Now I was almost crushed with that grieving and determined to send him some message by Lar if she would carry it.

Lar was just rising when I found her in Yima's shelter. She was full of complaints, being stiff and sore from her hard ride. When I told her my wish she gave me a sharp, appraising look. "I have been told your story, Sair. You do not blame your father for your marriage and all that followed?"

"My father was always very kind to me, more perhaps than he should have been. But as he was weak before my will, so I could not hope for him to stand against the will of all Eezore, past and present. After all, marriage sales are the custom among the Shokarn. Oh, Lar, no doubt he thinks me dead . . ." I did not finish for the tears threatened to rise again.

She nodded. "I will take him word and gladly, Sair, but you must make the message brief and safe and I must read it before I carry it. Letters between Yarmald and Eezore can be dangerous to those who bear them."

Lar found me a scrap of paper and sharpened a quill. With that I wrote, "Dearest Father, I am well and happy and love you still." After that I could think of nothing more to say unless I told him all, enough to be a book and not a letter Lar could safely carry.

I stood staring out the window, remembering the courtyard garden and the library and the tower room and the rides in my father's carriage. My tears fell on what I had written. Lar slipped that paper away from me, blotted it and folded it very small to slip in a secret inner pocket. Keeping my face averted, I told her the best way to my father's house.

* * *

At sunset we all gathered at the Zildorn. The floor had been cleared of all that was movable and strewn with dried crushed Gobal leaves. They had a sharp bitter smell when trod on. In the middle of the room, a circle of white candles was set out with a triangle of blue ones within it. At the very center was an iron caldron. The room itself was filled with a soft orange light from the glow of the setting sun on those red rock walls.

As we entered, we formed ourselves into a circle around the candles. Since we were many in that space, there was much talk and laughter and also some jostling and shuffling before we found our places. Then Quadra raised her hand for silence and stepped forward to light the oil in the caldron, from which there rose a sweet, heavy smoke. After that Jephra and Yima came from opposite sides of the circle to light the candles.

I looked about me at that circle of women. It was the first time I had seen all the Hadra of Semasi together in one place. They had put off their work clothes and were wearing long, soft robes or skirts and seemed transformed in that warm light. Most had washed and oiled their skin. Many were bare-breasted and wore those symbols of triangles and circles, on chains or thongs between their breasts, or wore amulets of birds or beasts or female figures. Their hair was braided or decorated and they wore jewelry at their wrists and ankles, in their ears, and on their foreheads, as well as around their necks. Halli had helped me dress for that occasion, but I wore a modest robe that covered both my breasts. I was not yet ready to bare myself to so many eyes.

After a deep silence when all stood with bowed heads and closed eyes, Yima began to pass around a blackwood bowl of Gobal leaves. As each woman wished to speak, she took some of those leaves, stepped forward, crushed them and threw them into the caldron fire. With that the fire would flare up and a sharp tang fill the room.

"Oh, Great Mother, please help us to be strong and not be cruel."

"Oh, Great Goddess Shimuir, she who makes light, please help us hold the power we will need against whatever comes."

"Oh, Manayistra, Mother of Waters, please help us to be clear and clean in this work."

"Oormog, Great Oormog, Sister of our souls, spirit of caves and tunnels and all dark places, please help us to use our wisdom and remember mercy."

"Harimair, Sister Spider, help us to bind together all our strength in one tight web that cannot be broken."

Their voices went on for some time. When at last there was a silence and no more came forward to speak, Quadra gave a nod. Mirl and Kedris took away the caldron by its handles, stepping quickly over the candle flames. Then Quadra stripped off her robe, laying it carefully over Jephra's arm and herself stepped naked into that central triangle of light. She raised her arms, chanting words I did not understand, then turned to each point of the triangle. She was answered by the others in the same words and for some time the chanting echoed back and forth. Then there was again a moment of silence.

After that, all threw up their hands and turning their faces toward the ceiling, said together, "As it must be." By then the day had darkened to evening. In the flickering light of the candles, the pattern on the ceiling leapt and quivered, the colors surging and melting into one another. I stood transfixed, staring upward until I heard those about me move. When I looked down again, Quadra was kneeling in the center of the triangle, her head bowed low on her chest, swaying and chanting softly to herself. She did not glance up when the others left. Each woman as she went out drew in the air with her hand, making the circle of blessing.

* * *

Once outside I ran to catch up with Tarl. She slipped her arm around my waist, and we walked together in silence to the edge of the sea cliff. There we stood listening to the ocean until the moon rose over the mountains behind us, silvering the waters. I turned back to look at Semasi glowing in that pale light and thought of Quadra.

"Will she stay there through the night?"

"At least till the candles burn down. Sometimes it is very lonely being councillor."

"How did she gain that place?"

"It was not gained. It was thrust upon her. We begged her to be councillor for one was needed here."

"Were there no others to choose from?"

Tarl shook her head. "To be councillor one must be over thirty and better over forty. Not all of those years have the calling. Yima is too sweet and Jephra too stern and judging. Quadra has some quality I have no words for, but I would follow her into the very fires of Damlin itself if she said we must go. Jephra, I would not follow past the lodi orchard, in spite of her stern stares." Then Tarl shook her head and putting her hands over her face, she mumbled through her fingers, "Oh, Little Sister, I am ashamed of my reckless temper that outspoke me so cruelly last night."

"Come, Tarl, I think Quadra has forgiven you. Also, she has much else to think on." When she made no response, I put my hand gently on her arm. "I think you love her almost like a mother."

"She is more mother to me than my birth-mother will ever be." Tarl answered angrily and turned away.

"Is your mother living?"

"She lives in Zelindar. I do not wish to speak of her."

After that there was a stiff silence until I asked, "What does it mean to be Councillor to the Hadra?"

She dropped her hands and turned to look at me with that sol-

85

emn manner she sometimes took. "One who is Councillor must sit in for and give council at all discussions. For decisions of grave importance, she must fast and meditate in solitude to open herself to the powers. That is what Quadra does tonight. The council does not have to go by her words. It can choose another course, but it must first listen carefully and have good reason."

That night Tarl and I slept together in my stone hut. The candles were still lit in the Zildorn when we passed.

* * *

AFTERNOTES

Council ; Council Circle—In cities like Zelindar, council members are chosen to represent different districts, and meetings are held at prearranged times. In small settlements like Semasi council is often all those dwelling there, and any can call a meeting.

Escuro River—The wide, deeply curving river that runs for most of the length of Yarmald, passing along the eastern edge of Zelindar and emptying finally in the tropic southern swamplands below Bayrhim. Barge and raft traffic take goods along it from north to south. It is considered to be the sacred heartline of Yarmald as well as its main waterway and is looked upon with awe and respect and also a sort of humorous affection. Many settlements are built along it by both Hadra and Koormir and its flow irrigates most of the farmland of the peninsula. In the north the Essu grounds and the Council grounds are located on its banks. Most of the year it is shallow and easily crossed, but it is apt to flood suddenly in spring and fall.

Kerril — A large, twelve-stringed instrument, sometimes held across the lap and sometimes played with the base of it resting on the ground. It has a deep melodious tone and can be used for intricate harmonies.

Redline — A line of force and power, that is also an actual painted line, separating the Yarmald Peninsula from the Zarns' lands. It was laid down by Hadra and Koormir together, seeking to protect Yarmald from Shokarn invasions and goes from the northern tip of Yarmald at Felduir Point to the far southern tip past Teerhault inlet. For further information concerning the making of the Redline read *The Redline of Yarmald*, book 596 of the Hadra Archives.

Mishghall — The oldest and largest Kourmairi city in Yarmald. Being very favorably situated on a gentle bay, it is a ship building center as well as a center of commerce and culture. Its desirable location has made it a target of Shokarn conquest and it was held by the Zarn of Eezore as a slaving and shipping center, until it was recaptured by the Hadra and Kourmairi together at the time of the making of the Redline. For more information read *The Redline of Yarmald*.

Tashkell — All the lands beyond the Rhonathren Mountain Range. Because of the steep, forbidding nature of these mountains, little is really known of this area, although Shokarn and Koormir both have many tales of this region. There are even old legends of the Shokarn having originally invaded from Tashkell.

PART 8

DEPARTURES

I woke early. The sky was still gray, save for a few streaks of pink glowing on the horizon, yet already I could hear voices and the sound of horses. I knew the Hadra were meeting at dawn in the public circle. Tarl should be wakened, but I had no heart to do so. Instead, I raised myself on my elbow to watch her sleeping. Her dark hair lay loose on the pillow, wavy from yesterday's tight braid and her face looked soft and open. With pleasure I could have watched that way for some time, but my mind must have touched on hers, for suddenly she opened her eyes and looked straight into mine. She did not speak, but pulled me down tight against her, wrapping her arms and legs about me. For a while we lay still together, sunk in that deep body touch. Then I slept again.

When I woke next Tarl was up and dressing, her hair already braided and her boots laced. I jumped up instantly and came to stand before her. "Did you think to slip away and leave me sleeping?" I asked sharply.

She nodded without looking at me. "It seemed simpler that way," she said and went on dressing. She would not meet my eye.

I grabbed her arm. "Tarl, I must go with you," I said urgently.

At that she pulled away. "No, Sair, it has been decided by Council that you cannot go."

"But I have a right to be there. For what was done to me by those men, I have a need to go."

"It is for that reason, Little Sister, that you cannot go, not even to the river. Your anger and your pain are so fierce, you would pull us off center and upset the balance. We need to focus all our energy, all our Kersh without distraction."

"They have terrible new weapons, Tarl. They will demolish you."

Tarl shook her head and laughed without humor. "The more terrible their weapons, the more destruction they bring on themselves." Her voice was grim.

I felt her slipping out of my power. "Tarl, if you can leave me this way, you do not love me."

With a shout she grabbed both my arms and shook me forcefully. "Stop this, Sair! Do not play on my heart. It already hurts to leave you." Then she loosed her grip and pushed me away. "Do you want to weaken me, Sister?" she asked fiercely. "Or will you give me strength to go? This is a thing that must be done if any of us are to live safe between the Redline and the sea."

I felt a sudden rush of shame for what I had been doing and looked down at the floor. "I am sorry, Tarl. I had no right."

She took my chin firmly in her fingers and turned my face toward her. "I need you now, Sair. I need you to send me off with love. This is no game that we ride out to." At that moment she looked sad and weary, almost old. I felt a pull of pain in my heart.

Sobered and afraid, I pressed my fingers to her forehead and said with all the powers I could draw upon, "All my love rides with you, Tarl. Whatever strength I have is yours."

She gently touched my hair. "You are with me in my heart and spirit, Sister. You are bound into my flesh. But in my mind, for the balance of things, for the Cerroi*, the circle of fate that we live within, it is not what matters." She made a circular gesture with her hand. "In my mind you must be no more to me than any woman they have abused, women that I do not know and never will. For the Great Balance we cannot go to the line in anger. Do you understand?"

All this seemed quite different from the turn of her words with Quadra by the fire, but I nodded, knowing that even if I did not understand, I must accept. There was a moment of silence between us as she stood staring off into some distant place, then with a sudden, quick nod Tarl shouldered one of her packs and signaled me to take the other. We walked unspeaking toward the circle, not even touching hands, though we touched in other ways.

Just before we reached it I turned and said, "Tarl, I am going off on my own journey. After all that has happened to me I need some time alone and cannot sit here awaiting your return." Until I spoke those words I had not known myself that I was set to do this thing.

"Good," Tarl said gripping my arms. "This must be your time." She gave me a hard kiss and a harder hug, the weight of our packs falling awkward between us. As she stepped back she handed me a knife. "Take this with you. You will need it wherever you are going. I made it with my own hands."

"But you will need it even more," I protested.

"I have another in my pack. Take it for me."

I strapped on the knife and followed her. When we got to the circle it was filled with movement. Women and horses and dogs were milling about in a cloud of soft, red dust. A fire had been started for roasting potatoes and nuts, and for brewing those endless cups of tea. Bright banners* of red and blue and yellow, looking like a flock of birds, leaned against the central Gobal tree. The Hadra were brushing their horses and loading them, braiding their manes and tails with feathers and ribbons. It seemed as if all Semasi were already there, and clearly we were late.

Halli rushed up to greet us followed by her horse, Ishta. "I almost came in search of you," she said breathlessly. She spoke to both of us, but it was Tarl she looked at, laying a hand on her arm. Tarl responded with a long hug, that only ended when Timmer came running down from the high pasture and pressed his head against her side.

I had much wanted some heart-touch with Halli before she left, but she and Tarl set instantly to talking of that day's ride, so that I felt closed out and soon slipped away. When I looked back they were standing close, their heads bent together as they brushed their horses.

In spite of all those preparations made the day before, it was almost noon when the Hadra rode out of Semasi, and that, only after many rounds of kisses and blessings. Just before they left I saw Jephra sitting on her horse apart from the others. She was gazing out to sea with such a look of sadness on her that it wrenched my heart. As I wore no jewelry, I had nothing on me for token save the spiral shell from my first time of swimming. This I carried always in my pouch. On impulse I went up and thrust it in her hand, saying quickly, "Go with love, Mother." Then, for just an instant, I laid my face against her knee.

* * *

Most of the settlement rode out that day, not more than ten of us remaining in Semasi. When I had done with my kisses and farewells, I ran up the path to the top of a small hill above the village. From there I could watch that little band of women riding out to meet an army, all in their bright colors, with their banners flying and their horses dancing under them. Tarl and Quadra rode at the front. In twos and threes I watched them pass below me, winding down the narrow road to the river where they would meet with the women of Ishlair, and after that, with the Zarns army. I sat for a long time after they were out of sight, watching the road by which they left, and at last fell asleep in the sun. I had planned to leave that day on my own journey, but when I woke it was almost dark, and I was cold and stiff.

The night birds were hooting already from the hills when I wandered back into the central circle. All the others had left save for Zarmell. She was still tending the fire and stirring the contents of a large pot. Seeing me, she set down her spoon with a smile and reached out a hand.

"Well, Sairizzia, are you calmer now? Will you have some tea?"

"Yes," I said gratefully, and sank down on a rock, not caring this time if she mocked me. I drank my tea in silence while Zarmell stirred her pot. My mind was still on that distant road. At last, I nodded my head toward her brew, asking my question without words.

"Potions, potions for healing," she replied to my nod. "Things that can cure the spirit as well as the body. I have no Kersh, no Hadra powers. I am an outsider like you, Sairizzia, so this is my way—to be a healer. It is a thing I can do and a power none can deny." As she spoke, she shook more leaves from her pouch into the pot, and thrust some branches on the fire so that it blazed up again. "Often Neshtair become healers. Sharven made that same choice, but she went to live in Ishlair instead. It is she who will heal them at the line, while I have potions made ready for their return."

As she went back to her stirring, I sensed a long silence coming and wanted her to speak more. "Who is Sharven?" I asked, hopeful of some story.

Zarmell stared into the fire making no answer for some time. Then she spoke suddenly as if just remembering my question. "Sharven . . . oh, yes, Sharven. Who is she, indeed. A very powerful Neshtair. She is healer, not only to the Hadra at Ishlair, but to the Kourmairi of the river settlements as well. No doubt you two will meet sooner or later." Zarmell set down her spoon and came to stand before me with her hands on her hips.

"Sharven and I are as sisters though we are no blood kin. We even look alike: big women, women of bulk and substance — stature, not all muscle and bone the way you like them." With that she pinched me and laughed. I struck at her hand, but she took no notice and went on.

"Yes, we look like sisters, but we are not even from the same city. She is from Maktesh, and her escape was very difficult. You must get her to tell you some night by the fire. She was uppercaste, even danced for the Zarn once, but that was when she was a little skinny thing, a nibbit*. However, that is her story and she must tell you herself.

"Since coming to Yarmald she has chosen to become healer and herb woman and is very good at her work." She stopped and gave me a sharp look I could not read. Then, frowning, she went on. "We are strong women, Sharven and I, yet neither of us has any Kersh. But you . . ." Suddenly she picked up her spoon and shook it at me. "You will have it! I see the mark of it already!" She shouted this with a strange mixture of envy and triumph and then rushed on. "You could hear the speech of minds almost from the start. You came here young enough. They will train you."

With those words, she waved her spoon so wildly I drew back, sure she would strike me with it. Her intensity frightened me. I had nothing to say into that flood of words and so held up my cup for more tea.

"Yima leaves," she said with sudden gentleness as she poured from the pot. "The root is for dreaming, for visions, but the leaves are for soothing the soul." Her voice was as soft then as it had been harsh before. Smiling, she came and sat next to me, putting her arm around my shoulder.

It was truly night now. The sky had darkened, and the darker mountains rose in front of it as flat black shadows. Against them, the lights of Semasi looked few and scattered. Zarmell's fire blazed like a bright heart at the center of it all, and I felt strangely comforted by her size and the warmth of her body against mine.

"You are sad, Little One," she said softly. "And I have talked too much and too wildly."

I sipped my tea for some moments in silence and then remembering my old promise to myself, I asked, "How did you come here, Zarmell? In what way did you leave Eezore?"

"Aha, so you finally have time to ask. I thought you so bound up with Hadra lovers you had no time for words with a Neshtair."

"Zarmell," I said impatiently. "Tell me your story or not, but do not tease me more."

She sighed and nodded. "Ah, yes, yes, I have a sharp tongue and sometimes it outspeaks me. Tarl is not the only one who should feel shame for her words." She glanced away with sudden shyness and asked, "Do you really wish to hear it, Nibbit?"

I put a hand on her arm. "Yes, Zarmell, I have wanted to ask since I first knew you came from Eezore and were not Hadra-born."

She got up to poke the fire again and stir her pot, moving about so restlessly that I almost lost hope of her speaking, but at last she settled on a rock beside me. "Like you, I was born Shokarn in Eezore, but I am working-caste. You have seen the brand on my forehead. This also is mine." She unlaced her wide leather wristlet and showed me the caste tattoo, purple against that lighter patch of skin.

"I was always muirlla, always. Even from the time I was very young. I did not have to come among the Hadra to learn that." She gave a snort of angry laughter. "They did not invent the love of women, though sometimes they act as if they did. But in Eezore it is your death if discovered, so I learned to be very careful.

"Because I was young and strong then, I worked at rough jobs, often men's jobs. Women who are working-caste have more freedom in some ways. There is no need to keep them unspoiled goods for some fine husband." She spit into the fire. "There were always other women like me on those jobs and sometimes we met in secret with each other. But I found no happiness in that. They secmed too much like men. They may have thought the same of me, for I was a tough sort then. So I was always looking and hoping, but carefully, for there was much danger.

"There was a shopkeeper on a street close to where I lived. I passed her every day. She was young and pretty and always smiled at me. After a time we began to greet each other and trade a few words. One evening, taking all my courage in hand, I stopped at her stall. With a low bow I said quite formally the words I had practiced so many times, 'It would please me much to know you better.'

"She did not take offense, but smiled sweetly and answered, 'That would please me, too.' It was almost as if she had been waiting for my words.

"Trembling, I held out my palm to her in the sign of friendship. She drew in it the sign of the muirlla, all the while looking into my eyes." As she spoke, Zarmell took my hand and opened it flat. With her fingers she traced that sign in my palm; I remembered having wondered at it red-painted on the walls of Eezore. For what seemed like a long time she stared at my palm, as if searching in it for the past before she went on. "I looked down expecting to see that mark burned into my flesh like a brand. My hands shook. I could not believe my great good fortune, and yet, was much afraid, more so than I had ever been even at dangerous work. It was not just the risk to my life that made me tremble. It was this new adventure opening before me. I blushed and grinned and looked down at my feet while she told me the way to her rooms.

"Quickly I went home to bathe and deck myself in the only good clothes I owned, a white shirt with red embroidery and a long skirt of a red and orange patterning. Dressed so, I thought myself fine enough for anything. I even brushed out my hair, a thing I had not done in weeks and put a flower in it. Back in the streets, I went with my heart high and full of joy, thinking I had found my love at last. When I knocked, the door opened on a dim room, and two guardsmen sprang at me. They began slapping me about, making accusations.

"Death was clear in front of me. I knew I must move quickly. They both were drunk enough to be unsteady on their feet and thought me a great fool, not much to deal with. After all, one does not send the Zarn's army to bring back one muirlla. But I had learned much keeping life in my body on the streets of Eezore and I always carried a knife. They asked me foul questions and poked at me with their swords. Then one, for sport, thought to see what I had under my skirts. He came close enough so I could give him a hard knee in the groin. As he bent in pain I had my quick knife twice in his back. With a groan he dropped to the floor. I grabbed up his sword. The other guard had time for one shout only before I had him through the gut with it. He was not expecting any trouble, only thinking to have some fun before delivering me to death."

She spat again and said harshly through her teeth, "All this Kersh is fine and honorable, but there are times I would rather see their guts spilled out before me on the floor." With that she gave an angry laugh. I nodded in agreement, knowing well enough what she meant.

"I did not wait to see what that one shout would bring, but ran to hide in the sewers. These I had knowledge of from my work. Soon I could hear many feet running above me and the sound of shouting, so I knew I was being hunted. That is how I escaped Eezore, crawling through the sewers of the city in my only good clothes. I was many years safe in Yarmald before I could bring myself to wear a skirt again. The rest you know, Sairizzia, for you yourself have come the long road to cross the Redline."

She sighed and leaned back, shutting her eyes. "I have often wondered about the little shopkeeper, if she betrayed me or if we both were watched and reported to the guard. Perhaps she died tortured in the square, thinking me the traitor. Oh, well, if that is so, she is long since at peace, and I am glad enough to be here."

"Did you ever find your true love, Zarmell?"

"I never looked again, Nibbit. Yima was my first love after I crossed the line, but there have been many others. Here I am free to love women without fear. Many women, as many as I want. That is enough for me, more than enough, Sair. That is heaven." She laughed. Then she pinched my arm again. "Well, Little Sister, will you share my cloak tonight? I have had my eyes on you for a long time and now you are well again."

I drew back, shocked and offended. "I am with Tarl," I told her indignantly.

Zarmell shrugged. "Well, only for warmth and comfort then. I know well enough where your heart is. But Tarl and Halli will share cloak this ride, of that you may be sure."

I looked about me. It seemed dark and cold beyond the light of the fire. Also, the charm of the night was upon me. I had no wish to sleep alone in my small stone hut with only my fears of the coming battle to keep me company. "Only for warmth and comfort then," I answered. She made no reply, but raised her eyebrows at me and went to bank the fire.

When we lay naked together in her cloak, Zarmell seemed all mountains and valleys to me, large round forms so different from Tarl's tight muscled body. I was shivering by then as I had been too much exposed to the sun that day, so Zarmell wrapped her arms about me, pressing me close against her breasts and belly. I could feel the warmth from her body burning into mine and giving comfort. She put her face against my hair, telling me to sleep. For a long while I lay rocking in that cradle of bodily ease. Then a heat came between my legs and with it a restlessness.

"Zarmell," I whispered. She made no answer. I whispered her name again, then spoke aloud. Still no reply. I took her hand and slipped it between my legs. That hand lay there, large, warm and motionless, making me more desirous, but giving no relief. It seemed I had what I had asked for—warmth and comfort only—and now it was not enough. "Zarmell," I said louder, pressing my legs insistently against that sleeping hand. For a while there was no response.

Then very slowly her fingers began to move like some small creature exploring on its own, a creature unconnected to that large still form. Sensations ran up my body so that I shivered again, but not with cold. With her other hand she drew the hair back from my neck. I could feel her teeth there in small sharp bites. Her hand at my private self moved faster now, her fingers inside and delving. When I tried to turn, she threw her leg over mine, pressing me down with her arms so that I found myself held firmly under her sensuous weight.

"Lie still," she whispered in my ear. Her bites grew sharper and her hand moved faster, taking me to the edge of pleasure. Just as I was at the point of struggling, she flipped me over with her easy strength.

I felt her body on me, soft and heavy. She spread my legs and her large breasts brushed down my body to settle hot and full between my thighs. When her head pressed up against me I gripped her fingers, pushing them into me. I would have taken her whole hand inside had it not been much too broad.

With a sudden and amazing shift I was riding a wild horse, leaning far forward, galloping across an endless field. The speed was terrifying. It would surely kill me. I would fall and die. But I shouted to the horse, wanting to go faster still. The hoofbeats on the ground rushed up through my body, wave after wave. I could not contain it all. I was breaking apart, coming loose in the wind. With another sudden shift I was riding the great breakers of the ocean, a fierce joy in me as they crashed against the shore. One, higher than the rest, bore me up screaming and then drew back suddenly, beaching me on the sand.

I lay still that way for what seemed a long time with only the murmur of the waves and the sound of my own voice receding. Deep in my belly there was a core of warmth. At last Zarmell turned me around so that I was lying on top of her, bound in her arms. I clung to her as to an island and pressed my face into her breasts.

"A wild ride, Little Sister," she said softly, caressing my back with damp, gentle fingers.

"How did you do that?" I asked when I could speak again.

She laughed. "I only took you where you asked to go. Is that not true?"

It was, indeed, true. I felt a deep easing in my body and in my spirit, too. Then suddenly I thought of Tarl, riding to that strange battle. I sat up with a cry, guilty and in pain. "She may be killed and I lie here thoughtless, taking my pleasure."

Zarmell hit me lightly with the back of her hand. "And would it lend her strength if you beat yourself instead?"

As I still sat there shaking my head, she pulled me down impatiently. "No, Sair, she would be glad for you. Believe me, in some ways I know her far better than you do."

I turned to caress her in turn, but she shook her head. "Not tonight, Nibbit. We are both too tired. And, besides, I came with you on that ride. It was surely one of the best." There was much pleasure in her voice and some pride, also. I curled up against her. This time we slept.

We were roused in the early morning by Yima, poking at the fire.

97

"I am sorry, Daughters. I had no wish to wake you. I only meant to warm myself a little."

Zarmell laughed and winked at her. "Come, Yima, you also meant to see who I was sleeping with." Yima grinned at us both.

"Well, Zarmell, I see you have finally caught Sair in your cloak." Saying that she poked some flames out of the coals. The flare of the fire lit the gray morning.

"Yes, Mother, and I live to tell you she was well worth waiting for." Zarmell seemed quite pleased with herself.

At those words I pulled away, not liking to be spoken of as a prize catch. "Tell me, Zarmell, who else are you casting your net for?" I asked her sharply.

"Many far and wide, Little Sister, but as truth be told, I have had my eye on Kedris for awhile."

I sat up shocked. "Zarmell, you must not. She is but fifteen and still a child."

"And do you think yourself an old lady at eighteen? I, for one, do not see much difference. But you need not fear for her, Sairizzia. She is quite safe from me. Right now she is enamored of her mother and will be of no use to anyone until that passes."

As Yima was shivering, Zarmell drew her under the cloak, and we hugged her into our warmth. She dozed comfortably between us, but I soon grew restless, wanting to be on my way. When the sun rose I slipped out from the cloak and poured myself some tea.

Yima opened her eyes. "You are up early, Daughter."

"I am on a journey of my own today if Sharu will take me."

Zarmell sat up. "Let us help you pack."

"Let me do for myself this day." I bent to kiss Yima gently and with rough loving knocked Zarmell back down with my shoulder. "Thank you, Sweet Sister, for the night," I whispered to her and slipped my hand under the cloak to give her nipple a quick pinch. She laughed and swung her hand, catching me with a sharp slap on my bare leg.

"Ride well and find what you need, Nibbit," she called after me.

I went to ask Sharu if she would take me, talking to her both in words and mind pictures. "I need to go on a journey and I am not sure where. Will you guide me and be my comrade and bring me safely back?" She pushed her head against me, then pranced about in little steps and pushed against me again. I had been answered.

I took little with me: a sleeping cloak, one change of clothes, some camp bread and dried berries in my pack, and a gut bag of water over my shoulder. I checked my pouch for sparkstone, strapped on my new knife and was ready. When I rode out of the settlement, Zarmell and Yima were fast asleep in each others' arms and no one else was stirring.

I left there with neither plan nor purpose, knowing only that I could not stay waiting in Semasi. I had no wish to ask another for directions fearing it would become their journey rather than my own. Worse, they might set to arguing among themselves which way to send me. Instead, I set off with a strange lightness of heart, letting Sharu or chance or the Goddess be my guide.

I was alone. I had not truly been alone since first coming to Semasi. In all my life in Eezore, I had never been alone. Always a whole city had pressed in around me. Only on my way to the sea had I been alone, but that was as a walking corpse. Now it was different. I was alive and full of joy, my spirits high and Zarmell's loving still riding in my blood. I sang and chanted wordless songs that sprang up from my heart. The day was new, the kiri soared overhead on a light breeze, and Sharu was warm and firm between my legs.

Then I remembered Tarl and Halli and Quadra and those other Hadra riding to meet their fate at the Redline. A cold fear came over me, a dark cloud that covered all the sun. I was afraid for all of them, but most of all I was afraid for Tarl, worried that I had weakened her with my own foolishness. I saw her in my mind as she had stood before me, telling me I could not go. /Be well, Sister, be strong, be safe./ I called out to her over and over in my heart.

Then the joy came on me again. A chant rose to my lips for the warmth of the sun, the pleasure of my horse-friend-guide under me, the slow curves of the road before me and behind. All that day I rode pulled between joy and dread, filled with whichever one took me at the moment.

At first we followed the way the Hadra had gone, taking the road down the hills out of Semasi, through the beauty and fragrance of the flowering-lodi. I feared that Sharu was trying to join the others, but by midmorning we had turned westward and crossed through marshy fields into low green foothills. Beyond them loomed craggy mountains, their rocky peaks red in the morning light. These I took to be the Timmers.

When we had gone high enough into the foothills, I could look back and see a wide river, no doubt the Escuro, curving below us, and even settlements along it with their neat planted fields growing in patches of green and gold. Then the road turned between the hills and the view was gone. Great old trees loomed over us now like a high tunnel of green, and the sun came through in golden patches.

I had given myself up to this adventure and did not question the way. When we came to a clearing with a stream, Sharu stopped to drink. I slipped off and went to sit by the stream. There I let the sound of the water flow through me until Sharu came and nudged my arm.

After that, as we went on, the road grew steadily steeper. The trees became thin and sparse. Gradually the land itself turned rocky. I could see nothing there to please the heart or eye, but Sharu pressed steadily forward to some goal of her own. Toward late afternoon we turned off onto another road that was steeper still, not much more than a hard path between the rocks. Now we were climbing the actual flank of the mountain. I slid from Sharu's back and climbed beside her, my hands in her mane. The tree cover had gone altogether for there was no purchase in that thin soil. Only low thorny shrubs clung to the rocks. The sun beat down upon us. My clothes were wet with sweat, and Sharu's neck and sides turned dark. The way was hard underfoot so that I stumbled often. When it became too narrow I stepped aside and let Sharu go up before me, dragging myself after her as best I could.

The rocky mountain top loomed before us now, rising straight into the sky. I could see no way through or over it and could not understand the eagerness with which Sharu pressed onward. She seemed to have forgotten me altogether and moved with purpose, so I could only struggle to follow, fearing to be left in that strange place. Hot, footsore, and weary almost past endurance, I was despairing of any change in that hard scene when the path veered sharply left between high boulders. Before us lay a great slab of fallen rock and beyond it was a gap through which I could see light.

With no hesitation Sharu crossed the slab and I followed. Her hooves rang loudly on the rock in that mountain stillness. We soon found ourselves in a high narrow gap, wide enough perhaps for two horses passing — a break in the mountain wall. When we stepped through this natural doorway it was into a broad meadow filled with grass and flowers, so lush with beauty after the barren harshness of our climb that I gave a cry of surprise.

The meadow was cupped by high mountain peaks which looked misty purple at that hour. Few trees grew there, only some sparsely scattered groves at the far edge. A stream flowed across the meadow, and on the other side I saw a herd of horses, more horses than I had ever seen together at one time.

Sharu called to them in the way of horses. They raised their heads to answer. She snorted and stamped and shook herself, so I quickly unstrapped my pack, fearing that she would leave with it still fastened to her back. She ran then without a backward glance and splashed across the shallow stream to join the others. They whinnied and snorted and pranced about her, greeting as horses do, then all dashed off together, running toward the far edge of the meadow.

Now I was even more alone, but I did not mind. There was a soft sighing wind in the meadow grass almost like a voice singing. I could hear the horses in the distance. The repeated call of the ta-ta birds echoed back to me from the rocky heights, their red and yellow brilliance flashing through the meadow. All that was company enough. I shouldered my pack and walked toward the stream. The flowers grew so thick by the water that I took off my boots to do less damage. It was there on a sandy bank I made my camp as the sky seemed clear enough to need no shelter. The sun was already setting full and red at the rim of the mountains, so for warmth I made a small fire at the water's edge with what little wood I could gather and ate some food. When the stars rose, I rolled up in my cloak and lay listening to the sighing of the grass and the music of the stream. Before I slept, I called out to Tarl one more time, sending her all my love.

Much happened to me in my two days in that meadow, but it has to do with spirit only and cannot be told in words, nor is it any part of this account.

* * *

AFTERNOTES

The Cerroi — The principle under which the Hadra live. I cannot explain the Cerroi, for I, myself, cannot fully comprehend it, but the Hadra speak of it as the Great Circle, the Law of Return, or The Balancing. At rituals, departures and other important occasions, they evoke it by making the sign of the circle with their hands. The clearest explanation I have heard is by Tarl, in Section III, Part 4.

Banners — The Hadra, with their love of design and bright-dyed fabrics have invented banners for every possible use. There is a banner for Yarmald, different banners for North and South Yarmald, banners for cities and parts of cities, a banner for each settlement and a personal banner for each Hadra. The emblem for this personal banner is chosen at coming-of-age. The designing and sewing of it is part of that ritual, though it can later be changed to reflect the experiences of that woman's life.

Nibbit — An affectionate Shokarn term meaning "little thing." It is often used for someone younger and smaller.

SECTION II – BATTLE AND RETURN TO EEZORE

PART 1 – PREPARING FOR BATTLE
Tarl's Account

    The following three parts are Tarl's account of these events, since I myself was forbidden to go to the battle. As Tarl cannot write, I have tried to record her story just as she told it to me, hoping to keep to her spirit, though the actual words are mine. Some portions of this were not easy to retell, especially that between Tarl and Halli concerning me, but I have done my best to be honest here. That portion, wherein Quadra speaks to the captain or the guards in Shokarn and they reply, was added by Quadra, herself, who also read the rest of this for errors. I wish to thank Tarl and Quadra, both, for their help in this work.
                                            Sair of Semasi

It was not until the middle of the day that we left Semasi. The preparations had been too long in the making. Restless to be gone, I rode out at the front with Quadra.

There were twenty of us mounted. We went with few extra horses and no dogs, not the usual Hadra style of traveling. On leaving, I laughed and shouted with the rest, holding my banner high and calling out farewells. But as soon as we were well on the road, I fell silent. A great weight was on me. I rolled up my banner and strapped it before me on my pack. When I glanced back at our small numbers winding down the hill, I saw the others silent also, closed in their own thoughts. Semasi rose behind us, soft red against the darkness of the mountains.

Flowering-lodi covered the hillsides. We went forward through a haze of pink and gold and white and every shade of green. All around us high spring was in its bloom. It seemed most strange to me to ride to battle in the midst of fragrant bursting life.

That first stretch of road is steep and winding, but very beautiful. Sudden changing views catch the eye. Flashing glimpses of the river shine blue and silver in the far distance. I love this wild northland around Semasi, more even than the soft southern valleys of Zelindar where I grew up. But I knew well we had not always held this land free and in peace. Armies and slavers had built the roads we went by. They would travel them again if we could not hold that line.

I felt Quadra next to me weighted by the same thoughts and more. Of all of us she alone had witnessed such a battle*. Though she tried hard to shield, still I caught glimpses and flashes of old horrors in her mind.

Heavy things stirred in her and with sudden bitterness she said aloud, "Such fools! Why must they try to swallow everything? Have they nothing better to do in this season of growing than to bring death upon the land?"

"It is their own deaths that will feed the earth," I said quickly and spit off to the side. But suddenly I wondered if I could hold steady to my place with death around me. I myself had seen no death other than what comes of age or accident.

"Ask the Goddess to steady you when you have need," Quadra said softly, seeing into my head.

Again I regretted my hasty words to her that night by the fire. At that moment she seemed to me more Hadra than I would ever be, and with more right to that name.

Knowing my thoughts, she laid her hand over mine. "All that must be set aside, Tarl. We need to work together now as one being."

For a while we rode on in silence. Our horses pressed close together as we passed down the steep, narrow portion of the road with all that shimmering day about us.

When the road flattened and widened, Quadra shook herself as if shaking off some heavy cloak. She turned to look at me. "I know it was hard for Sair to stay behind and hard for you to leave her. For that I am sorry."

"Mother, it was as it had to be. I saw that at the end though I argued hard in council. Her rage burns like a fire in her."

"And for Sair that is good and healing. For you it is like a drink of poison. I hope you are not too much infected with it."

All this was true, yet I would have given much for Sair to have been riding by me at that moment. I was about to answer when Quadra swung her arms around and said in a different tone, "All this land is like a blessing. The birds sing and the trees bloom. Let us enjoy it while we can."

At that moment Halli rode up to ask if I would come back and keep her company. Kedris came forward to ride by her mother.

Halli and I rode wordless for some time, sharing the beauty of the land with the same eyes and exchanging memories. When I asked her, "Will you share cloak with me tonight?" I heard her asking the same question in my head.

* * *

We rode hard that day with little rest. Not until the last part of our journey did the thinning moon rise to brighten our way. It was very late, nearer to morning than deep night, when we reached the meeting grounds by the river. Slipping from Timmer's back, I went forward on shaking legs to drink and bathe my face and hands. "Bless us, Mother, for we will need it," I said softly to the dark Escuro. The quivering reflection of the moon broke across her face. Then Timmer stepped up beside me, and all around us Hadra and horses were at the water.

Ozal was there to meet us and had lit a fire. The Hadra of Ishlair had already made camp, but we were weary. We did not try to meet with them that night. Instead we went quickly to find our own sleeping places. Halli and I chose a small grove of trees apart from the others for our tent and banners.

There, at last, we were able to lie together, close and safe between the cloaks. Our hands ran over the familiar textures of each others' bodies in the motions of love, but no heat came, none of the quick expected passion. Halli even slipped her hand between my legs, but I was closed and dry. With a sigh, she rolled away to where our bodies barely touched and gently took my hand.

"Has it gone?" she asked with sadness.

"For you, too?" I asked in return.

"For me, too," she answered.

"Perhaps it is simple weariness," I said with more hope than belief.

"No," she said softly. "We both know."

We lay silent that way for a while, our hands loosely clasped. The moon shifted overhead. I listened to the stir of horses and the soft voices of the Hadra who stood watch, grateful to those who were our eyes that night. I was close to sleep when a sudden anger stirred in me.

"She is a stranger and has come between us," I said harshly. With those words, I could see Sair again as she had stood before me that morning, willful and defiant. In spite of my anger, deep in my body I ached for her.

Halli nodded. "The stranger, the other," she answered. "She has caught me, too. There are not many 'others' in our lives." In the silence that followed, I could feel Halli gathering her thoughts. Finally she said, almost in a whisper, "Tarl, I had hoped we would become companions, you and I, before the closing of this season or by the next. Maybe that was too soon. Maybe it will not be."

I felt the grief of loss at those words and answered quickly, "That might still happen."

She shook her head. "I think we will always be comrades, Sister, but not companions. Not if the fire of our loving has slipped away so easily."

I still felt the struggle of something rising in her, something she wished to speak, yet feared. At one moment she was clear as glass and at the next clouded with shielding, until at last the words sprang out of their own force. "Tarl, I want a child, a baby. I want a daughter. The hunger is in my body and stirs itself almost like a pain. I need to be ready before the next spring Essu, but I can think of no other Hadra in Semasi I could companion with. Perhaps when this is over, I will go back to Ishlair with the river Hadra and spend some months among them. If something there seems hopeful, I might well stay the winter."

I felt a sharp grievance toward this unknown child who was taking Halli from me. Yet I knew it was I, myself, who had made the distance. "Oh, Halli, what if the one you choose will not come back with you? Then we lose both the child and you." I pulled her close against me. "I do not want to lose you, Sister. I wish I could make my passion flame up to hold you."

"You cannot lose me, Tarl. We are deep-bonded on other levels besides passion. Also, Semasi is my home. I will always come back to Semasi."

"And what if there is none to companion with in Ishlair or elsewhere?"

"Then Semasi will be bond-mother to my child. In Zelindar, there are many daughters, but in Semasi she will be the first one. Surely she will find enough mothers among us to keep her warm."

I shook my head. That is not how we do for our daughters. "Halli, how long have you wanted this child?"

"The thought has been forming in my mind this past month, but for longer, much longer, she has been growing in my spirit."

That I should have known nothing of this, told me how far apart we had traveled. I drew her head against my breast and wrapped my arms around her saying softly, "As it must be." When I fell asleep at last, the first gray of morning was already softening the darkness.

In spite of our short sleep, we were up by midday. Stumbling out of the tent, I heard my name called and looked up to see Serl among those of Ishlair. Gladly I went to hug her. We had been good friends while growing up. A Kourmairi from the coast settlement of Noshan, she had chosen very young to come to Zelindar and live as Neshtair among the Hadra. I knew she had left the city shortly after I rode north.

107

We stood for a few moments talking of our new lives. Around us camp was loud and busy as Ishlair and Semasi met again, though with none of the wild freedom of the Essu, where we race and wrestle and throw the dice. Instead, there was a hard sense of purpose among us, a knowledge of fate moving. As we parted, Serl said with a bitter laugh, "Well, old friend, we could have found some pleasanter way to meet again, you and I."

The camp is at a wide bend of the river, a natural meadow of river-grass that curves back against the trees. It is not so grand as the great sweep of the Essu grounds, but closer to the line and with space enough for our needs.

The Kourmairi I knew to be camped upstream from us, just out of sight. Their close presence made me uneasy. I did not care for men so near our rituals and baths. Seeing the Kourmairi at festival, beating their men at horse racing, that was as much contact as I cared for. Sometimes it was hard for me to believe we were of the same stock,* of one blood, so to speak. Yet, I had to set aside my feelings. It was not, after all, for pleasure we had come together there, Hadra and Kourmairi. It was under threat.

Part of a bargain our foremothers had made, was the pledge that when the line was endangered, those Kourmairi living closest would be warned and all would gather at the council grounds. Among Hadra, word given is word kept. That old pact was drawn and fashioned when the Redline was first laid down. The Hadra, themselves, agreed to stand the line and protect Yarmald against the slavers and the Zarn. In return, no Kourmairi could go armed in Yarmald. Also, any woman among them, who wished to do so, must be free to come live with us and be Neshtair, whether for a year or for life — any woman, be she wife or daughter or mother. This pact we had held to, Hadra and Koormir alike, no matter what our differences.

Standing by our tent, I noticed a woman from among the Kourmairi, making her way down the river bank to our camp and wondered what she sought with us. When I saw her returning some time later with Quadra and Manorkis, I knew she had come to fetch them to a Kourmairi council meeting, as Manorkis is Councilor in Ishlair. I felt some strangeness at the thought that soon those two would be sitting down in council among men.

* * *

As soon as we had eaten and bathed in the river, the choosing began. This was no easy thing to do. We had to decide who among us could best link their Kersh together to make a flow of force, a tight seamless web to hold against a very different power.

Quadra and Manorkis had returned from the Kourmairi. They helped keep order among us while we discussed and argued and threw the pebbles to ask guidance from the Goddess. First we had to choose a number. Too many different entities could not bond and too few had not the power. At last, we settled on the number eight, four from each settlement.

I was afraid for Halli and hoped she would not be chosen. Yet, I knew she must be. She was the strongest empath among us, skilled as a weaver and a binder. As the circle began to form, I caught Quadra's arm and said with haste, "Halli is too sensitive. She should not stand the line."

Quadra shook free of my hand and said sternly, "Tarl, that is not in your hands." Then more gently she added, "Have some faith in the Goddess. She chooses with us today."

I knew Quadra to be right and so was not aware of blocking Halli's name in the circle until Halli, herself, slipped in beside me and pinched my arm. "Let be, Tarl. I am no child that needs to be guarded so. You have not the right to stand between me and my fate."

Confused and embarrassed, I turned away mumbling, "As it must be."

At last, after our names had all been many times around the circle, Halli was chosen empath as I knew she would be. I was chosen for my force. Quadra was to be our leader, and also our speaker as she had some knowledge of Shokarn. Ozal, the fourth from Semasi, was picked for her steadiness. From Ishlair it was to be Hestor, Nais, Kama and Roshair. It was done. Many words had been spoken in that circle, enough to deafen us, but I think it was the throw of the pebbles* that marked us in the end.

Kedris, when she found herself not chosen for the line, gave a cry like a wounded bird. She slumped forward as if to fall and then as suddenly jumped back to shout at us, "But I must go! I must stand beside my mother and help shield her. Why else am I here?"

109

At that, there were many Hadra voices raised. In the pause between, Kedris said loudly, "The rest of you lay burdens on Quadra. I lift them off. She is the one who will have to speak for us. That weight will all be hers. She needs me to stand next to her and ease it." When our voices were raised again, Kedris shouted over them, "There is no need for discussion! I am meant to go!"

For just a moment I felt a sharp pain in my head. I knew then that Kedris was showing us her powers. Only for Quadra would she do something so forbidden.

Manorkis reached forward, taking Kedris by the shoulder. She spun her about until they were eye to eye and said sternly to her, "Do not try mind-bending again, Child! It endangers us all!" Then in a much softened tone she added, "Come, Daughter, we do not need to battle against each other here. Soon enough we must stand together against the Zarn." She took Kedris' hand in her own and, turning to Quadra, asked, "Is it truth she speaks?"

Quadra nodded slowly, staring wordless at Kedris as if seeing her with new eyes.

"Then if Quadra needs her, perhaps we should let her go," Manorkis said looking around from one to the next. "Kedris can be the link that binds the pattern. Is there any that stand against it?"

Kedris stared hard at each of us. There was a tense silence. When none stepped forward to deny her, she dropped her head, tears of relief shining in her eyes.

Hestor was standing next to me and said in my ear, "The Goddess moves in strange ways this day."

With her words I felt a chill. Great clouds were rolling across the sky. They came from the east, laying patches of darkness over us in their course. I thought of that army, also moving from the east and my throat tightened with fear. They were probably crossing the Drylands at that very moment. So few, we were so few—nine bodies with no shield or weapon against all those men and arms— flesh and spirit only on that line. We would meet the next day, of that I felt sure.

* * *

The choosing being over, we had need to do a clearing. This is a time of reckonings and settlings, a thing the Hadra do when they go together into danger. It is for clearing away old differences so our Kersh will not be clouded.

As I went in search of Halli, Jephra beckoned me to join her. She was sitting with Quadra on a rounded boulder at the river's edge. When I came near, she laid her hand on my arm. "Tarl, I would make peace with you. There is an old bitterness between me and the world, between me and this life, that sometimes you have unfairly felt the sting of."

"And sometimes deserved," I answered, for I felt quite humble at that moment.

"And often not," she said gently. Never had I seen Jephra in such a turn of mind. She went on, speaking so low I had to bend my head to hear her. "I would heal that now if I could, Daughter. If you would let me."

I nodded, saying to her in my head, /Do what you will, Mother. I shall be glad of it./ She pressed her hands against mine, palm to palm in the sign of friendship and kissed my forehead. Then she leaned forward and kissed the double triangle between my breasts that is my birthpiece*. I kissed her in return and felt a clearing in the air between us, such a clearing as when a quick rain falls and is followed by the sun.

When I turned to Quadra to ask her pardon, she said quickly, "If once more you ask forgiveness for your words, Tarl, I shall cut a willow switch and beat you with it. I have already forgiven you more times than I have patience for." Seeing my look of surprise, she laughed at me. Suddenly I, too, was laughing with a new lightness of heart. Soon we were all three laughing together, even Jephra. For that moment I sensed a sistering with those Hadra, whose age and closeness to each other had so often made me feel young and apart.

Then Quadra grew serious and turned me so that we faced each other. She put a hand on either side of my face and looked into my eyes. "It is not what lies between you and me, Tarl, that you have to struggle with, or even what lies between you and any other Hadra. It is what lies in your own spirit. You must keep your Kersh very clear and not muddy it with anger. It will soon be used in ways you have not tested before." She dropped her hands to press one against my chest and the other on my belly, saying, "Be sure to keep your powers centered here and here. Do not let them be scattered with

111

the wind." The old lessons of childhood came back, but with new meaning.

"Are you not afraid?" I asked her.

She frowned. "More apprehensive than afraid. It is an ugly business."

"You are the only one among us who has seen it before."

"And I wish to the Great Mother I might not have to see it again. It was very terrible and this time it will be worse. What gives me strength is knowing what will happen if we do not stop them at the line. But it is nothing great or glorious, of that you may be sure. We do what we must do."

"It will soon be over, Mother."

"By the Goddess, I hope so." She hugged me tight against her, the first time she had ever done so, and then took Jephra, too, in her embrace so that we were all three bound together by her arms.

After that, I went to settle with Halli and with Kedris. Between Ozal and me, there was nothing to settle. We were as born comrades. I found Kedris sitting back from the river between some trees. She was holding her head in pain from trying to drive our thoughts. Sensing me, she looked up and said in my head, /Forgive me, Tarl, for wishing to bend your will./ I saw her again as the sweet gentle Kedris, who could be asked for anything and would give it gladly. But I knew now that other powers moved behind that sweetness.

"I know it was for Quadra that you did that and now you, yourself, carry the pain of it, so I cannot be too angry." With those words I sat down by her and pressed my palm to her forehead to draw out that pain. After a time I said, "I am sorry, Kedris, for all those times I treated you with arrogance." I said those words for the clearing, yet, as I said them, I felt a wave of love released between us.

There was much I could have said to Halli, and she to me, but when I found her, we did not speak. Instead, she drew me into a sheltered space under the low-hanging branches of a tree. There we sat, very close, staring into each others' eyes. We sat that way in silence a long time, sharing all that had ever passed between us until shouts and the sound of hoofbeats told us that Ballis had ridden in. Hadra were calling out that the Zarn's army would likely reach the line before noon of the next day. The last set of pebbles, it seemed, had been thrown and patterned.

I needed some time to be alone from all that had passed that day. Crossing the river, I waded along the far shore until I found a shallow sandy place. There I lay down in the water and, resting my head on a rock, I let the Escuro flow over and through me. Overhead the great clouds passed, marking their changes of light and shadow on the land.

* * *

That night we sang, Ishlair and Semasi together, around the fire. They were old songs, songs of line-keepers and holders of other times, songs that go back to the beginning of the line and help us remember. At the end, Ozal sang a new song, made for us that day.

When the singing was over, we made a great circle around the dying fire. There for the last time we called upon the Goddess, the Great Mother, by all the different names we knew for her. We had already made our own private altars and spoken our own words to her many, many times since coming to the river.

Later, I went with Roshair for the night. Of all the line-keepers, she was most stranger to me. We shared a little loving and so passed some energy between us and made a bond. But I could not sleep. All night those great clouds passed through the country of my mind.

The next morning, those of us who were chosen line-keepers drank at the river and bathed, but did not eat. Then, with the others, we went toward the line in a great wave, Hadra and Kourmairi together, for so it had been decided in council. At a small rise overlooking the line itself, Quadra raised her hand and stopped us. There, we sang and shouted and danced and beat the drums. Altogether we made such a noise that the Goddess, herself, must have heard and taken notice.

At that moment, I did not grudge the Kourmairi, but was grateful for their presence. Indeed, I would gladly have welcomed a hundred more. I looked around me with love in my heart for all who were assembled there, but far too soon Manorkis blew the conch shell. The others drew away, back to the river. Only the nine of us were left together on the knoll. The silence was heavy after all that sound.

Kama on one side of me said with a grim smile, "Well, Sister, the time is upon us."

Ozal on the other said, "Love and courage be with you, Tarl," and I told her the same.

Halli I did not look at, but sent her love and courage from my heart. Kedris looked so young to me. I knew she would not be the same when this day passed.

We all polished our birthpieces and kissed them for Mothers' Luck, then kissed each other on the lips. Those of us who had not already done so, stripped off our shirts and footwear so that the energy might flow unhindered through our bodies from the earth.

Bare-footed and bare-breasted, we nine stood in a circle, hands raised at head height and pressed palm to palm, breathing together, long deep breaths, over and over, until we were one body, one breath. We did not evoke the Goddess. We had called whom we could call and that was done. Now it was only ourselves and what we could hold between us at that hour, for from outside our circle, from beyond it in that other world, came the sound of men and horses. As we broke the circle to walk to the line, we said together, "As it must be."

* * *

AFTERNOTES

When Quadra was no more than fifteen years of age and still living in Zelindar, she had witnessed and taken part in a battle along the wild coast of Teerhault inlet south of Zelindar and east of Bayrhim. The Zarn of Nhor had sent boats from the port of Nhor in an unsuccessful attempt to invade the tropical southern coast of Yarmald. More on this is written in book 830 of the Hadra Archives, *The Siege of South Yarmald.*

The Hadra and Kourmairi Racial Connection—Originally, the Hadra were gathered from among the Shokarn and Muinyairin, as well as the Koormir. By intermixing with the Kourmairi at the Gimling to conceive their daughters, the Hadra have become far more Kourmairi in blood and appearance, in spite of the frequent occurrence of new Neshtair among them. Even so, Hadra and Koormir have not much love for one another. A wary respect is maintained between them by careful adherence to old agreements and by distance. The Koormir are distrustful of Hadra powers and, perhaps, jealous as well, especially the men, but they rely on the Hadra to keep Yarmald safe from Shokarn invasions. In turn, the Hadra, at least those of the northern settlements, look to the Koormir for such things as metal-working and glass-making, particularly the Koormir from the old established cities of Mishghall and Koormi. Contacts, however, are brief, for a Hadra's powers begin to fade if she stays too long among men.

Tossing the Pebbles—A thing that can be done in many ways and for many purposes. At the Essu, it is a game of chance, played with much cheating and loud banter between the players. It can also be used as a tool for divination to reach into the uncertain future or a way of seeking guidance from the Goddess on some heavy matter. This last is mostly done in a ritual manner, often in connection with Council or High Council or some long established ceremony. Sometimes though, it is quickly called for at a moment when there is no clear thing to do and action must be taken. Hadra and Koormir have different styles for reading the toss and even Hadra from north and south differ in this. The reading itself is beyond me to describe here, for it is very complicated and I, myself, have no clear understanding of it.

Birthpiece—A silver neckpiece made to hang on a chain or thong, consisting of double-triangles, or of triangles and circles, with inserts of precious stones. It is given to a girl at birth, usually by her bond-mother, to insure closeness to that child, but sometimes by a woman who has a special place in the life of the birth-mother. The giver and the child are then considered to have a life-bond.

A birthpiece is thought to have magical properties of power and protection for the wearer and is seldom removed. It is often rubbed and kissed in times of danger and occasionally lent to a loved one going into peril.

PART 2

THE ZARN'S ARMY
Tarl's Account

The Zarn's Army — at last we were to see these men who thought to invade our land and lives. I felt a rush of anger and heard Quadra's voice in my head saying, /Breathe and count, Tarl, keep clear at the center./

At the sound of that approaching force, we quickly left the knoll and went to stand on the Redline. There we spaced ourselves close enough to touch fingers, but not so close as to crowd each others' powers. Quadra stood at the center. Kedris and I stepped to either side of her and Halli moved to stand beside me. When all were in place we were enough to span the road and reach as far as the edge of trees.

The road there passed through woods, a part of the old forest not cut in any memory and undisturbed by raids. Huge oaks and Gobal trees pressed close together. Thickets of rithberries covered the road banks with hard-thorned branches and white blossoms thick as snow. Only a small corridor was cleared through this growth for the Redline itself. This made a narrow space of action, far better for us than meeting the Zarn's men on some wide field where our small numbers would have been scattered and our power thin-stretched. Still, this grove of ancient trees seemed almost sacred, an ill-suited place for such a clash.

There are stretches where the Redline has almost faded from sight and others where it has darkened to brown like old blood, but here under our feet, it was a bright clear red. It had been re-done with the help of the Kourmairi after the last fall Essu. I felt a twist of grim humor at the thought that all unknowing, we had made the line fresh-painted for this meeting.

A steep hill lay before us which hid the army from our eyes, but we could clearly hear the shouts of men and feel tremors from the hooves of many horses. Even if they had come in silence, we could have felt with our Kersh the advance of so large a hostile force.

"Quick, a last kiss," Hestor called. She was at one end of the line. That kiss, passing from Hadra to Hadra, was our final chance of closeness with each other, for at that moment, the army poured over the rise. It appeared as the crest of a wave that did not recede, but rolled forward on and on, rank after rank of black and gold with metal flashing in the sun. A deep groan rose from among us.

Quadra raised her arms and said in the old ritual way, "No armed man of Eezore shall pass this line our foremothers laid down for us. As it was before we took first breath, so it shall be long after we are blown to wind."

Then she opened her hand and a crystal blazed with light. Bright colors flared in all directions, touching on our faces, the road, the trees, and even the still distant soldiers, so that they shouted in surprise. Together we took up Quadra's words, repeating them until we had raised a chant. Palm to palm, we pressed our hands against each others' hands at shoulder height to make a flow of energy between us. That contact shook my body with such force that I was more in awe of its power than of the huge gold-flecked black snake that bore down upon us.

The smartly moving guard rode at the front. Before them they carried a tall banner on which was stitched a figure that seemed the very embodiment of the spirit of war. I heard Ozal mutter, "They have the effrontery to carry Rha-ais* right into our faces," and Quadra replied quietly, "The Goddess was here long before. She shall still be worshipped after that one is gone and forgotten."

Behind the guard came men-at-arms, dressed in brown, and the supply wagons guarded by more men riding. At the center of this pack, one behind the other, rolled three strange looking weapons, great dark tubes mounted on high-wheeled wagons and drawn by four heavy horses each. These were most ominous, as was this whole array of power. Yet, there was also some amusement in seeing this huge beast of war assembled to bear down on so few in so far a place.

I heard Quadra next to me thinking, /They have done themselves up to besiege a city. This Zarn has learned nothing from his father's losses./

Ozal said aloud, "It seems a shame to waste such a fine force. Surely they could be doing something useful."

When the men were close enough to sight our nakedness, there was much shouting and pointing. Mocking, derisive laughter rose from their ranks.

Hestor muttered grimly, "Let them have their jokes for now. Soon they will not be laughing."

The noise was such that the captain had several times to shout for order. Finally he swung his sword in anger and there was silence. When he had regained control, he rode forward signalling all to follow. From his horse, he called out to us to clear the way and made no sign of slowing. Indeed, he would have ridden over us, followed by his whole troop, but a few feet from the line, his horse swerved slightly and stopped. All who rode in back had to make a rapid halt, being almost at each others' heels. Many angry shouts and curses were followed by a loud command from the captain. Then, in clouds of dust, the army wheeled on the edges of the road to re-form their ranks.

At the next advance, the supplies and men on foot stayed back. Only the mounted front lines moved against us. They came forward at a trot with swords drawn and raised, and again, swerved before the line. I could clearly feel an impact and a tremor. Between the Hadra on the line, there ran a force like living lightning.

118

The air was thick with anger now and loud with the snorts and cries of horses as the guard wheeled again. This time, they drew far back before they turned at the captain's shouts and rode toward us at a hard gallop, spurring their horses and beating them so that those poor creatures were flecked with foam and blood. Yet, again, they could not pass. Half-crazed at being ridden with such force into an unseen barrier, the horses reared and spun about, some throwing off their riders. Then everything was pain and confusion, for some men were down and hurt, and others were riding forward over them in a third and fourth charge. Finally, the captain commanded the front row to ride in swinging their swords. Suddenly there were wounded men lying before us, bloody and screaming. Like a blow, I felt their pain and the pain of empathy from other Hadra. Most of all I felt the pain from Halli, who screamed silently in her head. I struggled hard to shield and keep control.

The captain ordered the road cleared and the wounded pulled back. Then he rode forward himself. I saw in the confusion of his face, a war of fear and anger. He came straight at us, but this time stopped before being forced to. "In the name of Yorin, Great Zarn of Eezore, Son of Haniffal, Ruler of all lands between Balmori and Sildaire, I command you to clear this road."

I could hear Kedris thinking, /That name must be longer than the Zarn is tall. It is a wonder he does not trip over it on rising./

Roshair on the other side of me muttered, "Pompous horsefart!" I had to struggle not to laugh.

Quadra kept her composure. Taking a step forward, she said in formal style, "In the name of all those who dwell in Yarmald, we ask that you take these men home and set them to useful, peaceful tasks while they still live. You cannot force this road, though you come with a thousand men. There are old powers working here." Then she reached forward to hand him our proclamation, for in such cases, Hadra words must be written as well as spoken.

He snatched it from her, read it quickly, made some rude oath and threw it under his horse's hooves. When he answered he seemed less a commander and more an angry man, unused to such resistance. "Queen of witches, take your slavey women with you back to the hills. Be afraid, for we have fearsome weapons that can make holes in the earth the size of trees and turn you to ashes where you stand."

Behind him, his soldiers were shouting, "Why talk? Let us blow them away and move on!"

Quadra raised the crystal again so that it flashed on all assembled and said slowly and clearly, "Hireling of the Zarn, there are no queens among us, no slaves, and no women. We are all Hadra here and have powers, as you have already seen. I warn you that whatever weapons you turn on us shall turn back on you. Their terror shall be your terror. Believe me, I have seen it all before."

I knew Quadra to be forcing her mind on scenes of the old battle. I used all the shielding power that I had to hold my own. Several Hadra groaned aloud, but I felt Halli next to me linking with clear strength to Quadra's words. The captain looked white and sick. He shook himself as if to shake free of some loathsome weight.

/Will they go back?/ Kedris asked silently.

Quadra shook her head and said aloud in Kourmairi, "I think not. No matter what awfulness I paint for them, they are caught between the fire and the flood. If they go back to Eezore unsuccessful they will be tortured and executed there. That much I can read from this one's head."

Now there were more shouts from those soldiers most impatient to move forward. But some, also, were calling to go back, saying there was nothing blade and fire could do against witches' powers.

The captain himself seemed uncertain, though he spoke harshly. "I tell you one last time to clear the road or this entire army will ride you down. You will be crushed where you stand."

Quadra took one more step forward so that she stood at the very edge of the line, saying, "Then you must try me first, Captain."

"Witch's tit!" he shouted at her and leaned from his horse to give her an angry shove. With that he was knocked back and almost unhorsed. A cry of surprise rose from his men. While he held his arm in pain, Quadra stood quietly with her arms crossed.

"Captain, hear me. I have seen this all before. Turn your men around and take them back to the Zarn of Eezore, while they still live. No armed man of Eezore can cross the Redline. As it was a hundred years ago, so it is today."

When there was no response, she shook her head and said in a very different tone, "Please, Captain, take these men home. Everything I have said is true. I do not wish to watch this one more time." There was a terrible grieving in her voice. ·

For an instant I saw a softening in the captain's face. Then the voices in back of him rose louder, urging quick action, no doubt threatening us with rape and dismemberment as well as flaming death. With a smile that seemed to conceal some secret pleasure, he turned and gave command. The whole troop parted as if by a knife, one half drawing off to either side. This left space for those strange weapons to be drawn up beside each other and aimed at us unimpeded.

The weapons were fearsome enough to look upon and should have left me trembling, yet, at that moment, it was not fear I felt. In spite of all my training, in spite of Quadra's warnings, it was my anger that took control. Hearing the threats and taunts, I thought suddenly of Sair and what had been done to her by just such men, perhaps the very ones before me now. A hot rage rushed up in me. Heedless of any danger, I stepped forward past Quadra.

The full force of my Kersh shook me and I shouted, "Take all this garbage back to the Bargguell where it belongs!"

With no word, the captain spurred his horse and rode at me, sword raised for the killing. Quadra pulled me back with a sharp word of warning. All in an instant, the captain was lying before the Redline in his own red blood, his horse leaping away wildly. There was a roar of rage from the men watching.

"Cap your anger, Daughter, or you will draw their fire," Quadra said forcefully as she gripped my arm and drew me back between the others.

Shocked at the outcome of my rashness, I held tight to Halli and to Quadra, trying to re-weave that line and bind myself into it. I drew on all the force I had, to mend what I had torn, and felt the other Hadra straining with me to hold the power clear and strong.

When the captain did not rise, there was much confusion in the ranks. Then a command was given and those tubes were raised. Another shout was followed by a great blazing flash of light and a blast of sound that shook the very earth beneath us. The impact was such that I was rocked on my feet and almost lost contact with the others. For a moment all was like the darkness of an earth storm, where nothing can be seen. Then flames burst out. Rocks, branches and the burning parts of bodies rained down from the sky.

The destruction was so sudden and so total that it numbed the mind. Huge clouds of smoke rose over the scene. Through this, men and horses ran in all directions, flaming and screaming. Great trees, those giants of the old forest, had been torn loose and tossed about like twigs, shattered and splintered as if the earth had shaken and ripped apart. Whole blocks of the road itself had been thrown up in the explosions, and men lay crushed beneath them, crying out.

Over the sounds of chaos, I heard Ozal say loudly, "It is finished. The Zarn's army has nothing left for us."

Then I saw Halli slump forward across the line. I tried to reach her, but such waves of pain coursed through my body that I could not move. A sudden sound caught my attention and I turned to see half a man screaming from what was left of his face. With that, all before me turned red, then black, and then red again. For just a moment, I knew the pain I felt was the pain of others. Then the pain was mine. Then it no longer mattered. It was all one pain and I was caught in it. When all turned dark again, there were arms around me. From that black space came terrible shouts and screams, the smell of burning flesh and wave after wave of agony.

Whoever held me said, "Breathe, Tarl, breathe. Shield yourself. Breathe." She said it over and over. Choking and sobbing, I struggled to breathe. Slowly the pain abated and my vision cleared.

When I turned, I saw it was Sharven who gripped me in her strong arms. I leaned back against her and for a moment there was peace. Then the pain was back. Sharp screams tore from me, that went on and on until, with a quick slap across my face, my wits returned. I opened my eyes to see Jephra before me, with her hand raised.

"Once is enough, Mother," I said quickly.

Next to me, I heard Quadra say, "It is the anger. It left her open and drew their fire. Now it draws their pain."

Around us the smoke thinned and the scene began to clear. Halli was being carried to the river by holders. Hestor and Roshair were leaving, supported by other Hadra. Many of the army's horses had crossed the line and stood about bewildered with their reins hanging. Those men still able to walk, seemed dazed and aimless, but one dragged himself out of the rubble, stripped off his weapons and threw them down along with his coat.

He came staggering toward us with his arms raised, saying in faltering Kourmairi, "I will not go back to Eezore. I was forced to come here. This horror was not of my choosing. Let me cross the line and you may do with me what you will. Kill me if it pleases you." Plainly he was mad with desperation.

Serl moved to bar his way, but Quadra raised her hand and said, "Go where you will, Brother. As you harm none, none shall harm you." He stumbled wearily across the line that just before had blocked an army.

Serl picked up his coat and tossed it after him shouting, "Take this with you. These hills are cold at night."

Seeing how the wind blew, two others stripped off their weapons and crossed the line. When a fourth tried to do the same, Serl called out to him, "Go back to the Zarn, man of Eezore. You will never live in peace with us here." When he took two more steps toward the line, watching her all the while with sideways eyes, Serl stepped in front of him. "Have you learned nothing from all this death and wretchedness, man of Eezore? Go back and leave us in peace." I doubt he understood her words, but her meaning was plain enough. He stepped back and turned away, slowly picking his way through the bodies until he was but a tiny figure in that smoking ruin.

Then Serl came up and said some words to Sharven. Sharven beckoned to Loris and Imyuri, both of Ishlair, and said to me, "Go with them to the river, Tarl. You are in much need of healing. I will soon be there to help."

Other line-keepers were being helped away by holders. Halli had already been carried off to the river, but I could not leave. I stared down at the tattered and shredded banner of Rha-ais that lay on the ground before me as if bound to that scene by some strange power.

Then Serl and Sharven crossed the line and went among the remnants of that army. Sharven marked those men or horses who could not be helped or healed. Serl followed like the mower, cutting throats, a work of mercy no Hadra could have done. She moved with a strange dead look to her and tears running down her face. What troops were still living and able to move, backed away with dread from those two.

I watched for some moments in a haze of pain, then with a cry, I went forward and picked up a knife abandoned on the ground. My heart felt somewhat hardened to the sufferings of men, but the suffering of horses I could not endure. Where I saw horses struggling, I hacked them free from the tangle of reins and harness, and helped pull them to their feet. Those that could no longer rise, I left for the kindness of Serl's blade, my heart like a cold stone in my breast. I went on hacking with a desperate strength until I felt a hand on my shoulder and turned to see Quadra's face.

"Daughter, I have never given you command as Councillor, but now I do. Go with these Hadra to the river, for until you leave, I am not free to do so."

When I saw the deep weariness on her face, my madness fell away. I let Loris and Imyuri guide me like a broken child through the still smoldering rubble. Quadra went with Kedris. Jephra took her other arm to give support. I saw that Quadra had scarcely strength to walk. She seemed all bent with pain and age.

At the line I turned for one moment to look back over that desolation. We had won, if such a thing could be called winning. Semasi was safe again, all Yarmald was safe, but as yet I could feel no rejoicing. I thought of Quadra's words, that there would be no glory in it and much that was ugly. My ears still full of the cries and moans of the wounded, I turned and went with the others toward the Escuro. We left Sharven and Serl to their grim work.

There by the river, holders and line-keepers were gathered for healing. My heart leapt with fear when I saw Halli laid out at the water's edge with her eyes shut. I tried to go to her, but Loris restrained me with a hard grip on my arms, saying, "She is already being cared for. Tend to your own healing, Sister. You have nothing to give another at this moment."

With a blind bitterness I turned to Quadra and shouted, "I knew it was too dangerous for her! Halli is too sensitive, too much an empath!"

"And that is the source of her power," Quadra answered wearily. "She was needed there at the line. Goddess knows, Daughter, it was dangerous for all of us, even for you. Would you have asked someone to keep you safe away?"

Jephra added, "She has her own ways she needs to move. You must stop trying to protect her from her life."

When I would have said more, Kedris told me firmly, "Enough, Tarl. Quadra has as much need of healing as the rest of us."

I nodded and gave myself over to Loris and Imyuri. Imyuri stripped off my pants and eased my aching body down gently on the river bank. As Loris poured water over me, she began to chant, "Oh, healing waters, bare away our pain." Other holders took up the chant until, up and down the river, that song mingled with the songs of the Escuro herself.

When I heard Sharven's voice, I sat up to speak with her and there, a little ways downstream, sat the man who had first crossed the line. At the sight of him a sudden rage shook me.

"Wretched pig! What are you doing here? Why are you watching us? Go away!" At my shout the man looked up, dazed and bewildered. I saw that he had not been watching, that, indeed, he was scarcely aware of anything.

Sharven came to squat beside me and said, "That man is badly hurt. He is holding his burned arm in the healing waters."

I looked at his arm and turned away again. I had seen enough horrors for one day. Sharven said some words to Mirl, who rose, crossed the river and guided the man further downstream until he was out of sight.

Then Sharven turned back to me and asked, "Tarl, do you want some yima root?"

"Why not?" I asked with a pained laugh. "Surely I need to be away from this for awhile. Make it a strong dose, Sharven."

With that she took some red powder from a small pouch, mixed it in a cup of water and held it out to me. "Drink it all in one swallow for this batch is very bitter. Is this your first time?"

"No, I have traveled that road many times." I drank it as she told me to and made a face. It was, indeed, a bitter dose.

She nodded and put her hand on my forehead to gently push me down. "Let what happens, happen now, Little One. You have done all you can do. The rest is being taken care of."

Imyuri kissed me on the forehead and said, "Let yima and the waters of the sweet Escuro enter your spirit, Sister."

I shut my eyes, saying in my heart, Oh, Mother of waters, take me away with you. From outside the haze of yima, I heard voices and felt many hands on me, massaging, caressing, drawing out the weariness. There were no faces or names in that place, only wondrous hands, hands that moved over every part of my body, and the chant of voices, and the flow of water, and a rush of brilliant colors under my eyelids, swirling and re-forming with each touch. I was barely conscious when they wrapped me in my cloak and carried me to our tent.

* * *

AFTERNOTES

Rha-ais — The cult of Rha-ais, the God of war and battle, has become the official religion of Eezore, supplanting all others by edict of the Zarn. It is under the banner of this God that the Zarn fights his wars, but the worship of the Goddess, the Great Mother of All, still continues secretly in the city, especially among the Koormir and the lower-caste Shokarn.

PART 3

HIGH COUNCIL
Tarl's Account

I crawled out of our tent in the noonday heat, leaving Halli still asleep. A terrible stench hung over the Escuro that usually smells so sweet and fresh. As I was still heavy with sleep and yima, I did not realize at once the cause of it.

Then shadows swept over me. I looked up and saw the birds-of-death dropping down over the hill, and with a wave of soul-sickness, remembered the battle. For a moment, I stood there swaying on my feet, holding to a tree for strength. Then I turned and walked slowly toward the line. I had a need to see.

At the rise of the knoll, I stopped. Below me, Hadra and Kourmairi together were clearing away the bodies of men and horses. The bodies of trees, uprooted and dismembered, lay scattered on the road. Where holes were blown in the pavement, bones and flesh fused to the melted edges. Looking down at that wreckage, what I felt was not anger, but something so cold, it was far to the other side of it.

Serl stood nearby watching, her face set and hard. She turned when she heard me and said with much bitterness, "Welcome, Sister, to the scene of battle. The Zarn should be here to see with his own eyes the results of his war. Better yet, he should be here to do his own house cleaning."

"That all was meant for us," I said, gesturing toward the road. "What sort of mind can turn to the making of such things?"

"Minds hired by the Zarn," Serl answered quickly and spit with anger. "We have killed the men and boys he buys and sells like

127

cattle, while the Zarn himself sits safe in his palace." As bodies and parts of bodies were dumped into a long, dug trench, she groaned and shook her head. "Poor fools. Poor, poor fools."

"Yesterday those same poor fools would have been glad enough to see us in that ditch," I spoke harshly for I felt little mercy in my heart at that moment.

Serl shrugged. "True enough. And with no pity. But what else do they know? What choices do they have? It is the man who sent them that I want to see before me on the road as screaming burning flesh." There was such hatred in her voice that I shuddered. Seeing that, she took my arm and said, "Come away, Sister. This is an evil place."

"I should stay and help here," I protested.

"No, Tarl, the Council met last night and decided that none of the line-keepers should bury the dead. One day's death is enough."

Relieved, I let her lead me away. As we went, she told me that High Council* would be called that day, since Hadra had come in the night, even from Osen* and Baltimere.*

"Then that was Karf I saw on the road," I said, thinking I had recognized her among the diggers.

"Yes, she rode in late at night with at least ten others from Osen."

So Karf was here. I had heard that she lived at Osen now. She had been my riding companion when we were younger. Growing bored and restless with city life, we had left Zelindar together and together explored much of Yarmald, not just the coast, but even far into the wild mountain passes, meeting danger as one. At that time we had pledged to ride as comrades all our lives, such pledges as one makes when one is very young. This seemed a strange, hard way to meet again. For a moment my mind slipped back into that other time.

Serl shook me by the shoulder. "Tarl, will you come with me and lie by the river?" I nodded and took her hand.

When we lay down together in the soft grass by the Escuro, Serl shook as if with sudden cold though the day was hot. Thinking to keep her warm, I pulled her tight against me, but she shook her head. "Sister, I fear not all the loving in Yarmald can ease this rage. There is a sickness that burns in me from all I have seen here." Then she pressed her face against my neck. We wrapped our arms around each other and lay still.

It was Sair I thought of when I shut my eyes and, suddenly, I was lying in a meadow high in the mountains. A clear stream crossed it, bordered by clumps of flowers, and many horses were grazing there. Over this scene, there rose a sky so blue it made the heart sing. All this I shared with Serl as best I could, for she had only a little mind-reach. For a while, we lay in peace. I was quite sure that Sair herself was in that meadow for I felt her deep in my heart.

We were awakened by the sound of drums. After that the shell was blown three times and then three times again — High Council. When we reached the gathering place, I saw the banners of Yhaghar and Sorren, settlements on the far coast, flying with the others. Serl, next to me, said with excitement, "That is all of us then, all the Hadra settlements of North Yarmald, represented to speak here at High Council."

We Hadra did not come together that day joking and jostling and shouting greetings as was our habit when we met. Instead we gathered somber and heavy, hardly speaking. When we had assembled around the flat rock, we bowed our heads, threw each a handful of holy water in the center as the bowl came round and said our words to the Mother. The smell of burning flesh was rank from those who had been at the road. There was no forgetting the reason for calling Council.

As the oldest among us, Azurmi of Ishlair was entitled to lead High Council. She went to stand at the center of the flat rock and said with bowed head, "Goddess, please guide our thoughts, our words and our actions in this circle." Then she shut her eyes, raised up a willow wand and asked, "Mother, who has need to speak here?" I knew these to be the ancient ritual words for starting High Council, though I was unused to such formality. In all my life, only once before had I seen High Council called.

With fixed eyes, I watched the willow wand as it seemed to quiver and strain, and then bend slowly toward Ballis. So marked, she stepped to the middle and took the branch herself, saying the ritual opening, "Hadra — Sisters, Mothers, Daughters, those I know and those I will know, I have need to speak here." After that, her words rushed out. "For three months I have been a spy in Eezore, living as one of the Zarn's guards. This war was all the talk in the city. It is said that the Zarn has no patience with defeat. He plans to march his army all the way to Mishghall and the sea and will send men, again and again, till he breaks through the line. At the moment, he is forcibly recruiting from the Balmori River settlements and has no care for lives. This one battle will not be the end."

Then she shut her eyes and raised the wand until it bent toward Quadra, who stepped forward, took the willow and spoke the opening words. She seemed to me much older than when we had left Semasi. She spoke slowly, looking past us as if toward the hills.

"Sisters, he will succeed at last. We cannot bear up under the weight of so much killing. All that pain will burn away our Kersh. And what will it do to our spirits and our souls? This one day was enough, more than enough for those of us who stood on the line and saw the work of those weapons."

Before Quadra was finished, Serl jumped into the center, not waiting for the sign of the willow or remembering to say the formal words. "There is no justice in men being forced to come here for their death while the Zarn sits safe in his palace," she shouted. "These weapons must be turned back upon the man who sends them."

At once there was uproar and confusion, with many Hadra shouting at the same time, "Can we do it?" "Have we the power? Who will tell the Zarn?"

Then Halli was in the middle also, and I heard her saying, "If no one else will go, then I will ride to Eezore myself with word, for never will I stand on that line again and cause such death."

I pulled her back, saying quickly, "You cannot, Halli. It would be too much for you. I will go to the Zarn, if it must be, and find others to go with me."

This time Halli did not protest, for she had no wish to go to Eezore and more than a little fear. It was desperation that had made her speak. Many in the circle shouted that they were willing to ride with me, Serl, Karf and Estral among them.

In this confusion, Azurmi pushed her way to the center and took the willow branch from Quadra's hand. With it, she beat at us, commanding, "Hadra, back to your places in the circle! Have you no regard for the Mother? Wait till you are called by Her!" I felt the sting of the willow on my cheek and shoulder and stepped back.

Subdued, we re-formed our circle and came to order. Now the discussion went with more heat and less formality. It seemed more like the Councils I was familiar with. Still, Azurmi held the wand and kept us from out-speaking ourselves too rashly or over-speaking each other.

First there was much discussion of whether we could gather our Kersh to do that thing over such a distance. It felt right and just when Serl had first spoken, yet now it seemed to me a vast stretching of our powers. Both the Hadra of Yhaghar and Sorren spoke strongly for it as they would be close in the path of the Zarn's army if, indeed, he reached Mishghall. Zeela of Osen voiced strong misgivings, fearing that being so far stretched, our settlements could not come together with enough speed to make such a force.

To my surprise, it was Quadra who said at last, "We have no choice but to try. If he sends out armies against us, over and over, he will break us in the end and all of Yarmald will lie open to him by such slaughter. If we focus all of our powers together, we may be able to form a shield that will send that destruction back to its maker."

At those words, Manorkis of Ishlair called out, "Then we must all believe this and let the Zarn know our will."

And Roshair shouted, "I call for hands on those words." Azurmi brought order again and a show of hands was made. Looking around the circle, I felt the chill of fate, for every hand rose along with my own. Even Zeela joined with us.

Then Azurmi pointed the willow at me and asked loudly, "Tarl, do you still stand by your word to go to Eezore, or should we seek another?"

"I will go," I answered quickly, fearing that Halli would speak if I did not.

There was some talk that followed then of my worth, not all of it easy listening, for some spoke of my pride and some of my rashness. The worst was a long discussion of my break of anger at the line. Through it, I was silent and said not one word in my defense, for it was all truth. There was nothing I could say. But it put me in a torture of embarrassment and made me long to be elsewhere, riding fast and far away on Timmer's back.

At the end, Azurmi looked me up and down and said dryly, "Well, it is not courage surely that she lacks, but sense." Yet, she was one that spoke for me to go, saying, "I trust, Tarl, you have learned from this to better hold your anger."

Quadra and Jephra and others also had spoken of my better qualities that would be useful for such a task. So when Roshair again asked for hands, though there were not as many as on that first vote, still there were more than enough to send me on my way and no strong voice blocking.

Now a great chill came over me, for I had, indeed, put myself in the path. Several of the younger Hadra and Neshtair spoke to come with me, but none seemed right. I did not trust Serl, her anger would be dangerous, and Karf was more foolhardy even than myself, and Mirl had not the endurance for the dangers of such a trip.

At last Ozal stepped forward and said decisively, "I will go with Tarl to Eezore. We are trusting friends and comrades. I am as steady as she is fierce. She will speak and I will be holder."

There was a cheer. I thought all was settled and that at last we could leave for home. Then Manorkis said to me in her clear commanding voice, "Little One, how do you plan to address the Zarn, since you know hardly one word of Shokarn, or have you been studying since we last met?" Manorkis had been my mother's friend and not always mine. She had scolded me much for leaving Zelindar and not staying in school to study when I had the chance.

I blushed deeply and had no words to answer with. Ozal, I knew, spoke no more than a few words of Shokarn, having refused to learn the "slavers'" tongue when her grandmother would have taught her. I was afraid again that Halli might try to go since she spoke better than most of us or, worse even, that Quadra would step forward.

Suddenly, Sair leapt to my mind. I saw her again as she had been the morning before we left, blocking my way and demanding her right to come stand with us against the Zarn's army. Before I had had time enough to think on it, I found myself saying, "Sair will ride with us. She knows the city and the language and has good reason for taking such a message to the Zarn."

This was followed by more talk, for many did not know Sair and some felt it unwise for a new Neshtair to be sent on such a mission. I myself could scarcely speak, for I ached to be on Timmer's good solid back, riding home. At last, there was agreement and Azurmi ended High Council with the old words, "In the name of all those who are gathered here, we thank you, Mother, for your aid and counsel."

The Hadra began to scatter and regroup. I saw Azurmi walk away with her arm around Quadra saying, "Sometimes these Hadra are worse than wild dogs. How have we survived them for so long, my dear?"

As I turned to go, Karf appeared at my side. "So you ride to Eezore, my wild friend. I wish I could go with you, but it has been decided otherwise by this Council, no doubt wisely. We are too much the mad fools together." With that, she hugged me with such force, it seemed my ribs would crack in her grip.

I stepped back laughing. "So, old friend, you have not weakened from living in Osen."

She raised her arms to display the muscles for me. "We have been building boats. Soon we will be bringing some to Semasi for trade, if you have anything worthwhile there."

"We are in need of boats for we have had no time yet for such work, but we are still too new to have much of worth to trade. Come anyway. There is beauty in our sea cliffs and our forests and we may find something to barter. Come anyway, Karf, because I would love to ride with you again."

"And I with you," she answered. We hugged again though this time I was more prepared.

The formal council was over, but meetings, plans, discussions and arguments went on all night around the fires. I went to my tent to sleep and, when the noise grew too loud, I pulled my cloak over my ears to shut it out.

The next morning on leaving, Sharven stopped me with a hug.

"Well, Mother," I said to her, "this time I have truly put my foot in the circle of fire."

She laughed and kissed me between the eyes. "Oh, Nibbit, you are a good dancer and will know which way to leap. The Mother's Luck ride with you on this venture, Tarl."

We were gathered and mounted early as all were eager to be gone. Much as I love the Escuro, I was glad to leave her that morning and did not look back. The birds-of-death were still circling overhead. Our horses, too, were glad to be turning home. They had been nervous and fretful ever since the battle. As we went, many of the army's abandoned horses came trailing after us.

I rode fast ahead of the others. When I was in a wild spot with no sound of voices or sense of human presence, I sent out a call to

Sair, straight from my heart, with all the Kersh I had left. /Come home, Sister, for I have need of you!/

* * *

AFTERNOTES

High Council — An ancient ritualized form of Council probably descended from the Asharha. It is only used when several settlements meet together and the questions being deliberated have grave consequences for the future. Unlike the informality of most Hadra meetings, much importance is given to the proper ceremonial words being spoken and aid is sought frequently from the Goddess before final decisions are made.

Osen and Baltimere — Two Hadra settlements. Osen is located on the inner bend of the coast opposite the lower tip of Felduir Island and Baltimere is on the Scarn River before it flows into the Escuro.

PART 4

PREPARATIONS
Sair Resumes

On that third morning I lay in my cloak a long while, watching the clouds with no more thoughts in my head than the flowing water. I could hear the songs of birds and the horses moving through the high grass and the rush of the stream that ran nearby. It seemed as if all the world's contentment lay in that meadow.

Then as clear as a trumpet I heard my name called. Instantly, I sat up and looked about me, though I knew myself to be alone in that place. The summons had to have come from within my head and from far beyond the pasture. Tarl!

I jumped to my feet to call Sharu, but she was already coming at an easy run. Hurriedly, I gathered up my pack and cloak and swung myself onto her back. The call had had such urgency that I was fearful and wished to be quickly home, not even stopping to look back with gratitude at that magic place.

Sharu moved with confidence at a long slant across the meadow toward the opposite side from where we had entered. Though I could see no way through that wall of rock, I trusted myself to her. When we came close to the barrier, there appeared a small break in the rock worn by some ancient waters or some weakness in the fabric of the stone itself. The pass was so narrow, there was room for one horse only, and the way down from there seemed precipitous, but Sharu went at a steady angle across the steep slope. It was not long before we came to the valley floor. When I looked back, I could see no pass above us, nor any way to it.

We went back a different way than we had come and it was not at the same pleasant leisurely pace as before. I pushed Sharu as hard as she was willing, listening always for another call inside my head. When we galloped into Semasi, all those left in the settlement rushed out to meet us. Though they greeted me warmly enough and even questioned me some on my journey, it was not me they waited for so anxiously. It was those who had been to battle. I joined the waiting, filled with my own fears for them. Over and over, in my head, I could hear the cry that had wakened me that morning.

It was not until much later in the day that I went looking for Sharu to rub her down and thank her for our journey. After that I wandered about restless and to no purpose until nightfall, when I joined the others in the central circle. No one seemed ready for sleep. Zarmell had made a fire and we sat up by it, long into the night, talking and worrying and tossing the pebbles to see which way the luck ran. Not wanting to sleep alone and apart in my small stone hut, I rolled up in my cape under the central Gobal tree and dozed there, until I heard shouts and the sound of hoofbeats.

It was still early morning with the sun just rising. Tarl was the first one I saw breaking through the morning sea mist. I ran to her heedless of all the others. She slid off Timmer's back into my arms so that we fell together and rolled about, hugging and coughing in the dust.

"Oh, Sister, Sister! I am so glad to see you! Did you hear my call?" she asked, when she had breath enough to speak.

"Clearer than bells and trumpets," I answered laughing.

When we stood up, she drew me away by the hand even before I could brush off the dust, saying urgently, "Come where I can talk to you alone. I must tell you what I have done, for you may be very angry with me, Sair." She gave me no chance to greet the others.

I was so overjoyed to see Tarl safely back, I could not imagine cause for anger. Without protest, I followed her to a rock ledge above the sea cliff, stopping often on the way to kiss and hug and touch and so assure myself that she was home unharmed.

When we were seated, Tarl seemed troubled and distracted. For a while she could not speak. As I had no clear reading of minds and she was guarding her thoughts, I could not guess the cause, but watched her face for signs. At last, looking out to sea, she told me all in a rush of words of the battle and the outcome of the Council meeting and what was to be my part, if I willed it so.

"Will you do this, Sair?" she asked me at the end.

I was both flattered and very much afraid, but from pride, I answered yes, that I would go, not giving myself clear time to think. At that, Tarl hugged me and seemed much relieved. Then suddenly a shadow fell across her face.

"Sair, are you very sure?"

I was not sure at all. I was full of doubts. But I had been left before, like a small child at the gate, when the Hadra rode off to meet the Zarn's army. I would not be left again. This time I would be the one to go.

"Very sure," I answered boldly, trying to hide my doubts as best I could and fearful that Tarl could read them.

She did not look me in the eye, but slowly raised her hands palms forward. Slowly I did the same and we pressed our hands together. "I will do this thing if you will," she said, and reluctantly I said the same. Then I felt a trembling inside, for I knew I had bound myself by Hadra oath.

"Will you share cloak with me tonight?" Tarl asked. I nodded, glad at least for that. "Good, then we will be together later. Now I must go to see how Halli does. I am uneasy for her."

With no more words, Tarl was gone at a slight run and I was left alone with my fears. I was now oathbound to return to Eezore. How had I given my consent, so lightly, and with so little thought? Had I been mind-bent by Hadra powers? Had Tarl laid a spell on my wits? I felt some anger at her, yet when I gave it honest thought, I knew it to be my own pride more than Tarl's doing. I sat a long time gazing out to sea. The water, that was usually such a bright and sparkling blue, seemed to me that day a vast waste of flat, dull gray.

* * *

That night, though she loved me and lay with me, in some way Tarl was not there. I sensed a change in her, a strangeness that I could not touch. When I told her my fears of Eezore, she held me close against her saying, "Ozal and I will be with you at all times. So long as you stay close between us, you are safe, that I can promise you. Our force can easily enough cover for all three of us, and we will be in Eezore no more time than is needed."

I thought of Zarmell then and my time with her. Suddenly I felt uneasy.

"What is troubling you, Sair?"

I shook my head and would not answer, but with little trouble she saw full well what I was confessing—or rather not confessing. "Do not be angry with me, Tarl, or jealous of Zarmell. It meant little enough."

"Jealous of Zarmell!" She laughed and nibbled on my ear. "No one can be jealous of Zarmell. She can take the lover right out of your bed and put her back there more loving than before. It would be a waste of heart to be jealous of Zarmell."

"And what of Halli?" I asked suddenly, remembering Zarmell's words.

Tarl shook her head. "We slept together as sisters only," she said sadly.

After that, she was full of teasing and affection, but when I asked about the battle, she turned aside all my questions so that I knew no more than before, and ended by telling her of my own trip instead. Of that, she asked me many things and, at the end, laid her head between my breasts saying, "Will you take me to that meadow, Sair? There is peace there."

"I cannot, Tarl. Sharu will not let me." That answer amazed me for I replied without volition, not even knowing the truth of those words until they were spoken. Perhaps it was selfishness, as well, for in a land where I was a stranger and knew so little, this had been my own private place.

Tarl drew away from me and seemed to harden. "So, you who are only Neshtair, have been to the fabled 'place-of-horses', and I, who am Hadra, am forbidden to go. We were not even sure if it was real or only some old tale, for none among us has been there. Then she sighed and laid her head down again. "Ah, well, as it must be. It is a great gift, Sair, and must mean some special thing for your life. Take me back there in your thoughts then if you can, for I have deep need of that peace."

She fell asleep, wrapped tightly in my arms while I opened my memory as best I could to those high flower-filled meadows with the herd of horses and the bright, slow stream.

* * *

For the next week, it seemed that all Semasi joined in preparing for our departure. Clothes were lent me and made for me, and for Tarl also, since she paid so little heed to her own. She gained several shirts and tunics. Even new leather riding pants were fashioned for her. This was necessary, for Mirl and Zarmell had spirited away her old shabby ones to the burning pile. Halli cut and stitched them with care from the hide of an old loved horse, who had died that spring*. Ozal had clothes enough of her own and had only need to pack, but for love and luck, Mirl made her a new green tunic for the ride. Ozal blushed with pleasure when she tried it on for our admiring eyes.

For concealment, my long yellow hair was cut short, though not short enough to reveal the castebrand on the back of my neck. My hair was then curled and rinsed with rithberries, so that it gained a coppery hue. I seldom had reason to look at my reflection, so when Halli drew me before the mirror, I was amazed at the stranger who stared back. I had lost my Shokarn whiteness. My skin had bronzed in the sun. With my curly reddish hair, I could have been Ozal's sister better than my own. I went to look for Tarl to find if she loved me still in my disguise. She took to laughing so at my appearance, that I ran at her and knocked her down and rolled her in the grass.

Later, I realized that it was the first I had heard Tarl laugh since she had come back from battle. It was not Tarl alone who was affected. All who had witnessed that dreadful scene seemed in some silent pain, especially those who had stood the line. They had come back to Semasi with the smell of burning death on them and, though the smell had gone, some other essence had remained heavy in the air.

* * *

There was some haste in the preparations. It was needful that we leave soon, before the Zarn gathered another force of men to send against the line. Yet time was also necessary for Tarl and Ozal to rest and regain their powers.

Since, by Hadra custom, all warnings must be written as well as

139

spoken, we had to draft a proclamation for the Zarn. My better knowledge of court speech made me useful for that purpose, as it is almost a different language from street usage. Quadra and Jephra and Tarl and I spent many long hours in the Zildorn together, arguing over what best to say to the Zarn, and how to say it in formal Shokarn. I was given the chore of doing the final writing. By the time we had it penned and sealed, we all were weary of the task, and of each other as well. At the end, Tarl stamped away, shouting angrily, "We should draw him a set of pictures! That would be plain enough for any fool!"

* * *

On the eve of our departure, some Shokarn coins that had been collected at the battle were distributed among the three of us for use in Eezore. There was a short informal ceremony held on the beach at sunset by the younger Hadra. Then at dark, Yima called us together in the Zildorn. We each held a candle and formed a circle with Yima in the middle.

When there was silence, she raised her arms and said as if speaking to an old friend, "Jahar, Goddess of Journey and Venture, please guide us on the way, for we can only see part of the path and never the whole circle."

Then she called Tarl into the circle. Tarl stood there, feeling foolish with embarrassment, while Yima kissed her on the forehead and said, "Jahar, Guardian of the Road, please lead our daughter Tarl on her path."

After that she made the sign of the blessing, Tarl stepped back and I was called. I stood frozen in place until Kedris nudged me and I found my feet. Yima made the same signs over me, then over Ozal, too. That being done, she beckoned Quadra into the center and she, herself, stepped out to join the circle.

Quadra held in her hand, a polished wooden box. When she opened it, there was an exclamation from the Hadra of the circle. I heard Halli say in an awed voice, "The passing of the Stones!"

Quadra summoned Tarl back into the circle, told her to strip to the waist and kneel. This Tarl managed with a little less embarrassment than before. When Quadra lifted out the necklace, she held it up, turning it for all to see. It had an elaborate setting of bronze or gold, almost like a medallion. The stones in it were large and unflawed, black, blue and red.

"Eyes of earth, eyes of sky, eyes of fire, these are the Tormesh, the Stones-of-the-Mothers*." With those words, she slipped the necklace over Tarl's head. "These were given to me by Azurmi, who is Keeper-of-the-Stones*, to pass to you. When you wear them, you speak for all the Hadra of the North, as well as being the messenger for High Council."

I found myself staring at the beauty of Tarl's breasts with those stones gleaming between. Quickly, I looked away again, before others could read my mind.

Quadra went on, "You must not take them off till you have given the Zarn our message and are safe home again. Then you are free of their weight and their power." Dipping her fingers in a bowl of water, she drew the Hadra triangle on Tarl's forehead and between her breasts. Then she raised Tarl to her feet, kissed her and made the sign of blessing. We all bowed our heads to the Mother and Yima signalled the circle over.

There was a cheer and Hadra pressed in to kiss and bless us. I found Quadra standing next to me. She leaned close and said, "Remember, Sair, do not go to Eezore with anger. It will endanger this mission, but most of all it will endanger your life. Find some way to leave it here, Daughter." She pressed my hand as if to press her message into my flesh. Though I much admired Quadra, I felt impatient at that moment with her advising. It was not the first time she had given me such warning.

All around me, younger Hadra were crowding close, saying, "Sair, now you are truly one of us." "Sair, you are very brave to do this." This went to my head like spring wine and I had little patience with admonishments.

Tarl was laughing and I heard her say to Yima, "Oh, Mother, if there is any more solemnity to this venture, I shall collapse under the weight of it. I think I would rather meet with the Zarn's guards or the Fires of Damlin than endure another Hadra ritual this night."

When at last I turned to leave, Jephra took hold of my arm as if she had been waiting for that moment. She drew me to a window bench and motioned me to sit. Having been subject before to her

141

sharp tongue, I had no wish for more and felt some fear of what she planned to say. She saw my thoughts and shook her head.

"Not so, Daughter, I do not always scold. Often my heart is hard, Sair, and for reasons I may never tell you, but there are some soft corners to it. This is no easy thing you do, Daughter, to ride back into that place that meant your death and we here are . . ." She could not finish, and I saw to my surprise that she was crying. Pulling a small packet from her sleeve, she held it out to me and said when she could speak again, "If you would wear something from my hands . . ." I unwrapped the packet and held up to the light a silver double triangle on a chain. It was much like Quadra's, only smaller, and with a red stone set at the center.

"It is a power piece and also a focusing device. If given in love and trust, there is some measure of protection in it."

I could not have been more amazed, but when I tried to thank her, she rose quickly and went out of the Zildorn, leaving me alone there. Slowly I clasped the chain around my neck. It was not easy, for my fingers shook.

With my hand, I pressed the neckpiece against my chest. At first the silver was cold on my flesh, then it took on a wondrous and comforting warmth. I sat for some time in the Zildorn, watching the candles flicker on those walls. This room had been my first home and shelter in Semasi.

* * *

AFTERNOTES

Since the Hadra kill no creatures, their only source of leather is from the hides of beasts who die, or from trade with the Koormir. This gives leather a rarity and value among them, so that they use it sparingly and with great care.

<u>The Tormesh, The Stones-of-the-Mothers</u>— This necklace is thought to have originated at the time of the making of the Redline. It is held to be sacred and is worn only at moments of grave importance, when it is necessary that one Hadra carry out a dangerous task agreed on by all the Hadra of North Yarmald. First, the wearer must have the "Stones" fastened around her neck at a ritual that invests her with their power. By doing this, it is as if all Hadra power and protection is focused on the wearer through the "Stones." After that, she cannot remove the Tormesh until the task is accomplished. For the time she wears it, she speaks for all the Hadra of North Yarmald, and they speak through her.

<u>The Keeper-of-the-Stones</u> is always the oldest Councilor of the North Yarmald settlements.

PART 5

THE ROAD BACK TO EEZORE

We slipped away in the earliest dawnlight, wanting no more farewells. Also, we hoped to reach the Drylands* by nightfall when it would be safe to cross. All had been made ready the night before, our watergourds, our food pouches and our packs. Dressed in our new clothes, with our horses eager under us, we were glad to be on the road at last.

Ozal, I knew to be a fine companion and each time I glanced at Tarl, I thought how beautiful she was and how glad I was to ride with her again no matter what the reason. So when the sun rose at last over the eastern hills, I felt a lightness of heart that amazed me. For that time, at least, the pleasure of the ride outshone its purpose.

Later, I came to think Tarl and Ozal had planned it so. Ozal sang her mountain songs without pause, starting a new one as soon as the last had ended. Tarl joined her when she could. At times they even coaxed me to add my voice. From this I felt a sharp, sweet nostalgia for my time of healing in the Zildorn when Ozal had played and sung for me there. If the songs faltered, Tarl quickly filled the silence with her talk of horses and, indeed, we passed many wild ones along the way. Sometimes they would follow for a distance, timid, yet curious. Then Tarl would comment on their shape and color and make her estimates of their endurance and their speed. There was much calling back and forth along the way between our horses and those wild ones.

For myself, I looked about with pleasure at this landscape in the full bloom of early summer colors. I had crossed it before, more dead than living, with the last cold of spring and was surprised to see Kourmairi farms and settlements where I remembered nothing. That death-walk to the sea seemed like some distant story to me now.

Several times we passed Kourmairi farmers on the road and they called out their greetings. They had heard news of the battle and all seemed pleased to see us. Some even stopped to ask a blessing for their child or make small offerings of fruit or flowers. For a while, we rode with flowers in our hair, eating sun warmed parmi-fruit* and sweet, newly baked tarmar cakes.

By afternoon the wooded hills began opening more and more to fields. We came, at last, to the Redline. All seemed so peaceful here, though I knew the scene of battle to be only a long day's ride south of us. Tarl and Ozal both slipped from their horses. To my surprise, they knelt on the line with bowed heads. Not knowing what to do, I moved off to the side and stood leaning against Sharu. After some time of silence, when they seemed to have forgotten me and all else in the world, Tarl stood up and said, "May the powers guard this line and close Yarmald to any who would enter here for harm." Ozal said the same. Then both together said, "As it must be," and remounted.

Ozal smiled at my puzzlement. "Whether that is truly a spell with powers or only old words, I do not know, but it gives comfort and does no harm. We say it each time we cross, hoping to renew the power of the line."

Once over the line we went with less gaiety. Now as we passed Kourmairi, they did not greet us, but drew aside and grew silent with fear. I could feel their distrustful eyes on my back as we rode by. The day grew hot and then still hotter. Soon the land lay flat on either side, harsh and dry, and we fell silent. There was no bird song there, nor any sound but our horses' hooves upon the road. Consumed by thirst, I drank my whole supply of water and from pride, did not ask the others for a share of theirs. At last, when I had given up all hope of change in that cursed landscape, there rose before us a small grove of trees. The horses turned in unison in that direction.

On entering the grove, I saw at the center of it, a pool of milky green. Ferns grew thick along the bank and a spring bubbled from between the rocks at the far side. My mouth was too dry to speak.

145

With a groan, I slipped from Sharu's back and stood trembling in that welcome shade. Horse and human together, we gratefully drank our fill. Then, as the horses went to graze, we washed away the road dust, refilled our watergourds and made our meal by the pool's edge. Afterward, Tarl and Ozal stretched out to nap on the mossy bank, inviting me to do the same.

I shook my head. "We are in the Zarn's lands. I am afraid."

"The horses will watch and keep us safe."

I shook my head again.

"Sair, we must ride through the night. You need some rest."

"I will lie down in a while," I said. The others slept, but I could not. I pulled the wilted flowers from my hair and sat leaning against a rock with my own troubled thoughts to keep me company. The light mood of that morning had drained away. I felt at last the full fear of what I had pledged to do.

* * *

Not until late that day did we remount to ride again. As we approached the Drylands, the earth itself grew very strange. The grass thinned. Knobs of rock broke through the surface much as if bones of land were breaking through its skin. These knobs grew larger as we progressed and took on many varied and fantastic shapes. Sculpted by wind and rain, they had a likeness to the legendary gnomes and goblins from the old tales. Everywhere the ground cracked into ravines and gullies and finally canyons. The vegetation changed. What few trees grew there were bent and stunted. Small spiny plants that had been scarcely noticeable near the grove, now rose to great heights, their thorny branches reaching up into the sky like stiff green fingers.

It had grown mercilessly hot, so it was with relief that we turned at last to watch the sun set in a blaze of red and orange and felt the rise of the evening breeze. There would be no moon that night. As it grew dark we had only starlight and groundglow to guide us, but the horses had no trouble with the way. The shapes of rocks and plants grew more ominous. I might have been afraid, yet Tarl and Ozal seemed quite at home in that strange night. Ozal even sang again, though softer this time.

* * *

It was dawn when we stopped at last. I had been dozing over Sharu's neck and opened my eyes just once in that dull reddish light. Then I felt myself being lifted off the horse and laid gently down to rest. I did not even know we sheltered in a cave until late that day when I was wakened from an ugly dream by my own loud cries. By then the slant of the sun had filled the place, lighting all about, but not even its warm glow could dispel the heavy shadows that hung over me. That dream was much like the ones that had plagued me in Semasi. In it I had been struggling for my life, with my body held and bound. Around me, large shapes had moved in shadow so I could not see their faces.

The others had been sitting by a small cook-fire at the cave entrance. They came quickly at my cry. Tarl crawled over and curled up against me. "Let me hold you, Sair, until it passes."

Ozal pressed close to me on the other side, but I held myself apart. Their comfort was kindly meant, yet there was a coldness in me that bodies could not touch. At last, I shook free of them and sat up, leaning against the cave wall. Whether that dream spoke of the past or of things yet to come, or both, I could not tell, but a great fear was in me. It must be spoken of before we rode one step closer to the walls of Eezore. At that moment, Semasi and all that was Semasi seemed very far away.

I stood up slowly, pressing my back against the cool smooth stones, finding some comfort there. Clearly, the time had come to say aloud all that had been working silent in my head since our rest by the spring.

"The Zarn," I said starting slowly. "We three think we are going to demand an audience with the Zarn? To take him a warning and command his will? Do either of you understand what the Zarn is?" I stared down at them, turning from one to the other. Standing, I was in shadow, and they were still in sunlight. It seemed we were in different countries. They sat gazing up as if waiting for me to finish my strange speech and resume my place between them.

"He is more than a king in Eezore." I went on, speaking faster now and louder, willing them to hear. "The Zarn is like a god. All bow before him—all! How am I to stand up and say your words when I should be prostrate on the floor before him?"

147

At that Tarl gave a snort of disgust and shook her head. "Sair, the Zarn is also a man like other men. Why puff him up so greatly?"

"Tarl, the Zarn is absolute ruler. All lives in Eezore belong to him. Even highborn Shokarn, who lord it over merchants and farmers and workers and slaves, are themselves as slaves before the Zarn. No one demands to speak to him. All are beggars there. He holds the power of death over every person in that city and the lands beyond."

Scenes came to me then. I could see again that river woman thrown on the Bargguell, a slave being tortured in the public square, a man beaten for falling under his heavy load, some guardsmen executed. And always my father explaining that in some way they had displeased the Zarn. I know my father tried to shelter me from such sights. What more might I have seen without that shelter?

Suddenly I was shouting and gesturing wildly with my hands. "You do not understand! You cannot, you cannot. Ask Zarmell. She knows. You Hadra have always lived free. You have never lived with power over you, power over your bodies and your lives. How can you know what that means? You saw the horrors of that battle, Tarl, but what do you know of the fears that drive men to such battles? Zarmell understands. Eezore has branded her. Eezore is branded on me, also. And I am one of the lucky ones, born uppercaste. But even I know in my body what it means when you do not own yourself." I was breathless from that flow of words, glaring down at Tarl as if she were the enemy, yet I hardly understood myself what it was I struggled so to tell her.

Tarl stared back at me, stricken. "Sair, I fear I tricked you into coming with us on this work. Do you wish to go back to Semasi?"

"No, no! Tarl, you are a fool. I want to go on. I must. I have my own need to do this. It is not that I am so afraid of dying. I am more afraid to stand up and look at that man who is not a man and say those words. Dying might be easier." I was shaking now as if to break apart and shouted again, "You do not understand!"

At that moment, Ozal grasped my arm to draw me down and pressed a steaming cup of tea into my hands. "Drink that, Sair. It helps to calm and mend the spirit."

In my upset, I had not even seen her pour the tea. "You Hadra think all the pains of the world can be soothed with a cup of yima tea," I muttered, but I sank down and held my cup obediently, pressing its warmth against my chest. My anger drained away abruptly and with it, all my strength. I began to tremble as if from fever. Tears welled up and flowed, then sobs shook me and I set down my cup. The grieving that swept over me was as great as the anger had been. It was not my grief alone. It was as if I had tapped into some vast river of human grief. I cried for us all, all those who have ever been bent helpless to another's will and all those who live their lives so. When at last the crying lessened, I drank my tea and grew calmer.

The Hadra watched in silence. When I could speak again, I said more quietly and with less anger, "You cannot understand such feelings, Tarl. We are different creatures at the core, you and I — born different. No one can ever use physical force against your being, and you have lived so all your life. For me, the knowledge of Eezore is born and bred in me, biting deeper than any castebrand."

Thinking perhaps that fear had unsettled me, Tarl put an arm around me to draw me close, saying, "Sair, we will protect you. I promise you will be safe with us. Eezore will not touch you." As she spoke, I shook my head and pulled away.

Before I could answer, Ozal said quickly, "Hush, Tarl. It is too late for such promises. Eezore has already touched her. Sair is right. Because of our powers, we cannot know — not in our blood. It is not tomorrow only that she speaks of, but whole lives spent that way, where those in power can steal your soul and make you dance to their will in fear for your life. And if you are foolish or rash enough to defy them, they will take your life in punishment, or worse, your children's lives."

She shook her head as if such a world was past understanding but when Tarl made to speak Ozal raised a hand to silence her and went on. "It is from the top of that pile of power that the Zarn rules, playing god over mortal lives. Not only Eezore is held that way, but all that we know of Garmishair, and perhaps all else on earth. I know, Tarl. I was raised on my grandmother's stories." With that she ran her sleeve across her eyes, and I saw to my surprise that she was crying, something I had never seen Ozal do. Almost in a whisper she ended, "That is what we ask Sair to stand up against."

Looking at them both, I saw them as separate and apart from

me, born with such luck not all the treasures of the Zarn could match it. "You Hadra are not human!" I shouted, growing desperate again in my strange pain. "You are something other."

"I am human enough," Tarl said angrily and jumped to her feet. Her face looked grim and hard. "Why sit here mourning for the world? Let us go do what we can to crack some part of that power." I stood up, too, and suddenly it was as if rocks had rolled off my back. I felt so light, I was dizzy, and put out my hand against the stone to steady myself. I had said what needed saying and was free of it. The Zarn, when I thought of him now, seemed a much smaller figure. No longer did he loom over Eezore and blot out the sky. Suddenly a wave of laughter swept through me, catching me helpless in its grip, as helpless as I had been before to that flow of tears.

"The Zarn," I said, when I could choke out the words, "the Zarn will be much surprised. No one has ever spoken to the Zarn in this manner. No one!" Then the laughter began again. Tarl and Ozal also were swept into it. "A surprise for the Zarn. We shall be a fine surprise for the Zarn."

We laughed together until we could hardly stand, staggering and holding to each other like drunkards. Then, as quickly as it had come, the laughter passed. Tarl shouted, "It is time to go! The Zarn awaits us!" and picked up her pack.

As we ducked out the entrance of the cave, Tarl bumped against me, and I took her arm. "I am sorry, Tarl, to have battered at you so." Now I could not understand my great anger, and why so much of it had been for her.

She grinned at me. "I may have learned a little from all that. Sometimes I am hard to teach." Then she gave me a rough kiss that had as much of pain in it as pleasure.

Before we left, I stood a few minutes with my face pressed against Sharu's neck, taking some comfort there. Then I swung onto her back and said in Hadra style, "As it must be," understanding, perhaps for the first time, the power of those words.

When we left the Drylands behind us, the countryside turned lush and the earth rich and dark. Orchards, gardens and grain fields grew in abundance, a sight to gladden the heart, but the people here seemed fearful and stayed far from the road. There were no greetings shouted now, nor even any insults, and no farm animals anywhere in sight. As we went, we passed more and more signs of conflict or disaster, abandoned wagons, burned buildings and the carcasses of beasts. A sort of pall hung over everything, and there was a constant smell of smoke in the air.

Far ahead, we could see the blue of a wide river winding across the broad green valley. This should have been a scene of beauty, but as we rode closer, it was made grim and ugly by charred ruins on either side of the river bank as if there had once been a village or small town there. The fields around were overgrown with weeds. There were no Kourmairi about and no farm creatures, nothing but waste and devastation, except for a small group of guards standing by the ruins of a bridge.

As they saw us approaching, they shouted and moved to block our way. I was gripped with fear, but when Tarl shouted back, "Hadra!" they stepped aside in sullen silence to let us pass. The river there was slow, but the water was almost to the height of the horses' chests. We had to pull our packs well up to get them clear of it. The bank on the far side was a hard, steep scramble.

I looked back just once. The guards had regrouped and were staring at us with hate-filled eyes. I remembered my ride in the farmer's wagon, the shouts of the soldiers and the smell of burning. I also remembered the barracks. I did not look back again.

"This is more of the Zarn's work," was all Tarl said, but I could feel her rage burning like a fire. Suddenly she leaned forward over Timmer's neck and rode off at a gallop.

I started after her, but Ozal stopped me. "Let her be, Sair. She will come back when she is ready."

* * *

We made camp two more times on our journey, the second in a rock shelter under a ledge. It was not far from the road, but well concealed by brush and the low hanging branches of trees. When I questioned Tarl, she told me the Hadra had many such places of concealment near the Zarn's cities and that they were from the old times.

When we rode away early the next morning, she left a small pile of stones by the road to mark the turning. "If we are separated in any way, we can meet at this shelter." I looked about and could see nothing in that landscape to catch the eye, nor did I think Tarl's small rock pile enough to mark the way.

As we rode, Tarl glanced at me several times to see how I did. Each time I nodded to tell her I was steady. At last I said with some impatience, "Tarl, there is no need to worry over me so closely. I have my own reasons to be on this road again and will do well enough what needs doing." After that we all traveled in silence with our own hard thoughts.

* * *

AFTERNOTES

Drylands — A long crescent of semi-arid land, stretching north and south down the length of Garmishair. It starts as a narrow strip northwest of Eezore, then broadens out until it curves below Nhor in the south, where it is at its widest point. The northern part, where I had crossed at night is fairly narrow and so not as dangerous, though even there it does not do to be caught waterless in full daylight. The vegetation in the Drylands is very strange, said to be different from the rest of Garmishair and from Yarmald as well.

Parmifruit — A small, early-ripening fruit of sweet and sour taste much favored by the Koormir. The shrub like parmi trees are often used for hedges and field guards as they are thick branched and have long, sharp thorns. It is from fermented parmijuice that both yors and quillof are made by the Koormir.

PART 6

THE ZARN

Not long past the middle of that day, we were close enough to Eezore to raise the bright yellow flag of safe entry and the Hadra flag of North Yarmald*. The city itself crowned the hill that rose steep before us and was surrounded by a massive wall of stone. Spread around it like a scatter of pebbles was a loose circle of smaller buildings, shacks and sheds, some of which reached in our direction. Beyond us, off to the left, towered the rotting heap of the Bargguell.

Watch-guards must have seen us, for soon after that outriders circled us, and we were met at the gates by a small company of guards. The gates were closed, something not common in the middle of the day.

When we stopped Tarl raised her hand. She spoke slowly, giving me time to repeat her words. "We are Hadra from the battle and must speak to the Zarn. It concerns his safety. Do not be so unwise as to shoot. As you must already know, any weapon so used will come back to your own harm. Please open the gates now for our passage." This was followed by a strange silence, for I sat staring speechless at the guards, caught in my old fears, until Ozal rode up to nudge me. Then Tarl's whole careful speech came out in a rush of words, a poor beginning surely. After that I vowed to remember my part in the business, no matter what I saw or felt.

As soon as I finished, there was much talking and arguing and rushing about among the guards. Faces came and went at the viewing slot, weapons were raised and lowered, commands were shouted back and forth, and Shokarn threw challenges to each other's courage, but none were willing to make the first hostile move. All this time Tarl and Ozal kept close on either side of me, but I was not much afraid of that bluster. From the talk around me, which I shared with them, I learned that news of the battle had, indeed, come home to Eezore and, with it, much fear of the Hadra. At last, after some final shouts, the gates were opened. We three rode into Eezore with guards before us and behind.

I sat very straight on Sharu's back hoping, to look proud and unafraid, while inside I trembled to pass through those gates again. There were many curious at all the doors and windows and on the street as well, but they stayed well back. Shouts of "Hadra! Hadra!" echoed from place to place. We went into the city with the way clearing before us and closing behind, until one man bolder or more foolish than the rest, or dared by his companions, ran up to grab at Tarl. He fell back with a cry. After that there was no more trouble.

When we had gone but a short ways, the guardsman who seemed in charge, halted our advance, and said nervously, "We must send word to the palace and see if the Zarn wishes to give you audience. You cannot ride this way any further."

"We will wait for word at the public fountain," I said, amazed at my own boldness, and turned Sharu in that direction. I saw no need to stand waiting in the street with the heat of the noonday sun bearing down, and our horses dry and weary. This time the guard followed after us, while two of their number rode hard for the palace.

It was good I knew the way to the fountain for not all the streets of Eezore were familiar to me. As I was somewhat recovered from the shock of being there again, I began to look about me and was surprised at how shabby it all seemed. Eezore was not nearly so grand as I had remembered, dirty even in those fine streets. Most of all, it was the misery of the people that I noticed. It pressed on me from all sides and I could feel the ache of it deep in my own body. I wondered if it had always been so bad. Even those Shokarn who wore fine clothes to cover it, gave off a haze of pain. Worst of all was the sight of slaves, especially women slaves. I did not envy my companions their Kersh. Glancing at them, I could see from their drawn faces they felt it even more than I did and were struggling hard to shield.

The fountain, at least, was as beautiful as I remembered, rising in the center of a large square. The square itself was surrounded by wide old trees and elaborate, ornate gardens. We dismounted at the fountain's edge to let our horses drink and cool our cramped and aching feet in the water. Though the guards muttered at this, they did not move to stop us. The curious of all castes and classes pressed around too close for my ease and all mixed together in an awkward blend, though mostly this was an area reserved for upper-caste.

The haughty Shokarn, surprised in their pleasure spot by this mob, seemed quite discomforted. They looked at us with contempt and made rude comments, but under this show I could feel their fear. Then one thin young man, who appeared especially haughty rode quite close and said with harsh mockery in his voice, "Well, I see some refuse from Yarmald has been dumped out here on our streets." I stared down into the pool to hide my smile, for I recognized in this "young man", Lar's long face and bony frame, and knew Tarl and Ozal spoke with her in silence.

The guards, meanwhile, made several tries at driving off those of lower castes until Ozal stood up and shouted, "Leave them be. They are not your cattle to be herded about." Though I did not translate, the guards left off their work in confusion. When I glanced at Tarl, she was bent forward as if in pain.

"Tarl, are you sick?" I asked with concern.

"Not sick of body, but sick at heart. Be glad you do not have our Kersh, Sair. Right now it is a curse. How do these people live with so much pain?"

Ozal reached across to her. "Give me your hand, Sister, and I will help you shield." I took Tarl's other hand and tried to focus on the cool, falling waters of the fountain.

After a few minutes Tarl seemed to recover. She glanced about her restlessly for some sign of a returning rider. As none appeared, she jumped suddenly to her feet and shouted at the guards, "If no one comes soon with word, we will go unescorted to the Zarn and ride up the very steps of the palace itself!" Before I could repeat her words which, indeed, I had no wish to do, a messenger in palace uniform rode up. We were given official summons to audience with the Zarn, the god-king of Eezore himself. I pulled my boots on over my wet, swollen feet and remounted.

155

Now my fears threatened to ride over me in force. I clung to Sharu's mane with both hands as if some safety could be found there. Ozal rode close beside me saying, "Breathe and count, Sair. Breathe and count. This work will soon be done. Then we can leave this cursed place. Breathe and count, keep steady at the center." I held to her words until some calm returned. But on the way, I saw little that we passed for I kept my eyes on Sharu's ears and my mind turned inward.

As we approached the palace, some of our crowd fell away. The streets grew wider and the buildings larger and more imposing. I could feel the coldness of power there and had to hold myself rigid to keep from trembling. Ordinarily, only highborn, slaves and guards were allowed in that part of the city, but a few of the lower castes still escorted us, emboldened, no doubt, by curiosity.

More guards met us at the palace steps, many from the Zarn's own private regiment. It looked to be a small army that had assembled there to greet three Hadra. They did not try to block our way, but one, with a rope, reached for Timmer's head when Tarl dismounted. Timmer reared back and snorted. The guard stepped away hastily.

Repeating Tarl's words as loudly as I could, I shouted to the crowd, "Do not touch our horses! It would be dangerous for you! Stay far away! They will wait for us there under those trees." As she spoke, Tarl pointed to a small park-like place off to one side. Timmer, indeed, looked dangerous with his ears laid back and his teeth bared. I hoped that the guard and all others were sufficiently afraid, for their fear was the only real protection our horses had. We left our packs with the horses, but first Tarl slipped the scroll in her belt pouch and took the Hadra banner to carry before us.

With our large escort, we climbed those endless steps. My knees felt weak. I wished we were truly riding up as Tarl had threatened. I would have welcomed Sharu's familiar warmth between my legs.

"And we could have left a few horse-piles for the Zarn as token of our passage," Tarl muttered at my side.

Ozal said from behind me, "If he wanted to see people, surely he could have made it easier. These steps are enough to wind a goat."

The steps were, no doubt, meant to impress all lesser beings with the Zarn's great might. The whole palace must have been constructed for that very purpose. It was certainly not a thing of grace or beauty. Rather, it appeared to be a huge block of gray-white stone, built of smaller blocks of gray-white stone. It covered a large stretch of the street and ran back for many blocks. Though there were parks and gardens at its edges, they did little to soften its grim austerity.

"If this ugly palace is the cause of all the suffering in Eezore, it is indeed, a waste," Tarl muttered through her teeth.

Ozal shook her head. "Think what we could make in Semasi with such stone worked in a different style."

When we reached the top at last, we were met by still other guards who after some argument, swung open the doors for us. Those great doors were very high, their whole surface being worked in wood and metal set with precious stones and skillfully wrought into scenes of violent battle. At the topmost corner was a huge figure towering over all the rest with a fistful of arrows in one raised hand and a fistful of lightning in the other. No doubt this was Rha-ais, God of War and Battle, who has been raised over all other gods in Eezore, as the Zarn is raised above all men. Below this there was one man, clearly the victor, who was larger in each panel than the others. I took this to be the Zarn, if not this present one then perhaps his father, or his father's father before him.

Again I was reminded of the power that resided there. I shivered. Glancing uneasily back at the street before passing through, I saw the haughty young "Shokarn" from the fountain, leaning against a tree. I stepped across the threshold, feeling in some way safer with Lar watching there for us. I could scarcely believe I was actually following the Hadra banner of North Yarmald into the Zarn's palace.

In my years in Eezore, I had passed the palace many times, but only once before had I entered. I was quite young and had come with my father for an audience with the Zarn. It was some special holiday and many of the uppercaste of the city had been summoned. The palace had been decorated with flags, banners, tapestries and many flowers. The audience was held in the great hall which was also well decked for the occasion. I remembered my father tugging at my hand, saying, "Kneel and bow, Sairizzia— quickly!" I had been too entranced with the scene to remember the careful instructions he had given me at home and was amazed at all those bowed backs. The Zarn, seated on his throne, seemed high

157

above us. I hardly dared glance at him. My father never took me back, though I begged him to many times.

This time the palace was not decorated and seemed almost as austere inside as out. Before we had gone more than a few steps down the main corridor, our way was blocked by a man of amazing height. He was dressed in such ornate magnificence that it was clearly a display of power. Holding up both hands, he said in fluent Kourmairi, "I am Kermakin, Minister to the Zarn of Eezore. He is occupied and cannot see you, so I am entrusted to take him your message. There is no need to proceed any further into the palace." These words were spoken with polite formality under which lay all manner of unspoken threats. I was relieved I did not have to translate and surprised that the Minister of the Zarn deigned to speak Kourmairi, a language so despised among the Shokarn.

Tarl answered coolly, not looking at this human barrier, but slightly past him. "The message I have from the Hadra of North Yarmald is for the Zarn himself and for no other. It concerns his safety. We cannot leave until we have spoken with the Zarn."

Kermakin replied instantly, "I have already said you cannot see the Zarn." This time the threat in his voice was clear.

Tarl shrugged and plainly looked away. "Then we must remain in the palace until the Zarn consents to see us. I am messenger for Hadra High Council and cannot go back until I have delivered my message to the one for whom it was intended. If you will not take us to the Zarn, we may seek him out ourselves in his palace." With this she made as if to take a step forward.

Kermakin flushed almost to the red of his robes and commanded the guards to seize us. They gave a shout and moved hard against us. Instantly, they were thrown back with as much force as if they had rebounded from an unseen wall. In spite of all I had heard of the battle, I was unprepared for this sight and almost as amazed at their helplessness as the guards themselves. They, meanwhile, were stumbling about, shouting, cursing and threatening us with all manner of harm while they retrieved their weapons and tried to reassemble into some semblance of order. The Minister stood staring at us, speechless with anger.

Tarl smiled slightly and this time looked directly in Kermakin's face. "Ask your master one more time if he will see us. I do not think he will want three Hadra camping in his corridors or hunting him down in his chambers."

Kermakin said some hasty words to the guards I could not understand, turned and went back the way he had come. We were left with our small army of nervous guards. There was a tense silence followed by several loud angry shouts and more commotion. Then a messenger came toward us hastily, saying we were to follow him to the Zarn. He was very white and seemed so fearful and agitated that his hands shook and his words were jumbled. I had expected Kermakin to return, but we did not see him again, then or later.

We were not led to the great chamber, but to a cold, plain room that still was larger than any building in Semasi. Our escort stepped aside for us to enter.

"This does not seem a friendly place," Ozal whispered.

"It must be where he summons criminals for sentence," Tarl said with a grim laugh. Then she opened a few buttons and folded back the neck of her tunic so that the Tormesh was clearly visible. The Stones-of-the-Mother lay bright against her dark skin. "I think we are here," she said to us both and stepped boldly forward.

I could barely see the room through my haze of fear, nor could I look at the Zarn at all, though I could feel his presence in my bones. Before we had gone more than a few steps, the captain of the guards shouted, "Stop! Kneel and bow to the Zarn!"

I told Tarl what was said and she answered, "I bow to no one but the Great Mother, and to her from love, not fear."

Ozal said, "I, too."

There was a silence. All things were suspended until Tarl whispered, "Translate, Sair."

I was sweating, yet chilled through with dread, struggling to keep my knees straight and not crumple to the floor. Trembling, I cleared my throat to speak Tarl's words, but they came out a strangled whisper that none could understand. When I repeated them, I spoke too loud, and "I bow to no one!" echoed fearfully in that large empty chamber.

Instantly, the Zarn gave an order, the guards sprang for us and were thrown back against the wall, shouting in surprise. This time I was expecting it and watched with pleasure. After that I was less afraid.

When some measure of quiet was restored, Tarl said with weary patience, "Zarn of Eezore, you cannot bind us that way, as you well know, if you have heard reports of your war. To try more force will only harm your men." She stopped to give me chance to speak and the words came clearer and easier this time. "We have a message from the Hadra of the North to deliver to you in spoken words and written ones as well. As soon as this is done we will be glad enough to leave. There is much misery in your city, Zarn, and it is no pleasure for Hadra to be here."

There was a long silence. The guards were on their feet again, but made no move toward us. Indeed, they seemed frozen in their places. I stole a few quick glances at the Zarn and then dared to look more openly. His eyes were not for me. It was Tarl who was fastened in his stare. She did not bow her head, however, or look away, but gazed straight ahead as if the Zarn on his throne were a distant mountain and she was seeking out the best road through the pass.

The Zarn, now that I could look at him, did not appear so fearsome or even so impressive. Kermakin, had he sat on the throne, would have seemed a more imposing Zarn. Though his throne raised him high above the rest of us, he was not, in fact, a very large man, not near the size of his Minister. I thought him of middle years, no older than my father, forty and five perhaps. He was extraordinarily white, his hands and face appeared never to have seen the sun. I know that some highborn Shokarn intentionally keep themselves shaded to preserve that valued pallor, but this seemed more, as if aided by powder. He wore a long purple robe edged with thick gold embroidery and fur, but aside from that, he did not look like a man attired to give audience. Indeed, he had the appearance of one who has been hastily called from elsewhere, even from his bed. Perhaps it was the terrible reports from his war that had persuaded the Zarn of Eezore to meet with uninvited Hadra.

It amazed me that I, Sairizzia, was staring unimpeded at the Zarn. Then I remembered Tarl saying, "Sair, the Zarn is a man like other men." So he appeared. Behind his cold, closed face, I could read impatience, uncertainty and even a little fear, for I had learned some in Semasi of tapping the minds of others. At last, he gave a slight nod to indicate that Tarl should speak, though he did not acknowledge us in any other way.

Tarl remained silent for a moment as if she had not noticed that signal. She was staring straight ahead, holding the banner before her. I could feel her gathering her powers and knew she intended to be very terrible. All the words were remembered in her head as we had practiced them in the Zildorn. She had nothing to read from as the scroll was sealed and must pass so to the Zarn. Even if it lay open before her, she could not have read it as she did not have that skill. When she spoke it was slowly and loudly, pausing at the end of each phrase, to give me time to translate. I tried to forget the Zarn's face, the guards, the palace, even the city of Eezore that pressed around us, and turn my whole self to repeating Tarl's words exactly as she said them.

"Yorin of Eezore, I am Tarl of Semasi. I am only a messenger here, but I am sent by High Council. As I carry the Hadra flag and wear the Stones-of-the-Mother, all the power of the Hadra of the North speaks through me.

"You have sent terrible weapons against us at the Redline. Those weapons all turned back upon the men who used them, as we warned they would. We have felt grieved and sickened to watch men die so horribly who had no choice but to fight there. It has been decided at High Council that if ever again such weapons are used on us by you, they will come back, not at the hirelings of the Zarn, but at the Zarn himself. This is a warning being spoken here, and a promise. We Hadra will use all the power we can summon together to drive those weapons back to him who sent them."

The Zarn made as if to speak, but Tarl spoke louder and did not stop. "You will have one warning only and you hear it now. Zarn of Eezore, if ever again you send such weapons against us, then no place, whether of wood or stone or iron, will shield your body from their terror coming home to you. This is a Hadra pledge." Then, in a quite different voice, she added, "There will not be enough flesh fastened to bone to make a meal of you for the birds-of-death if you ignore this message." I knew these to be her own words, but repeated them also. With that she held up the scroll saying, "That was the spoken warning and here is the written one, according to our custom." With that, she tossed the bound scroll so skillfully, it landed at the Zarn's feet.

The Zarn's men gasped and leaped forward but did not move against us. The Zarn half rose and said, "Go," the first word he had spoken to us. Tarl turned to leave, and we followed. The guards

161

were everywhere, but they drew back to let us pass and did not speak. Every step down that long room and through those corridors was torture, for I expected at any moment a sword or an arrow in my back. Instead, we were followed by the sounds of our own footsteps in that silence.

* * *

AFTERNOTES

<u>Hadra Flag of North Yarmald</u> — Three horses, much stylized, one black, one red, one white, each with a gold star on its chest and all on a background of bright green.

PART 7

PRISONER IN EEZORE

Once past the entrance with its formidable doors, Tarl stopped, rolled up the Hadra banner and thrust it, almost carelessly, under her arm. Then, arm in arm and almost at a run, we went down the long steps of the palace. Ozal was crowing joyously, "We have done it! We have done it! It is over! We have taken the Hadra message to the Zarn! Sisters, the work we came here for is finished!"

Tarl, on the other side of me, was asking eagerly, "What think you both? Did he hear us? Will he heed our warnings? Have we made him fearful enough to cease his warfare?"

To this I was silent, but Ozal answered quickly, "You were very fearsome, Tarl. I think he heard you clear enough. After all, he did not set his guards on us more than once. And when you spoke of flesh parting from bone, I felt him tremble. At the end he had the look of one who has chewed on a lemon and cannot spit it out."

"Well, it is hard to tell with Zarns. This one is already white as a cave bat. And he did not make me much answer."

"No, he is not long on speech, this Zarn. I wonder if he has more to say at other times."

"Surely a Zarn has need of more words than that to rule a whole country."

They went on in this way, bantering back and forth between them about the Zarn, but I could not share their gaiety. This was, indeed, the end. Likely I would never see Eezore again. Instead of joy, what I felt was a painful blend of grief and loss, mixed with an immense relief at being free of the palace. All of this left me numb — distant even from myself. It was as if some stranger moved inside my skin.

As we neared the bottom step, Tarl turned toward me and shouted, "Sair of Semasi, you are as brave as you are beautiful. Well done, Little Sister. The Hadra of the North will all be proud of you."

Ozal added, "Sister, you were very strong and very brave to speak our words so clearly into the face of power."

With that we reached the street and they hugged me, both at once, one on either side. A crowd had formed again or had never really scattered. It appeared to be composed more of lower castes than of highborn. Seeing our hug, the people answered with rough laughter, shouts and jeers. Several times I heard the word "muirlla", spoken more as a curse than as a name. Embarrassed, I pulled away, wanting to be gone from there. Tarl and Ozal appeared to take no notice of the tone of the crowd which, to me, seemed less fearing and more threatening than before. Indeed, those two looked to be playing to an audience, making a show with hands and gestures and trading line for line. Tarl took Ozal by the arm and shook her in a pretense of anger.

"Kneel and bow down to the Zarn, slut of a slave!"

"Oh, sir, I cannot for my back is too stiff."

Ozal in turn raised a mock sword. "Kneel and bow down to the Zarn, wretched wench!"

"Truly I would, sir, but my pants are too tight."

Then Ozal leaped up on a stone marker and shouted, "Is it true the Hadra sleep with their horses?"

And Tarl answered, "How else would they smell so sweet?"

"Is it true the Hadra sleep with each other?"

"Why else would they be so pretty?"

More rude laughter came from the crowd, whether or not they understood the words. Sporting and jesting in this way, Tarl and Ozal went to rejoin our horses, while I tried my best to keep close by them. For the moment, it seemed the class order of the city had broken down as the curious of Eezore followed after us. They overflowed into the streets, while the guards struggled to keep order and watch where we went. Never, in my many imaginings of coming back, had I pictured such a scene.

Once mounted, I wanted to ride for the city gates by the shortest way, but the others argued to go through the Vendor's Square. "What harm can there be, Sair, another hour or less? Goddess willing, none of us will ever pass this way again. The market of Eezore is famous even in Yarmald. We have Shokarn coins from the battle and may find something useful for Semasi."

Taking turns, they spun out more arguments than I cared to answer. I could not believe they would want to delay in Eezore even for a moment, especially after all their promises of quick departure. But those solemn, purposeful Hadra, who had faced the Zarn, were gone. In their places were two wild, country girls loosed in the city.

For myself, I was amazed at our good fortune to still be whole and free and wished to be quickly gone from there. "You are like children," I said angrily, not understanding their recklessness. "The market is on the far side of the city. I do not know the way."

Hadra, once they have set their minds to some purpose, are hard to turn aside. Ozal rode at my side whispering, "Only a quick look, Sair. We will not be long." Tarl, not discouraged by my ill humor, turned in all directions calling out in Kourmairi, "Who will tell us the way to the market?"

She went on in this manner until one woman, clad in a bright red tunic, stepped forward boldly, saying also in Kourmairi, "Come with me, Hadra, I will show you. It is too hard to tell, and I go there myself." As we started after her, she turned and said, "My way is short, but full of turns, so follow closely."

Our guide seemed no more than thirty and had surprising confidence in a city so full of fears. Her long stride easily matched our horses' steps, and so we quickly passed from the side streets into a maze of alleys that were crowded and very dirty.

The horses grew nervous in this press of people and buildings. I knew how they felt and would have been glad enough to ride off with them, free of the city streets. This seemed to me a trap, but I saw myself moving helpless with the tide of things. When the way grew too narrow, we dismounted and went on on foot. Timmer kept his own space as well as Tarl's by snaking his head about with bared teeth and flattened ears. Sharu raised her leg to kick if any came too close to her flank.

At last the alley opened out into a space of interlocking squares, lined with shops, booths and stalls. Many had only a blanket

165

spread on the street from which to sell and these shouted at us to take care with our horses' hooves. I had been to the market but once or twice before in my life and this part of it was not familiar. As I looked about us, I could see little that pleased me or seemed worth this risk. All was noise, confusion and dirt.

At least the people here were not so threatening. They smiled and spoke to us, many of them in Kourmairi and altogether seemed less wary of the Hadra. Perhaps it was the Zarn they were less afraid of, for the Vendors' Guild has some power in Eezore. The guard drew back out of sight. It is the one place in the city where they do not flaunt their power with such ruthlessness, for the market has its own rough guard. I had often heard highborn visitors in my father's house complain of the Vendors' Quarter, saying it was a dangerous place that should be cleared out and burned to the ground. Now I was witnessing for myself more freedom than I had ever seen in Eezore.

It is also true that women have some power there. It is said that many of those who work the stores or make the wares are widows or women deserted by their men and that some even are free women, having never been bound to any man. The one who led us appeared to be well known in the square. Many greeted her as she called out loudly, "These are the Hadra who have been to speak to the Zarn!" Again I heard the word "muirlla", but spoken more with wonder than hate. One small child even ran out to take Ozal's hand and walked with us some little ways before her mother called her back.

At last we stopped by a trinket and jewelry booth, where a small dark woman of older years reached out for our guide. She said impatiently in Kourmairi, "Anyice, you worthless piece. I have been waiting hours for some help here. Now you have brought back half of Eezore on your tail. What sort of a daughter are you?" Her words were harsh, but her smile was full of welcome.

"Mother, these are Hadra who . . ."

"So I heard you say quite clearly, for you did not whisper your way here." The mother stepped around her booth to better look at us, running her eyes up and down as if we were some merchant's wares, to be examined coolly and with care. Then she reached out her hand and boldly ran her fingers over the Tormesh and over

Tarl's breasts as well, saying, "That is a fine set of jewels you have there. I would trade much in my stand for those stones."

"You could not trade your whole stand and more for those stones, Mother. I would not trade them for all of Eezore. Those are the Tormesh, the Stones-of-the-Mother." Tarl re-buttoned her tunic to cover the necklace.

The old woman shook her head. "Ah, well, better bargaining next time." Then she gave us her appraising stare again. "So you are Hadra. Well, well, you only look to be three young girls and not so awesome after all, though I hear you have evil habits." With that she winked and laughed and then went on, "I rather thought to see tails and scales and claws from all the stories that are about. It is said that you fried the Zarn's army at the line, that you can blast and burn most fearfully with no weapons at hand. Is that a fact?"

I felt Tarl about to speak the truth, but Ozal interrupted and said coolly, "We do what we must, Mother, to defend ourselves."

"What do they say, what do they say?" a man called from the crowd. Though most in the Vendors Quarters seemed to use Kourmairi, this man spoke in Shokarn. I saw my chance. With pleasure, I repeated loudly in both tongues some news of the battle, such news as I thought would be impressive. Those who had been crowding us drew back, reminded again that Hadra had strange powers and were to be feared. I felt more safety with that distance — though, in truth, there was little of the hostile mockery here that I had so feared in the open streets.

While Ozal examined cloth, and Tarl bargained with Anyice for a string of red beads, her mother questioned Tarl shamelessly, asking things which to a Shokarn would have been rude and even shocking. These exchanges I did not translate. The woman clearly had no fear of Hadra powers or the Zarn's spies, either. Tarl, however, took no offense. She answered seriously or with jest as the mood moved her and never lost track of her red beads. All the while the woman watched me intently until, suddenly, I felt a chill and thought myself known through my disguise. Perhaps in some way this woman had been attached to my father's house or had taken part in the wedding preparations.

In a rush of fear I mindspoke to Tarl, /We must leave instantly. It is dangerous for me here. I am known./

But at just that moment, Ozal took her by the arm and pulled her

167

to the next stall. "There is fabric here as tough as leather, but made of woven stuff. This bolt alone could fashion riding pants for all Semasi, and we would not have to wait for the death of horses." Even Anyice and her mother turned to handle the cloth and give advice. As they all bent their heads over that fabric, I felt myself drawn to look up. A man stood watching me, a strange, half-frightened look on his face. It was Lairz Mordal, the man who had been my husband, though in very different clothes.

I did not question how Lairz could have seen through my changes, or why he would have followed me to the market. I only knew that it was Lairz, staring at me from a few yards away. My fear left instantly, and I was in a burning rage. My dreams came back. This time I would have my knife in his flesh and his blood on my knife.

With no word to the others I rushed at him, hot with fury and he fled. He turned and ran up an alley. I followed him out of the square, through smaller and narrower streets. We went heedlessly, leaving shouts and turmoil in our path, until I had him trapped in a closed alley. I grabbed his arm, my knife raised in my other hand. He turned toward me with a cry, and in that instant, I saw he was not the man I hated, and he saw I was not the woman he feared. How could I have mistaken him for Lairz? This man had only a fleeting semblance to him. For a long moment we stared into each others' frightened eyes. Then, with a shaking hand I resheathed my knife, stammering apologies. He seemed so relieved I was not whom he feared that he was hardly angry for the chase.

Just as he started to speak his story, there were shouts from around us, "Guards, guards!" and a hand was placed on my arm. I struggled, and the grip tightened.

"You can see she is no Hadra witch. She does not have their powers," the one who held me said. With that a second guard came and pinned my other arm. Not without some pain, I twisted about to see my captors. The first guard was an older man with a heavy beard and a thick hard face. I recognized him as one of those who had opened the palace doors for our entry. He clearly was in charge. The second man was younger, clean-shaven, not nearly so confident. The hand with which he held me shook.

"Stay back or I will blast you when my powers rise!" I shouted at them, hoping to bluff my way to freedom.

"Not likely, witch," the first guard said with a rough laugh and brushed my hair back from my forehead. He seemed puzzled to find no mark there. Then he pushed my head forward and pulled my hair aside. I shuddered for his hands on me reminded me of Koll.

"Shokarn, uppercaste," he said with some surprise, touching my castebrand. "Why are you traveling with that trash?" He raised a hand as if to strike me.

At that moment the man I had pursued spoke quickly in my defense, saying it was all an error and could easily be explained, but the second guard raised his sword at him. "Stay back, rat-scum! This is no error. This woman is wanted by the Zarn, and he shall have her. We can take you, too, if you care to come." The man backed away and vanished as if he had melted into the street.

"My friends! Tell my friends!" I shouted desperately in Kourmairi, hoping that he might understand and trusting the guards would not, for guards in Eezore are always Shokarn and have great contempt for the Kourmairi. When I turned in search of him, the alley and even the street beyond seemed to have emptied miraculously. There was no one to be seen in any direction.

"What will you do now, woman?" the first guard asked mockingly. "Clearly you have no power without your muirlla." He spat that word out like a curse. That was, indeed, the question turning in my head. I cast my mind out in all directions, hoping to touch on Tarl or Ozal, but met everywhere the vast confusion of Eezore. I remembered Zarmell's story, and wished these guards were drunk and careless, but they were very sober and alert with fear. They took my knife, bound my hands and walked me in front of them with drawn swords. I had no choice but to go.

As we went, there was some discussion of my fate. The younger guard wished to take me instantly to the Zarn, and so be free of me, but the older one insisted that the Zarn was in conference at that moment and could not be disturbed. "We shall put her in one of the deep cells for safeholding, until we have clear permission."

I sensed that the older guard wanted full credit for my capture and feared to have me slipped out of his hands by another. Though I hoped for a delay, it seemed likely either way that I would be brought defenseless before the Zarn of Eezore—the God-king

169

whom I had mocked and insulted that very morning with Hadra words.

Though the guards were rough, they took care not to harm me, whether in fear of the Hadra or the Zarn, I did not know. We followed old streets I had not seen before, and always my captors glanced nervously behind them fearing my companions. As we went I cast my mind out probing for them, but could make no contact in a city so full of other beings. Every step took me further away. I held back as much as I dared, hoping Tarl and Ozal might come riding after. The guards, with their fears, pushed me forward as fast as they were able. In this way we came at last to a strange entrance, scarcely visible from the street.

Its low stone archway was set with a heavy wooden door, the top of it almost at street level, so that we had to descend some well-worn stone steps to enter. Everything seemed very ancient and unused as if an old tomb lay on the other side of those rusty hinges.

"What manner of place is this?" I asked, holding back in dread.

"The old part of the prison that is carved from the rock itself. It is here we bring prisoners who can expect no visitors." The older guard smiled as if pleased with his answer.

"A dungeon," I whispered fearfully, remembering old scary stories of my childhood. Often enough I had passed the main gates of the Prison of Eezore with its ornate ironwork and its huge deathposts, never thinking I, myself, would end as a prisoner there. This back entrance I had not seen before, though I had heard there were several throughout the city. Well, there was much in Eezore I had not seen before that I seemed destined to see that day.

The guards unlocked the door and together struggled to force it open against rust and age. Inside was darkness. When I hesitated, they thrust me roughly before them through a doorway so low I had to duck my head. As soon as the torch was lit, I glanced about me in dread.

"But it is a cave," I protested.

"Whatever it is, it will hold you well enough till you are wanted. Move on now."

I was forced forward, going with only the light of that one torch, down tunnels and passageways that took many bends and turns. Hard as I tried, there was no way to mark in my mind the route we took. The city lay over us. I felt on my heart the weight of all that stone and thought myself surely lost to my companions. That was no doubt the purpose of our strange journey.

On the way we passed no other light and saw no person, though twice I thought I heard a cry or groan from some distant place. The passageways we went by were all hollowed from the rock itself though, whether cut by some ancient waters or by the hand of man I could not tell. There were times when the torch light caught on wondrous shapes and forms, things half-seen of beauty and strangeness. If I had not felt my life at forfeit, I might have found some pleasure in that walk through the depths of the earth. The guards, themselves, were afraid of that place, as well as afraid of me or what powers they imagined I could summon, and so went in silence for which I was grateful.

At last, after what seemed like hours and miles, they stopped and unlocked a cell door saying, "Here you will stay for now." It was no more than a niche in the wall and looked like many other cells we had passed.

"What does the Zarn want of me?" I asked, hoping to delay for a moment longer the locking of that cell door on all my freedoms.

"You are muirlla and an ally to the Hadra. This morning's work alone would cost your life. But most of all, the Zarn wants to know by what methods the Hadra get their powers. He wishes to make such a thing."

At that, I almost laughed aloud. "Make such a thing!" I exclaimed. "They do not make their powers. They are born so. If it was a thing that could be made, surely I would have some. Nothing will come of holding me here."

"So you say and I can well believe you, for plainly at this moment you have no powers, but the Zarn thinks differently. He is very determined to find the secret and will not mind having you torn apart with hot tongs for what he wants, if that seems necessary."

"Then he is a great fool and will get nothing for his troubles."

The older guard gave me a push. "You can tell the Zarn what you think of his wisdom when next you meet. For now, into this cell, girl. We have other work to do."

As they were leaving, the younger one turned back and said with some weariness, "Muirlla, it matters little, for either way your life is marked and will not end pleasantly." He did not speak with cruelty, but as a fact.

171

With obvious relief they locked me in and turned away, taking the torch with them. The first guard called back from the darkness, "May the Zarn have mercy on you, Muirlla!" It was all mockery for I knew this man had no mercy in his heart for me.

"You will not hold me here!" I shouted after them defiantly. Then as the light grew dimmer, I wanted to cry out and beg them to leave me one flare, but pride held my tongue. Their footsteps were soon gone, and I was alone in that place.

It was dark. It was darker than anywhere I had ever been, and I was more abandoned. Even the Bargguell seemed a kinder end. As long as the guards could see me I had held to my courage, but now that they were gone, what did it matter? There were only the rocks to hear me cry.

I gripped the bars, and with my face pressed against that cold metal, I wept out my heart for all that was lost to me. When there was pause to my grieving, a voice in my head said quite clearly, /So, girl, you have gotten yourself into this, you must get yourself out./ That voice was deeply familiar though I could not place it. Instead, I thought of Quadra and her warnings to me that I had not heeded and of which I had even been impatient.

"Well, Quadra," I said aloud to her. "You were right. And I am a fool. My own anger has put me here. All that you warned me of has come to pass. I was too arrogant to heed your words." Still I felt some anger at her for being so right, and that anger gave me courage. I shook the bars and shouted to the darkness, "Goddess, I will not die here! Mother, I will not die in Eezore! I have not gone so far or learned so much to come back and die in this place! Goddess, I will not die in Eezore!"

Clearly my best hope lay in reaching Tarl, for I was buried deep in the darkness of the living rock and had no way of escaping on my own. With that in mind, I groped my way along the damp stone for a cot I had noted in the torch light. It seemed better than standing pressed against the bars. Even with the total darkness, it was not hard to find in so small a space. With a groan, I stretched out my weary body. From the blanket there rose the smell of all the human misery that had been locked in that cell before me. In spite of that, I wrapped it tight around me. Still it was not enough to keep back the damp and cold.

As I lay shivering in the darkness, trying to set my mind on touching Tarl's, there were flickers and glimpses now and then in the great confusion of Eezore, quick touches quickly gone. I was close to tears again when, at last, I thought of the neckpiece Jephra had given me. Firmly I pressed it between my breasts and soon felt its comforting warmth. Whether, indeed, that stone and silver held some power of safety in it, or whether it only gave me focus for my thoughts, mattered little at that moment. I was ready to try whatever came to hand.

Now the contact was stronger, and I had some hope. Yet, each time I responded eagerly it was gone. Soon I was trembling and my mind ached with effort. Again that familiar voice said in my head, /Do not try so hard, child. Let it come of itself./ Now I remembered the source of that voice. It was as if Old Marl herself had spoken next to my ear. So many times when I was little she had told me that.

"Well, Marl," I answered, as if she were really there, "I am glad someone has come to be with me in this cell for it was very lonely." I spoke aloud to keep my courage. Taking heart from her imagined words, I composed myself as best I could. The blanket I threw back. It gave little warmth and reeked of old pain. Remembering the power of the Goddess, I said several times, "As it must be," and took some deep breaths. Then I lay very still with my hands folded on my chest, so still one might have thought me dead. I let myself float in the darkness. The warmth of the neckpiece seeped down into my body. Far off water was dripping on the stones and the rhythm of it became music. I thought of nothing. A strange peace came over me as if I could lie that way forever, warm and safe in the dark. The darkness itself, that had seemed so terrible, now became a friend.

Suddenly I heard Tarl's voice in my head, very clearly. /Sair, Sair, I can see you. I know where you are./ I sat up too quickly and the contact was broken, but I knew we had touched minds. Hopefully, she had seen both my cell and the entrance to the prison.

Now if only I were granted a little time, I might still be saved. But, almost as I thought that, I heard cries and shouts and the sound of struggling. As this noise came closer, I could hear a child's voice crying, "Do not hit me! Please do not hit me more." My cell door was quickly opened. As I blinked against the light that flooded in, a child was thrown through the doorway with such force that she fell to the floor. A guardsman, the same, indeed, who had first caught hold of me, held up a light over her saying, "Stay there for now, slut. You will get your proper beating when the slaves have been assembled." With no other words, the guard locked the door again. This time, by some mercy, he lit a torch in the hall before leaving.

So it seemed it was not my time after all. Quickly I gathered the child up and took her to the cot. Even in that dim light I could see her face was bruised and swollen. She was sobbing and shivering and seemed very young, not more than ten years of age. I held her close, giving what warmth I could. When she had calmed herself, I asked her what had passed.

"I am a slave and a serving girl here," she said between sobs. "I was so hungry, I took a little food from a prisoner's tray. They caught me eating it."

I saw easily enough from her way of speaking that she had eaten all of it with no intention of making that delivery. When I said this to her, she pulled away afraid. "Will you beat me, too?" she asked, looking at me fearfully.

"It is not my way to beat people. I think we must console each other. After all, Little One, for the moment we are both prisoners here." She smiled, reassured, but not willing to let her off so easily, I asked, "Did you not think that a prisoner might be hungry, too?"

She looked away and said softly, "I heard he was going to the Zarn. None who go before the Zarn have need for food again. It seemed a waste, and I was so very hungry."

"You have a hard wisdom for one so young," I told her, thinking bitterly to myself that if I had had some wisdom of my own, I would not now be sitting in that cell. "Even the condemned like a last meal," I added.

"Are they going to kill you, too?" She stared at me with fascination. "I heard them say you were also to go before the Zarn."

"I do not know, Little One. As it must be." I was trying hard not to think on it. And there were other things worse even than death that crept into my mind.

"But how will they do it?"

"What is your name, child?"

"Marilynda."

"Well, Marilynda, I have no desire to sit here pondering what methods the Zarn may wish to use for parting my spirit from my body. Now, we can talk of other things or we can sit silent."

Not able to be silent long, she asked with awe, "Are you a Hadra?"

I shook my head. "No, child, or I would not be prisoner in this place. I am a friend of the Hadra and hope they will see me safe from here. But I fear I may be lost to them out of my own foolishness." So I told her my story of how I came to be there, and she told me of her life while she huddled close against me, touching my neckpiece, playing with my new curls and saying many times that I was the kindest person she had ever met, probably no great compliment for there seemed little kindness in that place. In such manner, we strangers passed the time together waiting for our fate.

Occasionally, I would signal for silence. Then I would shut my eyes, press the neckpiece against my chest and search for Tarl. I was catching sight of her more and more often and sensed her coming closer. At one moment I saw her quite clearly, but not looking like herself—Tarl, but not Tarl—strangely dressed in rough Shokarn clothes. She seemed so real, I almost called out to her, but at that moment I heard sounds again and thought, "Too late. This time truly I am lost."

"On your feet, Muirlla. We go to the Zarn." It was the same two guards who had brought me there. Now they would have the pleasure of delivering me to the Zarn himself.

I do not know how the words came, but I found myself saying, "If you want me, you must come to get me. I will not walk one willing foot to that end." Not moving, I sat on the cot with the child in my arms.

I saw them hesitate, still afraid of me, unsure of my powers, or perhaps thinking I had some trick to use. I fixed them both with a hard stare to hold them back, but at last the older one said, "We must take her soon or they will send to look for us." As everything in Eezore is done from the greatest fear, they entered the cell and came forward.

With a cry, Marilynda struggled free of my arms. "Not to the Zarn," she shouted and leapt between us.

The younger guard swung his arm as if to strike Marilynda full force across the face. The older one, with a roar of anger, drew his knife and stabbed at her. In that instant, I felt a surge of power that

175

threw me to my feet. The guard with the knife fell back against the wall, himself stabbed as if by his own hand. The other doubled up, holding his head from the hard blow he had sought to deliver on the child.

I scarcely understood what had happened, but saw this to be my only chance and leapt for it. The guard who was stabbed, I went at first. Not caring if I killed him, I gripped his beard in my fingers and banged his head against the wall until he slid to the floor. Protruding from his chest, I saw my own knife, the very one that had been taken from me. Speedily I drew it out, and with my hands and the blade all bloody, turned instantly to the other.

The second guard was just straightening up with a groan. Quickly I had him with my arm around his throat. Holding the wet knife against him, I growled in his ear, "Be silent, or I will cut you wide open!" Surely the spirit of Zarmell was at work with me in that cell.

Marilynda, quick as a cat, had pulled some rope from the first guard's pouch. "They use this for binding prisoners. It will do for them both." Tearing a patch from her worn skirt, she helped me gag the guard I held. He did not struggle much for he was too afraid.

"Take his uniform, you will need it," Marilynda urged. "Take his sword, take his sword! Hurry!" Together we pulled off his clothing until he stood white and shivering like a plucked bird. Then with the rope we bound both men and turned them to face the wall. As the guard who was stabbed left me sticky with blood, I had many times to wipe my hands on my clothes before I could strip them off to pull on that uniform. This I did as quickly as I could with shaking hands. Marilynda stuffed my curls under the cap. She helped with everything, buttoning and fastening, and all the while saying, "Hurry, hurry, you must hurry before others come. This is our only chance."

As soon as we finished my transformation, Marilynda helped me push both guards under the cot along with my bloody clothes, though she strongly advised that first I slit their throats. "I cannot kill bound men," I told her angrily, glad not to have that on my hands. Yet, in truth, it might have been more merciful. They would not be kindly treated for losing us.

Still saying, "Hurry, hurry!" Marilynda pulled the blanket forward to conceal the bodies. I buckled on the guard's belt, and with a grim smile, resheathed my knife. He had had little use for it. The newly gained sword, I strapped on the other side and pocketed the keys. Then in an instant, we were out. I secured the cell door, and we found ourselves on the other side of those bars with the guards bound and locked within.

"But I do not know which way to go," I cried, peering into the darkness.

"This way, this way," Marilynda said impatiently. "Take the torch."

When I had the torch, she grabbed my other hand and pulled me down the dark corridor. Stumbling, half running, I followed as best I could, terrified that in our haste we would fall and lose the light. I could not understand how, at such speed, in the semi-darkness of that quivering torch she could recognize the turns and crossings. Still, I had to trust her knowledge for clearly I had none of my own. We changed directions many times all at a mad pace, and just when I was sure we were truly lost, the passage we followed ended in a low wooden door, the very same I had come in by.

I gave Marilynda the torch to hold and, steadying one hand with the other, fumbled disparately with the keys, not knowing which would turn that final lock.

"Give me the keys and hold the torch close," Marilynda ordered, thrusting the torch back into my shaking hand. She snatched the keys from me and shook the key ring until she found the one she wanted. Then, standing on her toes, she unlocked the last door to freedom. I stuck the torch in a wall bracket, and together we pulled with all our strength, struggling against those rusty hinges. I felt another struggling on the other side. When the door at last swung open, Tarl fell into my arms.

PART 8

RETURN TO SEMASI

I was much heartened to see a little daylight left. I had expected darkness after my long entombment. Tarl grabbed me in a crushing hug. "Sweet Sister, I thought you lost from us in this foul city."

"I am not so easily disposed of," I answered, and laughed with a sudden wild gaiety born of relief.

Tarl was rough-dressed, looking like a man, just as I had visioned her in my head. Beyond her I could see Ozal, also in strange, ill-fitting clothes, and our three horses all decked in saddles and bridles like some owned creatures of Eezore. My mind flooded with questions, but Tarl quickly pushed me away.

"We cannot stand here hugging in this way. Someone will notice. Guardsmen and townsmen have scarce cause to hug in the streets of Eezore. Mount and ride quickly, Sair. Our Kersh is not enough to protect you from all Eezore, armed and angry. And it will be harder now that they know you are Shokarn with no Hadra powers."

"But the Zarn's livery is a good cover," Ozal added. "This fading light will help hide her face and figure."

"She must come with me," I said, pointing to Marilynda.

Tarl shrugged. "Well, then she must. I will pass her up to you."

When the child was seated before me, Ozal slapped me on the leg. "Neshtair, I am very glad to see you alive and safe. But I must tell you, you have caused us more trouble than a barrel of snakes."

This was said good-naturedly, but I answered with anger, "And you—if you had not gone to the market to finger fabric . . ."

"Go now," Tarl said abruptly. "Do not be too fast in the city, but once past the gates, ride for your life. Meet us at the rock shelter. We will do what we can here."

"How will I know the place to turn? Your little pile of pebbles is not enough to catch the eye, and besides, it will be dark by then."

"Trust Sharu. Now go, Sister, and be safe."

"I do not know the way to the gates from here."

"I know," Marilynda said, tugging on the reins.

I pulled her hands away. "Hold to the saddle. I will manage the horse, and you will give me directions." I did not glance back as we left, but prayed we had not been noticed together. The saddle felt strange and hard between my legs. Sharu tossed her head from side to side as if to shake free of that unaccustomed metal between her teeth.

To my relief, the street seemed near deserted. I urged Sharu to a trot, going as fast as I dared through back alleys with Marilynda guiding our way. Even at that pace, our passage raised few looks for guards in Eezore are used for many tasks. It is not uncommon to see a guardsman transporting a slave girl for his own pleasure or others'.

Marilynda had a true knowledge of those back streets, and it did not take us long to come within sight of the walls. When we reached the west gate, I was shaking inside, but gathered up my deepest voice to shout, "I am taking this zuka to the Zarn's men on the Balmori River." A zuka is female trash. I knew the Zarn to be fighting a rebellion on the Balmori, and it is said men always have need of women when they fight.

The guard at the gate laughed and winked. "See that she gets there safely, soldier. Do not do too much tasting on the way." The other guards laughed heartily. It seemed to them a fine joke that I might stop and rape this child myself before delivering her into the hands of other men. I felt the fire of anger rush up my back, but made myself breathe deeply.

A pale, bony Shokarn youth rode over on the pretense of examining Marilynda and said, "Well, soldier, that is a pretty piece you are carrying off, but a trifle thin I think." Then Lar bent closer as if to pinch the girl's cheek and whispered, "Do not run till you are out of sight of the walls. Then go like the wind. I will make a commotion and distraction here at the gate." Aloud she said, "On your way, soldier!" and slapped Sharu on the flank. Sharu lurched forward, I saluted the guard as I had seen done, and the gate swung open before us. We were out of Eezore. Plainly we were not yet missed.

As soon as we were out of sight, I stopped to free Sharu of the saddle and bridle, hiding them in a ditch under some brambles. Sharu rubbed against me in a show of gratitude. All that was strapped to her now was my packs. I swung on her back and called to Marilynda, "Quickly, climb on in back and hold tight to my waist. From here we must make much speed." Already I could hear shouts and uproar from the city.

We rode fast for much of that night. Twice we heard horses behind us, and Sharu slipped off into fields and by-roads. Once there was a great commotion, shouts and cries, the flares of many torches, and the sound of voices calling, "They went this way." "No, that way." The noise was such that it seemed as if an army rode in pursuit of another army. Not far past us, they all turned back and rode with the same fury toward the city, still shouting, "This way." "No, that way."

After that the night was empty of human sound. We went at a slower pace. Scarcely awake, I clung to Sharu's back, and Marilynda clung to mine like a flesh-twin. It was still dark with only a little groundglow when Sharu turned from the road at Tarl's rock marker. In front of the shelter, I slid from her back like a sack of meal. Marilynda fell on top of me. I had just strength enough to unfasten the packs and pull them off. At this, Sharu shook herself all over, much relieved to be free of her burdens. Then with Marilynda's help, I dragged the packs under the overhanging rock. There I unrolled my cape and fell flat out on it, thinking at last to get some sleep.

That was not to be so easily had. Marilynda threw herself on me, saying, "Oh, Sair, you have saved me a beating and rescued me from that dreadful place. Now I will go with you wherever you go. Will I be a free person or a slave? I would be glad enough to be your slave." She petted and fondled and caressed me as if I were a large dog and kissed me until I grew quite embarrassed.

"Marilynda, it is you who have saved my life, and we have rescued each other from Eezore. There are no slaves in Semasi, nor would I want one. You will be a free person the rest of your days.

Now I must sleep for I am weary beyond words, and you must sleep, too. We have ridden all night."

For a few moments she lay still, but at the first sound she was in my arms again, trembling and sobbing, seeming full of fears. "Oh, Sair, I am a branded slave. They will come for me and kill me, for that is how they do." She said this while pressing my fingers to the slave brand on her wrist. I sensed she was playing on my feelings, yet this was no light thing. Young as she was, she still could have been killed on the spot, or taken back and tortured for attempting an escape. Fortunately, she had not yet been branded on her forehead.

With much knowledge and in detail, she told me what would have happened to her at the hands of men if she had stayed drudging in that prison. That she was still untouched, was surprising. It was good she was so small. Between the guards and the prisoners, I had heard such serving girls do not last long when they come to bloom.

I held her and reassured her, saying she would be safe with the Hadra. No such things would happen to her among us. But even as I talked, I longed for sleep. It was hard to fasten one word to the next. Yet each time there was a new sound, if the wind rose, or Sharu shifted, or a distant dog barked, she would be on me again with her terrors. At last I understood that this was a ruse for affection and said, "Marilynda, I will hold you close even if there is no danger." With a sudden show of pride, she pulled away and sat up.

"You sleep, and I will keep watch," she told me firmly.

I was glad for this arrangement and did not argue. Again, with some hope of sleep, I had just dozed off when she shook me awake. This time her terror was real and instantly became mine. There were shouts and the thunder of horses' hooves fast approaching our hiding place. I jumped to my feet, thrusting Marilynda behind me, just as Tarl and Ozal tumbled through the entrance.

"Stop this!" I shouted angrily. "You are frightening the child, and put us all in danger with this noise!"

"No danger," Tarl roared back at me. "We have ridden the guards around in circles this night, led them a dance out of Eezore and back again. Now they search for us by the north road and will not come this way again. You are quite safe." She struck her spark-

181

stone, and a reed torch flared up in a crevice of the rock face. In that sudden burst of light, she looked wildly disheveled, and I saw that her new clothes were streaked and torn. From her pack, she drew out a half empty bottle of wine and held it up before my face. "We are drunk, very drunk this night," she said by way of explaining her strange appearance. This shocked me. The Hadra seldom drink except at the Essu and at some ceremonial occasions. They are almost never drunk, as it clouds their powers.

"Have a drink with us, Sair." Ozal took the bottle from Tarl and held it out to me. I shook my head.

Tarl gave me a comradely blow on the arm, saying, "Have you no kiss for a lover, now that we have saved your life and are safely back?" She crushed me against her, sweaty, dusty and reeking of wine.

Turning away my face, I pulled free of her embrace. "You did not save my life; you risked it with your foolishness," I said angrily. "I saved myself from prison with that child's help, not yours." In that mood I did not know who Tarl was or what to say to her. Overnight she had become a stranger to me.

Tarl shrugged and laughed harshly, then threw herself down on the floor of the shelter saying with sudden pain, "Oh, Mother, take me home. Let me never see that stinking city again!" At that moment I was struck by how young she looked and how hurt. There was much sadness coming from her, but by now I was angered and in no mood to give comfort. She pulled out another bottle and drew the cork with her teeth.

"Come drink with me, Sair," she said more gently, as she patted the ground beside her for me to sit. Stubbornly I shook my head again. Marilynda said hopefully, "I will drink with you."

Tarl grinned at her. "Well, brat, come here then, for I cannot reach that far." When I started to protest, Tarl said, "Think of all she has escaped this night, Sair. Would you grudge her a little wine? What harm can it do?"

Marilynda drank several good swallows from the bottle, then threw herself on Tarl with even more attention than she had turned on me. I expected Tarl to push her away, but instead she tussled roughly with her.

"What is your name, wild thing?"

"Marilynda."

"Marilynda, indeed. What sort of name is that? The Hadra cannot call you Marilynda. We will change it to Marli. That has a better sound."

"Yes, Marli. Yes, if you say so I will be Marli."

With that she climbed on Tarl again and swarmed all over her, at first brushing against her breasts as if by accident and then, finding herself not scolded, quite openly stroking and fondling them. Tarl lay drinking from the bottle and smiling at her as if with pleasure.

I could not watch, but went to sit against the rock wall with Ozal, sharing at last the wine I had refused. Clearly she saw my thoughts and laid a hand on my arm.

"We all must deal with pain in our own ways, Sister. Kersh is a blessing. It is the source of our freedom and the power in our lives. But if you take Kersh into a city like Eezore, with such pain everywhere, then it becomes a curse." She shook her head and herself took a long pull from the bottle before she went on. "I can see that you love Tarl, but sometimes I wonder how well you know that Hadra. She is wild and daring and full of spirit. That much, even little Marli can see. But do you know how sensitive she is, Sair? What an empath? It is no accident that Tarl and Halli are lovers. Do you have any idea what that battle cost her or that trip into Eezore? It will be a wonder if she has not burnt out some part of her powers these last few weeks."

I sat for a long time staring down at the dirt floor of the shelter, seeing many scenes played out there in the quivering torch light. At last I said, almost in a whisper, "Thank you for that, Ozal." I felt I had been given something of much import to think on.

She turned and said next to my ear, "You were right, Sair. We were very foolish to stay in Eezore one moment longer than was needed. That was Hadra arrogance. I grieve for what it cost you and now am ashamed and sorry."

I was much touched, not having expected such a confession. Sick with weariness, I put my head on Ozal's shoulder and slept at last.

I woke, hearing voices raised in argument. It was dark. Someone had laid me down in my cloak.

Tarl was insisting, "But I risked Sair's life in my great fear for Halli and did not even think on it. I had no right to do so. When I think of what they would have done to her . . ."

And Ozal was answering, "They will do nothing to her, Sister.

She is safe here with us. That is enough, Tarl, you have said it all enough. Sair went to the Zarn for her own reasons, not for yours. She has told you that herself many times."

They repeated much the same thing several times more. I felt an urge to speak for myself, but fell asleep again before the words could form.

Sometime later Tarl woke me, slipping gently under my cloak. "Forgive me, Sister," she whispered. "For now, I do not know what else to say. Later, when we have time to talk together I will say more." Her voice sounded strained and weary. I pressed my fingers to her forehead in the blessing and felt some power for healing in them. She pulled me against her and said in my ear, "I was afraid for you, Sair, so afraid, afraid for your life and more. When I think what they might have done to you there . . ."

She hugged me even closer, and I knew she was crying, for I could feel the warm moisture against my neck. We had hardly slept together that trip, our minds being on other things than loving. Feeling now how much I had missed her body and her touch, I pressed gratefully against that warmth. Suddenly she threw the weight of her body over mine. Her breath thick with the smell of wine, she began kissing my face and neck in a way that promised far more than affection. Then, just as suddenly, she fell asleep.

It was late in the day when I opened my eyes again. Tarl was preparing us to leave. I watched her moving back and forth, thinking how much better I liked her sober than drunk. Then Marli began to follow her about like a puppy saying, "Where should I put this? What should I bring next?" I felt again that strange discomfort akin to jealousy and made scarcely any move to help while Tarl and Ozal finished tidying the shelter.

When we were outside and ready to mount, Marli declared loudly, "I will ride with Tarl. She is my Hadra."

Tarl smiled. She seemed pleased with this new affection. "Well, so be it then," she said swinging on Timmer's back and pulling Marli up behind her. After that, when we rode, Marli went always with Tarl.

Now we travelled openly by the road, for the others had no more fears, but I glanced behind us often and at any sound. As we rode, Tarl and Ozal drew my story from me, my capture and imprisonment and escape. Marli talked, too, and interrupted, telling her own tale and saying with much pride, "I jumped between them and would not let Sair be taken by the guards."

Tarl and Ozal, by turns, told of their own adventures and Lar's help in getting clothes for them and tack for the horses so they could go unnoticed in the city. As for the capture of the wine, they laughed so much I could make little sense of it, but that somehow Anyice had her part in those doings.

"The bolt of cloth is safe here in my pack," Ozal said, patting it, "and will make riding pants for all Semasi. That man you chased so hot and fast from the market searched us out to say you had been taken, a brave thing to do for he was much afraid."

In silence I pondered my sudden burst of powers. How had I done for that child, what I could not do for myself? Was it truly my own powers or Tarl's and Ozal's and mine combined, or did Marli have some part in it?

* * *

This time when we crossed the Balmori, a group of ragged Kourmairi were working at rebuilding the bridge, watched over by several armed guards. Most of the Kourmairi turned away from us, but one stopped his work to spit in our direction, muttering, "Dirty muirlla."

At this, Tarl laughed and said loudly, "Far better to be dirty muirlla and Hadra in Yarmald than to be Kourmairi in the Balmori Valley under the press of the Zarn's guards." The guards watched us pass in silence. They did not move to block our way again.

By late afternoon, we reached the far edge of the Balmori Plains and the beginning of the Drylands. Determined to stay awake this time, I rode next to Ozal and questioned her on all that grew there of which she seemed to have great knowledge. Also, it helped to ease my loneliness. Tarl, far from finding time to talk, now sought to avoid me altogether.

After a while Ozal called out to Tarl, who rode ahead of us, "Should we raise the Hadra flag? That would let the Muinyairin* know who we are and lessen the chance of attacks." In this way, I learned that other things besides plants dwelt in the Drylands.

"Are there really Muinyairin?" I asked in fear. That word was familiar from the legends of my childhood. In Eezore, children who are troublesome are told the Muinyairin will come for them in the night, if they do not mend their ways.

"Indeed, there are. They alone hold sway here. You are lucky they did not find you and set upon you when you walked alone through the Drylands that first time."

This thought sent shivers through me. "What manner of people are they?" I asked. "Are they loyal to the Zarn? Will they betray us?"

"Loyal to the Zarn? No, Sair, they are loyal to no one but each other, and that only at sword point. They are as fierce as the land they live in. A people who move and shift like the blowing sand, part Koormir, part Shokarn, they acknowledge neither one. Even the Zarn's guards will not ride after them. They are not kind nor gentle and think nothing of relieving those passing through of their goods, or even their lives. But they do not tangle with the Hadra. From us, there is no profit to be had, only trouble. They can not harm us and they know that. You are safe with us."

"And you told me none of this on the way riding out."

"You were half asleep, Sair. And, besides, would you have ridden happier if I had?"

All this Ozal told me with good-natured amusement, but after that, when I glanced fearfully in back of me, it was not just the Zarn's guards I looked for, but the silent and deadly Muinyairin as well. Marli, on the other hand, seemed more curious than afraid and asked enough questions for both of us until she fell asleep against Tarl's back.

* * *

We went on the next day, but slowly, resting often from the heat. Long before evening we rode clear of the Drylands. Later, when we made ready to sleep by the bend of a stream, Marli came to curl up against Tarl, and I moved myself away to another place. The ground felt very hard and cold to me that night.

By mid-morning of the following day, we came to the Redline and all cheered at the sight. Tarl swung down and opened yet another bottle, shouting, "We must stop and give thanks for the safety of these two." We joined her on the line and all drank from that bottle. Then she held it high to pour out some wine on the line itself and still higher to pour some on us as well. "For our sisters who are safe with us this day, thank you, Mother. To the power of this line, may it endure forever."

Ozal bowed her head and said more respectfully, "Thank you, Mother. May we never abuse the powers you have given us." Then she added the words for keeping the powers of the line.

After a time of silence, we linked hands and walked together across the line into Yarmald. In that manner, we continued down the road with the horses grazing alongside. Again the land seemed brighter, and the colors clearer once the line was crossed in that direction. There the summer flowers bloomed all along the way, dotting the fields with white and blue and yellow and even a few patches of bright red.

The shared wine had softened the pain of my jealousy and left me giddy. Singing and laughing as we went, we picked armfuls of flowers and put them in each other's hair, the horses' manes and tails, and finally anywhere they could be fastened. When a second bottle was empty, we remounted and rode at last into Semasi, quite drunk and decked everywhere with flowers. All of the settlement poured out with cheers to greet us.

* * *

In the manner of the Hadra there were parties and feastings and music to celebrate our safe return. No doubt many danced to exhaustion in our names, but I slept for the next two days and saw none of it.

The first evening I was up, I went to the Zildorn, hoping for some quiet. I was in no mood yet for festivities. Jephra was already there at the big desk with a pile of books before her. I thought to slip away again and not disturb her, but she saw me or sensed my presence and called me to her.

"I have been here reading stories and legends of the monsters that used to inhabit this northland. My sleep has been much disturbed of late by just such creatures." Her book lay open to a set of pictures. There were things of wings and scales and claws much like the stories Old Marl had told me as a child. Strangest of all was the huge Sea Serpent, its great fearsome head raised and its eyes staring. When I pointed to it, Jephra said, "That is the Morl*. They really existed once or so it is believed. There are legends recorded here of Morl swimming off this very coast in ancient times. It is these that come to me most often in my dreams." I gave a little shudder. She closed the book and turned to look at me.

"I am very glad to see you home, Sair, and have worn this next to my heart while you were gone, willing your safe return." She showed me the shell I had given her, strung on a leather thong around her neck. "That was a brave thing you did, Daughter, to go back into that city with no Kersh to protect you. Very brave."

I looked at her, puzzled. When I first came to Semasi it had been easy enough to read her feelings. They were quite clear and did not change. But in our last few meetings, she seemed different. "Jephra, I thought you hated me. Was I wrong?"

"Not hated, Sair, disliked at times, but that does not stop me from admiring courage." She shook her head. "Oh, Sair, much of it is not yours. I am a bitter woman. For the rest, this is a hard settlement. There is no room for luxury here. I saw you taking more than you gave and did not like your highborn ways. It pained me to see Tarl use her time with you, for she is one of our best, and Halli, too. And then, when you thought that about the work of slaves . . ."

I dropped my eyes and with a rush of pain saw again the slavery in the streets of Eezore. "Can you forgive me that, Jephra? There was much I did not understand then."

"If you can forgive me my meanness, Sair." I raised my head and, looking her in the eye, put out my hands cupped in the Hadra sign of forgiveness. She cupped her hands over mine and bent forward to kiss me on the mouth. Then she laughed suddenly and straightened, saying in a very different voice, "Well, I seem to be settling my debts of the heart all at once, though I am not planning to die. Still you must understand, Sair, it is not just that I have softened slightly, you have also become more useful here."

"Mother," I said humbly, "I have learned to work."

"I know, I know. I have seen you, and it is out of my own pride and meanness that I did not say." Then she looked at me intently as if searching my face for something. "I once loved someone who looked much like you, Sair, now that your hair is short and reddened. Her grandmother was Shokarn. She was killed by the Zarn's army helping some foolish Neshtair back across the line."

"Killed?" I asked, shocked, for I did not know the Hadra could be killed in that way.

"Yes, her powers of defense were not strong, though she had other powers, more than most of us. She was better with animals than any I have ever known, and was more skilled at growing things. She was much like Halli, with that same sweetness of nature.

"We were not far across the line. They came at us suddenly, many, many of them, and we had no time to link powers. I was not even near her at that moment. I had no force to stop them or protect her. They killed Dia and they killed the Neshtair, too. Then they did terrible things to their bodies. I was there and saw it." Her face was all twisted with old pain made new in the telling. I wanted to reach out and hold her, but she drew back. Her face changed again and she said in a lighter tone, "But I am lucky. I have a new life here and another love."

"You must love Quadra very much," I said softly.

She gave a strange laugh. "I love her as the ship lost at sea loves the harbor, if that can count as loving. Perhaps it is something else. Who else could live with me and give me some comfort and not be burned by my angers?

"Quadra was not always as you see her now—the sober and responsible Councillor. She used to be a wild one like Tarl, a wanderer and vagabond, always moving, even crossing the Drylands into Garmishair. She took no companion till late, after Kedris was born, and that did not last as she was too restless. For now she is content to settle here with me. This place is wild enough for her spirit, and she has done with wandering for a time. Yes, yes, I love her, and she gives me much. But Dia—Dia is still lodged in my heart like a sharp sliver of broken glass. I cannot accept her death and the terrible manner of it. I cannot, even now. Strange that I never saw before how much you look like her." Again I wanted to reach out and hug her, but abruptly she jumped up. "I talk this way to no one but Quadra. Why have I spoken to you of such things?" She sounded angry and turned to leave.

Quickly I took her hand and kissed it, saying, "Thank you, Jephra, for the gift of your words." Then she pulled away and was gone. I pressed my hands against my neckpiece. There had been no chance to tell her that it might well have saved my life. For a while I sat there alone, listening to the sounds of the sea and the distant music and thinking of all I had just been told.

As I was about to leave Halli came rushing in. "Oh, Sair, Sair. I have been looking for you everywhere. I hear that the Zarn's men captured you and locked you in their dungeon. You must come with me and tell me everything. Let me hold you awhile to know you are quite safe again." I went with her and spent that night in Halli's bed, for which love and comfort I was most grateful.

* * *

AFTERNOTES

Muinyairin — A wild, tribal people inhabiting the Drylands as well as the mountainous, northern regions of Garmishair west of Pellor. They are too fierce and nomadic to be subdued by the Zarns, and the Zarn-held cities are too well guarded to be overrun by the Muinyairin, so there is an uneasy truce between them, but travelers on the road are apt to fall prey to their raiding bands.

The Morl — The sea serpents of North Yarmald for whom the Morl River was named. Long believed extinct or legendary, they are rediscovered and described in Section 111, Part 3.

SECTION III – SEMASI TO ZELINDAR

PART 1 – SUMMER IN SEMASI

I was home. I was truly home. Never would I go back to Eezore. I was not a child of that dead city. I was a daughter of Semasi.

The first day that I felt rested enough to be up and walking, I went all through the settlement, looking, touching, smelling everything as if for the first time; seeing the way the streets curved around the buildings and followed the shape of the earth, the way the rocks lay one upon the other glinting in the sun, the way the sea always and everywhere framed our lives, filling our ears with her music and the air with her salt tang.

Wherever I went, I touched lovingly the stones that women's hands had set together to make shelter. When I reached the center of the public circle, I ran to hug the ancient Gobal tree, pressing myself against the rough warmth of its bark. The birds came calling and chattering, and I held out grain in my hands to let them peck at me. What touched me most was the sight of the Hadra, walking with ease and freedom through their own streets. That moved me to tears. I had learned more in that one day of being back in Eezore than in all the years I had lived there.

Going through the gardens, it seemed that miracles lay on every side of me. Never before had I planted a gardens and seen it grow. That those tiny green shoots had sprung from the dried seeds we had pressed into the earth, that those lush green plants I now saw crowding each other in the dark soil had come from those tiny green shoots—all seemed like magic. Almost I forgot the hard, sweaty work that had brought this to bear, not work for slaves surely, but work for free people.

We had returned into the midst of summer's plenty and summer's work. The berries were ripening on low bushes in clusters of red and purple jewels. The gardens and orchards poured out food in abundance. The building, too, was at its height, for all must be done before hard weather came, the rains and snows of winter. The storage barn must be finished in time for fall harvest, the roofs of most of the older buildings were in need of repair, a common house had to be built in addition to the dining hall so that we could come together in the cold, as well as our private shelters having to be remade or constructed new. "And all this the Zarn has interrupted with his war," the Hadra muttered with disgust as they went about their work.

I had my own small house to build and had chosen a site for it at the edge of the settlement nearest the ocean. The Hadra warned me it would be too cold there, but I was drawn over and over to that spot and so had begun to gather rocks. Often after a day's work, I would stand there on a small knoll to watch the evening come and feel the spirit of that place.

* * *

The Hadra were so pressed by the season, I had little chance to talk with them unless we worked together. Ozal labored on the barn all day and into dusk. Quadra worked and planned and gave advice, seeming to be three people, and Jephra also, though now she smiled and greeted me when we passed. Halli went as one in a dream. She did her work in silence, staring ahead as if seeing something none of us could share. Tarl, I hardly saw at all. I tried to have some patience in my pain, for it was not me alone that she avoided, but all of us. But Marli—Marli was everywhere and gave us no peace. Marli among the Hadra was like a goat among the horses or a snake among the fish—always the cause of trouble. She was wild and careless, her new freedom like a bottle of quillof, drunk too fast.

She left the food bins uncovered, crushed the berries, pulled plants from the garden or trampled them, and tormented the animals. Her work, she left unfinished or refused it altogether. If scolded, she laughed and ran off or turned angry and spiteful, saying, "I am not a slave any more to be ordered about." Tarl, she still followed with admiration and with her, Marli did not act so badly. Indeed, Marli seemed the one person Tarl herself kept company with. I felt some pull of jealousy when I saw them ride off together.

With the rest of us, Marli made herself a monster. Even Yima, she had no respect for, making ugly faces and calling her "old witch" and other names. But she quickly learned not to throw things when the first clod of earth returned on her own head.

Yima shrugged, saying, "I have seen better and I have seen worse. She will change." Yet I could feel her hurt and knew she would have been glad to befriend the child.

Quadra, too, Marli would taunt and disobey. "You are not my master. I am free now!" she would shout at her as she flew off to some other destruction.

Shaking her head, Quadra said to me, "It seems wrong to use Kersh on her, yet I am much tempted."

I felt the cause of these troubles. "I am sorry, Mother, to have brought this wild thing back to Semasi."

"No, no, Sair, you could not have left her. Whatever trouble she is to us, I would rather see her here than in Eezore. It will all come right soon enough."

I came one morning to the Zildorn in search of a book and found Quadra holding Marli pinned to the chair, trying to speak with her. The floor was littered with books. Marli was struggling, kicking and shouting wildly, "I will not listen! I will not, and you cannot make me!"

Quadra was saying firmly, but without much patience, "Marli, if you are going to live among the Hadra, you must understand. There is certain work to be done and shared. You have your part in this and can not . . ."

Marli saw me and cried out, "Sair, save me!" as if she were drowning. These were the first words she had spoken to me since we rode home together.

I shook my head and glared at her sternly. "Listen to Quadra. What she says is true."

"Where is Tarl? She will not allow this. She never treats me like a slave. Call Tarl! Call Tarl!"

At that, Tarl strode into the room in a wave of anger. "Why have you called me?" she asked, standing by the doorway with her hands on her hips and a scowl on her face.

Marli stopped struggling. "Quadra tells me I have to work like a slave girl again."

"No, Marli," Quadra said wearily. "I told you, we all must work so that life here can go on. You have been ducking and dodging your share so that it falls on others. It is you who have treated the rest of us as slaves."

"Why are you so disrespectful to Quadra?" Tarl asked sharply.

Marli, loosened from Quadra's grip, jumped up and ran to Tarl. There, she dropped to the floor and fastened herself to Tarl's legs. "Oh, Tarl, you are the only one here who is kind to me."

Tarl unfastened her not too gently, pulled her up and held her away with both hands. "Do you love me, Marli?"

Marli nodded eagerly.

"Then why," Tarl asked, speaking very slowly, "Why in the name of the Goddess have you caused me so much work and so much trouble? Can you not see that I am the one who most often follows upon your trail and mends the pieces? Marli, I had no wish to spoil your new time of freedom and so watched and waited, silent, hoping you would learn of yourself how to be Neshtair. But I see you must be told. You do not know how to live as a free person."

Marli looked down at her feet, covering one with the other. Tarl shook her. "Look into my eyes, Marli." Marli looked up slowly, but could not meet Tarl's gaze. "Girl, this is no easy place to live. Everyone must help. If you can not find it in your heart to do so, you must leave. I brought you here; I can take you away. You will be sent to live with the river people. Then you will not see me for a year or more."

Marli burst into tears. "Oh, Tarl, do not send me away! Please, please, tell me what I must do!"

"Why are these books on the floor?"

Marli looked wildly around the room as if some explanation were to be found there.

"Tell me!" Tarl shook her again.

"I threw them there," Marli said in a whisper, looking down again.

"Good. That is a start. First, you must pick up these books and put them back in place. After that we will talk of other things that need doing." When Quadra and I slipped away, Marli was dutifully replacing the books while Tarl leaned against the wall watching through half-closed eyes.

For the next few days Marli followed everywhere after Tarl, clutching at her hand and saying, "What must I do? What must I do now?" She was as slavishly diligent as she had been willful, and I was not sure which I preferred. After a while she regained her spirit, though not her troublesome ways, and so in her own way became part of Semasi.

At some moment Quadra noticed me watching her and said with a wry smile, "It is well for us that Marli has a hero. Only for Tarl would she have changed so." I felt again the hurt of Tarl's distance and thought to speak to Quadra on it, but my pride stopped me. She read my thoughts and put an arm around my shoulder. "She loves you, Sair, but she is in great pain. She has gone deep inside herself like a wounded creature that goes to hide in a cave. Tarl was so afraid for Halli. It is Tarl, herself, we should have feared for."

"Quadra, can you do nothing for her?"

"All I can do now is watch and wait and answer when she needs me. It is all you can do, too, Daughter."

* * *

We were not the only ones to be welcomed home. A few days after us, Lar rode into Semasi to much rejoicing, saying that her usefulness in Eezore was at an end. "I have been seen with the Hadra too often, most especially at the moment of Sair's escape. I made such a fine commotion that they suspect me of some mischief. If I had not slipped out of the city, I surely would have been taken soon for questioning." She did not seem regretful. "It was time enough for me to leave Eezore. The city was sickening my spirit. Tanyi is still there, and it is Osen's turn next to send someone as spy. For myself, I am glad to be away and very glad to be home."

This time, she had stopped to wash off her whiteness on the way. Joyfully she stripped off her Shokarn clothes and stuffed them in her pack. Stretching out her arms and turning up her face to the sky, she shouted, "Let the sun have my body now! I will be my own dark Hadra self before this summer ends." Then she turned to me. "Sair, I have a message from your father. I have seen him and spoken with him." She bent to riffle through her pack.

When she stood up again, she held out to me a small square of paper, grimed with travel and folded many times. Trying to steady my shaking hands, I took the paper from her and unfolded it with care. There I saw written in my father's own hand:

"My Dearest Daughter,

I thought you dead by your husband's wishes and in my great grief fell ill myself till news was brought to me of your escape. Now I am well again. Believe me, Sairizzia, if I had but known the cost of that marriage, I would have kept you living single with me all my life, no matter what the talk. But all that is rain long since fallen. It cannot be gathered up again.

When you rode through the streets of Eezore, I saw past your disguise. Oh, how I longed to rush out to greet you, but I knew the dangers and stayed well back. You looked well and strong that day, more like a man than like the girl I knew. Oh, Daughter, I do miss you grievously, yet doubt we shall ever meet again. I am too old and timid to venture where you have gone and must warn you not to return to Eezore for any reason. This time surely it would cost your life. There is notice posted for you everywhere, and the guards have questioned all

who knew you. I doubt I can write again for your friend is leaving soon, and the house is watched.
Know that I love you still, Sairizzia, and always will. I think of you every day many times.

Your loving Father"

All this was written in small cramped letters, on a tiny and much-folded scrap of paper, in my father's familiar hand. So he had been there among the crowd that day. I could have reached out and touched him one last time. Mindless, I stared at those words while all who were gathered there dimmed and quivered in my tears. I would have remained so, but at last Lar tapped me on the arm, saying, "Well, Soldier, how is our little zuka? Not giving you too much trouble, I hope."

At that, I came back to myself with a rueful laugh. "More trouble than you could possibly imagine," I answered, mindful of Marli's mischief.

Marli, herself, was quite surprised when she saw that the Shokarn youth, who had ridden up to examine her at the gate, was actually a Hadra spy. She pestered Lar with endless questions until at last Lar shouted her away.

Yima, of course, was overjoyed to have her granddaughter home again. They went about whispering and giggling together like young girls, or more like new lovers, and in my loneliness I felt some envy. But my father's letter, short as it was, was a joy to me. I took it back to my hut and fastened it to the wall, placing pots of flowers all around. There I could read it every day.

* * *

Some three or four days after Lar came back, I was shocked to see a stocky young man with a rough bush of dark hair and a curly red beard, walk casually into the settlement. I expected a loud outcry, but much to my surprise, he was warmly greeted by the Hadra. There was much talk of "Seronis, Seronis." Voices called out excitedly on all sides. I gazed everywhere, but could see no Seronis. At last, I realized that this stocky bearded "man" with the

197

large dog was the Seronis they spoke of—Seronis, back from her travels and the true owner of the hut that for a short while had been my home. I did not rush to meet her. In fact, I felt no welcome whatsoever and wished her still walking in the far north.

Back at the hut, I thought to gather up my few possessions and clear the space for its owner, but made scant move to do so. I had no will for it and no thought of where to go and did not wish to ask. When at last Seronis, herself, sought me out, she found me sitting there sad and dejected, staring at the floor with my cat Esla in my lap.

She gave a hearty laugh and said, "Well, you do not look to be overjoyed at my return. It is easy to see why. Sair, you have made a wonder of this place that I left much neglected." Even that praise left me saddened, but when she said, "Do you think we could live here together for awhile?" I looked up full of hope. Then I saw again her beard, not a disguise, but her own, a rough bristle of red and black that so repelled me, growing on a woman's face. Still I had few choices. I could live with her beard and be thankful for shelter or I could move elsewhere. I was embarrassed, for I knew Seronis could read my thoughts, but for that moment she chose to ignore them.

"I would be glad to," I said quickly, looking elsewhere than at her face.

"So, Sair, will you invite me to sit down?" I blushed and hastily drew up a chair. She sat down and slowly filled and lit her jol pipe, all the while looking about her with evident pleasure. Then she leaned forward suddenly and fixed me with her eyes. "Now, for some arrangements. I hear you have two lovers. That should be enough for anyone to manage. For me, I am at a time in my life of being celibate, and so I think we can manage this small space well enough without crowding each others' beds.

"You have made of this rough hut, a bright home. It gladdens my heart though I, myself, could not have done so. If you will take shelter here for awhile longer and keep it beautiful, I will be glad to share it with you. For my part, I will try to keep order and not destroy that beauty. Also, I have a good hand with a saw. That will help keep us warm when winter comes."

I was much gladdened to hear that I had shelter through the cold and so the changes I had to make did not seem too hard. And, indeed, our troubles came not with each other, but with our animals. They each had considered themselves sole creature of the hut and were not pleased at the intrusion. The first time Barlauf entered, Esla jumped to the window sill, hissing and spitting and upsetting my pots of flowers, which crashed to the stone floor. Barlauf lunged about barking, until Seronis could catch him in her arms and struggle him to the floor. Even then, he was hard to silence.

After several more such scenes, I despaired of a solution, thinking one or the other of them would have to go, most likely Esla since she was the real intruder. But by week's end, much to our surprise, they were sleeping together. Esla had discovered that this strange beast made a warm, soft mattress, and wherever he lay she would come and settle on him, purring with pleasure.

Meanwhile, Seronis and I had made a sound bargain with each other. For my part, I enjoyed cooking a good meal and setting a pretty table and always kept fresh flowers in the pots. But this was not forced on me or expected, nor was it always done. Each thing, Seronis received as a gift, and her pleasure was part of my reward. So for a time I was the wife in Seronis' small hut that I had never been to Lairz, and that became a joke between us. At the same time, I was learning much skill from her. I had grown strong, and we worked well together. I helped her raise poles, repair the hut roof, and fashion chairs and benches for the eating hall. We even began setting the loadstones for my house, the first time ever I had handled rocks.

Seronis was good company. She knew how to be silent, how to listen and, when she talked, how to tell a fine tale—and she had many fine tales from her long walk in the north. She, herself, was curious about Eezore and so questioned me at length about the manner of life there. Sometimes I even talked to her about Tarl to ease the pain, and about Halli, too. Often we would continue late into the night, sitting on the stone stoop, Seronis sucking on her jol pipe, Barlauf lying at her feet, and the ocean roaring below us.

Many of the stories she told me she had told, also, at gatherings in the eating hall or recorded more formally in the account* she as working on at the Zildorn. But one night, when it was even later than usual, she leaned forward suddenly and said, "I have not written this, Sair. I have told no one else." We had been silent for some while before that, yet I had remained sitting on the stoop, held by the spell of the night, though I was weary and much in need of sleep. Now I was instantly alert.

"Do you know of the Asharha?" she asked me. The way she said the word, the air between us trembled, but I shook my head. "The Asharha are the Old Ones," she went on. "When we speak at rituals in the ancient tongue, it is their words we use. No one knows where they have gone or why. We are not the original people of this land. The Koormir are dark, and the Shokarn light, and we both came here long ago from other places, but the Asharha were here before us— long, long before. They were smaller than we are and yellow-skinned, golden almost. That is what the old legends say, and that is how I saw them." At those last words a chill went up my spine that was not from the sea breeze. Things were stirring and whispering in the night around us. I said nothing, but looked at her intently, waiting.

She lit her jol pipe, staring into the night. Barlauf whined and came to lay his head against her knee. At last she went on. "I was looking for the first Hadra gathering place. It is believed to be north of here, but that is two hundred years or more gone, and they did not stay there through two turns of the seasons, so I had little hope of finding it. Instead, I found the First Ones.

"It was late afternoon. I had been walking all day and had passed little of interest, at least for the purposes of this journey. The land itself, of course, is always of interest. Just as I was near to looking for the night's stopping place, I saw to my delight a bald-headed hill rising before me. Instantly, I thought to climb it, knowing that from that high place, I could better view all the land around.

"Needing to reach the summit before sunset, I pushed myself hard, climbing fast against the closing day. This was no easy task. There was not a clear path to follow, in fact, there was no path at all. I plunged into thick woods, and all the land around me disappeared. My way was blocked by heavy underbrush and rocks and the low hanging branches of the evergreens—all of which made me question many times if I truly wanted to do this thing. But I have a curiosity in me that drives me on, sometimes to foolishness. Even old Barlauf here could hardly pass through that dense growth. He growled and grumbled for much of the way.

"Not till I broke through the final fringe of trees did I see naked rock again, or catch sight of any land beyond the hill. Being almost at the end of my endurance, I was glad to come at last into the open. I thought that by lucky chance I had emerged in the right place, for soon I found a path worn into the stone itself. Later I was to see there were many such, leading from different directions. This path I followed with great excitement, a sense of being led, going where so many feet had gone before.

"The path quickly brought me to the end of a great spiral of rocks that seemed to crown the hilltop, rocks of enormous size, clearly placed there by human hands and human intention. I knew this to be a very important find and tried to look at each rock carefully as I went, but I was drawn faster and faster toward the center. The outer rocks bore no carvings, or weathering had worn them down, but soon I began to see spiral designs and traces of writing. At last, whole words emerged, some even that I knew, words in the ancient tongue, words I could read and spoke aloud there, trembling with awe as I did so. The central rock of the spiral was all covered with designs and letters, many that looked to have been carved over other, older carvings.

"I could hardly believe my good fortune at such a find and wanted to rush back to Semasi with word of my discovery. Shaking with fatigue and excitement, I climbed up on the central rock and so stood at the very top of the hill.

"Looking about me, I could see more even than I had hoped. The land stretched north and south far into the distance and west even to the ocean itself, for that hill lay in a gap between the mountains. Only toward Garmishair did the dark green mountains block my view. At my feet, the great rock spiral wound around the dome of the hill.

"I stood there watching while the sun went down on one side of me like fire falling into the purple sea, and our lady moon rose on the other, gold and silver over the dark mountains that hid Garmishair. The moon was full that night and very clear. When the moonlight grew strong enough to cast shadows behind every rock so that a second, darker spiral seemed joined to the first, then suddenly 'they' were there, the Ashara. They did not come, they made no sound. They were simply there, one by each rock, moving in some ancient ritual of the moon, chanting or singing though I could not hear them. They did not look at me or speak to me or make me any sign, nor could I have touched them. I did not see them as I see you now, but more as I see mind pictures in another Hadra's head. Yet it was a true seeing. I was there, and they were there, doing what they had always done at the fullness of the moon."

With that, Seronis stood up, took something from her pouch and unwrapped it. This she handed to me. "It is a stone chip fallen from that central rock."

I took it and examined it, turning it from side to side. It appeared to be a chip of ordinary gray stone with no markings whatsoever. I pressed it between my palms. It was cool at first. Then as it warmed to my touch I saw them, moving in their ritual dance. They did not come clear to me, but moved as patterns of shadow and light. The stone felt suddenly hot in my hands. With an exclamation, I quickly handed it back to Seronis. Carefully she wrapped it away again. I was trembling with the impact of her words and the suddenness of my own vision. The night air felt very cool.

"I do not wish to write of this, and yet I know I must," Seronis said sadly. "The Hadra sent me north as their eyes, and I accepted. But I have seen what happens. There are not many Asharan sites in Yarmald that I know of — some ruins, a few carved stones. People come there to picnic or meet their lovers. The curious come to dig. There is no place there for the spirits of the Ashara and they have long gone.

"If I write of this in my report, Hadra will come from Zelindar to poke about and dig and measure and record. Then the Koormir will hear of it also and come. If that happens, will there be any place left in all Yarmald for the spirits of the Ashara, the Old Ones, the First People?" She leaned forward and looked at me intently as if I might have some answers, but my words were frozen in me. With sudden urgency she told me, "Say nothing of this, Sair, not to anyone, till I have searched my heart on it." Mutely, I nodded.

Later when I tried to ask her more, how they looked and if she stayed the night and by what way she came down, she shook her head. "There is no more to the story. I was there, and they were there. It is that simple and that strange. There is nothing more to tell." When my curiosity drove me to further questions, she got up and walked away into the night, not returning until long after I had gone to bed.

The Ashara haunted me after that. I went to the Zildorn, but could find little in those books. I asked discreet questions among the Hadra about the ancient tongue and the First People, but could not discover much more than Seronis herself had already told me. Much regretting my fear, I asked to see her stone again. She shrugged and said she had misplaced it. When I begged her to describe again her seeing of the Ashara, she looked at me as if my head had cracked, and it was all of my own wild invention. Anything else I could ask her. She would tell stories over and over if I wished, but the Ashara she never spoke of again.

* * *

Though we lived together and often worked together and saw each other almost every day, still I could not accustom myself to Seronis' beard and that is why, finally, I was taught to shield. Mostly, I tried not to look at it, but sometimes it caught me unawares. One night after dinner, I sat contemplating that growth, wondering why she did nothing to remove it.

She turned and looked at me. "But why should I, Sair? For whose eyes? For what purpose, since it chooses to grow on my face? Would you have me shave like some man?"

Embarrassed to have been caught in my thoughts, I opened my mouth to answer. "Because you do not look . . . It does not seem . . . That is not what . . ." All my reasons dissolved. The reasons belonged to Eezore. Plainly the other Hadra did not care. Many of them had face hair of their own they did nothing to disguise.

Seronis jumped up and paced around the room for several minutes. Finally, she came to stand in front of me. "Sair, you are welcome to think what you like about my beard, and whatever else you please, but I do not like to have it intruding on my mind. I must teach you how to shield, so we can both have some privacy in this place. I cannot live with your head flapping open in that manner. That uproar will drive me back to the hills." All this she said with considerable annoyance, which was unusual for Seronis.

I replied with hurt dignity, "I would be glad to learn. Then I could go among the Hadra and not be subject to their ridicule for my own private thoughts. It is no fault of mine they have not taught me."

203

She nodded. "Well, so . . ." she said in a softer voice. "For the most part they have done well with you, but they left some unfinished work."

She drew up a chair in front of me. "I am only an ordinary Hadra with such powers as we all have. I am not an adept or even a strong empath, such as Kedris or Halli or Tarl, but I think I can show you a few things. I will teach you as I was taught, or at least as I remember it. Are you willing?"

"Yes, please," I said, nodding vigorously.

"Now first, Sair," she told me with much seriousness, "this cannot be used for deception, for that is quickly known, as well as being a real abuse of power. Shielding is only to give each other peace and privacy, a little quiet from another's mind. Do you wish to try this now? Say when you are ready."

I nodded again.

"Then look into my eyes and think some powerful thought that has much emotion with it." She flinched when I thought of Lairz and said quickly, "Close a door between us, a heavy oak door, and at the same time, keep thinking those thoughts. The door is not thick enough, Sair. Add some planks. Add still more. Now nail them together."

I struggled to do as she asked and felt as much strain all through my body as if those were, indeed, real planks being dragged forward and not things formed in the mind. I thought it would suffice when I had all those imagined planks hauled up and nailed together, but I heard her saying, "Now some stones. Lay some stones up against it. More, Sair, more, pile them up against that door." My arms ached with this labor, and so did my back, but most of all my head ached as if there were a rope noose around it, being drawn tight. I wanted to cry "mercy," when I heard her saying, "Now make of all those stones, one solid black stone slab. Black, black, as dark as a clouded moonless night, as dark as a cave, as dark as . . ."

At that moment I thought of my cell in the Zarn's prison. Seronis shouted, "Good, good, that part you have. Now you must make it thick and solid and learn how to close and how to open it. This is a beginning. Next we must practice."

"Not now!" I cried. My head pained as if to crack with all that learning. I went and threw myself down on the bed, crying.

Seronis came and sat by me full of concern. "I was too rough with you, Sair," she said stroking my back. "You see, I am no teacher. Maybe another would do better."

"No," I said insistantly, "I am ready. Tomorrow we will try again."

So for that next week and more, we practiced every night, closing and opening the portals of my mind. I began to learn the art of it, though sometimes Seronis had to say, "Pay attention, Sair. Your thoughts are leaking out."

Whenever I despaired of it, she reassured me that I was making progress, until at last she thought me ready. Then she sat me down and said with mock seriousness, "Now look at my beard and think your worst of it. We will see how well you have learned to block."

I stared intently at that offending growth, but all I could see was that Seronis looked to be her own familiar self. The reddish hairs that curled along her jaw line, seemed quite at home there. I was delighted and wanted to tell her instantly, but I used my training well and kept the barriers in place.

"Well?" she asked, after a long silence.

"Well, what?" I countered.

"What terrible things are you thinking of my beard? You are shielding well. Nothing comes through."

I shook my head and laughed. "Now you will never know that or any other thought of mine unless I choose to tell you."

* * *

AFTERNOTES

Seronis' account, complete with maps, charts and diagrams, as well as careful descriptions of trees, plants, rocks, mountains and all manner of new creatures she had seen on her travels north, was to be sent to Zelindar for inclusion in the archives.

PART 2

YIMA

I was working with Seronis, learning to handle heavy stones as together we topped a wall of the common-house, when there was a long scream followed by many cries. We jumped from our scaffolding and ran with other Hadra to the cliff edge. Yima's body lay twisted and broken on the sand far below us.

Hadra ran for the beach, some scrambling down the cliff path, and others calling their horses and riding fast by the road. By the time I reached them, Zarmell was already kneeling by Yima in the sand, her face streaming tears. "Oh, Mother, Sister, my heart, I will mend your bones. Lover, I will heal you. Do not leave us."

Yima's face was gray. Her limbs were turned at terrible, strange angles. Barely able to speak at all, she whispered, "No, no, too much is broken, Nibbit. I have been strong all my life. I could not live patched and mended." Her words sounded as if they were being forced through water.

Zarmell was shaking her head desperately. "But we will heal you, Mother. We will make you whole again."

"No, Zarmell, no, Sweet One, it is done." Then Yima turned a sudden twisted smile on the rest of us and said, "The sweetest berries grow always at the edge." I understood then the strange purple "bruises" on her hands and face, and saw the basket fallen beyond her, the berries crushed and scattered on the sand.

The pain came on her then. Her eyes shut, drawn tight with it. She gave a terrible groan, a shudder shook her broken body, and blood ran from the corner of her mouth, mingling with the berry juice that darkened the sand.

Then she sighed as if released and was gone quicker than the turning of a bird in flight. As we felt her spirit leave, a moan went up from all the Hadra together. Zarmell loosed the soul-tearing death scream of the women of Eezore, and threw herself down in the sand. Quadra quickly seated herself by Yima's body and pressed her ear to her chest. After a time she straightened and shook her head.

"Nothing, there is nothing. It is truly over."

Many things happened then at once. Mirl rode back up to the settlement to fetch whatever was needed for the burial. Jephra quickly gathered Zarmell in her arms, saying over and over, "I know, Sister, I know," while she held Zarmell tightly and rocked her back and forth. Several Hadra called out, "Lar, where is Lar," until all had been reminded that Lar had left for Osen two days earlier and would not be back that week. She had gone to speak with the Hadra of Osen, since their time had come to send someone to Eezore in her place.

Quadra, meanwhile, took hold of Yima's hand and bent forward as if Yima could still hear her. "Go easy, Mother," she said softly, stroking Yima's forehead. "Go gently, go gently. Do not be hasty. This is too sudden for the soul. Go gently, Sweet One." For a moment Quadra turned to the rest of us, shaking her head. "It is a miracle she lived to speak at all from such a fall." I looked back up at the sea cliff wall. It was, indeed, a miracle, for the edge of it towered more than a ten-person height above us.

The other Hadra, by then, had sunk to the sand in a loose circle around the body. After a time of silence, they began, first low and then louder, to sing the death chant, swaying together with the weight of it. Wave after wave, it was like the sound of the sea giving voice to grief and went on and on as if there would be no end.

When Mirl returned at last, she carried a huge basket of greenery and flowers, as well as Yima's cloak, some oil and other needed things. Gently and tenderly, with many tears and loving words, Yima was laid out on her cloak. Her broken body was washed and oiled and her hair combed out and braided. This work was interrupted often, as one Hadra would sob out her grief and another would take her place by the body. When all was done, her body was straightened, flowers and leaves were laid over her and the cloak folded around her, bound at both ends. Through all this, Zarmell screamed and struggled in Jephra's arms, trying to tear at her own face and arms with her nails. When Ozal, Mirl, Seronis and Halli made ready to lift the body, she wrenched herself free crying, "No, let me carry her this last time!" Mirl stepped back to make room for Zarmell at the front. Together, those five lifted Yima's wrapped body, and the rest of us followed after.

It was all too sudden. I could not believe that Yima, who had just been with us that morning at breakfast, was truly gone. It seemed like a play, sad, but not real. Surely tomorrow Yima would be in the dining hall as usual, laughing and telling us stories of old Semasi. Also, I was amazed at the haste with which the Hadra were putting away their dead. It felt heartless to me and lacking in respect, in spite of all their tears. In Eezore it is customary to sit with the body at least a day and a night, sometimes more if the person is of great import. Still, I went with the others and did as I saw them do.

Singing the death chant, we slowly made our way from the beach to a place of mounds halfway up the hill. This I had seen before, but thought it to be an ancient place of worship. Now I saw it to be an old burial ground that seemed to have gone unused since the time of the first settling. The grass grew high and the rocks were green with moss.

There we dug a shallow pit and gently lowered Yima's body into the earth. Quadra said three times, "Blessed be the daughter who comes home to the Mother at last," and all around, the death chant rose and fell like the waves of the sea.

More leaves and flowers and branches were laid on top until Yima's cloak was covered. Then came the earth, the true burier. With that first shovel full, Zarmell screamed again and threw herself over the body, flinging back the dirt with her hands. For a moment no one moved or spoke. The only sounds were Zarmell's fearful cries, and the clods of earth falling. It was the first time I had ever seen the Hadra stand helpless. Then Seronis nodded to Ozal. Together they went forward and lifted Zarmell away. At that her wild strength seemed to fall from her and she went to lie quiet on the ground in Ozal's arms. For a while longer we stood silent and unmoving. Most of the Hadra were crying. From below came the long moan of the ocean. At last Quadra gave a nod, the shovel was passed, and the burying continued.

We each in turn threw on a shovel full of earth, until all was covered and mounded up. Then began the rocks. With every rock placed, some words were said.

"Good-bye, Yima."

"May Jahar guide you on this last great journey."

"May Harimair weave you a tight cloak."

"May Shimuir light your way."

"Good-bye, Mother."

"Good-bye, Yima." Now the sobs were loud around me, though I myself could not cry.

When, at last, there was a great mound formed, Quadra raised her arms, and we came together in a circle. Chanting again, we began a slow stamp-step, first in one direction and then the other. Mirl played the flute, Ozal the kerril, and some Hadra I scarcely knew, beat the drums. This circle went on and on until I lost all sense of time and place. Whose voice sang or whose body moved, I no longer knew. I could have been a seabird or a tree or a wave in the ocean.

Finally we stopped, perhaps at some signal or perhaps from exhaustion, I could not tell. When I had recovered my wits enough to look about, I saw Tarl staring intently at me from across the circle. It was the clearest contact I had felt with her since we came home from Eezore. Her own mind was closed and shielded, but she was probing mine. Catching her eye, I asked in her head /Sister, where are you?/ Just at that moment the circle broke, and the Hadra all went to gather wood for the funeral fire. I turned to look for Tarl, but she had slipped away.

After a large enough stack of wood was made, the Hadra drifted off to their separate places to mourn alone. Only Zarmell, Jephra and Quadra stayed to keep Yima company. By evening, all had gathered again by the burial mound. We formed ourselves around it in a spiral like a great snail, with the oldest at the head. Beginning with Quadra, we told each our memories of Yima: sad stories and happy ones, adventures and jokes, and whatever else came to mind. There were many more tears shed, but now there was laughter, too. When it came my turn, I spoke of how Yima had showed me the city of Zelindar while I lay healing and told me to go there if I could.

"And when I walk those streets, I will remember Yima and see them for her, also," I ended. Yet even saying this, I shed no tears. I watched all dry-eyed and from a distance, as if observing through a window.

When it came at last to Marli to speak, she was rubbing sand into her arms in the manner of Eezore and crying so that she could scarce be heard. "She would have loved me, but I would not let her," she said over and over through the sobs, rocking back and forth and rubbing her arms until the blood came.

At last Kedris stayed her hand saying gently, "Marli, she loved you anyhow." Then she drew Marli into a hug and held her close.

As youngest, Marli was last to speak. For now, the words were over. Hadra came forward to heap the wood against the mound. The fire, I was told, was to help free Yima's spirit. When the stack was made, it was Zarmell herself who moved to light it with her torch. A great cry rose from all who watched as the flames leaped up, roaring and flashing against the night.

Everyone sat up until dawn feeding the blaze and keeping Yima company on the first part of her journey. Many more stories were told, though no longer in any formal order. To my surprise, much wine, quillof and beer was drunk. "It helps the tears to flow so that they do not come and choke us after," Ozal explained, in answer to my questions. When it grew late, Ozal played her kerril, and Mirl her flute, until the sun rose. Then the Hadra began leaving. Only

Zarmell stayed this time, and Jephra with her. I myself staggered home to sleep. I still could not believe Yima so quickly gone.

* * *

In Eezore, mourning was for a year if it was a close relative who had died. In that time, you could not sing or dance or wear bright clothes or go to any parties or even laugh much. Marriages were not made then or any formal courting done. All this constraint was hard enough if you had loved the person much and doubly burdensome if you had not. In Semasi, the work went on as usual. The Hadra way of mourning was not by constraints, but by rememberings, by bespeaking the person often, saying her name many times and in many ways.

"Yima would have said that."

"Do you remember those stories Yima used to tell of that last winter in Semasi?"

"Were you here the day Yima . . . ?"

If someone made a particularly fine piece of work, she said, "This is for Yima."

When Ozal planted flowers at the edge of the public circle, she said, "These will bloom each year for Yima."

Over the door of the common-house that was being built, Seronis carved, "To remember Yima, who was grandmother to us all."

Even Marli wrote out Yima's name in stones before the dining hall. So Yima was always present among us although she was gone, and I heard, at that time, far more of her life than when she had been living.

When Lar came home she was inconsolable. I did not see her much, for she was like a sharp restless wind that blew through Semasi from one end to the other, and I was bound in place by rocks and poles as I struggled with the building of the common house. But one day she came and stood behind me, watching while I laid stone. It made me nervous to feel her eyes over my shoulder. When I turned, I saw she had a crow on her wrist. Its wing was bound with a splint. She knelt down beside me, holding the bird out for me to see.

"It came to me with a broken wing when I was in the high pasture. I have been healing it. It is the first thing I have cared for

211

since Yima died." The crow cocked its head from side to side, watching us both as if following our words.

Even after it mended, the bird stayed with Lar. It became a familiar sight to see her long frame striding through Semasi with a crow on her shoulder or flying overhead. It was as if some part of Yima's spirit had come back to keep Lar company.

* * *

Two days after Yima's death, Tarl came to look for me mounted on Timmer. "Sister, I saw your eyes across the circle asking where I am. I am not here, Sair. I am not here for you or for me or for anyone. My soul has been poisoned and I must leave for a time." I saw that her packs were already strapped on Timmer's back. Not waiting for a response, she rode out of Semasi without a kiss or touch or anything to soften her going, nor did she once look back.

Yima was dead and Tarl gone. When I tried to draw close to Halli, she had a strangeness on her. Her eyes were dark-circled and she seldom laughed. Once I went crying to her for comfort from missing Tarl. She shook her head, saying, "Sister, I have no comfort to give. My heart is burnt out in me." She took my fingers and pressed them to her forehead, saying, "This is what I live with".

I gave a cry and recoiled in horror, for I saw bodies running in flames and smelt burning flesh. "Oh, Halli, is it always so bad?"

She nodded, "I thought it would lessen with time, but it has been getting worse. Quadra says I must go to a Hadra asking place for guidance, for she can give me none."

I held her, wanting to give what comfort I could, and we sat together silent until night came. Next day I was ill from the horrors in her mind. Later that day Halli left also for the hills with no goodbyes.

Now Semasi felt to me full of strangers. Even Kedris was distant and distracted, seeming much changed by the battle, and Seronis was often absent, writing her report. Some of the younger Hadra seeing me so sad would have befriended me, but I did my work, held my pain close against me and preferred to be alone.

At last Zarmell came to me saying, "Child, you will make yourself sick this way." She put a hand on my arm. I shrugged and pulled away. "We both suffer a loss. Come share my cloak with me tonight that we may lessen each other's pain."

"Zarmell, so soon!" I cried, shocked.

"Nibbit, if it would bring her back for a year, for a month even, I would never pleasure myself with anyone again. But nothing I do or do not do in this world will bring her back, not even for an hour. And where she is now, it matters not to her what I do here."

"I have not the heart for it, Zarmell."

"Ah, well," she sighed. "I thought we could give each other a little comfort." She went away shaking her head. In my pain, I did not even offer her my arms for the night. I did not have even that much for anyone.

If not for Seronis, I might have gone on for some time in this state. But one morning, as I was sitting at breakfast, staring absently into my tea cup, she jumped up with a shout, knocking back her chair. In two strides, she stood over me and shook me so roughly my tea spilled across the table.

"Go! Go walk in the woods! Find some high place from which to look down on your troubles! Sair, I cannot live with your moodiness another day!" She threw her chair back against the wall with such force it splintered and she left her breakfast unfinished on the plate.

This shook me out of myself. I left everything on the table as it was, even the spilled tea and with scarcely the strength to set one foot before the other, I began climbing up into the hills above Semasi. The path I chose was hard going for the way was very steep, but that was well. It kept my mind on my feet instead of on my griefs. For the whole climb, I did not think of Tarl or Halli or the Zarn of Eezore or even Yima's death. I thought only of where next to step.

Finally, I reached the place I had seen from below, a ledge or outcrop that had seemed right for my purpose. Standing there, I could look down on Semasi from a fringe of dark pines. Behind me the ridges rose rough and jagged, the gray stone face looming like the walls of a fortress. In front, the hillside dropped away steeply and Semasi lay below me, bright and safe in the shelter of her fields. Beyond her stretched the endless sea where the blue deepened into purple by late afternoon. The sea cliffs I could not see until the sun dropped and the red of it turned the last bend to flaming orange.

I sat in that place for most of the day, letting the scene sink into my senses and thinking no thoughts. Only once did an idea touch me. I saw that someday, we ourselves would be like the Ashara. In some far future, others might stand where I watched from now, look down at the ruins of Semasi and say with reverence and awe, or with contempt, "The Hadra lived here once." That thought chilled me and gladly I went back to thoughtlessness.

As the first few lights came on, I started down hastily, not wanting to be caught by darkness in a pathless place, but the return was too sudden. Seronis looked up when I came in, meaning to greet me. I shook my head showing I needed silence, and she, who had walked alone all through the northland, understood well enough. She scooped me out a bowl of tarmar and covered it with hot, spiced vegetables. Then she went out on the stoop to smoke her jol pipe and watch the evening come.

I sat for a long while, bent over the bowl, smelling that fragrant steam. Then I ate very slowly, looking at each color, savoring each taste and remembering again that life had some joy in it. When the stars came out, I dragged my mat outside. Lying there under the night sky, I thought of how Semasi had become my home and it struck me suddenly that I had never thanked the Hadra. They had healed me and taught me and sheltered me, and I had never thanked them. I was swept with waves of guilt and gratitude. Two who mattered much had gone away, and one I could never thank on this earth, but at least I could make a start.

Suddenly my grief for Yima broke through and I could weep for her at last. I wept for the Yima I had known and the Yima I would never know. I cried until my body ached with it, rolling back and forth on the mat and pressing my face into it to not wake Seronis with my grieving. I cried also for Marl: I even cried for the mother I had scarcely known. At last I fell asleep exhausted in the wetness of my own tears under the bright summer stars.

Next morning, I set about thanking each Hadra who had helped me. No one seemed to comprehend what I thanked them for or why. At last Seronis said with rough humor, "Leave off with the thanking, Sair. It grows wearisome. Do you think yourself so special? We would have done the same for any Neshtair. It is part of being Hadra. Some think to thank us sooner and some not at all. It matters little. Either way, we do what we must and what we can." In some way her roughness eased the guilt of my ingratitude. After that I did the thanking in my heart and not aloud.

* * *

One morning, as I was in the Zildorn, searching again for some hint of the Ashara, Marli came flying through the doorway, shouting, "Sair, Sair, can you forgive me?" I looked up startled at this disturbance. In my time of pain, I had forgotten her existence.

"For what?" I asked, staring at her as if she had fallen from the ceiling.

She threw her arms about me saying, "Jephra says I should ask your pardon, and you would understand."

I squirmed in her tight embrace. "Well, Jephra may well be right, but you must give me some hint, Marli."

"I have treated you badly since we came here. It was you who saved me and carried me away, and I have never thanked you."

At that I started to laugh. Marli was thanking me, too late, as I had done with the Hadra. Well, all things come round in the world. As it must be, I thought with amusement. "Yes, Marli, yes, I forgive you. I suppose we must all forgive each other in the end. Now loosen your grip a little so I can breath."

"Will you go riding with me? I am lonesome."

"Why not," I said, closing my books. "I am lonesome, too." Carefully, she helped me put the books back in their places.

It amazed me when I looked at Marli to think she was the same child who had escaped with me from Eezore. With good food, she had begun to grow and some of her woman form to blossom out. She was not ten, as I had first supposed, but twelve and would be thirteen before the winter's end. In another year she would have been considered a marriageable woman in Eezore — though with the Hadra, coming-of-age is marked by first blood, regardless of years. If she had stayed in the city, this next year would have seen her with a brand on her forehead and little chance of ever gaining freedom.

After that time, I went riding often with Marli and taught her how to swim. I even showed her secret places in the woods that Halli had shown me, pledging her to silence. In this way, we two outsiders, Neshtair from Eezore, formed a bond, though I did not much trust that friendship. I had already seen how fickle and fragile it could be.

PART 3

THE MORL

I missed Tarl so that sometimes my bones ached with it and my teeth clenched, yet I would not send out my thoughts to pull at her. I was Neshtair enough not to do so. But sometimes, I went at night to sleep by the sea cliffs because I felt closer to her there and less lonely hearing the sea.

One morning, I was wakened there at dawn by Tarl, herself, tugging at my cloak. "Move over, Little Sister. It is cold out here."

With a cry of joy, I wrapped her tightly in my arms and cloak. Then I told her without words how I had missed her and she told me the same. We touched each other's bodies as eagerly as if we had each four hands or six instead of two. As it grew warmer, we threw the cloak open to the morning mist and loved each other with the fire of absence, the first time in more than a month our bodies had come together in that way.

Tarl slept after, and I lay watching, warmed by the pleasure of her closeness. Yet I was troubled, too. She looked thin and drawn and I felt the pain still in her after all that time. When she woke at last she looked into my eyes for a long time, weighing some heavy matter in which I had a part. I sensed her troubled thoughts, but she was shielding hard so I could not read them. At last she said slowly, "Sair, you are the one I was guided to ask. There is a thing I must do and I cannot go alone. I am too afraid. Will you come with me?"

I was so glad to have her back, I answered instantly, "Anything, Tarl. I will go with you anywhere." Yet my heart was beating very fast. If Tarl was afraid, what must it be?

She put her fingers to my lips and shook her head. "Wait, Sair, this time you need see it all and think well before you answer. You must not pledge me a quick yes till you know what is being asked. Eezore itself may seem easier." She took away her fingers and kissed me gently on the lips. "And it must not be from pride. Your pride tricked you before into a hasty answer, and I let it be for my own use. This time I must be honorable."

With that, Tarl lay back and pulled me under the cloak with her. For a long time she said nothing while I lay against her, trying to still my trembling. Then she began very softly, "Little Sister, I went away because my soul was sick. I could not be with you nor anyone. First, the battle with the Zarn's army, all that suffering and death, horrors I had not imagined in the worst of dreams. Then the trip to Eezore, a city so full of pain, it broke for a time my power to shield. Afterward, I could not clear myself. It was as if I had eaten rithberries of the spirit. The poison was all through me. When I rode out from here, I could not even say good-bye.

"I went to a Hadra asking place high in the Timmer Mountains. There I ate no food, drank only a little water and took some yima root. The dreams and visions that came to me were the same ones over and over. Look into my head, Sair."

I shut my eyes and put my fingers on her forehead for the strongest contact. Instantly, I groaned and snatched my hand away. My head was full of monsters, huge creatures, dark and slimy, twisting and turning in a pool of dark waters. My stomach leapt with fear. I was shaking, and Tarl held me tight.

"We go to fight them?" I whispered.

"No, Sair, to swim with them. Hadra do not fight with other creatures."

"What are they?" I asked, still in a whisper.

"The Morl, the sea-monsters from the old tales. They were be-

217

lieved extinct since none living had seen them, yet from my dreams and visions, I know they still exist. The Morl are real. They will come in to mate in the caverns by the sea below the Morl River. We go to meet them there if you are willing."

Before I could say more, Tarl sat up suddenly throwing back the cloak. She gestured to the sky with her hands as if the Great Mother Herself were looking down. "Oh, Sister, I know not why the Goddess has sent me such an answer when I only asked for guidance, but truly this is what I saw again and again, the creatures of the deep. It is as if I am bonded to them, as if they sing to me deep in my blood like some old music that has the power in it. I would have gone alone. I tried to, but they are too awesome. Each time my courage failed me. Yet I can read no harm in them, no will to hurt, however frightening they may seem." She turned back to catch me again with that piercing look. "Be careful, Sair. Be very sure if you decide to come. This is no light thing."

I wanted to shout, Tarl, I cannot do this! The words were between my teeth. Instead, I drew back from her and turned away, keeping a shield between our minds.

This will be my death, I thought, staring out at the cold sea. Then I remembered that I had already had my death twice over, once thrown by others on the Bargguell and once by myself into the sea. This woman next to me had saved my life, even struggled with me for it. These past months of pleasure and freedom I had had because of her. If I lost my life now, going with her, it was in some way a debt paid and no great thing. Yet, even with that thought, I could not shake my dread of those creatures, nor say yes with a good heart. Even less could I say no and let Tarl go alone, or force her to ask another, knowing she had been led by the Goddess to ask me. So for a while I was pulled back and forth like the waves, and whenever I was ready to make one answer, the other one rushed in to wash over it.

Never had I done a thing for love before. All my life I had been stubborn and selfish and that had been my strength. Now another strength was needed. I lay watching the sea as if my answer were to be found in her blue depths. Oh, Mother of Waters, I whispered in my heart. At last one thing came clear above all else. No matter what my fears, I would not let Tarl go alone.

Taking a deep breath, I summoned all my will and said, "I have thought on it in silence for all this time, Tarl, and my answer is still the same. I will go with you wherever you ask." As I spoke these words, the morning light struck on the sea, turning it bright with life.

"Are you very sure, Sair?" She turned me to meet her eyes.

I held tight to my shielding and said as calmly as I could, "That is my answer, Tarl. There is no need to ask again. Each time will be the same." Once again I had bound myself to Tarl in danger, but this time from love, not pride. I made the Hadra sign meaning "In your hands, Goddess."

Tarl, also, made the sign and our fingers met. For a long moment she held me fastened to her by hand and eye. Then with a shout she leapt to her feet, tossing off the cloak. It caught in the morning breeze and was swept almost to the cliff edge before she snatched it back. "Let us make ready at once," she called out, seeming as full of joy as I was of doubt. I did not ask where we went or for how long, but followed after her, will-less now that I had set my will on its course.

All the preparations were made by Tarl as I had no mind for it. I stayed out of sight, not wanting to answer Hadra questions and after a while went out to the meadow to confer with Sharu. She let me know that she would carry me where we went, but would not go near the sea-monsters. To make that clear, she snorted and stamped her hoof and shook her head. Afraid as I was, still I had to laugh.

Before mid-morning, we fastened our packs to the horses and were on our way, going south by the coast road. Though I tried hard to hide it, I went with a heavy heart. When Tarl turned to say, "We have not far to go," that did little to cheer me.

At those times I thought to look about me, I saw the way was very beautiful. The road we took followed the edge of the cliffs. As there were few trees, we could see far out to in three directions, up and down the coast and even across to Felduir Island. The mist had broken and the island rose green and gold out of a blue-green sea. Seabirds skimmed the water, flashing silver in the sunlight. There was a steady ocean breeze that lifted the horses' manes and blew our hair back from our faces. It was a fair bright day. I only wished we were riding out to some more joyful task.

Mostly I went silent, but Tarl made talk enough for two. She told me stories of Felduir Island that I cannot now recall for I had no heart to listen. She also told many stories of Semasi that at another time, I would have hung on eagerly. She talked much of the Morl, though I did not ask. Each time I saw again in my mind that pool of dark waters, I shivered and set a hard shield around my thoughts. Tarl made no comment on my new-trained power.

At a sharp bend of the coast, we passed a road turning hard left and curving steeply down between the mountains. "The coast-to-mountains road to Ishlair," Tarl informed me. Later, our own road turned inland for a ways, and we had to cross the Morl River. At this point she was only a clear narrow stream. When we stopped to drink, Tarl gestured at it, saying, "The Morl is friendly here and gentle, but further on she flows through the Timmers. Springs and creeks from those mountains make her fast and turbulent, for she goes a narrow rocky way between them. Some of the wildest land in Yarmald lies in those steep gorges." I nodded, hardly listening, but glad for any chance to stop. Later I had cause to remember her words.

Shortly after that, our road curved back to the coast. We rode on, with the sea always shimmering brightly on our right. Far to our left, the constant Timmers rose steep and dark, covered with evergreens. After some hours had passed, and Tarl had run through her store of tales, we came around a bend to see the way before us blocked with boulders. The road itself turned sharply to the left. The horses stopped. Tarl put her hands over her eyes. "I must feel the way," she said. "I have not been this far before." For a long while she sat silent as if listening to some inner wind, then said abruptly, "We must stay along the coast. This road leads into the foothills now."

"But there is no more road," I protested.

"We will walk and let the horses follow."

We made our way between the rocks. The horses ambled after us, stopping sometimes to munch at the sparse clumps of grass. Tarl went like one dream-tranced, always listening. She stopped now and again, turning her head as if to catch some signal. Neither of us spoke. Suddenly, I felt a sharp alertness in her. With excitement she whispered, "They are close below us now."

There was no way down for horses and seemed none for humans either, but Tarl was not dismayed. She strapped on one pack, tossed me the other and told the horses to go and graze. Then she walked back and forth along the edge of the cliff until she found something she called a path, though it looked like no way at all to me.

"We can climb down here. It seems not so bad," she said cheerfully.

I could not understand going to death in such light spirits and said crossly to her, "Tarl, you are mad! You have eaten too much yima root!"

With that, she turned and gave me a hard angry look. "The whole way here you have been like a Kourmairi chi-goat on its way to the death pen. Sair, you said you would come and that it was of your own will. When I would have asked further, you blocked me with shielding. If you had no heart to do this, you should have said so in Semasi. It is no fault of mine that you are here. I think it might be easier to face the Morl alone, than to drag you one more unwilling step. Stay here with the horses and wait." Then she shook her head and said in a very different voice, "Perhaps, after all, I am to blame. I should have seen your mood and had the wisdom to ask another, though truly you were the choice that spoke to me. Well, you may have gone as far as is needed for this thing."

She turned as if to leave. With a cry, I threw myself at her, gripping her arm. "Wait, Tarl, I will go with you!" At that moment I had less fear of the Morl than of Tarl going alone to face them.

She shook me gently. "Well then, Little Sister, we must go in better spirits to meet the Children-of-the-Sea. They have seen no two-footed creature for many a long age." With a quick kiss on my forehead she added, "I do not think we go to our deaths, Sair. That is not my sense of things. But if it is indeed to be our last day, should we not meet it with joy?"

My heart made one of its sudden turns. It no longer mattered if I lived or died. I did not care. My fears had lifted. I felt very light as I followed Tarl over the cliff edge.

We slipped and slid, struggling down that terrible steepness, helping each other over boulders and through thickets of brambles. Only at moments, did we catch a glimpse of the sea, our destination. Then we sank again in weed and brush and plunged on blindly, until, at last, we staggered out upon the beach.

As I caught my breath and looked about me, I saw what had kept the Morl secret from human eyes. To our right, as we faced the ocean, sea cliffs jutted out into the water past the beach, and before us ran row upon row of rocky reefs, sharp as teeth, stretching a far ways along that piece of coast.

"This is a place none can come to, neither by beach nor boat," I said.

Tarl answered in a strange voice, "Only one dream-summoned can find the way. None will come but who are meant to."

The tide was drawing out now, leaving its patterns of sea-foam, line upon line across the sand. Long breakers crashed endlessly against the far reefs, shooting up spray and foam in bursts of dazzling white. I found my eyes caught by their restless motion, but Tarl turned her back on the scene. For a while she stood silent again in that listening way. Then she nodded, as if to herself. "They are here. They have come in with the tide."

She took my hand. I went with her easily now, making no more resistance. We followed the beach to the left, past great ledges of smooth rock, carved and polished by the action of the waves. At the water's edge stood the bend of a sea cliff, higher than a fortress wall. As we skirted around it, the sand sloped steeply down and the sea rushed in. There, under the roof of a cavern cut into the cliff base itself, was a large, deep pool—wild with motion. It was almost dark, after the brightness of the beach. We both gasped. Even in that dimness I could see them roiling the water. One huge beast rose up and fell back, splashing us both. We leapt back in fear.

Tarl gripped my arm. I could feel the trembling in her hand. "The Morl! The legendary Morl! They are here! We have really found them!" We stood staring at the sight before us. The water was a turmoil with bodies that rose and fell. Huge heads gaped for a moment and were gone. They were not of a size to break a boat upon their backs or swallow a sailor whole, but they were terrible enough.

"Quick," Tarl said. "We must take some yima root before we are fear frozen to this spot."

So saying, she slipped off her pack and found a cup. Rather than pouring fresh water from her drinking gourd, she scooped up some sea water, muttering, "Life from the sea, blood of the Mother." Into this, she shook a double portion of red powder from her pouch and stirred it with her finger. We said together, "As it must be." Then she swallowed her part and passed the cup to me. Her hand shook. It looked like dark blood quivering in that wooden cup. I drank quickly and coughed from the force of it. Salt water and yima together are a bitter brew.

Now there was nothing left but to strip off our clothes. My fingers felt so numb that I had much trouble with the fastenings. When I was done, my garments all lying in a small heap at my feet, I felt more naked than if I had stood clothesless in the streets of Eezore. I looked over at Tarl. She seemed to me more beautiful than I had ever seen her, the reflections from the sea sparkling and spiralling up like moving bands of gold on her dark skin, as she bent to gather everything together.

"We must pay some heed, Sair. When the tide comes in again, all this could be swept away." I had no thought at that moment for such small matters and would have left clothes, packs and cup, all where they lay, though clearly the mark of the last tide was higher than the place we stood upon. Tarl had more sense than that. She stuffed our clothes into the packs and thrust them into a high rock crevice for safekeeping. Then she took my hand again, and we went to the edge of the pool.

From there, we were close enough to see eyes and scales. The Morl did not snap or slash at us. They seemed hardly aware of our small human nakedness so near them. Always moving in one direction, they circled the pool in their strange dance, curving up and over each other, then plunging down again into the dark water that shook and burst with their motion.

They were not so huge as I had first thought, being each no more than the length of five or six persons and perhaps the thickness of three. The yima was taking effect. I could see that their great ugly heads were also marvelous, that their eyes were flecked with gold, that their scales and skin had a shimmer of iridescence on them, small rainbows that caught in the slanting light. All this had been true before, but I had been blinded by fear.

I took a deep breath and turned to Tarl. We held up our hands to each other, palm to palm. "I will do this thing if you will," she said to me.

Trying to keep my voice steady, I answered, "I will do this thing if you will." So, in this way, we were oath-bound.

"As it must be," we both said again. We stepped to the smooth rock lip at the edge of the pool, and I felt Tarl release my hand. To the Mother, I thought, and let my body slip forward.

I had only an instant to be amazed at the warmth of the water, then I was knocked sideways by the impact of a smooth hard body against mine. The sea closed over me. Bumped and buffeted, I struggled in panic until my head cleared the water. I found myself face to face with a great dripping head and open jaws. The surge of the water threw me helpless toward those fangs, and I knew they would surely meet in my death. But as suddenly as it has risen, the creature curved away again and was gone.

I did not scream or shout, but hurriedly drew in great gulps of air. I was still living. Nothing ripped or tore at me. Perhaps, I was not to be made a meal of so soon. Still I was surrounded by bodies that churned about, striking against me and knocking my breath away. Even if the Morl meant us no harm, I should be crushed in their press if I could find no method of moving with them.

When I could force my mind into a place of calm, I put my arms at my sides and let my legs flow in back of me. In this way, their motion drove me forward as they rose under me and plunged away again. Now I was not so afraid of water over me, for always, I was carried up to air again. Their heads, crested and gilled and scaled, would rise, curve over each other and curve down again. I went with them, will-less as a leaf on the current.

Gradually, my terror eased. I became part of the Morl—a long, slithery creature, moving through the water in endless curves. Then one of those beasts came up, eye to eye with me. It stayed besides me as we moved. I felt our minds touch. With that touch, I saw scenes in my head of wild coasts and storms and sunny islands and wondrous, bright worlds under the sea such as no books had ever shown me. To better see inward I shut my eyes and stayed some long time travelling in those other realms while my body moved at the will of another.

When, at last, I opened my eyes, the sun was slanting in. The cavern was full of deep rich colors; reds, blues, purples and greens, gleaming like jewels from the scales of the Morl and even from the cavern walls. There was music, too, more than just the music of the yima. The Morl were humming. The sound reverberated from the stone walls of the cave and through the churning waters like the lowest notes on the stringed kerril, but much sweeter.

All this while, Tarl and I had kept touch with each other. We were as one mind or a joint spirit in two bodies. Though I could not see or touch her, we were so bound, I sometimes forgot which one of us I was. I saw through her eyes as well as my own and so was not afraid for her.

The motion of the circle was not so violent now. One Morl slid up next to me, pressing and curving against my body in a way that could only have been a caress. As I had grown much braver, I wrapped my arms and legs around that sleek form, shut my eyes and went with the creature, not minding the water over me, even able to take some pleasures in it. Suddenly, I was back in some ancient time, in some ancient body that might have once been mine. The music was all around me, not a few strings on the kerril, but a chorus of such beauty and volume, not all the instruments of Eezore, together, could have equalled it. The scenes from the sea became my own world that I was swimming through. There was language, too. For that moment, I could hear the speech of the Morl and knew its meaning, though it was not words as we use them, but something far deeper—closer perhaps to the speech of the Mother.

Finally, the dance of the Morl slowed to a lazy motion. I loosened my grip, and my companion slipped away. The day had turned. The sun was slanting lower, showing new colors on scales and fins. Water was pouring back into the cave in a great rush. As the tide rose, the sea creatures began slipping out over the smooth stone edge of the pool. They were returning now to the open ocean. I felt Tarl leaving with them, being drawn away. Frightened, I shouted at her to wait. She was no child-of-the-sea, but a daughter of earth who could quickly drowned in the inrushing tide. I think the Morl must still have been singing in her head. She had no ears for me. Stumbling to her in the deepening water, I grabbed her arm. She cried out and struggled with me, seeming spell-bound, while the Morl brushed against us in parting as they swam by.

I shook her, shouting her name over and over until, at last, her eyes touched on my face with some knowledge of me. "Tarl! The tide is turning! We will be caught!"

By then the water was knee deep at the edge of the pool and rising fast. It pulled and sucked at our legs like a living thing that wished to drag us away. I knew if we went with the tow, we would be dashed helpless against those reefs that edged the coast.

Tarl still seemed dazed and resistant as I pulled her from the pool. I had just strength enough to gather our packs, but her cup slipped through my fingers. On the next wave, I saw it sucked out to sea. With a cry, I thrust Tarl's pack into her arms. "Hold tight and keep moving!" I shouted over the rush of the waters. Using my free hand, I pushed her forward.

Slipping and stumbling, we made our way past the base of the sea cliff through waist high waves, that threatened at any moment to smash us into that wall of rock. Once past that obstacle, we struggled up the beach to the rock ledges. Each step of the way, we were pursued by water that sucked the sand from under our feet as we went. There we were able to pull ourselves out of the tide's reach. It was none too soon, for as we scrambled to the top, the waves began gnawing at the base of the ledges. It seemed that most of the beach would soon be swallowed by that hungry water.

Shaking with fear and exertion, I drew Tarl down beside me onto the rock ledge, put my arms about her and held her close. We lay there tight-pressed together, with our legs between each others' legs, as if we were one thing and had no bones. After a while my trembling ceased. As Tarl still seemed lost and far away, I began rocking her, crooning her name again and again to call her spirit back. A very different fear moved in me now. I needed that human closeness to break the charm and pull of the sea. As we had been part of the Morl, so now we became part of each other. We melted together into the smooth rocks that sill held some warmth from the sun. For a long time, we lay joined in that way.

At last Tarl shivered and sat up. I saw she had come back to herself. The sun had already set. Only its afterglow reddened the horizon and poured a last cup of gold on the dark sea. I struggled to my feet. Tarl gazed up at me frowning with concern. Gently she touched her fingers to my body. Looking down, I saw myself covered with scrapes, cuts and bruises, the marks of fins and scales.

"Nothing that will not mend," I said quickly. I knew I would gladly have suffered far more than that to swim with the Children-of-the-Sea. I stared out at the ocean. Now that we were safe, and I had no more cause to fear, I felt a sadness, a grieving, a sense of loss pulling at me like the tides. No longer could I understand the speech of the Morl. Their music had receded on the waves. In all that vast water, there was no sign of them anywhere.

"Was it the effect of yima only, or did we truly speak with them?" I asked.

"It was yima that opened the doors and let us hear. Yes, Sair, we have spoken with the Morl and shared mind-pictures with them, also." She was silent for a while, staring out to sea. Then she added softly, "Thank you, Little Sister. I could not have come here without you."

When Tarl stood up beside me, I was swaying on my feet. She looked at the horizon that was fast darkening and then up at the cliff. "We will never make our way there before night," she said shaking her head.

"I could not climb that hill now if we had yet four hours of light," I answered, for I was filled with a great weariness as if all the ocean had poured into me and then poured out again.

Too tired to eat, we dressed in what clothes were still dry, wrapped in our cloaks and stretched out close together on the hard, smooth rocks, for this was the only safe bed we had. The evening was cooling fast. Far off I could hear the Kiri calling to each other. The first stars were just breaking through the darkening blue. Lying there, mindless and weightless, I felt as if born new into the world. Some part of my spirit had been touched by the Morl, some part that I had had no knowledge of before. As I was dozing off, Tarl whispered against my hair, "This is the first time since we came back from Eezore that my soul has felt clean." She fell asleep then with her fingers in her mouth like a small child. Not in all our time together had I seen Tarl look so peaceful. I watched her until the darkness came to close my eyes in sleep.

227

PART 4

HALLI

The next morning, we dragged ourselves the last weary way over the top, scratched and footsore from our hard climb. The horses met us there, overjoyed at our return. They whinnied and snorted and rubbed against us in such a frenzy of affection as to make our progress difficult. When we reached the road and could mount again, we rode for a long while in silent companionable closeness, sharing, without need for words, scenes of our time with the Morl. Then suddenly, I felt Tarl clouding over. I expected some heavy words from her. Instead, she asked abruptly, "How did you learn to shield, Sair?"

"Seronis taught me. I had bad thoughts about her beard, and that disturbed the peace of our home."

"Ah, yes, her beard. That must be new for you. I doubt that many women in Eezore wear their natural face-hair. And what do you think of it now, that beard?"

"That it is part of her. That it becomes her like her hands or her nose. She would be less Seronis without it."

"Who would have thought Seronis could teach such a thing as shielding. It is not easily done. Halli would have been a better teacher."

At that I felt some anger on Seronis' behalf. "Halli neglected to teach me. Seronis did the best she could with what material she had."

"Yes, yes, she taught you well enough, so well that you could lie to me from behind that shield."

"Never!" I shouted at her, really angry now. "Never! I never lied to you, Tarl. I told you I would go with you wherever you asked, and that was true. For love I could not let you go alone. I did not say I would be joyful or unafraid in the going. I tried, but I could not do so, not even for you."

Her face softened quickly. "Indeed, you had much courage in the face of your great fear, Little Sister. I wonder if any other would have come with me, into the jaws of the Morl. You even saved me from the pull of the sea and in so doing balanced out our life-debt. If not for your will and your strong arm, she surely would have had me, for I had no will of my own and no sense at all." With those words, she reached across and took my hand.

We rode again in silence, but now I felt Tarl's heavy thoughts between us. Several times I sensed her start to speak. At last, she loosened my hand and said with grave formality, "Sister, I have need to talk with you."

The horses stopped, and Timmer turned so that Tarl and I faced each other. I nodded, waiting, not wanting to intrude. After a while she went on as if each word cost her a struggle. "Sair, I am no longer who I was when we first met. Some part of my powers have been burned away. Before I left, I already suspected as much. It was made clearer to me at the asking place. I suppose that was the price of standing against the Shokarn army and then so soon, using my Kersh to hold against a city. It was too much too fast." Her voice had a sad hollowness in it. "I think mostly it was the battle and my rush of anger at the line. In my rashness I broke with the Cerroi, the Great Circle, and left myself open to harm. I was lucky I did not pay with my life there, or worse yet, bring hurt to another Hadra. Quadra had warned me. Still I could not contain it. The captain's rage tapped my own. I could have gone against him with my bare hands."

"But, Tarl, he was an evil man. He brought that evil with him. Why should you be punished so for your anger? It is not fair."

"Fair?" She gave a strange humorless laugh. "No, it is not fair. It has nothing to do with fairness, not as you would think of it. It is a balancing out of things on a far larger scale. The Cerroi is the Circle of Fate, the law of return that holds our lives. As we cannot be harmed, so we cannot will another's harm. In both cases, the hurt comes back to the sender. It is like the suru, the small curved blade of wood that children throw. It comes back to them out of the sky."

I shook my head, all my old anger flaring up again. "I say the captain deserved his death twice over for what he wrought that day!"

"Not by my hand. It was not mine to do or even wish. Think what gross monsters we Hadra might become if there was no seal on our powers. You said once you did not think us human. Sister, we are both more and less. The power that guards our lives also binds our hands. Even if a guardsman killed my lover right before my eyes, I could not down him with a sword — could not — it would come back to my own death and would not harm him."

"Is that the justice of the Goddess," I shouted, "that you should pay for another's misdeeds?"

"No, only for my own," Tarl answered wearily. "As to the Goddess, who are we to think we can understand her will or her ways? We are only her children, not the judges of her justice. We need to ask humbly and open our hearts to her."

I had other angry words ready to burst out, but stopped, remembering Tarl's own argument with Quadra before the battle about the limits of Kersh. She had learned with pain and was speaking now from the opposite side of the river.

I gave her back my hand for comfort, but did not look her in the eye, fearing to see the loss there. "What powers are left you, Tarl?"

She shrugged. "I do not yet know all of it. Perhaps I could hold against an attacker or two, but never again an army or a city. Of what remains I am not sure. Living will tell me better."

With a rush of guilt, I knew my own pain had been part of the anger for which she paid. Now I understood clearly why I had been forbidden to go to the line. "Will you miss it very much?" I whispered.

She was silent a long while seeming to stare into some inner space, then turned a sudden wry smile on me. "I can talk to sea monsters, the legendary Morl, soul to soul, but not to the Zarn's men. Should I regret it? Oh, Sair, I think I had too much pride in that power. It was I, Tarl, standing alone against that army or that city. My pride is one of the things you like in me, but I can plainly see it does me harm."

I looked at her with tenderness. "Tarl, I will still love you even if you cannot halt an army with the power of your mind."

"Will you really?" She laughed and seemed lighter. Her thoughts came through unclouded. "Thank you for hearing me, Little Sister. I had thought it such a dreadful thing. Now that it is spoken of, it seems not so bad. After all, I can still mind-talk with horses." She leaned forward, and Timmer broke into a run. We galloped around the last bends and up the long slope toward Semasi.

Just before we rode into the settlement itself, two hawks circled over us. At their shrill screams, Tarl threw back her head and answered. They swooped lower, answering her scream for scream, until at last they landed on a tree in front of us. We stopped our horses. Tarl leaned forward to gaze at the birds, and they stared back at her unblinking. For a long time they remained eye-locked in this manner, woman and winged-things, regarding each other across that space. Finally Tarl made a sweep of her arm. The birds rose to the air, sounding their wild cries again. Tarl gave back one last answering cry and then said with a toss of her head, "I may well have gained as much as I have lost."

"Remember your pride, Tarl!" I called after her, but she was already riding on ahead and could not hear.

Halli met us at the far edge of the settlement. Shouting for joy, she ran to greet us. "I felt you coming! I told them you would not be long!" We jumped down to hug her close and as we stood all three clasped together, she saw in our minds where we had been. "The Morl! They are real! You have seen them!"

"We have more than seen them," Tarl said grinning. "We swam with them. For a while we even spoke their language. Oh, Halli, my spirit is clear again! It was all a great wonder, and Sair was very brave!" Tarl took Halli's hands, pressing one to my forehead and one to her own. We showed her without words all that we could of our adventures.

Halli pulled her hands away and shook her head. "They seem truly wondrous and amazing, but it is a good thing, Tarl, that you asked Sair to go and not me. Nothing, nothing on this wide earth could have dragged me into the water with them. I think you are both quite mad and I am very glad to see you safely home." With that she kissed us both quite forcefully. Then we walked into Semasi holding hands, with Halli in the middle. The other Hadra rushed up to greet us and ask our story, but Halli pulled us forward, saying, "You can tell them later. Right now I have need of you both. I have called a small circle and want your support and advice added to these others'."

Halli's circle was already gathered under the central Gobal tree and the Hadra shifted to make room for us. They did not yet question us, for clearly this was Halli's time. Still I could feel them probing at the edges of my mind. Quadra was there, and Jephra, Ozal, Mirl and Kedris, as well as two Hadra I did not know, Nais and Shavit, whom I later found to be from Ishlair.

They all greeted us warmly and drew us down between them. Halli reseated herself and leaned against the tree as if needing its strength. "I was just telling them how it has been for me. Ever since the battle with the Zarn's army, my spirit has been in pain. Men, burning alive, come into my dreams and appear even in my waking time. It is as if in some way I am answerable for their deaths."

There were many muttered protests to this until Tarl said loudly, "Halli, those were the Zarn's own weapons. It was no fault of yours!" This seemed to me much as I had answered Tarl when she spoke of the Cerroi, but I kept my silence.

"Yes, yes, that is what I told myself over and over, thinking to lessen the pain, but it grew worse. I came to Quadra, crying for advice. She told me to go to an asking place. This I have done, going to the Black Rocks* at Delmar Pass. The message that came clear to me there was to have a child now, to make a new life as soon as I am able, a new life to hold against all that death. I plan to go to this fall gathering and ask the Goddess to fill my womb."

At that there were many exclamations. Tarl shook her head with some force. "Halli, you were going to wait till the spring Essu or till next fall! You still have no companion!"

"We will all mother this child, Tarl. She will be the first daughter born to us here in Semasi."

Jephra shook her head also. "It is not the way of the Hadra to have a daughter with no bond-mother for her."

There was some heated discussion then as to the rights and wrongs of the matter. Nais and Kedris seemed much in favor of this child. Tarl and Jephra were equally opposed.

At last Quadra stood up saying, "If the Black Stones have spoken, perhaps we should listen. That is a strong asking place. It may be that we Hadra are too bound to our ways. After all, there are many of us here and no babies. I think she will find care enough in our arms."

Several nodded. Halli jumped to her feet saying, "With so many mothers, I will be lucky if I am allowed to hold her at all."

"And I will get to see a baby born," Kedris called out with delight.

It seemed settled until Tarl made more objections. Halli stepped over to her and said with some impatience, "Tarl, you went away to ask your questions and have acted on your answer, even in the teeth of danger. Please give me the right to do the same. I cannot live haunted this way any longer." I saw that Halli, for all her sweetness, was as head-set as any Hadra and would have her way.

Tarl would not meet her eyes, but stared down at the ground and said stubbornly, "I thought you asked for my advice. I see you only needed my consent."

At that Halli seemed suddenly close to tears. She put her hand on Tarl's arm. "Please, Tarl, I need your help in this. Those killings are breaking my spirit."

"I withdraw my objections," Jephra said loudly.

"I, too," Tarl said almost in a whisper. "As it must be."

Halli said more gently to her, "I thought to ask you to ride with me to the fall Essu and be my holder, but if you do not wish to, there are others I can ask."

"I will gladly be holder for you, Halli," Tarl said humbly.

Then Halli turned to me. "Sair, will you ride with us and be holder also?"

"Yes, gladly," I answered. I had been afraid that once again, I would be left behind but instead we three were to ride together.

After a few more words Quadra made the sign of the blessing and the circle broke. Several of the Hadra went to touch Halli on the forehead and set their palms against her belly for Mother's Luck. Then Halli walked away arm in arm with Nais. I felt a touch of loss and sadness sensing they were lovers, yet also felt much joy for Halli.

* * *

Later, Halli came to find me. I was consulting with Seronis on work to be done at the common-house. Wordless, Halli took my hand and drew me away. She had a power on her. I did not question or resist, but with my hand in hers, climbed the path to the high north meadow that rises over Semasi and the sea cliffs.

That meadow was a place of life and beauty, full of flowers and birds and butterflies, all their colors dancing in the wind — the very opposite of the charred field of death that had haunted her so. She led me to sit on a large flat rock that had the look of an altar-stone. As there were no trees in the meadow, we could see from there all the land rolling away before us, the woods, the Tarmar fields, the gardens, the red stones of Semasi, the sea, even the Timmer Mountains and, far to the north, the very peak of Harimair, the great sacred Spider Mountain itself.

"You will see," Halli said intently as she settled by me, "Tarl is not the only one who can summon creatures." Like metal flashing in the sun, there was some fierceness in her that I had never seen before. She motioned me to be still, shut her eyes and sent her mind out over the meadow.

At first, all I sensed was a strange unnatural stillness. Then, as if she were spinning out golden threads of power into the air, birds came twittering and singing, tumbling out of the sky. More and more of them were drawn by her silent call until the air was thick with the rush of their wings. A feathered multitude, they dropped down and settled on our heads, hands, arms, and even in our laps. Butterflies came, too, soft and brilliant, tickling over our faces and fingers. Even a great, dark bird-of-death swooped down to land on the ground in front of us. It cocked its head to look at Halli. I felt it to be conversing with her in words I could not hear. All about us was a wild chorus of bird song, the bright flash of wings and beaks and the brush of feathers. I sat very still, hardly breathing, though with my eyes I tried to look everywhere at once. Never had I seen so many birds together in one place. For a while I lost myself in their midst, feeling, for that time at least, freed of my earthbound limbs.

After some time had passed, Halli raised her hands to release them. Gradually that wild company flew away. I watched awestruck as they melted into the sky, leaving only some few feathers as mark of their passage. For a long while neither of us spoke. Then Halli took my hands in hers. "Sister, I see us going different ways soon and wished to give you some gift of myself, something to remember me by." With that she took up my hands and kissed them. I had to shake myself free of the spell of the birds to thank her. I saw she was watching me with a strange half-smile on her face and some mischief in her eyes. "Well, Sair, you are a very different person than when you first came to us and had to struggle so with the word 'muirlla' as if it were a sharp bone stuck in your throat."

I laughed, thinking of my old self. "Much of that is your doing," I said.

"And some Tarl's and more of it your own."

"Are you . . . are you . . . ?" I wanted to ask her if she had some jealousy of my being with Tarl and if that had any weight in her wanting this baby.

She caught my thoughts. "Some, perhaps, but not much. There is between you and Tarl something I cannot touch. I may be able to call birds out of the sky, but I would not swim with sea monsters. Not even for Tarl would I have done that, not even for love of her. Only you, Sair, could have done such a thing."

At that I shook my head and laughed again. "I did not go to the Morl with much good spirit, that I must confess. My knees shook the whole way. Tarl called me a chi-goat and nearly left me at the cliff top, threatening to go on alone." I turned then to look into her eyes. "And how goes it with you, Little Sister? Are you lovers with Nais? Is it healing for your spirit?"

She nodded. "It is fresh and new and very sweet still. She is helping me to mend."

Leaning forward she kissed me deeply. Then she leapt to her feet and ran down the meadow through a blaze of flowers. I sat a while alone in that place, looking out over the land and listening to the birds sing. I could still feel the touch of feathers on my skin, and when I shut my eyes, the Morl rose gleaming from the dark waters.

That night Tarl made a fire in the central circle. All of Semasi gathered around to question us. We told the story of the Morl many times, until I fell asleep with my head on Halli's shoulder and my hand clasped in Tarl's hand.

AFTERNOTES

<u>The Black Rocks of Delmar Pass</u>— A Hadra asking place, thought to be of Asharhan origin and therefore to be imbued with particularly strong powers for guidance. The Hadra consider personal messages received at an asking place to be of grave importance as they may, in some way, be a direct communication with the Goddess.

PART 5

THE MAKING OF A CLOAK

Once it was decided that a troupe of us would travel to the fall Essu, some joy in living returned to Semasi. There was a thing to plan for and to talk about. Though the Zarn's war and Yima's death were not forgotten, at least there was else to think on.

After much discussion, Hadra style, it was agreed that Halli, Nais, Tarl, myself, Mirl, Ozal, Quadra and Kedris should go, as well as two Hadra I hardly knew. When Quadra protested that she could not wisely be away so long, the council named Jephra to be Councillor in her place until she returned.

When she still seemed uncertain, Seronis said decisively, "Mother, it is for our good as well as yours that you need to have some pleasure and some time of your own. The council asks that you go."

Zarmell added, "Sister, it is no virtue to take the whole world on your back. Besides, all these children promise to be good while you are gone." This last made Quadra laugh, and so it was decided.

As to the rest, except for Marli, they were glad to remain in the settlement. Seronis said she had travelled enough that year and would be pleased to stay home and play wife to Semasi for awhile. "Only you must take my report safe to Zelindar and give it to Jorkal, who is Keeper-of-the-Archives there, as well as a letter to my daughter, who for now is living with my mother in the city." This I promised to do for her, thinking that her daughter was a story Seronis had not told me yet.

When Zarmell was asked if she wished to go, she shook her head saying, "Not me. I have no wish to see men this year and no need of a baby, but I shall miss Sharven. Tell her to come in this direction soon. I have discovered some new roots and herbs, I would like to share with her."

Marli, however, begged to go, though Quadra counselled hard against it, saying, "There are too many dangers for one so young and so new to freedom." For a few days Marli cried and sulked and became almost her wild, willful self again until in exasperation Quadra shouted at her, "Go, go then, but do not come back! You are not worth the trouble you cause us here!"

At that Marli burst into tears and would not be consoled until Zarmell took hold of her saying, "Stay here with me, Nibbit. I promise you we will go to the spring Essu together in grand style."

* * *

Though Halli and I were not lovers at that time, still we were good friends again and much together. When the trees were beginning to turn gold on the hills, and the days of the Essu drew near, she decided I must make myself a new cloak for Festival. "That is when most Hadra make theirs," she told me.

237

Mine was a very old one, borrowed from Ozal and quite worn. Still I protested, "Halli, I know nothing of making cloaks. This one does me well enough."

"That one is sad and shabby. Besides it must be returned before winter. It will be too cold to make one when you come back from Zelindar. Sair, it is not at all fitting for you to appear in rags at your first Essu."

I threw up my hands. "I do not even know how to start or what they are made of."

"Trust me in this, Sair. I will show you each step of the way, but you shall do it all yourself and learn."

I surrendered to her will, seeing that as usual with the Hadra, I had no choice. Moreover, I knew I should be grateful she would take this time for me. After that, it was a few days before Halli herself was free. By then I was anxious to begin.

Here in Semasi you do not send servants out with a bag of coins to fetch some of whatever it is you need. Because I had lived so long in Eezore, I was still not accustomed to thinking of each item of use as something that had, sooner or later, to be made — most likely by myself. It had never occurred to me to wonder how the Hadra came by the cloaks that were so much part of their lives.

Those cloaks were their moving houses. They kept them warm in winter, being very wind resistant, as well as keeping them dry against the rain. Cloaks could be shade from the summer sun or could be made into a lovers' nest. Two tied to trees could be fashioned into a tent. They were never thrown away. A four-year cloak became a winter blanket. When it was too worn for that use, it was cut up to make packs, carrying bags and horse rags. So now, I was to make my own cloak, and weave myself deeper into the fabric of Semasi.

When Halli at last was ready for cloak-making, she said, "First, we must cut some Harleepai and leave it to dry." We each strapped on a troga, a long sharp blade. I went with her to a high field some ways east of Semasi where there was a wide, shallow pond. She explained to me that this Harleepai only grew in marshy places and along the edges of slow shallow waters. What Harleepai looked like and how it could be fashioned into fabric, I had no idea. To all my questions she answered, "Wait and see."

When we reached the Harleepai beds it was, indeed, an amazing

238

sight and like nothing I could have imagined. Harleepai grows in clumps, each single stalk like a green club almost the size of a leg, with a fleshy, translucent exterior. These "clubs" looked to have no substance, but Halli assured me they had a good core of fiber under their pulpy surface. Other Hadra were gathering Harleepai on the opposite side of the pond. We called to them and waved. When I saw Lar's crow circling above them, I was glad. In my heart I wished her joy for that day.

As we stood before the first clump, Halli said, "It takes ten to twelve clubs to make a whole cloak, but since the Harleepai are sacred to us, we can cut no more than two stalks from any clump. Also we must say words of thanks to the plant and to the Mother for her gift." All this she said seriously, almost solemnly. When I first raised my knife she told me, "Make one clean cut clear through. It causes less pain." I was amazed and a little amused that the Hadra had made ritual even out of this simple task, but I went with her from clump to clump and did as she did, saying the words and leaving my little mound of pebbles before each plant to mark where we had been.

By the time we had cut and gathered up six clubs each, our clothes were soaked through with their juice which left a pale green stain on everything. The Harleepai were already wilting and shrinking in our arms. I felt as if I had killed some strange green creature and now carried parts of its dying body. I was much relieved when Halli stopped in front of a large flat rock saying, "This will be a good pounding place." We laid out the stalks to dry, careful so they did not touch each other. Halli told me, "In two days we can come back, and turn them for drying. Then in another day or so, we can come back to work them."

I asked if we could not take them home with us, but Halli shook her head. "Harleepai must always be worked by the water where it is cut."

When we came back to make my cloak, we brought with us pounders and scrapers and water scoops. At our approach, a great cloud of flies rose with an angry hum. The thick green flesh had dried to a flaky black crust which we scraped away with some difficulty. Now began the real work of pounding out the fibrous core, turning the work over and over to make it smooth and even. When this was flat, but not yet thin, the most skilled and troublesome task still lay ahead, that of piecing together and shaping the cloak itself. Harleepai must be pounded so that the edges of the pieces catch and overlap each other until they become a whole fabric without lumpy seams. While this is being done, scoops of water must constantly be poured over the work to soften the fibers and make them supple.

For this we stripped. Our naked bodies were soon very wet. A strange crust of pale green gathered on our skin looking like scales or lizard hide. Halli chanted as she worked, old chants that were for the pounding. Also, she gossiped and chatted and told me stories of her life in Zelindar, much about her mother and bond-mother that I had never heard before and about her sisters as well. She had three blood-sisters and two bond-sisters. They were all very close. It had been hard for her to leave them and she hoped some of them would come to live with her in Semasi, at least while the baby was small. I shuddered with some strange dread when she spoke of that baby and would not talk about it, though clearly she wished me to.

It took all day from early morning until almost sunset for us to fashion that cloak. When at last we trimmed the edges with our togas and laid that damp, supple fabric over some bushes to dry, we were both very weary. We went arm in arm back down to Semasi, singing and leaning on each other for support, seeming drunk from our efforts.

That night I had an edge of hunger on me from all that work. When I took my seat with the others in the dining hall, I saw before me Tarmar and vegetables one more time. In a bad humor I said, "I would give much for a plate of red meat with good, dark gravy to sop my bread in." I spoke hastily, without much thought.

Instantly, Halli drew away from me. "Oh, Sair! How could you think of eating meat, the flesh of living creatures!"

It was almost like a cry of pain, but at that moment I was weary and hungry, and so had little use for Hadra virtue. I answered impatiently and with the same ill humor, "Because it tastes good!" As I said this, I became aware of the other Hadra staring at me. The force of that stare set me to eating with nervous haste, hoping they would do the same.

Instead, there was total silence until Halli laughed and said mockingly, "And so no doubt would you, Sair, if you were cooked long enough, yet it does not seem sufficient reason to have you butchered and strung up for sale in the Kourmairi market square." At that there was a roar of approving laughter from the others.

Flushed with embarrassment, I threw down my fork, leapt to my feet and dashed out of the dining hall, stumbling over bench legs in my flight. Outside I was able to cool my anger in the night air and contemplate my empty stomach, thinking how my rashness had cost me my dinner. For being too hungry, now I would have nothing to eat. But later Halli sought me out to apologize for her mockery. She even brought me a bowl of food which I ate gratefully. Tarmar and vegetables had never tasted better.

The next day I went alone to fetch my cloak and carry it down to the dyeing pots on the beach. There I went from pot to pot, sampling and comparing. Other Hadra were dyeing their cloaks that day, some golden yellow, some dark red, some moss green. Finally, I chose the deep blue of the zuleberries for mine. This new cloak was much admired. Though I knew it to have some lumpy seams, still I was very proud of my work.

It was not just the making of cloaks that occupied the Hadra before Festival, but also the making of mizzi beads. In fact, for the last week or so before we were to leave, all other work was abandoned. Though there were some coins minted in Zelindar, as well as in the Kourmairi cities of Mishghall and Koormi, still there was no official currency for Yarmald. Mizzi beads were one accepted form of exchange. Everyone going to the Essu wanted her pouch full, especially those planning to ride on to Zelindar. Even those who were staying wished to send their friends with a little pile of beads to bring them back "a bolt of fabric" or "a new set of knives" or "some pretty trinkets to wear."

The beads were made of mizzail clay, which ran in a vein from Semasi northward and nowhere else in Yarmald. The clay was a dull gray-blue when first dug, but when fired with a little sand and then polished, it turned a lustrous blue-green. This mizzail had to be dug and carried home, then rolled and cut and pierced to make the beads. Some Hadra even stamped their beads with their own designs. All the tables of the eating hall were taken over by this work. Firing pits burned on the beach day and night.

For that week I was sooty most of the time, my fingertips burnt and my eyebrows singed. But at the end of it, I had my own pouch of beads to take that were not too badly made. The last night we baked great piles of trail bread on rocks still hot from the firing.

* * *

The fall festival, the Essu, was to be held that year at the Kalturin ritual grounds. It was a very ancient place from what Quadra had told me, with signs of markers from an earlier time, a time before the Hadra and even the Koormir. Perhaps the Asharha of whom Seronis spoke had marked that ground and gathered there. It lies below Semasi on the Escuro River between Ishlair and the Kourmairi settlement of Logarsh. The people of the north would come to it, and those from elsewhere who wished to travel that far, Hadra and Koormir alike. It was at the Essu that the children of the Goddess would be conceived. I had sat several hours in the Zildorn with Quadra, reading and asking questions and so thought myself prepared.

* * *

Never before had I seen the Hadra ride out for pleasure. I had first seen them coming back from an expedition into Garmishair and had watched them ride off unwilling to battle, but had not witnessed a departure of their own choosing. It was like a great moving tapestry. Anything and everything that had color to it was fastened on horse and Hadra: bright clothes, flags and banners, bells and flowers and ribbons and long sashes newly dyed with the cloaks. All the jewelry that each Hadra owned she wore and all she could borrow. Extra horses came with us, whichever wished to go, and a pack of dogs danced around our feet. Music played in Semasi as we left and music went with us on the road: flutes, drums, bells, a Kerril, several ferls and many other instruments I did not know the names of.

Riding out, I was carried by the gaiety of the others. I proudly wore my new blue cape though it was too warm a day. My hair had grown long enough to be fastened back with beads and feathers, Hadra style. The pouch at my side was heavy with mizzi beads. I felt very grand and looked forward with pleasure and excitement to the Essu. But as the day went by and we drew closer, I began to feel anxious and afraid, closed into myself. There were more and more people on the road, many of them men. They shouted out coarse greetings and seemed loud and rough. I rode close to one Hadra or another, feeling none of the safety I was used to in Semasi. The Hadra seemed unafraid. They shouted back as loudly and in the same spirit.

That night we made camp on the road. Though I lay safe in the tent between Tarl and Halli, my sleep was restless and my dreams invaded by the sound of men's voices. Next morning we ate a slow and leisurely meal. Not until well after midday did we reached the Escuro. Splendid in our bright array, with our banners flying and our horses prancing, we made a fine sight as we rode into the Kalturin ritual grounds. There we were met with cheers, shouts and greetings. I looked about me amazed and with some dismay. Nothing Quadra told me had prepared me for this sight.

PART 6

FALL ESSU

All was a great confusion. There seemed to me no plan or order anywhere. Music, color, dust, noise, and a profusion of smells each made their assault upon the senses. People and animals were everywhere and small children raced wildly through the scene. Yet even in the midst of this madness, a brisk trade was going on. Stalls, booths, and tables had been set up, each with its own bright flag or banner flying over. There crowds gathered and thickened, flowing from one stall to the other, shouting and gesturing as they went.

From my brief time in Semasi, I had forgotten men. Now they were all about me, more men than I had any wish to see, men on foot, men on horseback, men drunk and lying on the ground. Though they appeared to threaten no immediate harm, still I had my fears.

Drink appeared to flow in abundance there, great quantities of yors and quillof being consumed and other liquors I did not know the names of. I was offered cheer from every side, but shook my head, still fearful of their drink. Even some Hadra were drunk and staggering about. A few had already fallen in a stupor. This shook me more than all the rest, for never had I seen the Hadra drunk among strangers.

At first impression, the Essu had the appearance of a vast crazy house loosed from its walls. In Eezore such a scene would have been full of dangers: thefts, fights and stabbings being common there in crowds. Armed guards would have prowled about cracking heads, and none too careful who they chose for targets. Here there were no weapons and no guards. All seemed friendly enough in a mad way. Hadra strolled about arm in arm with Kourmairi river women, kissing in the manner of new lovers. Men and Hadra joked and shouted with each other. They raced horses, tossed the pebbles and flipped cards, wagering all manner of things. Hadra friends from different settlements rushed together to hug and wrestle, rolling on the ground, as if at any moment they might turn to public lovemaking unashamed. Those I had thought to be my friends, quickly scattered, going to find other friends or walk among the booths or join the drinking. I was left to myself, bewildered and alone—abandoned in the midst of chaos.

As I stood gazing fearfully about, a man bumped against me with intention. When I turned he grinned and shrugged. Then making a mock bow, he asked if I planned to seek pleasure at the next night's Gimling. Frightened, I backed away and went to seek Tarl for shelter.

Tarl, however, had no thoughts of me. When I found her, she was wagering Timmer's speed against some river man's horse and seemed already drunk. She put up her cloak, and the man his fine new boots. There were shouts to make way, which was not easily done. Then they were off with Timmer well ahead. I did not see Tarl again for some time. By then she was very drunk indeed, and laughing wildly. She showed me her new boots which were too large and offered me some quillof.

Seeing there was no help in Tarl, I went in search of Quadra, hoping to find some sanity with her. Quadra was not so easily found. At last I saw her dancing arm in arm in a circle of Kourmairi women. Some of them seemed quite taken with her. She had her head thrown back and appeared to be enjoying their attentions. Together they were circling a small fire and looked to be making a game of leaping through the flames.

Quickly I slipped away. Clearly there was no comfort to be had from Quadra either. It was as if the whole town had gone mad and I went to complain to the magistrate, only to find the magistrate as crazy as the rest.

After that I wandered about alone, fearful and close to tears until Halli found me. She had been drinking, too, but was not yet so lost in it. She drew me into a little shelter of trees and bade me sit next to her, offering to share her bottle of yors. I no longer cared what the effect might be and drank it gladly. When we parted, the day was already darkening and I, too, was not so steady on my feet. My head was freer though and I was less afraid.

Soon the flares were lit. The Essu grounds leaped and danced in their light, more fantastic even than before, but I had lost my worries and, no doubt, most of my good sense as well. From then on, whenever I was offered quillof or yors or a puff of jol, I accepted. In the end, I had drunk and smoked far more than I could carry. It was in this state that I staggered about the Essu grounds until at last I saw the banner of Semasi* and, nearby, Tarl and Halli's own banners flying. They had set up our tent for which I was most grateful. I fell to the ground and crawled inside. There, without even washing or unfastening my bedroll, I fell asleep with all my clothes on, even to my boots.

Still in my rumpled clothes, I woke next morning to an empty tent. Someone had kindly taken off my boots and covered me. I changed my clothes, then blinking in the morning light, I stumbled out into the great swirl of the Essu.

The scene was even livelier and wilder than before. Many must have come in the night or early that morning. As I looked about I could see more booths, tents, banners, horses and children than yesterday. But now, I was not so timid and could even look on it all with a little pleasure.

Being still thick-headed from drink and dirty from our long ride, I made my way down to the Escuro. The banks of the river were crowded with children. I had to force an opening for myself, but they moved aside with good natured bantering. I dunked my whole head several times and came up at last feeling clear and sober. Now I felt ready to sample for myself some of the wonders of the Essu. It was clear that I would have no Hadra guide. I was in my own hands that day and vowed to be more careful with my drink.

With all there was to see, I was drawn this way and that. At last, I settled on a troupe of acrobats from Osen, each dressed in a network of bells and flowers. While I stood watching, someone came from behind me and put hands on my shoulders. I turned expecting to smile at a familiar Hadra. Instead, I was met by some strange man's face. Before I could shout, he saw the double triangle I wore, for this time my shirt was open at the neck. "Hadra," he muttered, looking frightened. He leapt back in such haste that he stumbled on his own feet and was quickly gone in the crowd. I felt much pleasure in that borrowed power. It was clear, though Hadra and Kourmairi came together at night under the eye of the Goddess, Kourmairi men did not take liberties with Hadra in the day.

I had no thought of buying a shirt, but went where the brightest colors called and so stopped at a weaver's booth all strung with tiny wind-bells. Seeing me pause there, the woman held up a shirt and shook it at me, hoping to capture my attention.

"Hello, Pretty. A new shirt for the Essu? This one would look well on you." When I did not respond she held up another. "This would look even better. Yes, truly this one was made for you." That second shirt was such a thing of beauty — blues and greens and a soft sand color shot through with streaks of brilliant crimson — that I was held by it. The weaver smiled broadly, seeing her fish so easily hooked.

"How much for this one?" I asked, fingering the weave which was soft as rabbit's fur in my hands.

"What do you have?"

"Mizzi beads."

Her eyes brightened. She named such a high number that I poured out my whole pouch on her table.

"No, no," she said in disgust, pushing them back at me. "You are supposed to bargain at an Essu, not dump out your whole purse. If you go on at that rate, in an hour, you will have an empty pouch and little to show for it. Where are you from, girl? Have you never been to an Essu before?"

Confused and embarrassed, I said angrily, "No, I have never been to an Essu! I escaped from Eezore and am Neshtair in Semasi now."

At that the weaver smiled again, but this time with real heart. "Ah, yes, Sairizzia of Eezore, Sair of Semasi. Come here by me." She took down some wind-bells and fastened them in my hair as she spoke. "Yes, yes, I have heard much talk of you, even here. It is said you went back afterward to scold the Zarn to his face. Well, my brave one, you must have this shirt, for surely it was made for you. I should be proud for you to wear it. Take it now and, in return, give me whatever you make well with your own hands."

"I make nothing well," I said staring down at my stone roughened hands. "I made these crude mizzi beads and am only just learning to set stone."

"Good, then you shall come next spring to my settlement and help me set stone for my little hut. There I shall make you many shirts. It is all very well to have a husband and children, but I am still Hadra enough to need a place of my own, however small."

"You are a Hadra?" I could scarcely credit her words.

"I was. Did they not tell you of Tizzel the shirtmaker, who married for love? When I did that, my own mother said, 'You are as dead to me as if I never bore you!' Terrible words indeed for a daughter to hear. She got over it when the children came. I miss the Hadra sometimes with their wild ways, but they are too stern and fierce for me. I am happier here. I have six children and they are like flowers in my garden." With that she laughed. "Well, that is not always true. On some days they are like a sackful of toads dumped out on the floor. But I manage well enough. My husband helps with everything. He feels very lucky to have caught me." Then she shook me by the shoulder, saying, "Shut your mouth, child. You will catch flies in it, or something worse."

Embarrassed to have been gaping at her, I asked quickly, "Are all your children daughters?" That seemed, to me, quite a quantity of girls in one house.

"No, the last two are boys. A Hadra's powers diminish if she lives among men. Still, I have not altogether forgotten my origins. When they are old enough, my daughters will go to the Hadra for training, so they can make their own choice of lives. They may even live for a while with my mother. My first child is almost of age and has long been ready and eager. My next child has no wish to go so soon. She would rather stay by me and learn to weave, so with her, we may wait till later.

"Come, that is enough of me. Gather up these beads for they are cluttering my table and try on your shirt, so I may see how it becomes you." When I had it on she patted and stroked me all over as if to settle the fabric, saying, "Very pretty, very pretty indeed."

"This bead you must keep, Tizzel," I said, pressing it into her hand. "It is the best I made." She smiled and put it in a little pouch at her neck.

"Come now, my sweet fool. I will teach you how to shop at the Essu. When we get to a booth, you will signal me your choice with a nod. I will bargain for it with your beads. You will see easily enough how it is done."

"Will you leave your booth untended?" I asked with concern.

"Oh, yes," she said carelessly. "We may cheat each other at the Essu, but we do not steal."

At the end of an hour my pack was full and my pouch not half empty. I had seen and learned much in that time.

At last Tizzel said regretfully, "Now I must go back to work. I cannot afford to play all day, no matter how the company pleases me." When we were in front of her booth again, she kissed me on both cheeks and quite forcefully on the mouth, saying, "I will see you in the spring then, Sair. You have only to come to the village of Namakir and ask for Tizzel, the shirtmaker."

"But what if I cannot get there? I will already be wearing your shirt."

"Then you will send me a message or send me something you have made, for surely by then, you will have learned a skill. Or send me a poem if you write."

"That does not seem fair to you," I protested.

She threw back her head and laughed. "Do you think yourself the best judge of that? You worry too much, Little One. Leave something for the Goddess to attend to. I would rather you came yourself and set stones, but for the great turning of things it matters little. Wear that shirt in happiness, Neshtair."

Later, I met Halli walking arm in arm with Nais and several other young Hadra. She laid a hand on my arm and said with admiration, "Surely one of Tizzel's shirts and the finest I have ever seen. She is truly a mistress of her craft. How much did you bargain for it, Sair? It must have taken half your purse."

"The bargain was to go to Namakir next spring and lay stone for her if I am able. She said she would make me more."

Halli whistled with surprise. "Well, she must like you much for she makes no such soft bargains with the rest of us!" The others laughed and winked. I saw I was being both teased and flattered.

We stood there chatting for a few minutes. I discovered that all of them, except Nais, planned to go to the Gimling that night and make their first baby. The way they giggled and clung to each other, they seemed more like city girls than Hadra to me. I felt awkward with them all, even Halli. I was about to move on when there was a sudden loud commotion and much shouting. Halli took my arm, and we all rushed together to see the cause of it.

There was another race starting, this one with many horses. Tarl was again among the riders. It was more organized than the last, to be run in a loop with starters, judges and crowds of people watching. I had to push through a crush of bodies to reach the front, determined this time to see Tarl race. She was stripped to the waist, her pants already torn and dusty. Timmer was dancing sideways. I saw her lean far forward to whisper in his ear, while he held his head turned as if to listen.

There were three other Hadra in the race besides Tarl and six men. The woman standing next to me said they were to run the loop five times. While I stood watching several more false starts were made, then suddenly they were running. Timmer went easily at the center of the pack, seeming to make no more effort than when he ran on the beach at home. Finally, at the fourth turn, Tarl leaned forward over his neck and gripped his mane. Timmer broke from the pack, passed the horses in front and ran the last lap almost alone. He went twice more around the loop to slow his pace.

All about me people were shouting and throwing flowers. Tarl in that circle seemed like a stranger. Then, as if suddenly remembering my existence, she rode up to kiss me and pulled me up on Timmer's back. In this way we rode around the loop together in front of all those people.

Afterward, I left Tarl trading her newly won saddle for a set of stone-working tools and wandered on by myself. By now I was hungry, having eaten little the day before. The smells of food assailed me from every side. Food stalls were plentiful, and vendors walked about with trays, shouting the virtues of their wares — fried fruit, meat pastries, cheese-covered vegetables and honey-dipped sweets. At first, I sampled cautiously, nibbling what was offered by a passing Hadra or asking a taste of this or that at the stalls. Soon I grew more daring and ate with abandon, enjoying flavors which were not to be found in Semasi. After that, wherever I went, it was with some sticky edible in hand.

As I was passing a booth with several Hadra lounging in front of it, Ozal among them, a familiar voice called out, "Well, Sair, I am glad to see you safe in Yarmald. The last I saw of you was your rapidly departing back. Then that poor man you had so terrified came to tell us of your capture by the guards." I turned back in surprise to see Anyice with all her shiny trinkets spread out around her. This time she was in a blue robe with orange trim, bright enough to catch the eye even there among that feast of colors.

She reached out and took my hand in a firm grip, pulling me close. "I was just telling Ozal that your trip to the Zarn seems to have had effect. Before that all was talk of a new battle to be mounted with more men and more weapons, though none, I can tell you, were eager to go. The stories from the last battle are still passing mouth to mouth. They become more terrible at each telling. For a while there was at least one deserter a week given over to the torturers.

"Since your visit he is training more guards, but that, I hear, is for protecting the city rather than making mischief elsewhere. Perhaps, for a change, he fears for his own skin. All this, of course, is guess work, since I do not live in the Zarn's pocket. Some of your own people may be able to tell you better."

Ozal said quickly, "Anyice, this is welcome news and we thank you for it."

Anyice gave a bitter laugh. "Yes, and if there are any spies here, those words will cost my life." Then she shrugged. "Ah, well, it matters little. Being here at all could cost the same."

I was amazed to see her here in Yarmald, seeming just as she had been in Eezore. "Anyice, how were you able to get safely past the guard patrols and the Muinyairin?"

She shrugged again as if it all were nothing. "I come every year to the Essu, sometimes twice. The guards are easy enough if you know their patterns and have a little money to slip in at the right time. As for the wild ones, I am part Muinyairin myself and so we have worked out our own bargains. They, themselves, would not think of putting down their weapons to come trade with Hadra and Koormir. But they are glad enough to send me with some goods in exchange for seeing me safely through. They have their ways, and I have my uses. I help move things about. Those red beads Tarl bought with Shokarn battle gold, came first from the Hadra city of Bayrhim." She laughed, plainly pleased with herself. Then seeing all eyes fixed on her, she quickly added, "But still it is no easy journey. It has many perils."

Ozal shook her head, "Anyice, when will you come live with us in Yarmald instead of risking your life this way?"

"Ozal, old friend, always the same question, always the same answer. I will come when my mother dies or decides to come with me. I will not leave her, for I am her only daughter. Her sons are worthless. She will not leave Eezore for all her people are there. Yarmald would seem wild and strange to her. As it is, we do not do so badly in Eezore for we are both clever traders. If a woman alone could move freely there and have wealth and power, I would soon be rich with a grand house and many slaves and servants at my call. But as it is, I would have to hire a nordir* to be my pet and pretend to be my master. That I am unwilling to do. Besides, it is dangerous."

"Well, do not come here looking for slaves and servants, Anyice. The only way I could wish to serve you, my dear, is in bed." The person who spoke was a big, solid woman, who looked to be neither Hadra nor Kourmairi. She was standing off to the side. I had not noticed her before.

Anyice turned quickly to her and said with some heat, "And there, Sharven, I do not wish to be served by any, not man nor woman. To accept such service would soon make me the slave. I do well enough alone. The rest of the world looks, to me, like a great piece of foolishness with all its chasing and wanting."

So that was Sharven. Glancing at her, I saw that she did, indeed, look like Zarmell, alike enough to be her sister. She laughed with good humor at Anyice and asked, "Well, since you spurn our loving and you cannot be our master to live as a mighty highborn among us, how will you do here?"

Anyice answered instantly as if she had already thought on it. "I will get a wagon for my horse. In that way, I can be a traveling merchant, going up and down the length of Yarmald, north in the summer and south in the winter. I will get to know all the settlements, staying only as long as I want and moving on when it pleases me. When I come, everyone will run out and shout, 'Anyice, Anyice, what wonderful things have you brought us this time?' They will all open their houses to me. I will not live in one place and be Neshtair to the Hadra, that I know."

There was much bantering back and forth after that. As I turned to leave, Sharven came up and took my arm. "So you are Sair. I have wanted to meet you since I first heard of you coming to Semasi. Walk with me a ways." I was glad enough to do so, and we talked of many things until I thought to give her Zarmell's message.

"Ah, yes. I am missing her also, but I have some gathering of my own to do first. And then too, it is a long way to Semasi on horseback. I have not much love for those creatures the Hadra prize so much. As none is bonded to me, I have to go asking favors. Somehow it hurts what is left of my Shokarn pride to ask favors of a horse. But, in time, in time it will happen. I would much like to see Semasi. Yes, tell Zarmell I will come." So we parted with no thought in my head of what would soon pass between us.

There was much that amazed me at the Essu, but the sight I best remember, even now, was of Yassi standing on her horse's back, circling the field at a run. She sang and shouted and called out to the men to match her. Though she was Kourmairi, she seemed to me wilder and more reckless than the Hadra themselves. At last she was thrown when her horse stumbled, but she fell lightly, rolling forward and leapt back on as if it had all been for show. I turned and turned to keep her in sight. Afterward, my neck ached from so much watching.

Later, when I was sitting at a small fire-circle with Tarl and Halli and Halli's friends, Yassi rode up at a gallop, leaping off almost at my feet. "Is there room for a Kourmairi in a Hadra fire-circle?" she asked with insolence. Without waiting for an answer she sat down close to me while the rest moved over to make her space.

Though she sang and laughed and talked with the others, most of her attention was on me. She sat pressed against my body and said things in my ear whose intent was unmistakable. This made me blush and squirm enough to wish her gone, yet I could not help but find some enjoyment there. Feeling flattered, I was almost tempted by her invitations. I knew I would get little attention from Tarl or Halli that night, but I had pledged to be holder for Halli and did not wish to be distracted from my promise. Also, Yassi was too insistent. I was reluctant to be bent so to another's will. Each time she asked I shook my head. Still, I did not move away.

When the music started, and others rose to dance, Yassi pulled me to my feet. She did not dance apart as was the style there, but held me close as if we were one body. I could feel her blood pulsing against mine. It was both exciting and disturbing. When I tried to loosen her grip, she pulled me tighter still, as if that were my desire. Then suddenly she swung me out quite freely, so that Tizzel's little bells all rang, making the others clap.

After that she made a pattern of our dance, first close and then so far we scarcely touched. Only our finger tips kept the connection. I let her do as she pleased and lost myself in the dancing, drunk with the night and the music and the motion of bodies. It was early evening. Flares were already lit. There were many fires and many, many dancers on the field all moving in that flickering light.

Then a gong rang. It signalled the time to prepare for the Gimling. All dancing stopped. My sweat ran cold on me. I felt a sudden chill all through my body. Yassi asked me one last time. When I refused again, she laughed and said boldly, "You shall get no better offer this night, of that you may be sure." Then she swung up on her horse and rode off at a run.

On the way to the Escuro for the ritual bathing, I asked Halli about Yassi, wondering why she remained a Kourmairi when she seemed so like a Hadra.

"Ah, Yassi . . ." Halli shook her head. "No, Yassi is not like a Hadra. It is her wild ways that fool you, Sair. But there is far more to being Hadra than riding well." She was silent for a moment as if gathering her thoughts and then said, "Yassi likes to play Queen among the men, to dance before their eyes while they all circle around her like moths around a flame. She could not find that attention with us. No Hadra could give her that and none would wish to. Be careful, Sister. I see her playing you." Never had I heard Halli speak so of another.

The river was crowded with holders and bathers, Neshtair and Kourmairi as well as Hadra. Any who wanted a child but not a man, any who wanted a child of the Goddess, could go to the Gimling to meet their fate. Many times that night I heard the words, "As it must be" repeated.

While we bathed Halli and washed her hair, we chanted some ancient ritual words that Nais had the best knowledge of. I did not understand their meaning and did not ask, but along with Tarl, I repeated the sounds which seemed to me mysterious and beautiful. Afterward, we rubbed Halli's body all over with mazz scented oil, put flowers in her curls and a circlet of flowers around her neck.

Halli had already drunk much yima root and was wildly excited. For that moment, I too, was caught in her mood. Tarl and Nais were laughing. Halli's friends were nearby being bathed by their holders. It seemed but a joyous party by the river. Then the drums began. I suddenly remembered the purpose of this party. Fear clutched at me again. Halli sensed it and touched my arm. I hugged her against me, wanting to beg her not to go. How could we let gentle Halli out into that darkness, bathed, oiled and perfumed, not for one man only, but for many? We, her friends, had helped ready her for this. My body shook with its own ugly memories.

Halli pried herself away from me, saying gently, but with firmness, "This is different, Sair, very different. This is not something forced on me. I have willed this myself. I want this baby. These men are not here to hurt me. They are here to help. It is as if I summoned them." She took both my hands and kissed them. "It will be well, Sair. I will make a new life in this place. Be glad for me if you can."

I dropped my hands and stood looking at Halli, full of love and dread. Then quickly I kissed her on the forehead, saying, "Sister, may you find your child this night." I knew Halli had prayed and lit candles and tossed the pebbles many times to find Mother's Luck at this Essu, but I could say no more. I, myself, was close to tears. I had to turn away while the others said their blessings and wishes. Then those who were to stay for the Gimling linked hands on the shore, and the rest of us drew back from the river, carrying their clothes and jewelry. We left them in their nakedness with only leaves and flowers as adornment, for in that madness all else would be lost.

Already some of the flares were being doused. The drums played louder now, the only instrument that would be heard that night. I shuddered to think of those men even now advancing on the beach. Tarl and Nais, knowing my feelings, came on either side of me and put their arms around my waist. In that way we walked up to the tent together. There they changed their clothes and asked me several times if I would go out with them on their nightly rounds of the Essu. Each time I refused, saying I was too tired. I did not mention that rich mixture of food I had indulged in, which was just then having its effect. At last, they went off to drink together, and I crawled into the tent, sick, weary and determined to sleep at once.

It was a dreadful night for me. I must have slept a little, for I had frightening dreams, vivid but formless. When I woke it was to the sound of groans, cries, shouts, and the insistent, endless drums. The quiver of the flares threw leaping shadows about the tent, shadows that seemed full of threat to me. I rolled up the cloak and wrapped it around my head to shut out the noise but it came up through the ground into my body. I lay moaning and tossing as if in a fever. It was in this state that Yassi found me. She must have known I would be alone in the tent. She slipped in quietly, sat down on my mat and drew me gently into her arms, so that my head was resting in her lap. With her hands, she brushed my hair back from my sweat-soaked face and laid a cool, damp cloth over my forehead.

"I am here, Sair, and will hold you for as long as you need." Though at that moment, Yassi had me in her power, she did not tease or crush me against her. Her hands were gentle and soothing. She seemed a different person from the wild woman I had met that day. Talking softly, she asked me many questions, until at last she drew from me the whole story of my rape and my escape from Eezore. At that she shook her head and appeared to be crying.

"This can not be good for you, Sair. A woman so abused by men should not be at a Gimling. It was careless and thoughtless of your friends." When I tried to say more, she put her fingers against my lips. "Sleep, Sair, and I will sit watch for you."

I sighed and shut my eyes. Before I could sleep, Tarl returned. She seemed to be unsteady on her feet, swaying at the entrance of the tent. Yassi turned to her with anger and said, "Can you not see that Sair is being sickened by the sounds of the Gimling? It brings back all those horrors she has lived through. For shame! Is this how Hadra treat their beloved? They treat their horses far better, I hear. Pay attention, woman! She can not stay in this place another day!"

I was in an agony of embarrassment at Yassi's words, fearing that Tarl would think I had complained of her. Instead, though she had entered quite drunk, she sobered instantly and looked abashed. "The fever of the Essu was on me. I have been a heedless fool." She came to kneel by me, laying her head on my belly. For that one moment, we three formed a strange triangle.

Then Yassi slipped out from under me and stood up. "I will go now, Tarl, if you can be trusted. Do not leave her alone again. She must not stay here another night, that is clear. If you can do nothing, I will take her back to my village with me for it is not far from here and on an easy road." With those words, she ducked out of the tent and was gone.

Tarl touched her fingers gently to my forehead. "Little Sister," she said softly. "I have forgotten you here." Then wordless she stripped off her clothes, slipped in beside me and drew me close. We did not speak, but shared in silence. Kind as Yassi had been, I was glad it was Tarl who held me and no other. I quickly fell asleep in her arms.

I woke again when Halli came staggering back in the early morning. She was still wild with sex and yima, her eyes wide, her face flushed, leaves and twigs entangled in her hair, and her body scratched and muddy. The smell of her sickened me. She had brought the Gimling back with her into our tent. She stared at me intently, her eyes full of meaning I could not read. I cried out and had to turn away.

Tarl took me outside and laid me down, using my cloak for a cover and hers for a pillow. Before she went with Nais to the river to care for Halli, she said, "Do not leave, Sair. I will be back soon." As the ground was damp with dew, I was soon shivering and pulled the cloak tight about me. I must have dozed for when I turned next, Tarl was kneeling by me, watching my face with some concern.

"Sair, do you wish to go back to Semasi? If you do, I will go with you this day." I was touched, knowing what a loss that would be to her, but I did not wish it either.

"No," I said as forcefully as I could. "I wish to go on to Zelindar. I came as much for that as for the Essu."

"Then I will go to see what I can do. Wait here for me, Sair. I will be no longer than I must." I lay back feeling easier, now that I knew some help could be had from Tarl.

* * *

AFTERNOTES

Hadra Flag of Semasi — A giant Gobal tree in dark green, its branches stretching to the corners of the flag, the flag itself being midday blue.

Nordir — An appointed guardian, under whose "protection" a woman of great skill or ability may, in some limited form, enter public life in Eezore. Such men are supposedly selected for their honesty and virtue, but, in fact, are often corrupt and unscrupulous, even tyrannical — since the woman has little hope of recourse in the matter.

PART 7

THE RAFT TRIP

Tarl returned soon enough. To my surprise Sharven was with her. Kneeling at my side, Tarl said eagerly, "Sharven leaves on her raft this day to gather herbs along the Escuro and the Morl. Do you wish to go with her, Sair? If so, we can meet again at the Big Bend. Quadra and Kedris and some others are planning to return to Semasi after the festival, but Halli and Nais are going on to the city with us. No doubt there will be a whole troupe of women from the Essu as well. We can all ride on to Zelindar together."

Plainly Tarl thought this a good plan. Sharven, however, seemed doubtful. She peered down at me, not nearly so friendly as at our first meeting.

"So, Sairizzia, you do not like our Essu?" she asked in a mocking voice.

I sat up hastily, not wanting to explain. "Nor you either, it seems," I answered her sharply.

She shrugged. "I have four near grown children gotten so. At my age I do not need another 'Child of the Goddess' to care for. Besides, my herbs must be gathered before the rains come. I would have left sooner, but Annella, the river woman who was to help, sickened with pig fever. She is not yet strong enough for such a trip. Since no other is willing to leave the pleasures of the Essu, I have small choice." As she spoke, she looked me up and down with narrowed eyes. "Well, girl, can you pole a raft? Have you a good strong arm?"

I felt like a horse being measured for its uses. When I stood up, she even pinched my arm to feel the muscles there. "Strong enough," I snapped, knocking away her hand. "How soon do we leave?"

"You will go?" Tarl herself seemed doubtful now.

"Why not? This raft trip will take me far from the Gimling and do so quickly. What could be better?"

Sharven shrugged again. "Well then, as it must be. Wait for me upstream by the big white rock." She left to make ready, but it was clear she was not pleased with her new found assistant.

Tarl looked after Sharven, shaking her head. "Sair, you do not have to go. We can find some other . . ."

"No, let it be, Tarl. It will serve as a distraction. She does not have to be my friend. I will help pole, and she will gather herbs. That is enough."

Tarl watched me in silence as if considering this, then said with a sudden smile, "Well, Sair, you will be seeing some of that wild land along the Morl that can not be reached by foot or horseback. Even Seronis would envy you that."

Hearing her excitement, I could almost look forward to this unexpected trip. Then suddenly I remembered my chief reason for being at the Essu. "I am pledged to be holder for Halli. I must explain and ask her leave."

"Halli will understand. I will tell her for you if you wish."

I shook my head. "This I must do for myself." I touched Tarl's hand and ducked into the tent. For a moment the smell nearly overcame me. Then my head cleared. I groped around in the semi-dark for Halli's body. She was drugged and half asleep. I shook her gently, repeating her name until she knew me.

"Halli, I promised to be holder for you, but I can not do so. This place and what happens here will make me ill." The rest I told her from my head to hers.

/I release you from the holding, Sister. I am being well cared for. Go with love./ It was an effort for her to form the thoughts. I kissed her on the forehead. She lifted my hand, brushed it against her lips and fell asleep again.

So I was free to go. Of that I was glad, but I felt a sadness, too, as if in some way I had failed us both. "As it must be," I whispered. Then I strapped on my knife and gathered up a few needed things, leaving the rest for Tarl to bring. It was a relief to find myself out in the light again. Tarl still stood there waiting for me. I handed her Seronis' letter and manuscript.

"Put these safely in your pack, Sister. They do not need a raft trip."

She did as I said, then hugged me and held me close for a long time. When at last she released me, she looked into my eyes and asked wordless if I would be well. I nodded. Then she asked in the same way if she should come with me to the waiting place. I shook my head, saying I needed some time alone.

"You have done well to find me such a quick way out of here. Enjoy the Essu, Tarl. I will be safe now. We will meet down river and from there go on together to Zelindar."

As I said that magic name, I saw again the mind picture Yima had shown me of that wondrous place and heard her voice saying, "You must go to that city." In my head I answered /I am going, Mother./ Swinging my pack on my shoulder, I waved and walked toward the river, leaving Tarl standing by the tent.

The rock where I was to meet with Sharven was easily found. It lay around a bend out of sight of the festival grounds. I slipped off my pack and sat down on a log by the Escuro to wait. After some time went by, I grew tired of watching the water and happened to glance up just as a man was coming toward me. He hesitated when he caught my glance and seemed about to turn away, but a child ran up to him shouting, "Mica, Mica!" As he bent to speak to the child, something in his face and the tone of his voice seemed strangely familiar to me, in spite of his Kourmairi words. "Are you from this place?" I called out to him in Shokarn.

This startled him. The child ran off, but the man took a few cautious steps in my direction and answered, also in Shokarn, "No, from Eezore."

I called again, "Come closer so I may see you."

He came, but warily, keeping one hand hidden behind him. "Are you Hadra?" he asked with fear in his voice.

"No, I am Neshtair." He nodded, but that hardly seemed to suit him better. I looked at him intently. "Mica, do you not know me?" I asked, for by then I was sure of him.

He shook his head, puzzled and clearly wishing to be gone. Indeed, how should he know me? I had changed from a captain's lady of Eezore to a weather-hardened, sun-darkened Neshtair. Even my hair was different. I would not have known him either, having seen him for that one moment only, but that the child calling his name drew my attention.

"How did you come to be here?" I asked.

"I was in the battle and afterward crossed the line."

"Were you under the command of Captain Mordal?"

He nodded, watching me as if I might be some dangerous creature about to spring.

"How fares the captain?"

"The captain died in that battle."

"Dead!" I shouted. "Lairz Mordal is dead!" I gave a sudden hard bitter laugh. "So, I am a legal widow now and not a runaway wife. Well, I can not say that his death grieves me in any way."

The man had jumped back at my words. He stood staring at me, white-faced and trembling.

"No, no, Mica," I said quickly. "I am not a ghost or walking corpse. In fact, I am healthy and strong and well attached to my body. Come sit by me and talk. There is nothing here to fear."

He came then with a strange smile on his face and sat on the log. "So, you still live. I have thought of you often. The next day I went to look for your body thinking to bury it, but you were gone. I did not know what to think. How . . . ?"

"I walked to the ocean. I was not going to die with their garbage."

"You walked . . . ?" He shook his head. "There were stories, but who could believe . . . ?"

"Yes, I walked, from Eezore to the sea." I said this with a fierce pride, then added more gently, "Mica, I must tell you that you saved my life that night. Never could I have made that dreadful walk without your greatcoat and my clothes and that pack of bread. I still remember your kind words."

"Ah, yes, the greatcoat. I had a hard time explaining the loss of that garment. What happened to you then?"

"I was going to the ocean to kill myself. The Hadra rescued me and healed my hurts. Now I am Neshtair among them." Then I turned to look full at him. "And you, are you always so sad and mournful?"

"Oh, no," he said with a quick laugh. "It is only that I am afraid of the Hadra for I have seen what their power can do. That is why I was so wary of you." As he spoke he leaned back and looked suddenly younger. "Oh, what a wonder to see you again, alive and in Yarmald. No, I am not sad. How could I be? I wake in the morning thankful for my freedom and go to sleep at night the same. Here I can walk up into the mountains or swim in the river whenever I please, and none to stop me. I grow my own food. No man has power over my life. Next month I am to marry a woman I love, who has two children. Already they seem like my own."

"Was that one of them who came running to you?"

He nodded with a smile of pleasure.

"Mica," I said on sudden impulse. "If I should ever wish to have a child, would you father it for me? I would be too afraid of that . . ." I made a gesture toward the Essu grounds.

"That I can well understand," he answered. Then he looked down at his feet, embarrassed. "If you so wish it, I would be glad to," He said softly. "It would be a closing of the circle."

"Yes," I said with a quick, hard laugh. "You were the only man in that room who did not have me." Those bitter words sprang from my mouth unbidden, and he twisted his face away in pain.

"Forgive me, Mica, that was my own cruel jesting at myself." I put a hand on his arm.

He shook his head. "I am amazed that you can jest at all." Then he turned away and muttered, "Every time I think of it, I am ashamed that I did not fight and try to stop them."

I saw that it cost him much to say those words. "Mica, if you had been foolish enough to play hero against such odds, we would likely both have died that night. Instead, here we are in Yarmald, glad to be alive. You did what you could."

He turned more cheerful then and asked with a grin, "Do you ever miss Eezore or regret being gone from there?"

"Never," I answered instantly. "And you?"

"Not for one moment. It would not grieve me if all Eezore sank under the Bargguell."

At that I roared with laughter, and he with me. Then I told him some of my adventures, and he told me some stories of his life since crossing the line. By the time Sharven came, I had quite forgotten I was waiting for her.

"Ah, so I see you two already know each other."

We both looked up startled for we had not heard her steps. Then we answered together with one voice, "From Eezore."

"Let me see your hand," she said to Mica. Reluctantly, he held out the hand he had been hiding. I gasped at the frightful scar, but he shook his head, saying, "If not for Sharven's fine healing, I would have no use of it at all. This is a small sample of the Zarn's new weapons."

Sharven flexed his hand several times saying, "Make sure to keep rubbing lesh oil on it twice a day so that scar does not stiffen."

We said our good-byes. As I walked away, I remembered there was one more man in that room who had not had me, the man who kicked my "corpse" so freely. That one I wished well-fried on the field of battle.

* * *

As we stood on the shore making ready to pack the raft, a young man came running up the beach in our direction, grinning broadly. That grin was all for Sharven and not for me. When he reached us, she grabbed his arm and turned him toward me.

"This is my son, Sadar," she said slipping her arm around him. "And this is Sairizzia who will help me pole the river."

The manner in which she said "my son" was like a protective cloak thrown around him should I judge him to be just a man like other men. We nodded politely enough to each other, but his attention was all for his mother. He set to questioning her eagerly about the trip, where we would go and for how long, until he chanced to look down at the raft itself.

"Mother, will you be safe on this? Why not let me come with you and pole?"

Sharven cuffed him lightly on the shoulder. "My son, I have come through safely all my life without need of your cautionings. If you wish to be useful, you could help us load."

She gave him a hug which he reciprocated. Then we stepped on board and with no more protests, Sadar passed us all our bundles. These we lashed securely to the deck of the raft. The last thing he passed over was a small boat that he handled easily with one hand. Sharven called it a hiji* and, indeed, it looked more like a nutshell than a boat to me. It did not seem at all secure, especially considering Sharven's large size, but she seemed quite pleased with it. She treated it lovingly and tied it down with care, talking about it all the while. When everything was done and carefully inspected by Sharven, Sadar threw us the rope and stood waving as we floated off.

Poling away, Sharven muttered, "What does he mean? She is of stout orze-wood and bound together well enough for any waters." Then she gestured angrily for me to hold the pole in a different manner and went on as if to herself. "What foolishness. He knows that a boy near grown to manhood is not allowed to go gathering herbs. It is forbidden. These are women's secrets."

As we passed the Essu grounds, many waved and shouted. I kept at my poling and dared not slacken to raise a hand. Sharven waved back with seeming pleasure. Yet when we were around the next bend, she continued in a querulous tone. "The Hadra are snobs. I love them and have chosen to live among them. I would not do otherwise, so I have to deal with their snobbery, but they are snobs none the less." I did not know if this complaint against the Hadra had to do with Sadar or men in general or something altogether different nor did I ask. What little energy I had was needed to pole the raft. I was glad enough to be gone from that place and had no desire to interrupt some private argument Sharven held between herself and the Hadra.

After we left the wide Escuro to turn up the Morl, we had to pole hard against the current. I used all my strength to exhaustion. Still Sharven did not seem satisfied. I could not have lasted at this pace for long, but fortunately, she made many stops. There, we would drop our rock anchor. For those times I rested, having nothing to do but lie on my back looking at the sky and listening to the water slide under the raft. Sharven took her little boat, sometimes clambering aboard to paddle and sometimes towing it as she waded, depending on the depth of the water. She went diligently from side to side in search of what grew. Her secrets she did not share with me.

The landscape we moved through was indeed amazing and seemed impossible to travel except by river. The mountains there were cut by deep gorges, flowing with waterfalls that fed finally into the Morl itself. I saw many caverns and always the bluffs rose above us, sometimes on one side, sometimes on the other, with the river struggling a narrow pass between. Tucked behind the rocks were the moist shady glens where green things grew in abundance. It was there that Sharven hunted.

That first night, we tied fast to some trees, but did not go on shore. After Sharven had her day's gatherings stashed away, she made a fire in her big caldron and cooked over it some fresh caught fish. As she had no Kersh, she could not "talk" to fish and so did not mind the eating of them. For my part, it was the first flesh I had tasted since crossing the line. I sucked the bones clean and licked my fingers after. Next she made some tea, lit her jol pipe and told stories. After that she took out her double flute to play. I lay back on pillows with the river whispering under me, drinking yima tea, sharing the jol pipe, listening to music and watching the stars. At that moment, I felt as if my life was surely a gift from the Goddess.

Later Sharven teased me some about her "sister" Zarmell, saying, "Zarmell has a very wide cloak. How often has she wrapped you in it, Little One?"

"Once only," I answered boldly. "But it was a fine wrapping."

She winked at me as if we had a secret together. "I hear you have brought home a young Neshtair from Eezore."

I nodded. "She is a wild little thing and reminds me of myself when I was younger."

"And you are not afraid to leave her home with Zarmell? Beware, for she likes them any age."

At that I laughed. "Marli can take care of herself well enough. It is Zarmell who should beware."

Afterward, Sharven asked me to share her cloak, and I agreed out of curiosity. But when we lay down together, no passion rose between us and so we wrapped close for warmth.

Just as sleep was closing in, she whispered, "You are too skinny for me anyway, and too young, only a silverling. In that I am not like Zarmell."

The silverlings are the little fish of the Escuro, only a hand in length and no more than a finger's width. I did not mind, for that night, being a silverling. I smiled and curled against her back for comfort, glad to be far from the sounds of the Gimling. Rocked by the river, I fell asleep in peace.

For the next two days, we struggled up the Morl, often having to leap off and haul the raft by rope through shallow rocky places or past snags. Always the Timmer Mountains looked darker and steeper as we went, and the land around grew ever wilder. Though the sky above us was blue, there was much thunder over the Timmers far ahead. At last we came to a narrow place between rock ledges. There a huge tree had fallen, blocking the way. Try as we would we could not win past it. At last Sharven shrugged and threw up her hands.

"As it must be, Goddess," she said with a laugh. "You must have other plans for us."

And so we turned back the way we had come, but now it was easy. We let the river have its way and only poled when we needed to keep clear of some obstacle. Sharven sang and told stories. My weary body was glad of a chance to rest, but I regretted leaving that wild land. It had called to me, new and exciting, around each bend of the river.

Feeling quite daring one evening, I asked Sharven, "Did you really dance before the Zarn as Zarmell says?"

She grinned at me. "I did indeed, Silverling, but that was long ago. I was very young then and still quite small. I had a dancer's body, if you can believe that now. You could have put both hands around my waist with ease. At that time, I was a great fool and quite puffed up with myself, for men were much taken with me. I thought that to be a measure of my worth.

"I danced not once, but many times before the Zarn. He became quite enamored of me. Though that may seem flattering, it was, in fact, most unpleasant. The Zarn was bald and squat, as much like a toad as like a man. I, in turn, fell in love with the handsome young captain of the Zarn's guards and plainly let him know my desire which, of course, he reciprocated. So we had our moment of love but were quickly caught. The Zarn had spies everywhere. Things did not end well for the captain. It almost cost me my life as well. I was given ample time to cool my passion in a cold stone cell under the palace.

"Others who thought me fair of face and figure, saw me free of that place. I did not wait to repay their kindness with my favors, but fled Maktesh as quickly as I could. Later, I heard those who helped me came to the same end as the captain."

At this she stopped and spit with disgust. "Augh, it is all too ugly. I wish to talk no more of this. It happened in another time to another person. My body has changed, my mind has changed, even my name is different. That young woman who danced before the Zarn is long gone." Sharven quickly turned to asking me questions of Eezore, silencing my further questions with her own.

The first day back on the Escuro, we went slowly, for Sharven had many favorite spots to search out. As there was almost constant thunder and lightning from the direction of the Morl and a strange ominous feeling to the air, I soon grew uneasy and wished her back. But she moved from place to place with her gathering, seemingly untroubled by the signs.

Then quite suddenly, the sky above became a turbulent gray, the wind came up and all around us the light turned sickly green. I jumped up to call Sharven, but already she was paddling fast for the raft.

"I do not like the looks of this, Little One. Give me a hand with the boat."

She sprang on board. As quickly as we could, we lashed down her little boat and stashed away her day's gatherings. As I was bending to fasten a last rope, I heard a roar in back of us, and Sharven shouted, "Cut us loose, or we shall break!"

Without looking behind me I drew my knife and severed the rope that held us anchored. When I turned, I saw a wall of water as high as a house, bearing down on us, roaring and foaming. Terrified, I threw myself flat on the raft, gripping the lashings and expecting that dreadful wave to cover us. Instead, we tilted frightfully as if to turn over, rose up on that rush of water and lurched forward, tossed like a twig on the flood. Only a foot or so of froth and foam washed over us, though if we had not cut loose, we surely would have been smashed apart by the force of the wave. Now we were thrust at terrifying speed straight down the river on a furious head of water.

I kept tight hold and struggled for breath as the water surged around us. Next to me, I felt Sharven also clinging fast to the ropes. If either of us loosed our hold we were dead. Only that power of life which clings beyond hope or reason kept me to the raft, for soon my hands were numb, and then my whole body.

Other things shared that flood with us. Several times I heard the sounds of frightened horses or cattle, or felt their terror, once very close. Sometimes the raft was struck and spun about by logs or

267

perhaps whole trees, but I dared not raise my head to look. My own body was struck more than once by some object. Yet I had no choice but to keep tight hold and endure that battering.

At last, with only the faintest flickering candle of consciousness still left in me, I felt the raft drop below us and heard Sharven say through the rush of water, "We must be at the head of the marsh. It will disperse here." Still I did not dare move, for now we were spun and tossed about at random. When that wild dizzying motion slowed, I cautiously raised my head to look around.

We were in what I took to be a great marsh, though it seemed more like a strangely active lake with the water flowing and surging in all directions. Beyond us mist and rain closed in, hiding the now distant shore.

Sharven was already on her feet, unstrapping the poles. "Up, up, there is work to do!" she shouted to me. "It is a miracle we are still alive. Now we must strive to remain so!"

"But I have never poled wild water," I grumbled, struggling to my feet. My legs bent under me like saplings, and my hands were still numb from holding and rubbed raw from the sawing of the ropes.

"You had never poled at all before this journey. Curse me for a fool that I brought you! I wish I had Annella with me now. Keep us off the rocks and trees, that at least you can do, for it is worth your life. This craft can not take much more battering. I have no wish to try swimming in these waters with only a log to cling to."

For some time we poled in desperate silence, trying to keep clear of what floated with us or rose suddenly through those strange waters. Our only words were when Sharven saw fit to curse me or urge me on, shouting, "Faster, faster, or we shall be caught in it!" or "No, no, you fool, pole on the other side!"

I myself was speechless in my struggle with the flood. We were almost swept into rocks, logs, trees, and other things I could not even name that appeared suddenly out of the grayness of the fog. No sooner was one danger passed than another rushed at us.

The ache in my arms had become a torment almost past endurance when at last Sharven called out, "The tree, pole for that tree!" She had found another rope and managed to snag a branch before we were swept past.

"We are lost," she said as she tied us fast. "No trees grow in the middle of the Escuro. I have tried to follow the swiftest current, but all is a jumble of confusion here. The water runs backward and forward and sideways, giving scant guidance, and we have no sun to show us the way south."

All about us water rushed and swirled in a raging chaos. I could make no sense of the scene. I threw myself down on the deck exhausted while Sharven paced about, cursing and muttering and searching for signs. Suddenly she cried out in anguish, "My hiji! My hiji! My little boat is gone! She is lost in the flood, and I will never find her again." She sounded as bereaved as if a dear friend had perished in the flood.

Lying there bruised and battered, I felt scant sympathy. "By the Goddess, you are lucky to have come through those waters with a whole skin on your back. What is the loss of a little boat compared to that?"

"But she was made for me by old Mishi who is long dead. There will never be another like her."

I did not know if she meant the boat or the boat maker, nor did I care. "Sharven, where are we? Which way do we go now? We must get free of this marsh before dark."

The raft beneath us pulled and tugged at its mooring as if it would spring free, leaping first in one direction then another. It amazed me that Sharven could keep her footing. At last, she came to squat beside me.

"I can see nothing to aid us. When the water is normal, then the way is clear, for the Escuro is the deepest channel through the marsh, but now, what lies about us is like many crossing fingers and no sure way to go." She gave a deep sigh and was silent for a moment, then asked suddenly, "Sairizzia, you are lovers with Tarl and Halli both, are you not?"

I sat up suddenly and said with much anger from the sting of all her insults, "You have cursed me and called me a fool for these last terrible hours and now you want the names of my lovers! What sort of game is this, Sharven? We have barely escaped with our lives!"

"Yes, yes, I have a bad tongue. I promise to keep it reined from now on, but this is no game, Sair. Answer my question."

"Only Tarl," I answered grudgingly.

"And she waits for you at Big Bend?"

I nodded, not understanding and still sharp with anger.

"Good, good. Being lovers gives a strong connection and makes for better mind-sending. You must try to contact her for direction. By the Mother, there is no way I can pole us free of this maze unaided."

"But I have no Kersh."

"Bah, you can not do this and you can not do that. I think you have more powers than you know. I have been told that you can call horses silently and hear voices in your head. Now you must believe in this and try it. What other chance do we have?"

I looked around us and my anger melted. She was right. There was no other way. Signalling for silence, I lay down again and shut my eyes, trying to picture Tarl. I strained to touch her mind. At first, there was nothing but the terrible rush and drag of the water. Then I began to feel a pull toward the left, a strong pull. For a moment I saw Tarl, plainly worried, sitting on Timmer's back. Only that moment, then she was gone in the rush of waters.

"Well?" Sharven asked impatiently.

"Quiet," I said sharply, enjoying my small moment of power. I could not bring Tarl back, but the pull was still to the left. I sat up and pointed, saying, "We must go that way, but only for as long as it seems right. Then we must ask again."

Sharven untied us, and once more I took up my pole. Whenever the pull grew weak, we stopped and I mind-searched our direction again. In this manner, we zigzagged our way across that great flooded marsh until, finally, there was one course that was clearly deeper than the rest. Then we sat numb, exhausted, and silent, letting the river carry us through that drowned landscape.

Suddenly we came around a wide sweep and Sharven shouted, "The bridge is down!"

It was too late. We were driven helplessly against that broken part of it which hung down into the water. It caught us and spun us dangerously about, then almost flung us clear until it fastened tight at the back corner of the raft. We both struggled desperately with our poles and our weight and at last, fought free of it.

I groaned with relief, but Sharven standing next to me at the edge of the raft said spitefully, "What good are you? No river woman would have hooked us so on a bridge."

With a quick snap of my hip, I knocked her into the water before I had time to think. Immediately, I thrust out the pole for her to grab, and with my help she pulled herself on deck, soaked and sputtering.

"Why did you do that, Sair?"

"You cursed me again." Though I answered boldly enough, I was much frightened by my own rashness.

"Yes, so I did," she said mildly. Stripping off her clothes, she began to wring them out and spread them about the deck.

There was a long silence then for I was too embarrassed to speak. At last Sharven said softly, "Well, Silverling, before you think to try your tricks again, I must tell you that I can not swim."

Now I was truly shocked, thinking how easily she might have been swept away and drowned in those fast waters. I apologized to her once and then a second time. When I was starting on a third she stopped me.

"Enough. Maybe next time I will think before I speak, and you before you act. Here, come sit against me, so we may both be comfortable."

For a long while we sat back to back in companionable silence. Then, just as I began to fear that we would be caught afloat by darkness, we were swept around a great bend of the river and into the Hadra camp. Many Hadra ran out shouting to pull us in and bring us ashore. Tarl and Halli crushed me in their arms.

"Sair, Sair, we thought you lost in that great flood!"

"So we were. No doubt would have remained so, had Tarl not hooked us with her mind and hauled us in like a fish on a line."

"We had glimpses of you at moments and with that a little hope. Later, for some time, there was no sign at all. Then, when we found Sharven's little hiji-boat caught in the reeds, we thought you both drowned for sure."

"My boat!" Sharven cried as she scrambled up the shore. "My little hiji, she has come back to me!" There it sat as light and easy on the sand as if no flood had ever touched it. She turned it this way and that, examining it for injury and stroking it like a favored pet, all the while muttering, "So good to see you again, my sweet one. I thought you lost and gone from my life and here you are waiting for me, thank the Goddess. We will made many more trips together, Little One, never fear."

At last Halli led her away by the hand. "You must come and eat Sharven. You need some strength after your great ordeal."

Aside from Tarl, Halli and Nais, most of the women who crowded the shore to meet us were strangers to me, though I thought I recognized among them some of Halli's friends from the Essu. There were Kourmairi as well as Hadra, all greeting us warmly, holding out their hands to steady me up the bank. My legs were bending under me. I had only strength enough at that moment to stumble to the fire. There, many hands wrapped me in cloaks and laid me down. Filled with gratitude for the feel of solid ground under my back, I rested in that welcome warmth. It was there that Sharu found me. She came for reassurance, to rub her head against me and snuff her soft, hot breath into my ear.

While the Hadra celebrated our safe arrival, I lay too weary even to raise my head, but Sharven seemed in fine spirits. She sat by the fire telling of our perils with much elaboration and suspenseful detail. Shamelessly she made me the hero of the story, how I had cut us loose just in time, how valiantly I had poled in spite of her insults, how I had guided us through the flooded swamp with the aid of my Kersh. Altogether and in every way she said how brave I was and swore she would have been dead many times without my help. She even told of getting tangled in the bridge, and how I had pushed her in the water and reclaimed her with a pole. At that, the Hadra clapped and cheered and laughed uproariously, Sharven along with them. Lying there I though, not for the first time, what strange creatures these women were that I had come to live among.

* * *

AFTERNOTES

Hiji — A small boat for herb-gathering, made of oiled cloth stretched tightly over a frame of bent willow. It is shaped like the shell of a hiji nut, has room for one person only and is light enough to be carried in one hand. These boats are traditionally made by women who pass the skill on from mother to daughter. They are only used by women and much loved and valued by their owners.

PART 8

ZELINDAR

That next morning I was wakened by music so loud and shrill it pained my ears. I looked about bewildered, but could find no source for it. None around me were plying tools nor playing instruments. Then a tiny black toad, no bigger than thumb joint, hopped across my chest. Startled, I sat up to dislodge it, but not before it made a sharp trill. Now, at a glance, I saw a multitude of such tiny black toads. They were jumping all along the shore and even in our camp, the source, no doubt, of that great volume of sound that had pulled me unwilling from my sleep. I sat holding my ears and groaning. There was a deep ache all through my body. The flood had left me bruised and battered as if I had drunk too much yors or been thoroughly beaten on with sticks.

"What are they?" I called out to Halli when I saw her tip-toeing about, trying not to crush them.

"The ewee, the flood toads," she called back. "They come out for a little time after the flood waters go down, then disappear and are not seen again till the next flood."

Wanting no more encounters with the toads, I slipped out of my cloak and withdrew up the bank to the wood's edge, going as carefully as I could. From there I watched with some amusement. The ewee were everywhere along the shore, leaping and mating frantically and dying in the sun, so that the Hadra, with their great horror of harming living things, could scarce move about. Little progress was made toward breaking camp. At last, Halli took up Sharven's double flute. Picking her way upriver, she played a tune even shriller and louder than the ewee themselves.

Immediately the toads began to leave us, leaping over each other and rushing up the shore in a great crush. Where Halli stopped, they gathered around her as if she herself were the Queen Ewee. There they darkened the sand and with their loud trills strove to match the volume of the flute. The Hadra, able to move about again, clapped and shouted and roared approval.

When Halli returned she was much teased as "The Mother Toad"* which to the Hadra had some meaning I could not catch. At this she grinned and bowed, prancing about and thrusting out her belly as if already filled with child.

Now that we were free to pack, we went about it speedily. Even so, it took much time to gather up and fold away all that had been laid out to dry after the flood. Sharven even hung up some of her newly gathered herbs to air, for by some miracle not all of her sacks and safe-boxes had been lost to the Escuro. Two river-women I did not know, set to helping her repair the raft. In a few days, when the flood had receded, they planned to travel on with her to Zelindar, perhaps stopping along the way to do some trading. For myself, nothing could have induced me to set foot on that raft again or even venture too near the rush of the river. After her mockery the night before, I chose to stay well clear of Sharven, but as I bent to stuff my pack, she came and stood by me unnoticed.

"Well, Sair, how goes it with you this morning? Do your arms still ache from poling the flood? Are you quite recovered from our adventures?"

I looked up with a start and said angrily, "Sharven, why did you speak such nonsense of me before the fire? Was it to shame and embarrass me?"

"Not at all, Fingerling. There was much truth in all I said, more perhaps than I care to acknowledge. If ever you fancy a raft trip again, Sairizzia, I would truly be happy for your company."

"First you would have to learn to swim or learn to keep silent," I answered sullenly.

"Perhaps both, Sairizzia. Perhaps you shall teach me."

"I might teach you to swim, Sharven, but as to silence, someone with more patience than I must teach you that."

She laughed, not at all put out by my bad humor. "Swimming will be enough then. At my age it is hard to learn two things at once, especially something as difficult as silence."

With sudden shame I remembered my hasty action from which she might well have drowned and answered her seriously. "It is too dangerous to pole a raft and not know how to swim. I would be glad to teach you."

"So you would be the teacher this time, and I the student. Well enough, Sair. You will have your chance to even the weights." At that we both laughed. Then we hugged each other with good will and so made our peace.

While helping with some small task of departure, I reached for my knife. The sheath was empty. Then I remembered how that first terrible wave had snatched it from my hand. This time it was surely lost. The river would not likely bring it back to me as it had brought back Sharven's little boat. Ah well, as it must be. It had already saved me twice over. Perhaps Tarl would teach me how to make another.

It was well after midday before all was set to rights and packed away again. We were a large and noisy troop that rode for Zelindar that day, Kourmairi river-women as well as Hadra and many dogs and extra horses, too. Sharven looked up from her raft mending to wave and shout her good-byes from the shore.

275

With Tarl and Halli, I road out ahead and my good humor returned. Once more I felt myself part of the Hadra. The sun dazzled and all shone clean after the flood rains. It was good to ride on solid ground again and leave behind the mud-darkened waters of the Escuro, with its burden of debris and strange bloated forms.

* * *

Two nights we spent on the road. On the last day, I watched with interest the changes in the vegetation as we went through wide wooded valleys. There the earth lay about us peaceful and untroubled, so different from the lands across the line on the way to Eezore. I thought how good it was that in all that fair land, there were no armed men to make the roads dangerous and plague the farmers.

Catching my thoughts, Tarl said aloud, "It is the Hadra keep it so." She spoke with such fierce pride, I had to smile. Then I remembered that Tarl herself would not again be one to keep the safety of the line.

As the day wore on the hills flattened. At last, we rode for a time over a stretch of hot flatlands, almost like desert, though in the far distance I could see the land rising again. Under the weight of that heat, we went mostly silent, but when the hills ahead began to green, Halli, riding next to me, said joyously, "Zelindar herself lies before us in those first hills." Soon I began to see glimpses of white among the green. The land around us turned fertile again. We passed through field after field of Tarmar, stretching out on either side of the road, red-gold with ripening. As the road began to rise and the land grew hillier, these fields gave way to orchards and rolling pastures with many horses grazing. Far off to the right, I could hear the booming of the ocean.

By late afternoon the city was clearly visible, topping two hills with its white domes and spreading down the sides in the direction of the bay. I remembered Zarmell saying, "She sits like two big white nipples on the green breasts of the hills." The bay was curving in on one side of us, blue-purple in the slanting light, and the river lay silver on the other. Before us rose the splendor of Zelindar, much as Yima had shown it to me in my time of healing.

/Our city, the city of the Hadra,/ I heard Halli thinking. I could feel the excitement mounting, and the horses quickened to a fast trot.

There seemed no sure way to know where Zelindar began for there were no walls there and no gates, as well as no guards to shout orders and block the way. The change was gradual with the buildings growing thicker on either side, and the orchards more sparse, though not vanishing altogether. Before us the road branched out like many fingers which turned into streets.

From where the city sat atop those hills, any who advanced upon her, whether friend or foe, could be seen well before they reached her streets. When we came within sight, we raised our banners and rode four or five abreast, advancing in waves of fluttering color. Tarl named for me the different banners: of Osen, Ishlair, Yhaghar, and the Kourmairi city of Mishghall, as well as two Kourmairi settlements. It gave me pleasure to see our own flags of Semasi and North Yarmald flying among them. Zelindar must certainly have been aware of our arrival, for soon we were greeted by a whole troupe of young women, mostly Halli's sisters and her friends. They hugged her and petted her, rubbing her belly for Mother's Luck. Then talking excitedly about the baby, the winter and all their plans, they swept her away from us along with Nais, without a backward glance.

Tarl shook her head as she watched them leave. "All my daughters," she said forcefully, "will be born in Semasi." I looked at her with some surprise, never having thought to see Tarl slowed and swollen with child. Suddenly with a shiver, I remembered the bargain I, myself, had made with Mica.

Soon after Halli's departure, the others scattered, too, going their different ways in the city, until only Tarl and I were left together. Tarl had promised to be my guide in Zelindar, at least at the start and not abandon me as she had at the Essu.

The city of Zelindar was different from the city of Eezore in every imaginable way. First of all, there were no men, not anywhere in that city and no guards to be fearful of. Then, also, there seemed to be no grand avenues and no filthy side alleys, either. All looked clean and loved but nothing had been laid out straight or true. The stone-cobbled streets went up steep and narrow, winding in all directions with charming randomness. Everywhere, up and down the hillside, were terraced gardens of fall flowers and vegetables, all growing together in bright profusion.

I noticed a great variety of trees here, more than I had ever seen together in one place. "They have been collected from the far reaches of Yarmald and some from Garmishair as well," Tarl told me with pride. Even at this late season many were still flowering, and in the parks and circles, fountains bubbled and pools sparkled. All this gave the effect of a giant garden in which the buildings, mostly white stone domes, were set as ornaments. Here the large public buildings seemed impressive for their beauty rather than for a display of massive power, as in Eezore. Much care and skill had been put to their decoration with murals and carvings and inlays of colored stone. The city itself seemed comfortably cool and shady after the heat of the plains. I felt at ease there, but our horses were restless and fretful, feeling trapped in those narrow winding streets.

The women of Zelindar were a great surprise to me. Being used to the Hadra of the back country, I was unprepared for the Hadra of town. Except for their dark skin, they seemed to me much like the women of Eezore dressed in their town clothes—though some were still rough-dressed for work. Tarl laughed at my thoughts.

"These are the 'Zinda', the Hadra of Zelindar. They think themselves quite fine and consider us savages. They call us the wild ones, the 'Meerholt'*, and say that we eat with our hands and wipe them on our pants. They think we sleep with our horses instead of each other."

I smiled, for surely I had seen more fingers than forks since coming to Semasi. As for pants, I pictured Tarl as I had first caught sight of her on the road. Now I understood the cry of "Meerholt, Meerholt" I had heard several times as we rode. It was to announce our arrival. Indeed, I had caught some stares and glances, but they seemed only curious, not unfriendly—certainly not dangerous as they had been in Eezore.

We passed many of Tarl's friends on the way. Names were shouted and greetings exchanged while Timmer tossed his head and snorted. When we reached, at last, the house that Tarl had chosen to be that night's lodging, she told me we must send our horses back to graze on the plains.

"There is no food for them in the city. All the good pasturage is at the edges. Besides, it is forbidden to ride much further as the streets become too narrow. Past this point only those horses that help us in our work are allowed. Otherwise, everyone goes on foot, even the wild Meerholt who are married to their horses." The horses that had been so uneasy in the city, were now reluctant to leave us and turned back several times to snuff and rub against us. At last Tarl shouted at them, and they went.

With Tarl's friends we sat up that night until almost dawn, laughing and talking and smoking jol, exchanging news and gossip, telling of the war and the return to Eezore and the meeting with the Zarn. With each new arrival, I had to tell my story one more time. I talked my voice to hoarseness that night.

The next day, when we could finally rise, we went first to the archives to deliver Seronis' manuscript into the hands of the Archive Keeper. The archives were housed with the library in the largest Zildorn in Zelindar, a great white stone dome that crowned the second hill. The hill itself was steep, but once at the library there was no long forbidding flight of stairs to be surmounted. Instead, we stepped directly from the street through a graceful archway into an inner courtyard.

Jorkal, the archive keeper, rushed to greet us as if she had anticipated our arrival. I was surprised to see a young woman of near my age, for I had expected someone much older and more serious. With a shout she hugged Tarl and swung her about. Then, as I stood feeling estranged and awkward, she hugged me, also. The sweetness of perfume was in her hair, and that, along with the steep climb, made me so dizzy that I was obliged to lean on a column for support. When Tarl handed her the manuscript, Jorkal pressed it against her breast with both hands saying, 'Seronis' journey, written and delivered safe to us. What a great gift for the archives." Tarl entrusted her with the letter also, for it seemed Jorkal was neighbor to Seronis's family. Then she and Tarl fell to talking, and I was free to look about me.

There were more books there than I had ever seen, more books than in the Zildorn of Semasi and my father's library combined, as well as paintings, statues, and carvings on the walls, and thick multicolored tapestries that hung from the edge of the curved ceiling down to the floor. Some windows faced out on a bay, bright with boats, and others faced the Escuro and the hills. All about the room stood clay pots, filled with flowering plants. Others hung by

279

hooks from the ceiling. It seemed that a garden bloomed inside the walls.

Not knowing which books were permitted me, I wandered about delighted, looking at it all until Jorkal came to help. Then, finding little was forbidden, I grew greedy for everything I saw. Tarl soon felt restless and said she would come for me later.

The day passed far too quickly as I nibbled and sampled in that vast collection of knowledge, always with help and advice from Jorkal. In Semasi I had forgotten the pleasure of study for the joys of physical life. Now the passions of the mind returned to me.

When Tarl came, I was not ready to leave, but she said, "You can come back tomorrow, Sair. Now, we must go to see my mother. I have already sent word that we will be there soon." From the way she spoke, I could tell she thought it no great pleasure. In Semasi she seldom spoke of her mother and when she did, it was with some pain.

* * *

Monal's house, where she lived with her companion and her two bond-daughters, was a square stone structure, built into a steep hillside with many terraces and balconies. Tarl told me Monal was alone there for the moment since the others were away in the south. As we climbed the hill, I saw her standing in her doorway, watching — a solid woman dressed in a long blue tunic, who much resembled Tarl in face. She did not call out or rush to meet us. Her greeting, though polite enough, was formal with little warmth in it. It took no Hadra Kersh to sense her disapproval, not only of Tarl, but of myself as well. Mother and daughter, as they hugged, seemed to draw away from each other and their faces hardened. Even at that moment the resemblance was very close.

In silence we followed Monal to the lower terrace. There she seated us under a spreading tanquil tree and poured three mugs of simpi from a big pitcher. The tanquil tree was in full bloom of red and orange, its long branches arching over us like a flowered ceiling. The whole terrace was edged with beds of bright blossoms. The warmth of all these colors was strange contrast, indeed, to the coolness between us. Tarl seemed strained and nervous, but she spoke proudly of Semasi and all that was being done there. In this, she found scant support or encouragement from her mother. As for me, my tongue was frozen in my mouth. I added not one word. It was struggle enough just to sip my simpi without choking.

When Tarl paused, Monal leaned forward suddenly and said, "Semasi, Semasi. Why is it always Semasi? Is Zelindar not beautiful enough for you?"

Tarl nodded, then shook her head. I was amazed to see her close to tears. "Zelindar is very beautiful indeed, and I love it. It is always in my heart, the flower of our lives, but I cannot live here, Mother. It is too fixed. All has been decided, everything already set and solved. I must live in a place that is taking shape." Tarl got up and began to pace restlessly about the terrace, shaking her head. "There is enough and more than enough of everything here but space."

"Those sound like Quadra's words. I see that woman's influence in this."

"Leave Quadra be, Mother. I can speak well enough for myself." There was an edge of anger in Tarl's voice.

"And what will you do, Daughter," Monal asked mockingly, "if Semasi becomes a city like Zelindar?"

"Be happy for our success, but for myself, I would go further north and settle in a new place by the sea. Some, like Seronis and Lar, would come with me." I noticed with pain that my name was not mentioned. Yet I thought it true. Semasi was wild enough for me.

Monal set down her cup with such force it cracked. "Tarl, you are a wild thing, a prowling wolf! Even the name you took means wolf in the old tongue."

"And so it must be a good name for me!" Tarl said abruptly and turned away.

Monal shouted angrily at her back. "Why should my only daughter choose to be a Meerholt in the north? What have I done for such a fate?"

"Mother, do not give me the burden of all the children you might have had. You could have born other daughters who would have chosen to be city-bound here with you."

"I could have none after you." At that Tarl went to stand at the far edge of the terrace. From there she could look down the long hill to the sea itself.

281

It pained me to see Tarl treated so by her mother, as if she were a wayward child, not a grown woman ruled by her own will. In Semasi, I was used to seeing her met with pride and affection. I remembered Jephra saying, "She is one of our very best." Here in the city, she seemed to me tamed and diminished, like a wild horse in a fenced-in place. I would have been glad to have her away from there that very day, but we had agreed to stay until the Festival-of-Lights*.

When Monal saw that Tarl would not answer more, she turned to me. "Well, Sair, so you are the Neshtair I have heard so much talk of. I am told you lived as a highborn Shokarn in Eezore. There must have been comfort enough for you there. Tell me, why did you come to a hard place like Semasi?"

There was no kindly curiosity in her voice, only a dry mockery, so I kept silent and sent her strong mind-pictures of that night in the barracks. It pleased me to see her recoil. She did not speak for some time, but then she said in that same tone, "Why have you formed this strange attachment to my daughter? Does it not seem peculiar to you for Hadra and Shokarn to be lovers?"

At that I jumped to my feet, angry now on my own behalf. "Monal, do not question me like a river-woman questioning her son's future bride. I am not planning to marry Tarl, nor she me." I went to join Tarl at the edge of the terrace to show I would not be questioned more.

Monal called after me, "Well, I see you have the nairse of the Meerholt and their good manners as well." Then she picked up the fragments of her cup and went inside. So ended that day's visit.

* * *

Later that night as Tarl and I sat alone on the roof of her friend's house, looking down on the lights of Zelindar, she asked, "Will you be going back to the library tomorrow?"

This seemed an innocent enough question. I answered with great enthusiasm that I could return each day for a month and still there would be more to learn and see. I was going on in this way, praising the virtues of the library, when Tarl interrupted me in a voice so like her mother's it chilled my heart. "I, myself, might be more taken with the wonders of the library if I knew how to read."

"Oh, Tarl, I had forgotten you could not read. Let me teach you. I could easily do so. Then all the wonders and mysteries of those books would lie open to you, too."

"The world around is full of wonders. I have only to look about me. There is no need to find it in the pages of a book." She spoke with contempt but there was fear under it, as if she were a wild animal, and I had offered to build her a fancy cage.

I rushed on like a fool, not mindful of the signs, "But Tarl, think on it, you may someday be Councillor in Semasi. There is so much you will need to know. It is not right for you to have no skill at reading and be ignorant of books."

At that she jumped to her feet and stood looking at me for a long while, though in that dim light I could not read her face. At last, she said coldly, "I have no wish to be Councillor of Semasi and no need of a Neshtair to advise me in the doing of it." With those words, she turned in anger and did not come back that night.

After she left, I stretched out my cloak on the roof. For all my weariness I could not sleep. I lay there wakeful a long time, afraid that this might mean some terrible rift between us. But when Tarl returned in the early morning, she was gentle and contrite, in a quite different mood than when she left.

"Forgive me my rudeness, Sair. I am perhaps more like my mother than I care to think. What you said was true, but it frightened me. I had to go away and think on it."

"Tarl, none can force you to be Councillor. It will only happen when and as you yourself are ready. It may be you will welcome it by then."

"And perhaps, after all, I shall need a Neshtair to advise me." She smiled then and it seemed like a sunrise to me. "Will you still teach me to read, Sair? Councillor or not, I would be glad to discover what gives you such joy in books."

"Gladly, Tarl, gladly, as soon as you want, as soon as we are home again."

Tarl went to stand at the edge of the roof and stretched out her arms as if to fly. "I once asked Quadra if it was lonely being Councillor. She told me yes, and that it was especially lonely when there seemed none to follow after. Then she turned and fastened me with that look of hers and said, 'Kedris is the child of my body and I have much love for her, but you, Tarl, you are the child of my heart. You are my younger self reborn, my spirit twin, my daughter of choice.' All this, of course, warmed my heart, but when she added, 'I hope someday to see you Councillor in Semasi in my place,' I had a chill of fear. Her words felt like a great trap around me. When you spoke last night, it seemed like that trap closing. But you are right, Sair, none can force me."

Later, Tarl went down into the street to greet some friends, and I sat alone looking out over the city. It was not Yima I thought of at that moment, though I had thought of her often since coming to Zelindar. It was Old Marl. I felt her to be sitting beside me, her ancient body and her terrible old scars, sitting there looking down on a free city of free women, most of her own color, women who could never be touched by the slaver's hand.

"Marl," I whispered, "Marl, are you here?"

* * *

AFTERNOTES

The Mother Toad — This is another name for Gorma, Goddess of conception, pregnancy and childbirth. She is also considered the protector of mothers and motherhood and is often depicted as a great toad with her small human children nestled about her.

Meerholt — Derived from the Asharhan word for horse, it is used both affectionately and derisively by the Hadra of Zelindar when speaking of the Hadra of the northern settlements.

The Festival-of-Lights — The celebration at the turning of the year, for the return of light and warmth. Its origins may be northern, perhaps even Shokarn, for Zelindar does not suffer much from cold and darkness in the winter. This festival resembles the celebration of Lightsturn in Eezore, one of the few times when all casts mingle freely on the streets of that city.

PART 9

FESTIVAL-OF-LIGHTS

I was curious about that strange word Monal had flung at me. As I could get no clear answer from Tarl, I asked as many Hadra as I could the meaning of "nairse" and got as many answers. At last, I went to look in the big Book-of-Words at the library. "Nairse," indeed, had many meanings: strength, hardness, lack of care for manners, resilience, rudeness, obstinacy, nerve, courage, insolence, and more I could not understand. It seemed Monal had intended on insult and paid me half a compliment as well.

Being in the library reawakened my curiosity. I asked Jorkal what could be learned there of the Asharha, thinking that surely among all those books I would find some answers.

She looked at me sadly and shook her head. "Sair, I am sorry. The Book of the Asharha is in the locked case and cannot be given to a first-year Neshtair. Little else has been written. How is it you know of the Asharha?"

"From Seronis. It is all in her account."

"Ah, yes, Seronis. Seronis has been fire-touched. Who would have believed it of her. She seems a most unlikely one. But she should not talk so freely."

I could have wept with frustration to have a book so close within my reach, and yet forbidden. Again I met with that strange barrier of silence, for Jorkal would speak no more of the Asharha, turning aside all my questions. But she told me much else that day, talking for hours and neglecting her other duties. She poured us both a cup of yima tea and drew me to the wide stone sill of an arched window that overlooked the city and the bay. There I leaned back into some cushions, feeling a sense of ease and leisure I never knew in Semasi, for in Semasi leisure is only a pause before more work.

Jorkal herself seemed like a library with all she knew. I marveled at that in one so young, for we seemed almost of an age. "Have you read all these books, Jorkal?" I asked with admiration and a little envy.

"No, no, not all," she said laughing. "That would take a lifetime. Not all, but many. When I was a child my bond-mother was keeper here for some years, so the library became my other home and the books my friends. I vowed that I myself would be keeper when I came of age to do so."

"How long have you been here? Will you always be Keeper-of-the-Archives?"

"Oh, no, that is not how we do. I am serving the last part of my second three-year and training the next keeper. When that is over I plan to go to sea. There are Hadra ships now that go, not just up and down the coast of Yarmald and around the mainland, but out to islands far from our coast and even in search of other lands. We are charting the oceans, Sair. I want to go on such a trip, see all there is to see and help make the maps and charts that will be part of our record here."

The lure of far places burned in her eyes and made her hands tremble, but I wondered what she could find elsewhere as much to Hadra liking as Yarmald. I had my own painful personal knowledge of other places, but kept my silence, seeing how the excitement flushed her face and made her eyes shine.

"I would record it all as Seronis has done, writing my own account for our archives. Then I may do another three-year here as I do love this place and know it well."

In response to my many questions, she told me some of the history of Zelindar, how and when it was built, and how, before the Redline was completed it was burned once by the Zarn's army. Even the library itself was burned, though the books had been secreted away. Finally, with a sigh, she rose and went to fetch some books for me saying, "It is better told here by others. I cannot in these few hours weave for you the whole history of Zelindar and of the Hadra."*

Then she in turn began to ask me questions of myself, of Eezore, of my stay in Semasi, questions that followed questions with a sharp intelligence, like a wolf tracking down a hare. No one had ever questioned me with such purpose. I grew so weary the streets of Eezore swam before my eyes mixed with scenes of sea serpents and floods and women riding and always the sea cliffs of Semasi.

"Enough, Jorkal," I said at last. "I can speak no more. Do not try to wring water out of a rock."

She took both my hands in hers saying, "Then you must promise to write it all for our archives just as you have told it to me. We need a record of the Neshtair that have come among us, for that, too, is part of our history."

"No, Jorkal," I said quickly, "I do not think I can. I am no writer." I felt a little hurt, thinking that perhaps her friendliness had only been part of her work.

"But you must." She squeezed my hands harder and said laughing, "You must swear by the Goddess to put it all on paper just as you have told it here, or I will not let you go."

"Jorkal, that is no threat at all," I answered teasing. "You could hold me here forever if you cared to."

She grew quite serious then and fixed me with her eyes. "Sair, the Hadra have saved your life and loved you and sheltered you. Do this one thing for us." Just then her name was called. As she got up to go she leaned forward and kissed me lightly on the mouth.

* * *

As I sat leafing through the books Jorkal had left me, I felt a burning between my eyes. It was as if someone had pressed a hot thumb to the center of my forehead. Looking up with a start, I saw an old woman standing at the next table, observing me intently. She

287

was the darkest person I had ever seen with hair shorn so short, it seemed newly grown from shaving. Her clothes were random and ill-fitting, a raggletag such as clowns wear in Eezore. But there was no humor in her black eyes that stared straight through mine, into my very soul.

"So, you are Sair," she said at last. "I hear you can read minds, call horses, guide yourself through the flood waters on the current of a lover's thoughts and have even felled two guards with no weapons. That is more power than I have ever encountered in a first generation Neshtair. And who knows how much more lies hidden and untapped. Such untaught power loose in Yarmald is a danger to us all. Also, it could be put to far better use if trained. I would like to do this training. Come to me in the spring, Sairizzia, and I will work with you."

I was so compelled by the great force and power of her stare that I said instantly, "I would come now, Mother."

"No," she answered with impatience. "I have else to do these next months. Come in the spring. Then you will have been Neshtair one full turn of the seasons, and I will feel more assured of your true intent. I have little enough time left and no time at all to waste on those who will not stay. Besides, such knowledge is dangerous if taken back to Eezore."

I wanted to shout that never, never would I go back to Eezore, but some flash of light hurt my eyes and made me glance away. When I looked back the old woman had vanished clear away as if she had never been. I stared about, bewildered. How was I to find her? I did not know where she lived, or even how she was called. Perhaps that was the first test of my purpose.

When I went to ask Jorkal, she knew instantly who I meant. "Ah, yes, that is Anana. She lives nowhere and everywhere, but it matters not. When you come back in the spring, she will find you. She is one of the old ones, one of the last. She was a babe at breast when the Redline was first laid down. To have sought you out she must have much faith in your powers. You will be well taught, Sair, better even than many Hadra."

"As to faith in my powers, she said that untrained I was a danger to all Yarmald," I replied with some bitterness.

"Ah, well, Anana is not known for her politeness or her gentle manners. But you are lucky, Sair. She chooses few. In her hands you will learn all that is in you to learn. She will work you hard, drawing from you even your secret powers—though sometimes she will drive you to the edge of pain. No, not sometimes, often. She was my teacher long ago. If you can learn to bare the pain, it will be well worth it, but seek the gentleness you need in other places. And, believe me, Sister, if you become her pupil, you will need some gentleness in your life." She laid her hand softly on my arm, and I felt a message there.

Later, by accident, I found this description in one of the books I was perusing: "The anana: a small snake of bright green coloring whose bite is seldom fatal, but always painful. After the pain has subsided, the venom is said to cause visions of great intensity and unnaturally bright colors. In former times, witches were said to prize these snakes for the visions, seeking their bite and sometimes keeping them as companions. They are rare now for during the time of the witch-kills the Zarn's men hunted them almost to extinction."

So when the season turned I was to present myself to the Anana of Zelindar, suffer her painful bite and find my own visions. It would be a most interesting spring. It seemed I was to be a scholar again, but to a very different tutor. And I knew it was not just my apprenticeship to Anana that would draw me back. It was my bond with Jorkal, as well. Something in our spirits met and twined. I thought we had need to study more than books together, but that lay ahead in another season.

When I turned the page I saw a picture of a jewel-green snake, coiled and ready to strike. Its brilliant red eye stared up at me.

* * *

After our first ill-meeting with Monal, we did not see her much, staying more often with some friends of Tarl's. But as we had left our packs with her, we went back one evening to fetch some of our belongings. Both of us, I think, were glad to find her out.

Filled with curiosity, I prowled about the house, for I had scarcely seen it. It seemed full of finery. From some mad whim I called out, "Tarl, just this once, dress up for me. It would please me to see you in pretty clothes."

"What?" she answered with indignation. "Should I become a muirlla, a woman's woman, to please your fancy?"

I thought I had made some grave error, but while I was searching through my pack for a fresh tunic she did as I asked, borrowing her mother's clothes. When she stepped before me I was speechless. She was dressed in a long robe of soft birds-wing green with gold edging. Her dark hair, she had brushed loose from its braids, so that it stood out in tiny waves all about her head and face. Clipped in her hair and holding back some part of it, was a triple fish ornament of blue, green and purple in a gold setting. If the Goddess herself had appeared before me at that moment, I could scarce have been more surprised.

"Well," Tarl said with amusement as I was silent. I could not find my voice to answer. "Well, Sair, have you nothing to say?" On impulse I dropped to my knee and kissed her hand. At that she burst out laughing. "I see that all it takes is a few borrowed clothes to make a slave of you."

At that I jumped to my feet ready to fight, but Tarl backed away and held up her hands, saying quickly, "No wrestling, Sister. After all, I am in my mother's best. She would not be pleased. Come, let us go out and show my mother's Zinda friends how her Meerholt brat would look if she were civilized."

Before we left, I put on my new shirt that Tizzel had woven. Tarl added a few items to my costume so I would give the appearance of being town-bred and not "disgrace her." Then, arm in arm we strolled in the evening streets of Zelindar, looking like two proper Zinda instead of wild Meerholt from the north. There was some teasing banter from her mother's friends, and some from Tarl's, as well, but when I saw the admiration in others' eyes I must confess it pleased me.

When we re-entered the house, Tarl caught my arm. "So, you still think me beautiful, Sair?" I nodded eagerly. "Good. I was afraid that from too much seeing, I might have become ugly in your eyes."

This surprised me, for I had never known her to care. "Tarl, it was like a gift to see you go dressed so in the streets of Zelindar."

With a sudden change of mood, Tarl looked away and said quickly, "That may be, but now it is time for other things." Then she began to strip off those fine garments saying, "These are not mine. They are only borrowed. Their beauty also is borrowed.

What is mine is underneath and does not change with fashion, only with time." She put everything away with great care, exactly as she found it, not at all as she treated her own clothes.

When, at last, she stood naked before me, even the hair clasp gone, I thought I liked her best with no clothes at all. She held her body very straight and still as if presenting herself for my eyes, but when I moved to touch her she held up her hand to distance me.

"I can be Zinda for an evening, but at heart I am a Meerholt. That will never change, Sair. Do not ask me to dress that way again."

Her tone frightened me. I felt a catch in my heart as if a sword had come down between us and thought she would not let me touch her. But then she reached out her arms. When we came together, we were both trembling.

There had been little privacy for us since coming to Zelindar, so we made full advantage of this time alone. I followed Tarl up to the roof of Monal's house. There she pushed me down, almost roughly and I threw my body open to her loving. She descended on me with mouth and fingers and so tormented me with pleasure that I cried out and tossed and struggled under her, but with joy, not fear or pain. There was something fierce, even cruel, in her touch, punishing me perhaps for making a Zinda of her for those hours. I did not care, but took willingly whatever she chose to give.

Later, when we lay still together between the stars and the lights of Zelindar, she said softly, "Little Sister, it seems you are truly cured."

At those words, I felt a sudden twist of pain in my heart. Unable to speak, I pulled away from her and sat up. For a long while I stayed silent, staring down at that city where Hadra could walk free and unhampered through their own streets, even in the dark of night. They carried no such memories as mine, of that I was sure.

Several times I tried to answer. At last I shook my head and said slowly, "No, Tarl, it is not a thing one can be cured of like an illness. Instead, it is a thing one can, with great effort, learn to live past." Tarl said nothing, but when I lay down again, she pulled me to her and closed her arms tight about me.

* * *

For some part of each day I went to the library. For the rest I wandered about the city with Tarl, sampling its wonders. It amazed me to see a whole city with no guards or prisons and no sign of such restraints.

"How do the Hadra keep order if there are no guards?"

Tarl laughed at me. "What is the use of guards? You cannot use force against those who cannot be forced."

"But how can any be made to comply?"

"We have to shape our ways of governance in accordance to our powers. The Hadra do what is needed of their own will. It is no different here than in Semasi."

I asked no more questions of that nature, but enjoyed the beauty and freedom of those streets. For myself, I tried to observe how things were done.

We went often to the harbor and spent much time on the docks. Tarl wished to question the boat builders, thinking that boats would soon be needed in Semasi. I was quite taken with boats and all that pertained to them. I had never seen any in my time of growing up in Eezore, but had read of them in my father's books. I touched and examined everything, running my hands over the fine wood and asking so many questions of my own that it must have grown weaisome to those who worked there. When a friend of Tarl's came to take us for a sail in the harbor, then I knew myself truly Goddess-blessed. Even so I had my moment of fear when faced with water again. My last turn with it had not been kind.

There was a good wind. We went like a grey kiri, skimming the water with the salt foam in our faces. The sails snapped and billowed overhead. Schools of fish leapt before the boat and vanished back into the waves. I learned when to lean and when not to and how to keep my head clear of the swinging boom. I watched with interest the woman at the tiller, thinking I would like to learn the skill of it myself. There were other boats sailing the harbor that day, but none seemed as fine or fast to me. I vowed to myself that someday I would have my own, exactly like it.

Together, we explored markets and parks and eating places until I was in a daze of new impressions, but always I felt a restlessness in Tarl. "I am too much like Quadra," she would say. "However much I admire the Hadra, who have built all this, I cannot stay here long. My spirit aches to ride free again. If not for the Festival-of-Lights,

I would leave tomorrow." I knew the lack of bonding with her mother also pained her deeply, though she seldom spoke of it.

One night we came in quietly hoping Monal would be asleep. But she was sitting up by the dim light of one candle. She looked softer somehow and in pain. I saw Tarl start on seeing her mother and prepare to slip quickly by, but Monal put out her hand.

"Daughter, I have been sitting here alone, thinking some deep troubling thoughts this night. Much of it concerns what passes between you and me." She looked away, seeming about to cry and said sadly, "Tarl, it grieves me how we quarrel, when I want only to love you. When you are far away I think of many kind and loving things to say, but when you are here in the flesh, I only remember my anger at your absence. Then it is very different words that fall between us. I long for a way to mend this wound."

"I, too," Tarl said quickly and went to kneel by her mother's chair. "It is not to harm you, Monal, that I am in Semasi, but from my own true spirit. I have a need to live at the edge of things. That is who I am."

"Then let me love who you are for while you are here." Monal put her arm across Tarl's shoulders. "Do you still play the ferl? For now, music might do us better than words."

Tarl nodded and went to get the instrument. I was surprised, for never had she played in Semasi or even spoken of it. I slipped away then, knowing they had need of time together. Later, I fell asleep on the roof, hearing music rising from below.

The next morning on waking, Tarl glowed as from some inner light. "Monal has promised to visit Semasi in the spring as soon as the roads re-open. Perhaps Kassim, my bond-mother will come, too, and my bond-sisters, as well."

Mother and daughter smiled at each other across the table. It was the first breakfast we had all three made together. Afterward Monal even had a hug for me, though it was stiff and awkward.

* * *

In Zelindar, the Festival-of-Lights is held at the dark of the moon. It was for this we had waited. All that day, Hadra went to the public baths for purification. They also spent some time in a Kielness*, a house of visions, of which there were several in the city, but I was told I could not enter until my first-year was up. It seemed I had met again with one of those small barriers that let me know I would never truly be a Hadra.

By dusk all had gone home to dress. Monal offered each of us the loan of a long robe, such as was fitting for the festival. She even helped us dress, commenting, advising and making other offerings if something seemed unsuitable. At last, after many changes, I was robed in silver-blue, Tarl in white with a finework of gold thread and Monal in light lavender of a shade as pale as a moonmoth's wings. We none of us wore shoes or sandals, as all went barefooted on that night to keep touch with the earth. For the purpose of reflecting light, we decked ourselves with as much crystal and silver as we could find room for. Then Monal took the charcoal paste and darkened our eyelids. After that, we went to make ready our lights. By then I was trembling with excitement.

When it was quite dark, the bells were rung. All house lights and street lights were extinguished. From all over Zelindar, Hadra came carrying candles, torches and lamps. Lines of light wound down the streets of the city. The Hadra walked in silence this time with no drums or flutes or songs. Not even speaking, we went with only the flickering of lights and the soft sounds of steps. It was as if we were small streams of light flowing into rivers as we converged into larger and larger streets. Those rivers of light then flowed on toward the sea, until at last we all assembled in an arc of brightness at the shore of the bay.

There the lights were fastened to tiny rafts of thonwood and floated out to sea. Never had I heard the Hadra so quiet for so long. It was not until the very last light was floating that the singing began, the death chant sung in mourning for the old year, and afterward, a blessing-song for a safe turning to the new. The lights rose and fell with the swell, separating and converging, reflecting in the water so that the bay itself seemed afire. Still there were no shouts or cheers. After some time of silence, each Hadra bowed, saying softly, "As it must be." Then they turned to leave, yet even going back to their homes, they did not sing or dance. All went quietly, with only a few small candles among us to show the way. I thought everything had ended then. Even the lights we carried were doused when we reached our houses. For a while the whole city sat in silent darkness.

Then at night's-turn, the bells were rung again. The lights were all re-lit, Tarl doing that duty for the torch that brightened Monal's end of the street. After that, our ceremonial robes and jewelry were carefully laid aside. With much hilarity, we dressed in many, many layers of bright ragged garments, saved especially for this occasion. Teasing and joking, we painted each others' faces in wild colors, tied on sashes, and decked ourselves with bells. Even Monal took her part in this with good humor and many instructions, though she said several times, "I do miss Kassim at such a time. Whatever made her go away at Light Time?"

When we were all gaily decked and nothing further could be added, we rushed out into the streets, shouting, laughing and banging on pots. There we were met by all the Hadra of Zelindar, ringing bells, singing, dancing and waving torches to fill the nights with light for the coming year, against the dark of winter. I sang and danced in good spirits with the others, feeling far more ease and freedom in Zelindar, than I had at the fall Essu or even at the Essu in Semasi. This gaiety went on until dawn. In some ways this was also our farewell. The next day we were to leave for Semasi.

* * *

After saying a last good-bye to Jorkal, we made ready our packs, struggling to add the gifts we were given, as well as those we were taking home for others, to what we had already purchased at Fall Festival. Tarl laughed and cursed, saying we were no better than Zinda with all we had accumulated around us. She threatened to leave half her possessions until I pushed her from the room, saying I would attend to it myself.

As we left, Monal took one of Tarl's packs and accompanied us down the winding streets. She put her arm around Tarl's waist, holding her close as if reluctant now to see her go. We were soon joined by Halli and her sisters and others as we passed, so that we formed a small procession on our way to join the horses.

As I hugged Halli good-bye, I slipped my hand down to press against her belly. "Is the child really there?"

"Oh, yes. I have known since the Essu. Hadra can tell almost at once. We can sense another's presence."

Now that we were away from the Gimling, and I saw Halli

among her own, it did not seem so terrible. Indeed, she looked well and happy, not haunted as she had been these past months. Her face was flushed with excitement as she told Tarl, "I am planning to apprentice with a blacksmith, then with a midwife and perhaps a basket maker, as well, so I will have the knowledge of these things when I come home." Nais was to stay also, and together they would ride back in the spring. "When the roads open, I will come home to have my baby in Semasi." I did not tell her that I would likely be in Zelindar by then. I had told no one but Jorkal. Not even Tarl knew.

* * *

Many hard days' riding lay between us and Semasi, that I knew, and we were racing now against the winter weather. Yet, as we rode out into the flatlands, I looked back with longing many times at Zelindar, so beautiful with her white domes under the flowering trees. I was torn to be leaving and unsure of what lay ahead for me in Semasi, but Tarl had no such reluctance. She rode fast without a backwards glance, bending over Timmer's neck and shouting into the wind. Soon we cut off onto a sandy side road so the horses could run at their will. I leaned forward then, giving myself over to the pleasure of the wind in my face and Sharu's familiar strength between my legs. For that time at least, I had no need to think on the future.

* * *

Shokarn and the subsequent making of the Redline for the protection of Yarmald.

Kielness — A building designed for trance and meditation. With its high, narrow windows and central courtyard, it has little opening to the street. A first year Neshtair is not allowed to enter, but I am told there is much there to flood the senses: music — both drums and flute — bright paintings in concentric patterns that move and shift under the spell of the yima, incense, soft fabrics, flowing waters and fountains, and of course, flowers everywhere. I could only pass on the street and hear the music through the window slits.

My Dearest Jorkal,

    I have just read through this manuscript one last time and am sending it on to you with all its faults and errors. Seronis thinks to leave soon, and I need to have it ready for her. She has grown restless here among us. If there is sufficient thaw at winterbreak, she plans to walk south for Zelindar to visit with her mothers and her daughter there. This seems to me a fitting turn, as it was her manuscript I brought to you, when we first met. I will have mine well wrapped against the hazards of such a trip and have made a second copy to be kept safe here in Semasi. If we are locked in by weather, I will bring it myself when I come south after the springmelt subsides.
    Upon re-reading my first letter to you, I find it to be stiff and formal, such a letter as one would write to Jorkal, Keeper of the Archives. Now I wish to write another letter here at the end, to Jorkal of Zelindar, who is my friend and tell you some of what has happened here since last we met.
    As you see from reading this, I am planning to return to Zelindar. When we rode away, Tarl did not once look back, but set her face straight for Semasi, going as fast as the horses were willing. For myself, I could hardly tear my eyes away from the domes and trees of the city and looked back with longing many times. Still I felt strong loves and obligations drawing me back to Semasi and had need to make a completion of my life here.
    Semasi is very beautiful in its high place above the sea and has been my refuge since being forced to leave Eezore, but I am no country girl. I was raised in a city. Zelindar calls to me with its great Zildorn and its library, it's beautiful parks and fountains, the glory of the bay on one side, and the wide Escuro on the other. In my dreams I walk its winding flower-filled streets again. I wish to come back there to study at the library, as well as with Anana. It would gladden my heart to be a scholar again. Besides, I may be of some use recopying books for Semasi from the library of Zelindar, recording for the Hadra my knowledge of Eezore, and helping with your work at the archives. After all, I must find my own place of usefulness among the Hadra, having lived too long on their kindness.
    Also, I must confess to you, Jorkal, that I am no longer happy

here. Halli is gone, and Tarl I rarely see. We are only together when I am teaching her to read, that being an old pledge between us. For the rest, it is Marli she has chosen to be with. They go about together everywhere. It pains my heart to watch, as Tarl seems to have no time at all for me. After all we have shared together of love and danger, I find it hard to comprehend how she can turn away from me so easily. Tarl says it is I who have left, that I am no longer here with her or here in Semasi and that I have not been for some time. She says she cannot live the way that I would choose. We can hardly talk with each other on such matters, for it quickly turns to quarreling and anger so serious that other Hadra have begun to grumble. Quadra has even offered to give council for us. Who knows the truth of all this. Perhaps Tarl is right. Perhaps the Goddess sees the answer. Still, I know the truth of my own pain.

As for Marli, she has grown in great leaps these past few months and is as tall and strong-backed as any Hadra of her age. She seems a different person from the wild child who escaped with me from Eezore. Tarl teaches her all she has of skill with horses and the making of things and her knowledge of the woods. I teach her to read and write in both Shokarn and Kourmairi, and she has already written some pages of her life in Eezore. Quadra and Jephra give her what Hadra training they can, and Zarmell teaches her herbs and healings. She is the first child among us, though in truth, she is no longer a child. There is even talk of sending her later to Yhaghar, for the training of any powers she may have and perhaps on to Zelindar, which does not please Tarl much.

As for other matters, things have grown quieter in Semasi with the coming of cold. The Hadra have settled down to the making of cloth and beads and clay pots for the fire. I have tried hard to learn these things, though I have little skill in my fingers. We make most of what we need here, but window glass is still beyond us at this time. Goddess knows, there is little I miss from Eezore, but I would give much at this moment for one square of their clear glass. I would even settle for a piece of wavy stuff from Zelindar. As it is, we make do with oiled paper bartered from the Kourmairi. I think it lets in more cold than light. Ah, well, so be it. I would rather be sitting by a fire-hearth in Yarmald, than dining in the finest house in Eezore.

We have all been worried for Quadra lately. She has been ill, on and off, for much of this winter, due to the strain of the battle. Jephra and Zarmell between them have been hard pressed to keep her comfortable.

Three new Neshtair and several Hadra came to us before winterfall, and with their help we have completed the common-house that Seronis and I worked upon. Much to everyone's pleasure, they will stay on to settle here in Semasi. Many small huts and houses have also been finished in time for winter's cold, but my own little house will never be done. I have made of it a small open-fronted shelter, from which to watch the sea. On fair nights I slept there until it grew too cold.

Oh, Jorkal, how endless this winter seems. How much I long to sit by you in the sunny windows of the Zildorn, among those bright cushions and listen to your stories. Believe me, when spring comes, I will leave as soon as I am able. Mirl will travel with me for she is also going south, and perhaps Ozal as well, so I will have some company and some safety from the hazards of the road.

I wish I could ride straight on to Zelindar, but first I must stop at Namakir to settle some business with Tizzel, for that matter has been much on my mind. Then I will be free for whatever falls into my future. Would that I had the courage to set off with Seronis and be there sooner, but I know such a journey in the winter is beyond my strength.

I miss you, Sister, and will be very glad to hear your voice again. Perhaps spring will come sooner than I think. As it must be.

Your loving friend:
Sair of Semasi

(These letters have been recorded here with Sair's permission.)

Jorkal, Keeper of the Archives

THE RAGING PEACE
Vol. 1 Throne Trilogy
by *Artemis OakGrove*

$7.95

"Dykes on the prowl for nighttime reading, THE RAGING PEACE captivates."

—GCN

DREAMS OF VENGEANCE
Vol. 2. Throne Trilogy
by *Artemis OakGrove*

$7.95

"An overwhelming, breathtaking plot filled with revenge, violence and spiritual turmoil . . . far more than just another SM book."

—KSK

THRONE OF COUNCIL
Vol. 3 Throne Trilogy
by *Artemis OakGrove*

$7.95

". . . concludes the compelling fantasy of a love between two women that withstands the passing of centuries, the barriers of time and memory, reincarnation, earthly trials and spirit war."

—Bookpaper

TRAVELS WITH DIANA HUNTER
by *Regine Sands*

$8.95

"From the first innocent nuzzle at the 'neck of nirvana' to the final orgasmic fulfillment, Regine Sands stirs us with her verbal foreplay, tongue in cheek humor and tongue in many other places eroticism."

—Jewelle Gomez

A THIRD STORY
by *Carole Taylor*

$7.95

Ms. Taylor's wonderfully funny novel takes a candid look at university life and explores what can happen when the wrong people discover the heroine is a lesbian.

THE LEADING EDGE
edited by *Lady Winston*
introduction by *Pat Califia*

$9.95

THE LEADING EDGE is the hottest, sexiest book yet from Lace's Lady Winston Series. Journey through time from the world of an ancient-day Queen to a 19th century pirate ship skirting the New Orleans shoreline with a bloodthirsty crew of women bent on revenge to lurking the shadows in a modern-day New York bar in search of the perfect candidate to steal away to a forbidding red planet far from Earth. With contributions from Ann Allen Shockley, Dorothy Allison, Jewelle Gomez, Noretta Koertge, Merril Mushroom, Charlotte Stone, Cheryl Clarke, Artemis OakGrove, C. Bailey, Chocolate Waters and others.

JUST HOLD ME
by *Linda Parks*

$7.95

This romantic novel about women loving women, faith and determination will hold you fast in your favorite reading chair from the intriguing beginning to the hope-filled conclusion.

ORDER TODAY (clip or photocopy this coupon)

___ Copies of The Raging Peace (Vol. 1)	$7.95 ea. =	_____
___ Copies of Dreams of Vengeance (Vol. 2)	$7.95 ea. =	_____
___ Copies of Throne of Council (Vol. 3)	$7.95 ea. =	_____
___ Copies of Travels With Diana Hunter	$8.95 ea. =	_____
___ Copies of A Third Story	$7.95 ea. =	_____
___ Copies of The Leading Edge	$9.95 ea. =	_____
___ Copies of Just Hold Me	$7.95 ea. =	_____
Postage and Handling	$1.50 =	1.50
	TOTAL* =	_____

___ Enclosed check or money order
___ Charge my MasterCard/VISA

Acct. No. _____
Exp. Date _____
Signature _____

Name _____
Address _____
City, State, Zip _____

Send order form and payment to: Lace Publications, PO Box 10037, Denver, CO 80210-0037
Colorado residents add 3% tax. Thank you.